INCONCEIVABLE!

A NOVEL BY

Tegan Wren

A Division of **Whampa, LLC**
P.O. Box 2160
Reston, VA 20195
Tel/Fax: 800-998-2509
http://curiosityquills.com

© 2015 **Tegan Wren**
http://teganwren.blogspot.com

ISBN 978-1-62007-937-9 (ebook)
ISBN 978-1-62007-938-6 (paperback)
ISBN 978-1-62007-939-3 (hardcover)

For Patrick; without you, there'd be no story.

This book is also dedicated to all those who experience infertility. May you find a happy ending more beautiful than the one you've imagined for yourself.

TABLE OF CONTENTS

Part I

CHAPTER ONE

*S*uck it up, Hatty. You can totally do this. It's a bar full of booze hounds. No one's going to remember this tomorrow. My mental pep talk tore a small hole in the fabric of my fear as I squeezed past the people who had front row seats to Kamikaze Karaoke.

Eyes hungry for another disastrous performance peered over beer steins and wine glasses, waiting for me to trudge up the stairs at the side of the stage. On Saturday nights, Finn's attracted close to one hundred people eager to gape at tipsy singers crashing and burning as they fumbled through whatever tune the random song generator selected. I was the next victim, a prospect that was as exhilarating as it was terrifying.

At least Plato was the DJ tonight, sexy as hell in his fitted black shirt and jeans. Yep, he'd have my back. Extending his hand to me, he smiled broadly and ushered me into the spotlight.

"Go easy, okay?" I hissed at Plato, careful to stay back from the mic.

He raised his eyebrows, shook his head, and spoke to the crowd. "Let's see what the karaoke gods have lined up for Hatty."

Dear karaoke gods, please choose "I Will Survive" because I know it, and therefore I will, indeed, survive the next five minutes. Amen.

I held my breath, watching the zigzag lines scroll across the screens positioned around the pub.

My stomach sank when I saw the title flash in big black letters: "I Wanna Have Your Babies." *You've got to be kidding me—not this stupid pop song.*

Plato guffawed. "Hatty, are you ready to Kamikaze Karaoke?"

People in the audience stomped their feet and clapped, cracking a whip that set my heart at a full gallop.

I cleared my throat and stepped forward, determined to kick this ridiculous song in the ovaries. Someone whistled from one of the green pleather booths lining the wall. *Thanks buddy.* As the bouncing intro started, I focused on the cheesy music.

While I waited to sing, Plato grabbed me, pulling me to the side of the mic. He whispered in my ear, but the noise from the crowd made it hard to hear. "Princess, set the bar!"

"I'll set it sky high," I whispered back. His words of encouragement propelled my lips to the mic where I tasted the metallic screen moments before launching into the first line.

When I paused to grab a breath, some guy wearing a hot pink sombrero shouted unintelligible words while giving me a big thumbs up. Emboldened by this visual reminder of how hammered people were, I yanked the mic out of the stand and pranced—yes, pranced—across the stage. I'd learned a simple rule during my childhood in the Missouri Ozarks: when tackling a challenge, go whole hog. Wagging my finger and shaking my hips, I was damn near hog wild.

After I finished with the *mmm-mmm-mmm*'s at the end of the song, applause thundered through the room, rewarding my gutsy performance. I exhaled, full of relief that I'd kicked butt and taken names. Riding my wave of success, I blew a kiss, eliciting more cheers.

"Whoomp, there she is!" The Irish accent and early nineties hip hop reference told me it was my friend Sara shouting her approval from the back of the room.

Instead of joining her at our table, I strolled toward the bar for a fresh drink. Plato's beau, Sam, met me halfway. The tall Frenchman wrapped me in his arms.

"That was aces, Hatty! You're the queen of Kamikaze Karaoke."

"Be sure to tell Plato you've upgraded me from princess." I smiled, thinking again of Plato offering me that last-minute confidence boost.

Sam gave me a peck on the lips before heading back to his table. I swaggered to the bar and plopped down on a stool.

The young, eager bartender in his neat apron came over. "Riesling?"

"Actually, I'd love a chocolate kiss."

He nodded, then turned away to make the pub's famous hot drink.

"That wasn't bad… for an American."

My head snapped toward the guy sitting next to me. It was hard to see his face; he wore a scruffy brown cap and black horn-rimmed glasses that sat halfway down his nose. With his beat-up jacket and tattered maroon scarf, he looked like he rolled out of a field. Probably a farmhand from outside the city, though his accent was too formal. He kept his eyes glued to his beer.

"I'd like to see you get up there and sing that stupid song," I said, grabbing a napkin and dabbing the sweat that dampened my hairline.

"I'm bad news on a karaoke stage."

"You're in luck. I'm a reporter and I love bad news." Out of the corner of my eye, I saw his full lips turn up in a slight smile. It was gorgeous.

"Here you are, Hatty." The bartender slid a steaming mug in front of me.

"Thanks."

"A reporter?" Farmer Joe sounded skeptical. People always thought I was younger than twenty-two. Maybe it was my wavy brown hair that fell past my shoulders.

"That's right. I'm an intern at *The Morning Dispatch*. I graduate in May from Toulene's Royal University with a degree in journalism."

"What kind of stories do you write?" He pulled down on the frayed bill of his cap, making the shadows darken across his face in the dimly lit pub.

"My last story was a brief on road work in Roeselare. I do a lot of short pieces, which is fine. Gotta pay my dues before I can cover politics." My head buzzed with leftover energy from my performance, giving me above-average courage to chat up this handsome stranger.

He looked up at the TV behind the bar, the only one showing rugby highlights. The glow from the screen chased away most of the shadows obscuring his features. His eyes were big, alive. Underneath the accessories, his face had near-perfect symmetry, and I gave him extra credit for having lips that weren't chapped. Lots of guys in northern continental Europe got chapped lips the moment the weather turned cold. He pushed his glasses higher on his face, then raised the off-white stein. I studied his lips perched on the edge of it, ready for a drink of dark beer. So kissable.

"What's so exciting about politics?" he asked.

I gasped loudly, raising a hand to my heart in melodramatic horror at such a ridiculous question. "What's so exciting about politics? Everything! Legislatures determine spending priorities and set public policy. We all have to live by their rules." I leaned toward him and lowered my voice. "You know, everybody likes to focus on the executive—the president in the U.S. and the monarchy here. But they're just a distraction. Sure, they have a role to play, but it's comparatively boring. I'd rather cover the passionate debates among lawmakers." I paused, embarrassed by my effusive nerdiness. "I can't help it. I love the idea of being a statehouse reporter. I really want to stick up for people who don't have a voice."

"Now you definitely sound like an American. Also, the charming accent gives you away."

Charming? Eek! He grinned, and my hands turned sweaty. But something was off. Maybe it was *his* accent. Definitely upper class Toulene.

"Can't help it. I grew up in Nixa, Missouri, about four hours southwest of St. Louis. It's a small town, as American as they come." For the first time, he rotated on his stool, and there was his face. Holy cuteness. His eyes reached inside me with a searing intensity, and I inhaled sharply.

He leaned closer and sang softly. I recognized the opening lyrics to Journey's "Don't Stop Believin'." His singing voice was soulful and sexy, and something deep inside me responded, making my heart beat a little faster.

He stopped and looked me in the eyes. "That song's about someone who's alone. But that's not you. You're too lovely to be lonely."

A nervous laugh escaped my lips. "Are you kidding? Aren't we sitting in a sanctuary for the lonely?"

"I don't feel lonely right now."

"Me either." I blew into my mug, then took a sip. "Have you had one of these?"

"I don't think so. What is it?"

"It's called a chocolate kiss. It's peppermint schnapps and hot cocoa."

He reached over and picked up the steaming mug. His movement conveyed authority while his neat fingernails screamed uppity. They looked better than mine, damn it. After taking a long pull from the cup, he handed it back. Our fingers brushed together, sending a flash of heat through my body.

"Thanks for sharing a kiss with me," he said, reaching over and lifting my chin.

Our eyes met, and I couldn't tear myself away from his gaze. Yowza. Was he going to kiss me? Did I want him to?

"You guys know each other?"

I flinched at Plato's words—I hadn't seen him coming toward us—and pulled back. I sloshed a healthy dollop of my drink onto Farmer Joe's pants. We both reached for the stack of napkins, but I got there first.

"Sorry. Here, let me," I sputtered, dabbing at the wet patch.

I blotted along his pants, and my hand moved a little too close to the inside of his leg. A burning sensation rose up behind my ears. "Umm. I'll just let you do it."

I dropped the wad of damp napkins onto his open palm. Glancing at his face, I saw a half smile. I closed my eyes and touched my forehead, gently rubbing the area above my eyebrows as I always did when embarrassment overwhelmed me.

"Hatty, this is John. John, this is Hatty," said Plato.

With a click, the last piece of the puzzle fell into place, explaining why he looked all wrong in this bar and wearing these clothes. He was Prince John Meinrad, Toulene's most popular royal. Sitting in my favorite dive. Drinking from my mug. Listening to me babble.

No. Freaking. Way.

"So nice to meet you, Hatty. Thanks for letting me *distract* and *bore* you for a few minutes." He emphasized the words I'd used earlier to describe the monarchy.

"Nice to meet you too," I choked out, mortified by my dismissive comment about his family. I cleared my throat, nervous and not sure what to say to a prince. So, I spoke to Plato instead. "You guys are a thing? Have a thing? You met how?" Ladies and gentlemen, my sudden inability to put together words.

Before Plato answered, Prince John spoke up. "We met a couple of weeks ago at a poker game. Plato's helping me brush up." He removed a white handkerchief from his back pocket and wiped his glasses.

"Yeah, well he has a great poker face." I turned to my friend. "I can't believe you didn't tell me about this."

Plato held up his hands. "I gave you a heads up when I saw him walk in and sit at the bar right before you sang, but I don't think you heard me." *Oh. The prince is at the bar. That's what he'd said.*

"I asked him to keep it quiet," John said. "It gets a bit dodgy when too many people know who my friends are." Even after more than three years of going to school in this country, Toulenians' intermittent use of British slang still delighted my ears. It revived my middle school thespian aspirations and I wanted to respond, "Eh, guv'nah?"

"We'd better head to the back before anyone notices you're here." Plato reached over and grabbed my mug. In a couple of swallows, he erased the intimacy of the earlier moment—evidently my beverage was community property. "A couple of other guys are coming and we're going to play a few hands. Do you want to join us?"

"Maybe." Translation: *Spend more time with a hottie prince? Yes, please.*

Plato scuffed the toe of his shoe against the bar rail. "But just so you know, Jack's coming." *My stinking ex-boyfriend ruins everything.*

"In that case, no thanks. I don't want to bring any drama to your poker game." I looked at the prince. "I don't know if you're friends with Jack but he's a real jerk." My fingers fidgeted with the edge of my sweater. I wanted to end this uncomfortable stroll down Relationship Lane, but I also longed to stay by the prince's side a few more minutes. I coughed into my hand, again finding it hard to know what to say. "So, take care John. Or is it Prince John? Or Your Highness?" *Awkward like a boss.*

"Just John. Have a good night, Hatty."

My name in his mouth awakened more butterflies in my stomach. John slid the glasses back into place as he and Plato moved quickly toward the back room.

I made my way to Sara, stopping to say hello to two reporters from my newspaper. They made no mention of the prince—it seemed his disguise was effective.

When I got to the table, Sara was putting on her coat.

"You're not going to believe who I just met."

"Prince John. I saw you talking to him," Sara said with a wink. She was a world literature major and tireless romantic. "I can't believe you got a private audience with His Royal Highness. Did he stare into your eyes and steal your soul? He has a reputation for doing that, you know."

"Nope. My soul's still intact. Wait, how did you know it was him?"

"Please. Someone photographed him two weeks ago wearing a similar disguise at a bar in Paris."

"Umm, you need an intervention because you're spending way too much time reading *Xpress*. Did you know Plato's friends with him?" It still hurt that he'd kept it a secret.

"No, but I saw him walk with the prince to the back room."

"Did someone say my name?" Plato sidled up to Sara holding a couple of drinks. "Hatty, these are for you. Have a good night, my loves." He handed me a mug and martini glass containing a sloshy pink liquid before heading toward the rear of the pub.

"What's that all about?" Sara took the mug and sipped from it.

There was a napkin wrapped around the stem of the martini glass. I set the drink on the table, but kept the napkin. It was folded, not quite in half, and there was my name written in neat cursive. *What the what?* I flipped it open and read it. Feeling out of breath, I stuffed it in my pocket. "I guess Plato wanted to buy us another round. You drink up. I'll be right back."

I darted to the bathroom, slammed into a stall, and opened the napkin. My heavy breathing is all I heard as I read the words again:

I'll see your chocolate kiss and raise you a flirtini. John

Heat blazed across my cheeks. Digging in my purse, I pulled out a pen and a clean napkin I'd tucked away earlier and drafted my own note:

Hope you have an excellent hand because I've got a royal flush.

I texted Plato and asked him to meet me at the door to the back room. I trusted him to do me a solid and deliver my response to the prince.

CHAPTER TWO

H ere." My editor, James, shoved an advisory for a press
event across his desk.

"What's this?" So much for a work-in-the-newsroom
kind of Wednesday.

"The queen's going to be at a preschool today. Heidi's already
there to cover the press conference. I want you to leave now and
stake out a spot behind the building. Get as many photos as you
can as she walks to her limo afterward. Got it?"

"Sure."

Just the mention of the royal family revived all the
freakalicious feelings I'd had since Saturday night. Though I'd left
the bar on a buzz-filled high after our coy napkin exchange, my
euphoria faded in the harsh sunlight of Sunday morning. It was
probably no big whoop for the prince to flirt with me. If the
gossip magazine headlines were any indication, he was a ladies'
man. Every week, reporters photographed him with a different
woman on his arm.

"Get the snapshots with your phone. Do a good job and I'll
help you sell the ones we don't run to the tabloids."

I nodded. James offered because he was a merciless mercenary, not because he wanted to do me any favors.

His phone emitted a sharp buzz from its spot on the desk. Snapping it up, he stared at the screen. "Heidi says the prince is there instead of the queen." My nerves flared in a frenzy, but I tensed my muscles, hoping to hide my reaction. James raised his eyes. "He never takes questions from reporters during his press conferences. See if you can get a quote from him afterward. Anything unscripted is better than whatever bullshit he'll spew during his official remarks. Can you handle that?"

"Absolutely." I reached into my pocket and touched the napkin with the prince's note on it, savoring the tangible takeaway from our brief flirtation. I confess: I'd slept with it under my pillow every night. My ability to nurse a crush was epic.

On the short drive through Roeselare, I focused on taming my stomach, which refused to be quiet and still. *Show the prince you're a professional, not a spaz. Just do your job.*

Standing along the press line clutching my phone, I reeked of rookie. The more seasoned journalists had shiny black cameras mounted atop poles. We all prepped for a photo finish; the winner would be the journalist whose image of the prince got the most shares on social media. Smiling photos were good. Awkward snapshots were better. Much better. Catch him wiping his nose or making a weird face and you'd snag the grand prize: a fat check from Europe's biggest gossip rag, *Xpress.* The tabloid forked over thousands of euros for the best worst photos of the royals. *Faux pas means full pay, baby.*

Even though my editor and the gossip rags salivated over the awkward pics, my goal was to capture his brilliant smile and keep it for myself. I'd get some unflattering snaps in the process, and that would fulfill my professional obligations for this silly assignment.

On your mark. As I sized up the other reporters, I recognized a couple of *Xpress* photographers near the back door of the childcare center. They were the pros, but I'd inched my way into the primo spot. My position put me close enough to touch the rear bumper of the purring black limo that waited to whisk the prince back to the palace.

I held up my smartphone with its camera ready to go the moment Prince John exited the building. Would he remember me, the gal who was 'too lovely to be lonely?' A surge of nervous, jittery hope rushed through my body, making me lightheaded.

Get set. Thunder ripped into the quiet anticipation that had settled over the horde of reporters and photographers, but I held steady. A twinge of resentment threatened my focus as I thought about Heidi Braun, the senior palace correspondent from my newspaper, sitting comfortably inside the building covering the prince's visit. She might not get a quote, but she got to stare at his gorgeous face.

The back door of the childcare center swung wide to reveal a uniformed guard just as the dark clouds overhead opened up, releasing an instant torrent of blinding rain, the kind that's notorious in northern continental Europe. I stuck my phone in my armpit and scooped my umbrella off the ground. The sliding mechanism was stuck. I pushed and cajoled, but it didn't budge.

"Damn it," I whispered.

Go! The guard holding open the back door expanded a giant umbrella in a single motion and Prince John emerged. Shouting erupted from the reporters and photographers.

"John! Is Simone Thoreaux pregnant with your baby?"

"John, be a sport! Who was the woman with you last Sunday at the track?"

"Is the queen dying? Why haven't we seen her in weeks?"

I threw the umbrella into the grass at my feet, grabbed my phone from my armpit, and started snapping photos. My phone's camera clicks competed against the cacophony of shutter sounds around me and the pounding rain. Where the more experienced journalists had plastic covers on their cameras, I used my hand to shield my phone from the driving rain. I held steady as my teeth started to chatter.

The prince moved briskly down the path, staying under the umbrella carried by the guard. Was he actually smiling at the line of reporters?

"Sorry you have to be out in this, but thank you for coming!" he shouted in reply to all the nasty questions.

I waited to yell at him until he was right in front of me. I felt certain my words would prompt him to look at me with a "Huh?" expression on his face.

"We shared a kiss Saturday at Finn's!"

At my assertion, he stopped, then turned toward me with a quizzical look on his face. His gleaming smile was frozen and his perfectly sculpted eyebrows knitted together. I snapped photos continuously. *Cha-ching for James, and ooh, la, la for me!*

"I'm Plato's friend, Hatty!" I added, realizing he might not recognize me as a sopping heap.

His expression didn't change. There was no flicker of recognition or even acknowledgement he'd heard the second thing I'd said. It was disappointing. Maybe he'd been a bit schnockered Saturday night, thus explaining why he'd flirted with a nerdy girl like me.

He took two more steps to the limo and sat down. Just as the door was closing, the prince stuck out his hand and the guard leaned down.

Snap. Snap. Snap. My phone captured image after image of the guard turning from the car and walking in my direction.

I looked up at the tall, stoic man with the umbrella and saw my shocked face staring back at me in his mirrored sunglasses. My heart cranked into overdrive as I registered the authority embodied in his crisp navy suit and the clear plastic coil connecting an earpiece to a receiver buried inside his jacket. Had I done something wrong? I guess yelling we'd "shared a kiss" in front of reporters wasn't the smartest idea. Crap. None of my professors had touched on how to handle getting arrested while on assignment.

"The prince would like to see you." The guard's deep voice was quiet and urgent.

I nodded, and he reached out a big hand to lift the security tape. As I took the four steps to the limo door, the pack of reporters had just enough time to register what was transpiring. They shouted louder, and the camera clicks accelerated. By crossing the press line, I'd just become part of the story. And it was surreal, disconcerting.

I slid in next to the prince, unsure about the proper seating protocol for royal limos. The door closed behind me, blocking out the reporters and the chill of the late October rainfall. The guard got in from the other side and sat on a side bench, never changing the dispassionate look on his face.

From his red tie to his shiny, wet shoes, the prince wore the fashion opposite of his Saturday night disguise. My teeth chattered, and droplets of water dribbled off the end of my nose. My thin jacket was drenched, and my clothes clung uncomfortably to my body.

"Here, put this on," Prince John said as he removed his jacket.

It was a simple gesture laced with intimacy: his hands positioning the jacket over my shoulders, his fingers brushing against my dripping hair. I basked in his attention and let him adjust the coat.

"There. Are you warm?"

"Yes, but your jacket's going to be ruined. I'm soaked." Water dripped onto the collar from my hair.

"It's fine. I'd rather not see you freeze to death." He gestured to my hands. "May I?"

I nodded and he put my palms together. He briskly rubbed my fingers and hands, creating a cozy friction. Even though he wasn't exactly holding my hands it was close enough to make me lightheaded and giddy.

Seated next to him, literally enveloped in his generosity, I forced myself to remember my goal: getting photos and a quote. I wasn't here to moon over Toulene's hottest royal. It also didn't help that his jacket wrapped me in his scent: a mixture of soap, spicy aftershave, and mint. In one deep breath, I imagined him shirtless, going about his morning routine.

"Did you like the kiss we shared Saturday night?" I asked, laying on my Ozarks accent a little thicker than normal. It was the vocal equivalent of innocently batting my eyes.

"Of course. But what I really appreciated was your passion for covering politics. That and your incredible rendition of that awful babies song. So imagine my shock at seeing you along the press line just now." He raised his eyebrows like he expected an explanation.

"I hope you're not offended my newspaper sent an intern to help cover the event."

"Not at all. But I had the impression that stalking royals isn't how you intend to make a name for yourself."

"You're right. But I always try to do my best, regardless of how I feel about the assignment. I have to get a good grade this semester. And even if I graduate with honors, I'll probably have to start out doing more grunt work when I move back to the states in May." Grunt work for a Missouri newspaper meant more 4-H competitions and fewer limo rides with handsome men.

I hastily added, "I'm at the mercy of my crazy editor at *The Morning Dispatch*, and he gave me this assignment. He's also an American—totally obsessed with increasing coverage of royals and celebrities. I know there's an appetite for news about you and your family, and today's been fun, but I don't want to spend my life hiding in bushes, hoping to photograph you picking food out of your teeth. Not that you would ever do that. I mean, I'm sure you do floss and brush, just not in public. I'm going to shut up now."

He smirked. "Do you read the coverage of my family?" He leaned a bit closer and a flash of warmth crept up my neck.

"Not usually, but I see the magazine covers. Those photos can't compete with the real thing," I blurted without self-editing. Yes, horror of horrors, I'd essentially just told the prince he's way hotter in person.

An awkward silence crept into the space around us and I realized the driver needed to take me back to my car. I was dying to run to my apartment and change out of my cold, damp clothes before heading to the newsroom to review my photos and write a brief.

"Can you tell the driver to turn around? My car's a couple of kilometers east of the preschool."

John cleared his throat. "I'm sorry, but we can't take you home right now. When we travel on official palace business with the police escort, we have to keep to our route and schedule to ensure minimal disruptions to traffic. Once we get to Belvoir, I'll arrange for you to get back to your car."

"Sounds great. Thank you."

I glanced over at Grimmy McGrim sitting stiffly in the side seat close to John. Maybe he'd radio the police and make sure no one towed my car. This country cracked the whip when it came to parking and other vehicle-related violations. But the guard didn't move; his eyes and thoughts remained tucked away behind those sunglasses.

"Were the kids at the preschool excited to see you?"

"I think so. We played dress-up."

"Are you serious?" *How adorbs.*

"Of course! They had me wear a hat with a horse's mane on it. Then they wanted me to pretend I was sick so they could take me to the veterinary hospital."

"Did you cough and say, 'I'm a little hoarse? Get it, hoarse-horse?" It was out of my mouth before I could stop it. I'd inherited from my dad this ridiculous compulsion to inject stupid jokes and puns in conversations. It served me well as a journalist because I could channel it into the creative process of writing stories. But in real life, I just sounded like Super Nerd.

"Sorry. That was a really bad joke."

The prince flashed his gorgeous smile. "Hatty, this is only the second time I've met you, but I get the impression you don't censor yourself. Do you have any idea how fun that is?"

"Fun for you. Horrifying for me."

Our eyes locked momentarily before I looked away.

"Is it always like that? Cameras flashing, reporters yelling?"

"Yes. Part of my job is knowing how to deal with it in a gracious way that allows me to maintain some degree of privacy. That's why I take every chance I get to step outside this bubble and do normal things. Like going to a bar and getting to know some of Plato's friends."

I was one of Plato's friends. Electric currents ripped through me. *Get a grip! You're on an assignment for Pete's sake.*

The limo took a sharp turn and I looked out the window. We pulled through a tall, black iron gate at the rear of Belvoir Palace.

Some inspired architect conjured Belvoir from a fairytale. I gazed up at the towers topped with the beguiling battlements that reminded me of the bottom teeth in a jack-o-lantern's grin. At eye level, the manicured grounds sprawled away from the palace, a green grandeur, even in October, reserved for the royal family; a high brick and stone fence shielded it from public streets.

I realized I was holding my breath as the driver opened the door and helped me out.

"This is it. Home Sweet Beaver," John said, grinning at the well-known mispronunciation of the French name Belvoir.

"Does that mean you're Prince Beaver?" I realized a beat too late that what I said was a double entendre.

"I've been called that and worse. Are you sure you don't read the tabloids?"

I rubbed my forehead again. Even my reaction to embarrassment was embarrassing.

John led me through a service entrance into a dully lit passage. Despite our brisk pace, I tried to register each sight (faded green wood paneling in the hallway), sound (a woman singing in German), and smell (Toulene's airy, puffy bread in the oven). I drew in a quick breath when we passed a small, oval portrait of John's mother hanging on the wall. Her charity work and then her untimely death thrust Toulene and its royals into the international spotlight. It was a tiny country in the grand scheme of Europe, but the Meinrad family gained significant attention when Princess Beatrix died of ovarian cancer at age 29. John was only nine years old at the time. His father, who would presumably take the throne before John, hadn't remarried, and raised John and his brother, Henri, away from the public eye. That is, until the boys reached their late teens. They were handsome in all the right ways and exuded perfect manners, so they received more than their fair share of international press coverage from the gossip rags and TV newscasts.

We turned a corner and started up a staircase. The reality of being inside Belvoir was exhilarating. The royal family almost never let reporters in here. So, why the heck was he allowing *me* to traipse through the place? Regardless of the reason, I was in, and I hoped to score an exclusive story and an amazing photo with some flirting on the side.

By the time we got to the top of the staircase, I was huffing a little, though I tried to conceal it by taking controlled breaths.

"Sorry. Am I going too fast? Since I'm always darting in and out of cars and buildings, I've gotten into the habit of practically running everywhere I go." John waited for me to catch up at the top of the stairs.

"I'm fine. The wet clothes are making me a little slower than usual." The cold dampness of my shirt reasserted itself, and I shivered.

"We're about to take care of that." John had a note of delight in his voice. With his wide eyes and eager smile, he was brimming with the knowledge of some pending surprise. He was a man who knew how to fix problems, and enjoyed doing it. I'm sure it's fun to tackle challenges when you have vast quantities of money and power.

After traversing a series of short hallways, we faced a dead end with three closed doors.

"Is this your first time visiting the palace?" John stood with his back to the middle door, his hand on the knob.

"Yes. I'm mildly impressed so far." I laughed, unable to play it cool.

He opened the door. "After you." *Ever the gentleman.*

I stepped into a room that had a marble mantelpiece, a canopy bed decked out in blue layers of luxury, and a short, light blue sofa with navy pillows. Its sheer perfection froze me to the spot where I stood.

"Does anyone use this room? It's immaculate." I didn't want to drag my soaking self into such a clean space.

"It's one of the rooms we sometimes let photographers use if they want to do a shoot in the palace. Otherwise, we keep spare clothing in the wardrobe for just such emergencies." *Just such emergencies?* I kind of loved the refined, formal way he talked.

He disappeared around a corner that, from my vantage point at the entrance to the room, was hidden. It looked like he stepped through the wall.

"Come over here and have a look."

I carefully tiptoed through the room, afraid to drip on the plush rug or brush up against the furniture. When I rounded the corner, John had the wardrobe open.

"Riding clothes?" It was just a guess.

"That's right. We keep these here for palace guests who come for dinner and stay for hunting or riding. There's a linen bag in there for your wet clothes. I'll wait outside."

And he quickly slipped into the hallway, quietly closing the door behind him.

The hulking wardrobe nearly touched the ceiling. Green and pink rose-patterned paper lined its interior walls.

"That happens? You come to the palace for dinner and end up gallivanting through the woods in designer clothes?" I said out loud to the empty room as I gently touched the velvety fabric of a pair of pants.

Most Toulenian women were thinner than my U.S. size twelve, so I assumed most of these clothes would be too small for me. I sure didn't want to squeeze into tight breeches that would tattle on my every chunk and bulge.

I checked the tags inside the waistbands, and found a pair of jodhpurs that had potential. I peeled off my undies for fear their dampness might seep through and create unseemly wet patches around my crotch.

Putting on the old-style riding pants with the flare of fabric below the waist was like handing my thighs a megaphone: "We are *here* and we are *big*!" they seemed to scream from inside the overly bulky breeches. I just shook my head. There was no other choice.

On to the shirts. Only white. A perfect complement to my wet black bra.

I glanced at the canopy bed as I walked back through the room and wondered who might've had a fun romp there. A maid and John's father? Maybe he caught her by surprise one winter's evening. At the thought of this imaginary encounter, I exhaled loudly. I glimpsed at myself in the mirror, noting the black bra peeking through the thin button-up and my dark stringy hair drying in messy clumps. *No one wants to romp with this.*

I tentatively opened the door and peered into the hallway. John was on his phone, scrolling through something with an intent expression.

He raised his eyes. "You look brilliant!"

I extended my arms, looked down at my attire, and laughed at his assessment.

"You can't be serious."

He laughed too. "I mean it. I'm only sorry it's raining and we can't go for a ride now that you're dressed for it. Maybe another time. Let's go and see about getting you back to your car."

I nodded, but I heard the high-pitch whine of air seeping out of my happy little balloon. This unexpected adventure could've led to a brief interview or tour of the palace. But it seemed the inside of a guest room wardrobe was the only intimate encounter I'd have with Belvoir. Just as well. My deadline loomed.

He led me back through the maze of hallways, but stopped abruptly before descending the wooden staircase.

"Hatty. Have you had lunch? Do you want a bite before you leave?"

How 'bout them apples? Maybe I'd get my story-photo-flirting trifecta after all.

CHAPTER THREE

I wanted to jump at his invitation to stay for lunch but… "I'm supposed to have my photos from the daycare ready for an online story by 4:00 p.m."

"If I give you an exclusive interview over scones and coffee, think you could buy yourself some extra time?"

"I'm sure. Let me text my editor." I reached into the linen bag that held my wet clothes. "Oh no. My poor phone." I pulled it from the pocket of my wet pants.

It was waterlogged and didn't jump to life like it usually did when I pushed the home button. Panic gushed into my fingertips, forcing them to push the button repeatedly. My photos from the preschool were on there!

"Do you know the number? I can take you to a phone." He started down the stairs.

"Yes. That's great." Distraught that the phone—and photos—likely weren't salvageable, I dropped the dead device back into the bag.

At the bottom of the stairs, he veered left and there was a rotary phone in a small alcove in the wall.

"Will this do?"

"Once I figure out how to dial it."

James picked up on the first ring.

"Yes?" he demanded.

"Hey, it's Hatty," I said a little sing-songy, trying not to give away my editor's tone to John who stood a respectable distance down the hall, but remained within ear shot.

"Are you on your way back? Please tell me you got some good shots of the prince and the girl who got into the limo with him. It's all over Twitter and Instagram, though no one got a clear shot of her face. We have to get the story of the mystery girl. I bet he's seducing her at the palace right now."

"Well, *I'm* with the prince. He gave me a ride to Belvoir."

I registered the horror of James' words. Journalists becoming a part of the story was a major no-no. "He pulled *you* into the limo? Why the hell would he do that?"

I worked hard not to roll my eyes. "He's agreed to let me interview him. But I won't make the 4:00 p.m. deadline." I tried to sound like the seasoned reporters who held their own with the editors.

"Okay. Ask him who does his hair. I'm kidding. But definitely ask him about the little tart who was on his arm at the Carlisle racetrack Sunday afternoon. If you can get him to talk about this stuff, all the regional papers will run your story. They eat this shit up. See you soon."

"Fine," I said and hung up the phone. My toes dug into my damp shoes at the thought of writing a story about the prince's love life.

"All set?" John asked.

"You bet. Where do you want to talk?"

"In a big room filled with my ancestors. Come. I'll show you." He was already rounding a corner at the end of the hallway.

John led me to a room with a ceiling that was at least two stories high. Arched windows at the top of the walls ushered in natural light. The layout reminded me of a great hall I once saw while touring a German castle. The walls were painted a deep red, creating a dramatic backdrop for the room's many paintings.

I strolled inside and surveyed the artwork. There were portraits of serious-looking royals as well as pastoral landscapes that reminded me of the Ozarks. Bloody combatants were frozen in time on several canvasses marking major moments in Toulene's history. *No one does war like Europeans.*

As I walked deeper into the cavernous space, my heels clicked on the parquet floor, then fell mute when I crossed onto a broad maroon rug that ran the length of the room.

While I soaked up the paintings, John pulled two white chairs out from the wall, positioning them in the middle of the room. He handed me a black notebook and pen.

"Here. You might need these. I want you to get my quotes right. Most reporters fail at this basic task."

"Thanks. I'll do my best. Before we start, tell me about this room."

"It's called the Regents Room. If you ever tour the palace, you get to walk through here. But few people outside the family and close friends spend any significant time in here."

"So who's your favorite relative?"

"That's a tough choice because so many of them have fascinating stories. If I had to pick, it would be Uncle Fergus." He pointed to a painting halfway up the wall to our right. "He's the one standing in front of a mirror being fitted for a suit."

"Ahh. And why is he your fave?"

"See the woman in the painting crouched by his feet, checking the length of his pants? That's Emmaline, the royal seamstress. Despite extreme ridicule from his mother, Queen Helena, Fergus followed his heart and married her. Theirs was the first marriage between a member of our family and a commoner. The queen disowned him."

"Talk about harsh."

"It got worse. About a year after their marriage, he and Emmaline contracted typhoid. She died first at their shack on the outskirts of Roeselare. When Uncle was nearing the end, he had his neighbor wheel him in a cart to the front gates of Belvoir. He sat for two days in his own filth, and the family refused to send anyone to help him. When he died, the guards left him there and didn't dispose of the body until after dark."

I shivered at such cruelty. "That's criminal."

"My mum felt the same way. She had this painting commissioned during her first year of marriage to my father. I think it was her way of staking some territory with Granny. She had it unveiled in a public ceremony and my father apologized on behalf of the family for its treatment of Uncle Fergus and Aunt Emmaline."

"Wow. Your mom had some moxie."

"She did. Just like those two." He nodded toward the painting.

John's admiration of his relatives' sacrifice hinted at depths that lay beneath his camera-ready smile.

"I love the paintings that show Toulene's history. In America, we look up to you guys since you were the first ones who broke away from British rule," I remarked, as I took another sweeping glance at the battle scenes. "It's your ancestors' decision to set up a monarchy that makes Americans wince. You know, I always wondered, did the pilgrims consider sailing across the channel to Toulene instead of hanging a right to the New World?"

John laughed. "Good question. These battle scenes and the portraits of my predecessors give me perspective. Whatever crises they faced are now gone. The country remains. It reminds me I'd have to work pretty damn hard to muck it up."

"May I quote you on that?"

"Absolutely not." There was an edge to his voice. His expression was harsh and he clenched his teeth, creating a line above his jaw bone.

"In that case, may we begin the actual interview and speak on the record?"

"Yes. Go ahead."

"Why wasn't the queen at the preschool? The press advisory said she'd be there to promote her 'Read to Succeed' program." I looked him straight in the eye and smiled. *Charm and disarm.*

"Ask the public affairs office for a statement on changes to her schedule."

I was talking to a different person—the warm, winning personality had evaporated. Sitting in front of me was a polished politician who gave perfect on-the-record answers.

"Okay. Then, what did you take away from today's event that you'll share with your grandmother?"

"I saw how the program's helping children with learning disabilities. Parents get referrals for at-home interventions and therapies. Government revenue subsidizes the service, but parents pay a fee based on their income."

He placed his right ankle on the opposite knee, expanding his physical presence. Instead of intimidating me, it intensified my desire to know him better. His ability to handle himself so skillfully in this setting underscored how prepared he was to become king. He exuded power and it hit me in heady waves.

"The press release said it's only a pilot program. Why doesn't the queen plead her case to the assembly for more funding? If she really believes it's such a great program, why not request broader implementation?"

John sighed and rubbed his hand over his eyes, underscoring his frustration. "Can I speak off the record?"

"No. Off-the-record comments are no good."

"Then we're done. You're asking a legitimate question, but I can't speak to it on the record." For the first time since we'd met, he looked extraordinarily pissed. He stood, and I panicked. I wasn't done asking questions.

"Wait. Let's try this again." I capped the pen and closed the notebook. "We're off the record." I crossed my arms—I couldn't use off-the-record comments in my story.

"It's very complicated." He sat down, his facial expression softening. "We'd love nothing more than to strong-arm the assembly into a full-scale implementation of this program. And we can make the case quite easily. This kind of early intervention improves literacy rates. In your country, policymakers look at the percentage of primary school students who fail standardized reading tests and use that number to determine how many prison cells they're going to need in fifteen years."

I was a little impressed. He knew his stuff.

"Then, what's the problem?"

He sighed and crinkled his brow. "My grandmother is the first royal in decades to set out a serious policy agenda that goes beyond asking for an increase in the royal family's income. She wants to tread lightly because there are other things she hopes to accomplish besides full implementation of 'Read to Succeed.'"

I scooted my chair closer to him because, off-the-record or not, this was getting good.

"What other things does she want to accomplish?"

A loud bang made me jump. A tall older woman dressed in tailored pants and a sweater approached us. She looked familiar.

"John! I didn't know you were here… and with a guest. I'm sorry to interrupt. I was just coming in to think about how we want to decorate the hall for Winter's Feast. Who's this?"

We stood and I scrambled to set the notebook and pen on my chair so I could extend my hand. Before I managed to introduce myself, she spoke.

"Going riding? I think the weather will put a damper on that." Her eyes narrowed as she inspected my riding attire.

"Hatty, this is Aunt Elinore, the Duchess of Kortemark. Aunt Elinore, Hatty. She's a journalist and she's interviewing me about my visit to the preschool this morning. I'm sorry Hatty. What's your last name?"

"Brunelle. It's French," I said, finding my voice.

"French? You don't sound French. Nor do you sound like you're from Toulene," John's aunt said with certainty.

"You're right. I'm from the States. Missouri, specifically." I expected the inevitable glazed over smile that told me the person to whom I was speaking had no idea where Missouri was because it wasn't New York or California.

"I've been there. To St. Louis a couple of times. Very nice area with a rich history. It's the Show Me State, isn't it?"

"Yes. That's right."

Her words were pleasant, but her presence was overbearing. It was like I was back in fifth grade, sweating under the stern gaze of Mrs. Scott instead of speaking to the Duchess of Kortemark. *The palace guard ate my homework.*

"And when will you return to Missouri?"

"I'm not sure. I graduate from the Royal University in May. I'm interning at *The Morning Dispatch* this semester."

"Hatty, you may know Aunt Elinore has traveled more than any other member of the royal family," John said, steering the conversation away from me.

"I hope you felt as welcome in Missouri as I've felt the last three and a half years in Toulene."

"Indeed. Lovely to meet you, Hatty. And I'm glad to see someone getting use out of those pants I ordered. They emphasize your child-bearing hips." She floated out of the hall.

I didn't know what to say. Had the Duchess of Kortemark just told me my thighs were fat?

The awkwardness of her parting shot wasn't lost on John either. "I'm sorry. We never know what she's going to say."

"It's okay. It's just a tad startling to hear a member of the royal family call out my thighs." I forced a courtesy laugh.

"I don't think that's what she was saying at all."

I caught a glimpse of his wristwatch. "I'd better head back to the newsroom and write my story. But I still want to hear about your grandmother's agenda, even if it's off the record. Maybe some other time?"

"I'd like that."

"Before I go, my editor wants me to ask you one other thing—on the record. At the risk of sounding like a gossip columnist, who was with you at the Carlisle racetrack Sunday?" I gave him the most serious look I could manage given the subject matter.

"That was my second cousin, Prudence. Most people here don't recognize her because Pru's lived in Australia since she was five. It was the first chance I've had to spend time with her in ages."

"Was it a date?" I totally sounded like a gossip columnist. Or a jealous girlfriend.

"With Pru? No. I did say she's my cousin, right?"

"But I thought…" I wanted to say, *But I thought royals sometimes marry their cousins. It's like a thing.*

"Hatty, let me give you a history lesson. Some of Europe's royal cousins married to strengthen or extend kingdoms. These were strategic alliances. I have a little more say over the choice of my wife than they did." He grinned, enjoying how uncomfortable this conversation made me feel.

"Okay. Sorry I had to ask about that."

"It's fine. The press profits from speculating about my personal life." *Um, ouch.* "Off the record, they don't realize the most exciting thing I've done this year was join you and your friends at the pub."

"*That* was the highlight of your year?" I knew he was teasing me.

"I met you, didn't I?"

His words rang in my ears and my cheeks tingled, resurrecting the giddiness I'd felt the night we met at Finn's.

Quick! Say something! "If you thought playing poker in the back room at Finn's was fun, you should try doing a round of Kamikaze Karaoke with us."

"Let me know the next time you're on stage. I'll do my best to be there. Maybe we can share another chocolate kiss."

My heart stammered as he lifted my hand, turned it over, and kissed the inside of my wrist. So much more intimate than a kiss on the back of my hand. It sure beat the hell out of a stiff handshake, which is how my interviews usually ended.

CHAPTER FOUR

I n the harsh fluorescents of the newsroom, my fingers tapped across the keyboard. I included all the on-the-record details I'd scribbled during the interview. There were scone crumbs scattered on my notes; the taste of cinnamon hovered in my mouth. Because I ran out of time and didn't get to eat at the palace, John sent me out the door with a warm pastry wrapped in a cloth napkin. *Nom nom.*

A zing hummed through my arms, energizing me. Time to submit my story, go home, and comb through every moment I'd spent with the prince. I was in the throes of committing a cardinal sin for a journalist: I was crushing on him. Would he really come out with me and my friends for Kamikaze Karaoke? The possibility filled me with nervous excitement.

I wrapped up my story and hit "send." James was gone for the day, and Brigitte, the sleepy-looking night editor sat hunched over her desk, ready to nod off, per usual. While I waited for her to approve the story so I could leave, I got out my notes for an investigative piece I was writing. By the time I opened my spreadsheets, Brigitte was by my side. Even though she looked like she was teetering between wakefulness and a solid nap, she was a notoriously quick editor.

"James said you were going to write about being the girl in the limo." Brigitte handed me a print out of my story. "And what about the photos you took after the event?"

I held up my phone. "It's dead. I guess it can't handle its water." I'd plugged it into the charger on the off chance a steady flow of juice might revive it. I pushed the home button. Nada.

"Cripes. Well, then just go back and include a few lines about how the prince pulled you into the limo with him, took you to the palace, and gave you an exclusive interview." She walked away.

I went back to my story, hating that I had to inject myself into the narrative. I balked at the idea of pulling attention away from the preschool visit and the "Read to Succeed" program. Those elements were the essence of the story. My limo ride and brief time at the palace were a side show.

Still, there was no arguing with Brigitte. If I refused to expand my story, she'd roll her sleepy eyes and get James on the phone. I made the changes, got her to sign off on the revised draft, and drove to my apartment in Reines, a suburb of the capital.

As much as I wanted to deconstruct everything with my bestie, Tilda, my phone was a goner. And in truth, I simply wanted to soak in my claw foot tub and remember the details of the day: the way his jacket smelled, the look on his face when I walked out of the bedroom wearing those ridiculous riding clothes, the authority in his voice when he answered my questions, his lips pressed against the inside of my wrist, leaving a tingling sensation. I closed my eyes, inhaling the lavender aroma of the bath salts. My body responded each time I called up the prince's face and voice in my head, the collection of images and sounds looped repeatedly for my pleasure.

Rising from the tub, I wrapped a threadbare towel around my midsection just as a flash of light caught my eye. I looked through the crack in the curtains. More storms?

There it was again. Definitely not lightning. Something or someone was out there. My mom once warned me about weirdos who stalk reporters. I wondered if someone saw the story about me being "limo girl" and decided to look me up. I shivered at the thought of someone trying to photograph me getting out of the tub. I pulled the towel tighter and slammed my hand against the light switch as an unfamiliar jumpiness taunted my nerves.

CHAPTER FIVE

When I stepped onto my front stoop the next morning—a dreary October Thursday—an explosion of flashes and clicks stunned me. If I had any doubts about whether I was a part of the story, they evaporated in a flurry. I pushed and jostled my way through the crowd. Panic rose in my chest—the camera sounds and the movement of bodies made me think of swarming insects.

"Are you dating the prince?"

"Hatty, what did you do at the palace?"

"Are you John's new girlfriend?"

I recognized some of the dozen or so men from yesterday's press line at the childcare center. A scream threatened to burst from my lips as one photographer knelt down, a human obstacle between me and my car.

Wonder how much your photo is worth. Don't do anything stupid!

"Excuse me," I said, using my hands to part the group and open my car door. They moved aside without comment and I mentally gave them the middle finger.

Pulling away from the curb, I checked my rearview mirror. No one followed me, though a couple of photographers crouched in the street snapping pictures of the back of my car. Evidently, I was important enough to stalk, but not significant enough to chase. I found comfort in this knowledge.

Despite the unusual and disconcerting start to my day courtesy of the paparazzi, I realized the daily grind of reporting was going to feel especially dull after spending Wednesday with the prince at his palace. But the variety of assignments was one reason I loved journalism. I might interview a prince one day, and cover striking garbage collectors the next.

When I entered the newsroom, no one so much as looked up from their computer. I sat down at my desk and opened the notes for my investigative story. Paul, another intern, came over and tossed an envelope on my desk.

"What's this?"

"I don't know. The receptionist asked me to give it to you. You're famous now, you know," he said over his shoulder, as he walked away.

"Um, thanks?" I had no idea how to handle this new attention.

I looked at the envelope; I rarely received mail at the newsroom. I rubbed the heavy, creamy paper. Nice texture. My name was written in a neat script across the front. I opened it to find a note card inside in the same handwriting.

Dear Hatty,

Thank you for your article on my grandmother's early education program. I enjoyed speaking with you yesterday at Belvoir, and your article accurately reflected our discussion. Since your visit was impromptu and brief, I'd like to invite you back for a private tour of the palace. I'll send a driver to pick you up Saturday at 9:00 a.m. at your flat.

Sincerely,

John

The notecard fluttered from my hand onto the keyboard as my desk phone rang. I grabbed it.

"Are you okay? I've been trying to call you since last night. Please tell me there's a reason you didn't call and tell me everything about your new romance with Prince John." Tilda didn't pause for a breath.

"New romance? What are you talking about?" My stomach gave a restless turn.

"Haven't you read the other papers this morning? The Daily Scoop blog?" She sounded incredulous.

"No. I had a late night—"

"I bet you did!"

"Look, I got to interview the prince, then had to come back here and crank out my story."

As I spoke, I typed and clicked, trying to pull up the websites for the other papers.

I gasped. "Oh, no…" If the notecard from Prince John took my breath away, the story on the screen sucked all the oxygen out of the room. "What the heck?"

"Looks like you're the prince's newest conquest."

Prince John Whisks Journalist Away for Romantic Tour of Palace

By Xpress staff

October 17, 2013

As Prince John dashed from the Smart Start preschool Wednesday afternoon, he invited a young reporter to ride with him in his limo.

According to a source, this was not the first time the prince had met this particular newspaper intern.

"Someone told me they heard the prince kissed her at a bar," said a Smart Start staffer who asked to remain anonymous.

Xpress has learned the mystery woman is Hatty Brunelle, newsroom intern for The Morning Dispatch.

She's the latest in a long string of women seen in public recently with the prince who's on the rebound after his messy split from Claire Léglise, daughter of Monaco casino magnate François Léglise.

"Tilda. This is disastrous," I whispered.

"Well, is it true?"

"What? No. Yes. Kind of." I explained to her what happened, and how it must have looked to the other reporters as the guard pulled me into the limo with the prince.

"Tilda. I interviewed him at Belvoir. I was very professional." This stupid tabloid story completely stole my credibility as a reporter.

Paul approached my desk. "James wants to see you in his office."

"I've got to go. My editor's about to skewer me."

I hung up and walked into James' office.

"Close the door. Sit." He spoke in the same direct tone he wanted us to use when writing our stories.

He turned his computer monitor around, and there was the article I just read. "What's this?"

"I don't know." I hated confrontation… when I was on the receiving end.

"Do you know how this looks?"

"Awful. It makes me look like a ditz who's chasing the prince."

"Maybe. But it also looks like you've got an inside line to Belvoir. Your star at the paper's rising. Letting him drag you into his limo may have been the best move of your career. So, do you have a special relationship with the prince?" He leaned toward me with a wink.

"No. I met him for the first time briefly Saturday night at a bar. Then yesterday, he recognized me outside the preschool. It started raining and I was getting soaked. He had one of his guards bring me into the limo. That's it."

"I don't care how it happened. We want to give you your own blog."

"And what will I write about? My investigation into the environmental and health impacts of the smelter at Kortrijk?" *Yes! A platform for my investigative story!*

"No. You'll write about anything and everything involving the royal family. It will complement Heidi's coverage. Is that a problem?" His tone dared me to disagree. I watched in horror as my personal and professional lives collided at the intersection of Big Break Boulevard and Prince Charming Way.

"I need to think about it. Can I let you know Monday?"

"No. We have to strike while you're hot. Most interns would kill for this kind of break."

He was right, of course. But covering the royals was merely an amusing assignment. I went into journalism to take down corrupt politicians by brandishing my stick-it-to-the-man attitude. Blogging about the royals was like getting in bed with the man. Metaphorically speaking, of course.

"If I do this new blog, can I still do my investigative story?"

"Sure. Take a couple of hours this morning. But the blog is your priority. We want to promote it. This is going to change your life, Hatty."

CHAPTER SIX

After leaving James' office, I borrowed Paul's phone and texted Tilda. I asked her to round up Plato, Sam, and Sara for drinks at Finn's. Since it was a non-karaoke night, it wouldn't be crowded. Full of people or not, we loved this pub precisely because it wasn't like any of the other bars in town, most of which felt frozen with cold, modern décor and post-modern rock.

We sat in our usual booth at the back, sipping Toulene's famous red wine and speculating about my visit to Belvoir Saturday.

"Do you think he'll try to kiss you again?" Sara asked, already a bit tipsy.

"Absolutely not. This is strictly professional, and I'm not sure he even tried to kiss me last Saturday," I asserted.

"Your flirt-dar's broken. Of course, he tried to kiss you."

"Flirt-dar?"

"Your flirting radar. I was sitting across the room, and I saw him lift your chin and lean in for a kiss." Sara kissed the air with a loud smack.

"Sara's right. I think he's into you, girl." Plato's eyebrows bounced up and down and he grinned as though he had inside knowledge.

"You guys are crazy. This invitation to visit the palace is merely a courtesy."

"Perhaps. But I bet he thinks he can use you, that you'll do whatever he asks," Tilda said, ever skeptical of the royal family. The daughter of Kenyan immigrants, Tilda worked for Assemblyman Hans Aalders, a majority leader in the federal legislative body.

"Well, he can forget that, too. And they're the most powerful family in the country. Why do they need reporters in their back pocket?"

"Are you serious? They have a select group of reporters they use to plant stories. They think the press can sway the National Assembly and public opinion. Unfortunately, they're right, to an extent, though my boss doesn't care about the press. No offense, Hatty," Tilda said.

"None taken."

From the moment she heard about my encounter with the prince after my karaoke performance, Tilda questioned his motives. Even though she was a relatively recent law school grad and had only worked for the assemblyman a few months, she already had a firm grasp on the inner workings of Toulene's political scene and how the royal family figured into it.

I glanced across the room and saw my fellow intern Paul sitting in a booth, snapping photos of us with his smartphone. Without hesitation, I marched over to him.

"What are you doing?" I grabbed his phone and looked at the pictures. Most of them were close-ups of me. I began deleting them.

"Hey! That's my phone!"

"That's my face! Stop it." I slammed his phone onto the table. "Look, you idiot. I'm not the story. The royals are. Didn't you hear? James wants me to blog about them. So leave me alone." I turned and walked back to my table.

"Who the hell's that?" Plato inquired. As a graduate student, fellow American, and occasional DJ-for-hire, Plato knew lots of 20-somethings in Roeselare, and he was always shocked when we ran into someone he didn't recognize.

"Paul. Another intern at the *Dispatch*."

"You're such a badass. I hope the real paparazzi does try to come after you. You'll kill 'em." Plato didn't know about my lack of badassery when I'd gone toe-to-toe with the photographers outside my apartment building that morning.

I looked back at Paul sitting by himself. He was glaring at me and I mouthed the word *douchebag*.

"Look, I've been around John at several poker games," Plato said. "He's very chill. I don't think he wants to seduce you. His reputation for dating a lot of women is totally overblown. And I don't think he wants to use you to influence the legislative process. You guys are overthinking it. Back me up here, Sam."

"Oui. I agree. Hatty, you will be brilliant Saturday. He may give you another exclusive interview." Sam gave me his sweet smile. He was always the nicest man in the room.

"Sam? Can't you forget this Plato guy and run away with me?" I teased.

"Yes, to hell with Plato and the prince! We'll live in my medieval castle, grow our own grapes, and make wine." He punctuated his proposal by kissing the length of my arm. Flitting around a vineyard with a handsome gay man sounded kind of awesome.

"Well, no matter what Prince John's true intentions are, there's the little matter of my wardrobe, and what I'm going to wear Saturday. Tilda? Sara?"

"Would love to help, but I've got a date Friday night." Sara pressed her palms in the air in her favorite raise-the-roof gesture.

"Is it with what's-his-name? The one who's supposed to be a royal cousin three times removed?" Plato threw back the last of his drink.

"The very one," Sara said, standing from our table. "I've got to get home. The coffee fiends start beating down the door at 6:00 a.m., and I've got to be there to open. Hatty, I'm completely jealous you get to see your hottie prince again. Tell him your friend is dating his cousin-in-law on his dead mother's side."

"Will do. I'd better head out, too. Tilda, don't abandon me on the fashion front. I don't want a tragedy on my hands come Saturday morning."

"I always come to the rescue. I'll stop by your apartment tomorrow night."

As I walked with Sara down the sidewalk, anticipation swelled in my chest. What did I expect to happen Saturday at the palace? I had no idea.

CHAPTER SEVEN

E ven though the world knew I was the reporter the prince whisked away in the limo on Wednesday, the paparazzi's interest faded quickly. After a couple of the photographers decided to trail me Friday to the newsroom, coffeehouse, and back to my apartment, they saw just how dull the life of an intern was. By that evening, there were no more photographers hanging around my building. They had prettier people to photograph.

When Tilda came to my apartment Friday night, she suggested I wear my crisp, indigo jeans, a green V-neck sweater, and brown boots for my palace visit. She knew all about the complex I had stemming from a comment Jenny Marshall made sophomore year of high school: she said the clothes I wore made me look dudely.

Saturday morning precisely at nine, I walked to the street and met the nondescript black car that pulled up in front of my apartment building with no fanfare, fuss, or flash of cameras.

The driver got out and opened the door. I slid across the smooth leather of the back seat. Deep breathing helped me combat my nerves as we drove out of my suburb and into the capital city. We pulled into the same gate I'd entered the last time I was here.

A tall man with impeccable posture met me when I stepped out of the car. "Good morning, Miss. I'm Mr. Vermeulen. May I get your coat before I take you to the prince?"

I slid off my heavy jacket as I stood under an awning, trying to place his accent. Definitely not from Toulene. Belgium, maybe?

I handed him the riding clothes I wore home Wednesday. I'd washed them twice and taken great care with folding them. "I had to borrow these, and wanted to return them."

"Thank you, Miss."

He led me into the palace, and through the hallways and stairs I'd last traversed with John. Mr. Vermeulen walked at a much more reasonable pace, I noted. I recognized our destination at once, and smiled as John met me at the door to the red room with all the paintings.

The potential for awkwardness flashed in my mind only for a moment—whether to shake his hand or just nod or (gulp) hug him.

"Good morning, Hatty! How are you doing?" He was positively beaming as he wrapped his arms around me in a bear hug, making me feel like a long lost royal cousin rather than a journalist. With his body pressed against mine, warmth radiated down to my toes. Having his arms squeezing me felt scrumptious. I inhaled deeply, catching that mixture of mint, soap, and aftershave, the Holy Trinity of sexy man scent.

"I'm good. Thank you for doing all this." I waved my hands around. *Stop the gawky arm movements!*

"It's my pleasure. I'm sorry I didn't get to show you around Wednesday. This is the least I can do after you wrote such a lovely story."

"Thank you." Ugh. It wasn't meant to be a "lovely" story. I tried to write a straightforward account of our interview, the parts that were on the record anyway.

"Walk with me."

We took a leisurely pace, strolling along the closest wall. I stopped to examine the paintings up close.

"This room is where we hold our annual Winter's Feast, and it's also hosted a couple of royal weddings." He sounded like a tour guide giving the usual spiel.

The solemn eyes of the men and women in the portraits seemed to gaze collectively at a point in the distance, as though straining for a glimpse into the future.

"They look so serious. Do you ever wonder what made them laugh?"

"No. I've never thought about it before. What do you suppose made Great Aunt Helena up there unfreeze her frown?"

"Maybe she laughed at the desperation reflected in Uncle Comb Over's hairstyle." I pointed to the man in the portrait next to her. "I bet she gave him grief about it when he posed for the artist. Maybe she said, 'Why don't you just take it all off? You're not fooling anyone, you know!'" I laughed. And snorted.

Then, I froze. John wasn't laughing.

"Hatty. That's Uncle Gustav, a German count who married into the family. He died of an infectious disease that thinned his hair."

"Oh, gosh. I'm so sorry. I had no idea. It was stupid of me to say…"

John's laughter interrupted me. He pointed at my apologetic face and said, "Now that's funny."

I gently punched him on the arm. "I thought you were serious!"

We both laughed unrestrained like a couple of kids. In that unguarded moment, our laughter swirling together, my eyes met his. A current of attraction passed between us, charging the air, and I saw his eyes open wider to acknowledge it.

He cleared his throat and looked up at the portraits. "You've certainly imparted a new level of humanity to these stoic faces. I'm not sure I'll ever look at them the same way."

He was still smiling when he turned to face me. "Hatty, all of today is off the record. I mean, you're not on the clock. So, this isn't about work. Agreed?"

Dang it! I'd hoped to find a story for my blog during today's visit. Even though it wasn't the kind of journalism I wanted to do, I did want to give it my best shot.

"Yes. It's off the record." *Sigh.*

"Excellent. Let's keep moving."

We walked out of the Regents Room and up a wooden staircase.

We stood at the start of a long hallway. Farther down on the left, light poured into an open area with an overstuffed couch. We walked toward it, and I saw it wasn't just a single window that lit up the sitting area. One entire wall was made of glass, so you could sit and drink in the view. A flat screen larger than any I'd ever seen was mounted on one of the other walls. Heavy drapes hung at the edges of the window, ready to shut out the light for anyone who wanted to watch television.

"When we're home, this is where my dad, my brother, and I spend a decent amount of time."

"I can see why. What an amazing view."

The entire western end of the capital city sprawled out from our feet. Close to the palace and just beneath us was a massive lawn where a handful of peacocks preened, despite the cold. Beyond the palace grounds were three blocks of government buildings followed by houses that seemed to huddle together along each block. They all had the same steeply sloped roofs that were popular in Toulene.

We continued down the hall.

"We call this part of the palace 'The Flat' because it's the family's private apartment." John opened a wide door on the right. "And this is my room."

He's showing me his bedroom?

I stepped into an elegant space. It had a high ceiling and green, textured wallpaper depicting several scenes. They all featured caricatures of Asian men in conical hats with long flowing beards and moustaches.

A bed covered in a shiny green comforter took up one wall. A broad, light green rug provided a dose of warmth against the hardwood floors.

I pointed to the bed. "King size?"

"What else?" He winked, and my flirt-dar kicked into high gear. He didn't invite me to the palace as a professional courtesy. We were in his bedroom for Pete's sake.

"That's some serious wallpaper." *That's right. Take your mind off his bed.*

"It is, and it's there to stay. When your home's a palace, it's like living in a museum. I can't very well tear down hand-painted silk wallpaper from China that dates back to the 18th century."

"Well, you could, but I bet you'd suffer the wrath of the Historical Preservation Division."

There was a sunken sitting area by the windows where a golden harp gleamed in the morning sun.

"Do you play?"

"A little," he said, not meeting my eyes.

"Would you play something for me?"

"Sure. Except this really has to be off the record."

"Why? Afraid harp playing might ruin your playboy reputation?"

"Something like that."

He sat on the little stool and tilted the instrument back so it rested on his shoulder. He extended his arms and fingers, and strummed the strings. The sound throbbed through the air, delicate but also seductive. The sight of his fingers plucking the strings with strength and skill gave me an unexpected twinge of desire.

I sank into a small green settee and closed my eyes. The music was beautiful, so personal. He responded as he felt the melody and chord progression push faster in some spots, and then retreat to a slower and softer sound in others. The final notes hung in the air.

"I hardly know what to say... except that's amazing. How long have you played?"

"I started taking lessons when I was nine, after Mom died. She used to play. It's a way for me to feel connected to her."

This intimate revelation startled me; I suspected very few people ever saw this side of him.

"You're very talented. Why don't you play with the Toulene National Symphony?"

"There aren't many things about myself that I can keep private. This is one of the few. Remember—this is off the record." He smiled, but there was a warning in his expression.

"Yes, completely off the record. Thank you for sharing this with me." Disarmed by his openness, I felt compelled to reveal my new assignment. "And, if we're being honest here, then I need to tell you something. My editor at *The Morning Dispatch* is making me write a blog about you and your family." I physically cringed, crinkling my nose and squinting my eyes against whatever reaction my news might provoke.

"What's it called?"

My toes scraped against the inside of my boots. "First-Rate Royals."

"So, you're not covering the second-rate cousins?" His smile revealed total amusement.

"I know. It's a stupid name. It's what the paper wants."

"Well, maybe the world will finally get a first-rate look at our family. The article you wrote from our interview was accurate and fair. That's all we expect."

Expect? Had Tilda been right? Maybe he did invite me here to ask if I'd write stories to push his family's agenda.

He returned the harp to its resting, upright position. As he sat down beside me on the settee, my neck felt hot.

"Hatty, I'm having a press event Tuesday to celebrate the opening of the new airport runway. I'd like you to come." He gazed into my eyes with a sincerity that made my breath catch in my throat. The intensity of the moment bubbled with the secret chemistry of our attraction. Surely he felt it, too.

"Sounds great. I'd like to cover it." I looked down at my hands and blinked to clear my head. *Chemistry or not, don't expect any softball questions, buddy!*

"Excellent. I'll look forward to seeing you there." He stood and went to the door. "Let's go see the library."

"Now you're talking. Libraries are magical. I could spend hours surrounded by books. It's like hanging out with your closest friends."

"Then you'll love ours."

When we arrived in front of wooden double doors, John swept them open with exaggerated ceremony. The room had floor to ceiling bookshelves and a couple of those cool ladders that slide side to side.

John led me to a book under glass. It was open to a page with elegant handwriting and an illustration of a slender bird-like creature near the top. Its body curved into a C with its arms jutting out to hold a long, straight horn that extended from its mouth to its tail.

"This is a 14th century manuscript of the Magna Charta cum statutis. Scholars believe Phillipa of Hainault commissioned it for Edward III to celebrate their marriage."

"She commissioned a book for him? That's so romantic. I'd swoon over that kind of gift."

"Romantic? Hardly. It's a legal text."

I chuckled. "Maybe she wanted to start their marriage by laying down the law."

John looked at me, puzzled.

"You're not familiar with the expression 'lay down the law?'"

"Sorry." He smiled, but still looked lost.

"We use it a lot in the Ozarks. It means she was trying to show him who's boss."

"If that's what she was doing, she was ahead of her time by several centuries," he said, lifting the glass.

I leaned forward for a closer look. It was hard to imagine someone creating such intricate pictures and lines of text by hand without making any mistakes.

"We have this text on loan from Harvard until Monday. Curators from the national history museum are coming to get it, so they can put it on public display for six months." He replaced the glass.

"Wow. The perks of being royal."

"My father's a student of history. They brought this here at his request. He's always chasing some rare book or document."

After the library, we peeked in a large sitting room, three small parlors, a billiard room, and a casual breakfast area where the family members eat their meals in a more normal atmosphere. At Belvoir, that meant enjoying toast and fried eggs prepared by the cook while checking email on your phone. If my run-in with the paparazzi was any indication, the royals rarely experienced anything close to normal life when they left the palace. Next, he took me down several flights of stairs into a cellar area and flicked on a naked bulb overhead.

"These are the subterranean tunnels. During various wars, my family hid valuables down here and even sheltered prominent allies who needed protection. Now, they're abandoned."

I gazed into the three tunnels. Absolute darkness sat like a wall just a couple of feet from where we stood.

"This is Creepsville."

John touched my arm, making me jump. "You've got chicken skin."

"What?" I looked down at his hand holding my arm under the light. "Oh, you mean goose bumps. Yes, well. I bet a group of ghost hunters would have a field day down here."

"They've requested access to these tunnels. We get petitions from psychics and the like every year asking to investigate Belvoir, and we reject all of them."

"You're no fun. Wouldn't you like to know if there are spirits in here?" At the word *spirits*, a fresh crop of goose bumps sprouted on my arms.

"The only spirits we care about come in bottles. Let's move on."

We finished our tour above ground, stepping onto the wide stone patio out back. The peacocks had moved farther into the yard, beautiful even with their tails stowed.

"What's going on over there?" I nodded to a small section where three men were clearing out dry brush.

"That's going to be a garden. Granny has high hopes for it next year." He calls the queen Granny? I thought it had to be Queen Mum or something.

"Even though today's tour is off the record, may I do a blog post about your grandmother's intentions to start a garden?" It was such a lame story, but it was better than leaving empty-handed.

He squinted as he looked toward the small, dry patch of weeds and bushes. It appeared incapable of producing anything luscious and green.

"Yes. But let me have the public affairs office draft a press release."

"Wait. If they do a press release, everybody will have the story. Have them send it to me first and give me a five hour lead. Can you live with that?" It's like we were haggling over the price of produce at a farmer's market.

"Sure. I'll let them know."

"And tell the palace not to send out any pictures of the guys over there. Let me break in my new phone by snapping a few photos. At least that way, I'll have something no one else does." *I smell an exclusive!*

"Aren't you Miss Bossy Boots?" His voice rose with mock shock and I laughed at the nickname. It was completely out of character for him to say that, but also adorable.

"Bossy Boots? You have no idea."

"Sounds like he definitely wants something from you." Tilda huffed into the phone as she paused mid-run to hear the details of my palace visit.

"No! Everything's on the up and up. He showed me around and invited me to cover his presser Tuesday at the airport."

"Hatty. That project is a huge waste of money. If you go, you have to hold him accountable for the budget overruns and delays. His father forced the Department of Administration to hire a company that's run by close friends of the Meinrad family. In fact, they probably own part of it."

"Yikes. I'm sure the other reporters will ask those questions before I have the chance to chime in."

She choked out a laugh. "Don't count on it. The royals almost never take reporters' questions."

"What do you mean?"

"If you get to ask him questions, it's likely to be one-on-one after the event. He almost never opens the floor for reporters to shout questions at him."

My thoughts flipped into overdrive as a blurry idea came into focus: he's letting me ask questions because I'm an intern. He thinks I have no idea what I'm doing. That ticked me off. I began mapping out a plan to prove him wrong.

"Okay. I'm stopping by your office Monday to get some background. Let's bust this boondoggle wide open."

CHAPTER EIGHT

The granite tomb. That's what staffers called the National Assembly building, referring to the dimly lit hallways and cave-like alcoves. After an hour-long briefing with Tilda on the airport runway debacle, I left her office and headed to the library. I wanted to do some more research for my investigative story.

Of all the odd nooks and unusual spaces in this building, the library was my favorite. Gilded columns fit for a church conferred a holy status on the books lining the shelves between them. Ceiling art mimicking the heavens added to the spiritual aura. Libraries were my second home. As the daughter of a third grade teacher, I spent many hours sitting between floor-to-ceiling book shelves at her school, and even once fell asleep among the stacks. *Come, and I will give you rest.*

My ankles wobbled a skosh when my heels melted into the thick carpeting. I headed to the back room, a less impressive space, where I could search through the property deed archives.

I'd scanned the volumes on two other occasions, spreading out the old registers on the floor around me. As much as I loved how

Toulene's history unfolded with each entry, I needed to know a specific fact: who owned the land where the smelter sat near Kortrijk? This bit of information was one of several missing pieces in my story. Scientists from my university were also digging, literally turning shovels full of dirt to see if toxins were leaking from the plant into the soil. Others were investigating the incidents of disease and illness in the vicinity of the smelter. For my part, I was keeping tabs on the researchers and talking to neighbors.

Cracking open and carefully examining each register was my detective work. I. Loved. It. I may or may not have photoshopped a Sherlock Holmes pipe and hat onto my newspaper badge photo while I waited for an edit last week.

As I settled onto the floor toward the very back wall, I heard the door open, and then close with a soft click. Footsteps coming toward me? Yes, but in the row next to mine.

"Tell him he has to be more careful." It was a man's voice, hushed and rushed. "You've caught me at the assembly. Can we discuss this later?"

I silently set aside the papers in my lap and raised up on my knees. I slid out a handful of books at my eye-level. Gazing over the books on the other side of the shelf, I saw dark pants.

"Yes. Keep them away from each other." The voice oozed irritation.

I stood slowly, and removed another handful of books silently. Or almost. John's eyes looked back at me through the narrow shelf space. I gasped and dropped the books, creating muffled thumps.

"I need to go. See you soon."

John rounded the corner of my row. He wore his authority as well as he wore his dark suit. The determination driving his steps spoke to the power he wielded in this building. And all I saw was that impeccable hair, complete with the gorgeous bit of waviness in the front.

"Imagine meeting you here." I tried to sound contrite for spying.

"You're getting the hang of stalking royals, aren't you?" An intensity infused his voice and he didn't smile.

"Hey, I was here first. Maybe you're stalking me."

"How much did you overhear?"

"Not much. You sounded pissed."

"Pardon? I've only had water and tea today."

Damn British slang! "I mean you sounded upset."

He exhaled, relaxing a little. "May I join you?" He gestured to the ground where my backpack sat slouched and several books lay open. "What could possibly interest an American journalism student back here?" He picked up one of the books.

"Just a reporting project I'm doing that has nothing to do with any of you royals." *Thank goodness.*

"Will I see you tomorrow at the airport?"

"Yes. Will I get to ask you questions afterward?"

"You can ask me anything right now." His voice was low and he gave me a half smile, a flirty little firework that invited me to respond in kind. But there was no way I was going to pass up the chance to ask him a tough question.

"Why did your family pressure the Department of Administration to hire Hastert Construction for the project?"

"God, Hatty! Don't you ever give it a rest?"

"Hey, we both live on-the-record lives."

In a blur, he sprang toward me, his hand swiping across my left shoulder.

"Sorry. There was a spider on you."

"Ick. Thanks. Occupational hazard of hanging out in old buildings."

I peeked down at the offending creature. Spindly legs radiated from a body the size of a quarter. As I stared at the beast and scooted away from it, John took my hand and helped me up.

"Okay. That was a close call."

"I'll answer your questions tomorrow. All of them. Thank you for letting me interrupt your work."

A wave of shock pulsed through my body as I realized he was still holding my hand.

"No problem. I'll see you tomorrow," I said.

He squeezed my hand before letting it go. "Tomorrow."

CHAPTER NINE

I stood by the mult box where the radio reporters had their recorders plugged into the sound system to capture the audio of the dedication ceremony. The guards had corralled print and radio journos into a segregated area at the back of the hangar. We still had a sightline to snap cell phone photos, but the photojournalists and videographers were up on risers in a separate area nearby. Mine was a fun bunch with their made-for-radio wardrobes and frenetic energy.

When the event ended, Grimmy McGrim, aka Limo Guard, materialized and pulled down the rope that marked our area. He motioned to the reporters to exit, and everyone did. I hung back a moment. When all the journalists were gone, he nodded, and I followed him. In the hubbub of everyone leaving, no one noticed.

He took me through a side door that led outside the hangar. A black car, maybe the same one that had picked me up Saturday, was waiting.

"Come here often?" I asked the prince as I sat beside him in the back of the car.

"Only when I want to escape the press."

"Thanks for letting me invade your space."

"It's not an invasion. I invited you. We're going to drive to the palace, and you can ask questions until we arrive. Then, I'll have a car take you to the newsroom."

"Thanks. Okay. First question: why did your family pressure the Department of Administration to hire Hastert Construction for this project?"

"Really? You're going to start with that?"

I looked at him expectantly.

"You assume we pressured them. My grandmother merely sent the administrators a letter endorsing Hastert Construction because they have the strongest record of working with Turkish immigrants. We want to encourage these foreign workers to integrate into society, and employment is a big part of making that happen."

Okay. Sounded legit. Note to self: double check his assertions.

"Your family owns part of Hastert Construction. Isn't that a conflict of interest?"

"Double check your facts. No one in my immediate family owns a stake in the company. My cousin Gerhard Hohenstaufen of Germany is part owner but that hardly constitutes a conflict of interest. I stand behind my grandmother's decision to recommend them for the project."

"The runway project ran over budget. Twice. Why?"

"The cost of materials went up. Then, the assembly's new wage laws took effect. Public projects are subject to the whims of the market and the assembly. I know your friend Tilda works for Assemblyman Aalders. He can't change the wage laws and then get mad when companies that have government contracts comply with them."

"Why continue with the project if the costs were escalating?"

"This new runway opens Toulene to countries outside Europe. We can now handle larger planes. What I'm about to say is off the record: a major airline will announce next week that it will soon offer direct flights from the U.S. to Roeselare."

This was a big freaking deal. There had never been direct flights from the States into Toulene's capital or any of its other cities. I always flew in and out of Brussels. More tourists would be a game-changer for the country's economy.

"Will you give me an advance copy of the press release on the airline announcement without an embargo so I can break the story?"

"Let's see how you do with today's story first. If you do a fair job of explaining all sides, I'll see what I can do. Actually, I want to offer you something even better. Saturday, I'm going to Ghent for a private gathering. Would you be interested in joining me?"

I didn't have to think twice about my answer. I'd take any opportunity to spend time with him. Still, it struck me as odd; royals didn't let reporters tag along just for funsies, especially when it was something private. Tilda's warnings about him wanting to use me to plant stories rang in my ears. I'd just have to stay on guard and be careful.

CHAPTER TEN

I glanced out the train window, watching the fields of Toulene's farms slide by in a brown and yellow blur as we wound our way toward Ghent. John sat in a seat across from me. I had to admit he looked handsome even though a baseball cap covered his to-die-for hair. Two royal guards sat at the far end of the car. Otherwise, it was deserted.

The day after my airport runway story ran, John sent me a note complimenting my story and outlining the details of our trip to Ghent. I'd discussed the invitation with my editor, and James immediately insisted I go. The whole thing—passing notes, getting my editor's blessing to go with the prince to Ghent—had a whiff of middle school drama.

"Tell me about yourself. What was it like growing up in Missouri?"

My stomach knotted. I hated talking about myself, especially to someone I was covering. "Why do you care about my life?"

"Why do you care about mine?"

"It's my job. I care because readers care."

"But I hardly think it's fair. You know so much about me, and I know almost nothing about you. Other than the fact you think my relative's unfortunate comb over is funny."

I smiled and blushed, remembering the awkwardly funny conversation.

As the gentle rocking motion of the train helped me relax, I told John about my school teacher mother and my father who was an emergency room nurse.

"So you don't have any brothers or sisters?" He sounded surprised.

"No. My mom and dad always said they liked being able to focus on me. Sometimes I do think I have a sister-size hole in my heart. Honestly though, I would've taken a brother, too." I felt the pulse of a phantom pain I thought I'd tucked away in the recesses of my soul years ago.

"I'd like to have a large family. I loved growing up with a younger brother. And even though I had Henri, I wanted more siblings. I think if Mum had lived, there would've been a gaggle of us."

A gaggle of kids. In photos, his mother glowed, radiating an inner light that many expectant mothers possess.

"I didn't know her, of course, but I believe you. I imagine she would've had Belvoir overrun with beautiful, talented children."

John's earnest smile at my assessment hinted at his longing to know what might have been. Our eyes caught for a brief moment. Then, he cleared his throat, looked down, and studied his hands. His vulnerability and brief awkwardness were endearing.

Best to change the subject. "So, you have a degree in agriculture, is that right?" I mentally thanked Google for existing so I could read up on his background before today's adventure.

"Yes. I'm actually working on a doctoral degree."

"In farming?"

"Not exactly. It's in environmental science. I'm studying invasive species. Just look at this beautiful farmland." He nodded toward the windows. "Non-native plants and insects threaten this way of life. There's a farm out by the coast near De Haan where I do my research."

I had to silence my inner skeptic. She was rolling her eyes and wondering, *Is that some kind of Marie Antoinette thing where you go "play farmer?"*

"I'd love to see your work in the field. And I guess you're literally out in a field, right?"

He laughed. "That's right. How do you feel about getting your hands dirty?"

"I'm from Missouri. I'm not afraid of a little mud."

We chatted about the day he had planned, but he didn't share any specifics. First, we were going to a private gathering in downtown Ghent, then we'd visit one of the city's biggest tourist attractions. I'd done a fair amount of traveling around Europe since my arrival in Toulene three and a half years ago, but I'd spent little time in Belgium, which was right next door. I was excited to experience yet another country and language, though John reminded me Belgium and Toulene are similar in terms of the landscape, demographics, and culture.

When we arrived at the station, an SUV picked us up. We got in the backseat, and Bernard (Limo Guard had a name!) sat up front with the driver. The other guard got into a car behind us. Without a word, the driver sped off, weaving expertly through the heavy traffic.

"Is it always this crowded in the fall?" The volume of cars filling the streets was astounding.

"Yes. Ghent and Bruges are both popular with tourists right up until the end of November." John took out a small black book from his coat pocket. "Thomas, we can go straight to the foundation office."

It warmed my heart that John had taken the time to write out the details of our day in a notebook instead of relying exclusively on pop-up reminders on his smartphone like the rest of Europe and the U.S. I smiled as I imagined him bent over a desk writing out our itinerary.

"Foundation? What foundation?"

"Not long after my mother was diagnosed with ovarian cancer, she set up a private foundation. As you may know, she was born in Ghent and lived here until she was twelve. After her cancer diagnosis, she wanted to help the women here who were in a similar situation. She realized they didn't have the support she had because of her money and position. So, she established a place where they could go for financial assistance and therapy. I try to visit the support group from time to time."

It was such a tender revelation. In all my research, I'd read nothing about his mother establishing a foundation.

"Why didn't I find anything about this online?"

"She kept it quiet because she didn't do it for the publicity. I like to visit as a way to honor her."

I paused, carefully considering how to ask my question. "Are you going to let me report on this?"

"No."

"Then, why am I here?"

"Hatty, I want to get to know you better. And I want you to get to know me."

I swallowed. Loudly. His words tilted my world, aligning reality with some of the what-if scenarios I'd choreographed in my head since we first met at Finn's. What if he really, *really* liked me? Exhilaration rushed every cell in my body, and I stifled my overwhelming desire to scream.

But it was possible I was misreading him. "Get to know me? Why?"

"I have the impression you do your homework. So just think of today as research."

Hmm. Not exactly the confirmation I wanted, but I was still on high alert. All signs indicated that today was anything other than an ordinary outing with a source.

The SUV stopped in front of a building with a pointy roof and friendly façade complete with windows and cheery flower boxes. It was similar to many of the buildings we passed on our way here. The words on the glass door sprawled out in a cursive script, comprehensible only to those who read Dutch.

We walked inside, and a woman with big eyes and bright red lips greeted us with hugs.

"John! Who is this lovely woman?"

"Mette, this is my friend Hatty. I thought she'd enjoy meeting the family."

The "family" consisted of twelve women seated in padded pink chairs arranged in a circle. John hugged each woman with a tight embrace before introducing me. All but two of the women looked perfectly healthy.

"So lovely to meet you, Hatty." The woman, who looked pale and gaunt, wore a green silk scarf wrapped around her head and spoke impeccable English. "We're always begging John to introduce us to the women in his life."

What the heck? Clearly, they had the wrong impression. Or did they? My confusion ballooned. So did my worry. Like mental kudzu, unease grew and spread, enveloping every thought. His flirting might be an attempt to draw me in so I'd slant my reporting to favor his family. As much as I craved his attention, this was a sticky wicket. I didn't know his intentions. My stomach thrashed and rumbled.

Mette brought me a chair. John grabbed one for himself and we sat side by side. He asked each woman about specific details related to her medical treatment. He knew Rania was on her second round of chemo. He asked Treze if her new medication was causing her to have migraines as the previous medicine had done. His earnestness and sincerity pricked my heart. Sitting beside him, I noticed how his eyes softened. And they never shifted to his watch or the clock on the wall.

After the last woman, Eva, gave her update, she added, "I know you may not have time, especially since you brought a guest, but would you play for us before you go?"

Each woman in the circle smiled expectantly, and John stood. He walked over to a door, opened it, and wheeled out a harp. He set it near the circle and retrieved a small stool.

As he played quietly, several of the women swayed. Others closed their eyes. *This is why he doesn't play publicly. This is the only audience he needs.*

When he was done, the women gave him a farewell hug, a few added a peck on the cheek.

"How often do you visit?" I asked when we were back in the SUV. The driver knew where to take us next, though I had no clue where we were going.

"I come at least twice a year. Mette keeps me informed about each woman through email. Thanks for coming with me, by the way. I almost always come alone."

He spoke quietly, creating a seriousness and intimacy that surprised me. Even though the driver and Bernard were up front, it was a private moment. I physically jumped when John reached over and took my hand. John chuckled as though my unsteady behavior amused him.

"Hatty, relax. I invited you today because I want to ask you a question. Would you be willing to spend time with me on a regular basis?"

CHAPTER ELEVEN

I reminded myself to breathe, suddenly aware I wasn't taking normal breaths.

"What do you mean?" The moment was heavy, ripe with possibility.

"I mean I'd like to date you, or as we call it in our family, begin a formal courtship."

"Are you trying to woo me so I'll plant stories on behalf of your family?"

"Of course not. I'm trying to woo you, but my goals have nothing to do with journalism."

He likes me. *Likes* me, likes me. *Holy cannoli.* A minor bout of lightheadedness made me blink too much. "So, is this a date?"

"No. In order for us to go on a date, you have to sign a contract that protects my family's privacy and yours. Is that something you're interested in doing?"

"Are you asking me if I want to sign papers or if I want to date you?"

"Both, I suppose."

"Then yes. To both." The words slipped past my lips without

forethought. In that moment, I saw a seedling planted squarely in my chest basking in the light of John's attention. It bent toward the light of his humor, his smile, and his touch. I was so into this prince-slash-environmental scientist, he even influenced the metaphors that sprang to mind.

Before I managed to verbalize any of the hundreds of thoughts competing in my brain, the car stopped in front of an imposing cathedral.

"The church just closed to the public, so we have it to ourselves," he said.

"Is this St. Bavo's? It's one of the most famous cathedrals in Ghent, right?" It was the only tourist attraction I remembered from my online research of the city.

"That's right. Sint-Baafskathedraal to the locals. I'm impressed you know that. It's named for the patron saint of the city. We're going to see the famous Ghent altarpiece. Are you familiar with it?"

"I'm going to have to plead American on this one. I've never heard of it."

He laughed. "Don't worry. Unless you grew up near Belgium or studied European art history, you probably wouldn't be familiar with it."

We got out of the car and walked into a cavernous vestibule that swallowed us whole. Inside, the church showcased the ageless tension between light and dark with its interior design.

"I love European churches because they're nothing like the modern Protestant churches in the states where you have a stage with concert lighting and sound. Plus, our churches tend to be so light and airy."

"You'll find none of that American fluff at St. Bavo's," he said with a wink. John pointed to our right. "That's a pulpit made of white marble and oak."

Two curved staircases stood on each side leading to an elevated lectern behind which a priest would stand to deliver his homily. White marble statues of angels and mortals at the base of the massive structure created a striking contrast to the dark wood.

Most impressive of all was the enormous marble sculpture that served as a kind of roof over the pulpit. On top of the overhang, a gold cross stuck out from among the angelic bodies at an angle that made it appear poised to fall.

"It would be hard to disagree with someone who stood there and claimed to have God's authority. He would appear to be speaking from heaven down to earth," I said, lost in my thoughts as I tried to imagine an actual church service happening here in the 1500's. I shivered. "So, is this pulpit the Ghent altarpiece? Sorry. I'm Protestant to a fault." I gave him a shy smile.

"No. This is an impressive work of art, but the altarpiece consists of multiple panels of paintings. It's in a separate room."

He led me to an area at the back of the cathedral. We passed placards and wall hangings that, to my untrained eye, looked dark and Gothic with small skulls and words in a language I didn't recognize. Though I'd visited many European cathedrals, including the marvelous and memorable basilica in Krakow, this place was very different in its appearance and feel—colder and darker.

A man wearing neat khaki pants and a tie nodded when he saw us coming and opened a small wooden door. We entered a room that was more confined and intimate than a classroom, but too big for a closet. It had a floor to ceiling stained glass window that let light pour inside. There were two chairs sitting together in front of the most beautiful work of art I'd ever seen. And I'd toured the Louvre in Paris four times. Two side panels flanked the central painting. The side panels each held four individual scenes. At the top of the center section of the altarpiece, there were three paintings: a woman on the left, a man on the right, and what appeared to be a king in the center. Below that was the painting that caused my breath to catch in my throat.

"May I?" I asked, gesturing at the panels.

John nodded and I walked forward. Near the center of the middle painting was a raised altar with a lamb standing on top.

Though it looked very much like an animal, its eyes gazed at me in a calm, knowing way as small bursts of light radiated from the back of its head. Blood poured from a single hole in its body near the heart and splashed into a golden chalice.

"It's called 'Adoration of the Mystic Lamb,'" John said, almost whispering.

Hearing him speak softly, I turned my head. He was standing beside me. "You look so beautiful in this light."

Without hurrying, he reached his hand around my head and brought his lips to mine. We kissed in a gentle, rhythmic way that felt natural, as though we'd kissed before. Even so, my nerves danced, my stomach flipped, and my heart fluttered, bringing my senses to life; he tasted of mint and anise.

He slowly pulled away, opening his eyes to look at me.

"John..." I hardly knew what to say. Echoes of a first grade chant rang in my head: *first comes love, then comes marriage, then comes Hatty with the baby carriage.*

Before I had the chance to stumble around for the right words, he coughed and cleared his throat. "What do you find most interesting?"

And just like that, we were back to looking at the painting, as though we hadn't just crossed into new and thrilling territory. I yearned for the warm movement of his lips against mine, but forced myself to keep it together so I could focus on the altarpiece.

"I think it blends and balances the eternal with the ephemeral, heaven and earth. It's the retelling of the ancient story of Christ's death, but the imagery makes it fresh. Growing up, people at our church talked about Jesus being the Lamb of God, but to see such a literal portrayal of that metaphor is stunning."

There was a soft knock on the door. John went over and opened it. A small man wearing round glasses stepped into the room with us. He gestured to the chairs, indicating we should sit.

For the next fifteen minutes, he regaled us with stories about the painting and its history. Thieves had stolen, dismantled, and mutilated it. But since the end of World War II, Ghent had been its home. A group of artists from all over Europe came here and painstakingly restored it.

As we left, I took one last look at the bleeding lamb. It had witnessed our first kiss, and somehow, that made everything that followed seem ordained by God.

After we left St. Bavo's, we browsed the wares in several small shops. Yep, the day kept getting more bizarre—I was shopping with a prince. Thanks to his baseball cap and casual clothing, no one looked at us twice. Bernard, also dressed in plain clothes, was in the shop but kept his distance to avoid drawing attention.

I loved all the chotskies—the small figurines of Brussels' Mannequin Pis, snow globes that put Belgian landmarks in the middle of a blizzard, and miniature wooden replicas of the guild houses that lined the Graslei harbor.

John hovered over a table covered in pieces of lace. "The sign says these were all handmade in Belgium. Don't you think you need to take home some Brussels lace? Look at this one."

He held up a delicate section of lace. Vines, flowers, and leaves sprang from a central stem, all held together by threads thin enough to rival a spider's web.

"It's beautiful." I took it from his hand gingerly, not wanting to stress the lace.

We took it to the woman behind the counter. She must have overheard us talking in English.

She spoke to us with a heavy accent: "This is perfect for couple." She held it up and pointed to the flowers and leaves. "The pattern means many babies."

She smiled as she patted her abdomen. Heat instantly enflamed my cheeks. I busied myself digging for my credit card, a convenient way to ignore the implications of her words. I wanted to say, *Hey, lady. He and I only met for the first time a couple of weeks ago. We're not even really dating yet. I haven't signed the paperwork!*

When I finally pulled the card from the depths of my purse, John handed me a brown paper bag.

"It's a gift. It's the least I can do since you let me drag you out of the country today."

I suppressed the words, "You shouldn't have done that!" and merely smiled. "Thank you. I'll treasure this."

John took my hand and kissed the back of it. "Time to go. More surprises await."

CHAPTER TWELVE

J ohn led me down the cobblestone street with Bernard several steps behind us. He reached for my hand, and his fingers locked with mine. This wasn't the kind of neutered touch I remembered from the hallways of my middle school. This was a deliciously awkward feeling of skin against skin, warm and constantly adjusting.

We meandered our way to Korenlei where we stopped at the front door of a restaurant. The small flag hanging by the door had the words *Allegro Moderato* printed on it. Inside, the maître d' waited for us, apparently prepped for our arrival by one of the guards. He led us to a private room where a lively fire in the fireplace radiated warmth for the room's only table. We took our seats by a giant window that looked across the Lys River to the guild houses.

"Bon Appétit!" He quietly shut the door.

"Do you bring all the girls here?"

"Hatty. I know you think I date a lot of women. But can you imagine the kind of exposure I'd face if I did? I've only seriously dated two women. Both of them ended our relationship once the press found out and began following them around the clock. Once that happens, things change. I think you already had a little taste of that, right?

"Yes, but they quickly lost interest. I'm not fun to photograph."

"That has nothing to do with it. I called in several favors with editors and asked them to rein in the wolves. I also confirmed we're not dating."

"Seriously? I thought they left because I bored them to death. Thank you, then, because it was awful and uncomfortable. I don't see how you handle it so graciously. Aren't they after you all the time?"

"Yes, especially when I'm out with someone I'm dating. Even if we're dressed down and travel outside of Toulene, the press can still find us. They bribe people and lie, whatever it takes to track us down. It becomes much harder to enjoy a quiet dinner like this when you're worried about a photographer crashing through the window. When the tabloids figure out we're dating, I won't be able to stop them."

"Is that a warning? Are you trying to scare me off?"

"No, I'm being honest. The relentless coverage became a source of conflict with the two other women I dated."

"Did you love them?" I blurted it out before I could stop myself. I had no right to ask.

"Yes. One of them. I loved her very much. But, she wasn't willing to put herself and her family through the kind of scrutiny that comes with being in a relationship with me."

Who was she? My mind raced back to all the tabloid cover photos I'd seen of the prince with some "new girlfriend." Though I liked to read the covers, I rarely cracked open the magazines. The only woman I remembered seeing on multiple occasions was a princess from the Orange family in Holland. She was blonde and slender with impeccable features, exactly the sort of face that should be on the cover of magazines next to a prince. But her family is already under press scrutiny, so I couldn't imagine she had been The One.

"I'm sure it's an intense experience to be under constant scrutiny." Yeah, being on the journalist's side of the camera felt a hell of a lot safer. I wasn't looking forward to trading places.

There was a knock at the door.

"*Entrez.*" John spoke with a perfect French accent.

"*Beinvenue. Je m'appelle Jean-Paul. Que voudriez-vous à boire?*"

"*Je voudrais bien avoir seulement l'eau,*" I said. *You're not the only one who can parler a little français.*

"*Nous êtes prendre le Château Mont-Redon, Côtes-du-Rhône Rouge.*" John ordered the wine, and then the garçon left, closing the door with care. "I had no idea you spoke French."

"Oh, I started studying the language and culture in high school. It's my minor at the university. I've found a few occasions to use it during my time in Europe. It's kind of a drag English is the dominant language in Toulene."

"Yes, but most people speak two or even three languages. You shouldn't have trouble finding places to practice your French. By the way, I hope you don't mind the wine. Will you have a glass?"

"Of course. John, thank you for this. All of this. It's been a day I'll never forget."

"You're welcome. I do want to ask you about something, but I hope it doesn't make you uncomfortable."

He paused and I nodded. "Go ahead."

"The night we met at Finn's, you said you'd dated Jack. Plato said the two of you were together for about a year. Is that right?"

Lord, have mercy. Plato had probably told him everything, so I couldn't hide the truth.

"I'll give you the story, but only if you promise to tell me more about your past relationship." I craved information about the person against whom John would compare me.

"I'll tell you about Claire, but I asked you first. Plato told me a few details but I'd like to hear the whole story from you."

There was a knock at the door. Jean-Paul entered followed by a sommelier carrying a bottle of wine and two glasses. The sommelier put the glasses on the table, uncorked the bottle, and poured a small splash of ruby liquid for John to taste.

John took the glass and sipped. "*Oui, merci.*"

"*Que-est ce que vous voudriez?*" The waiter asked for our order while the sommelier finished pouring the wine.

John looked at me.

"*Tu vas de l'avant,*" I told him with a smile, trusting him to order for us.

"*Nous voudrions le stoverij, s'il vous plaît.*"

Both men left quickly.

"What's *stoverij?*" I asked.

"It's a meat stew, a classic Flemish dish. They add a nice bit of strong beer from one of the local Trappist abbeys. It also comes with pommes frites."

My stomach gurgled softly in response to the pending arrival of French fries. *You can take the girl out of the Ozarks, but you can't take the love of fries out of the girl.*

"Sounds perfect." I took a sip of wine. "So, here goes. Jack and I met on campus at the gym. I used to go workout after class to blow off steam, and Jack was always there. You know his real name is Jacques, right? But he likes everyone to call him Jack. Whatever. At first, I thought that was cute, but then it just seemed like he was trying to be someone else. Anyway, we started talking, and then one night, he asked me to go with him for coffee.

I paused to swallow.

"We quickly became a couple. I loved going to his rugby matches... until I didn't. I competed with rugby for his time and attention. One evening when he was supposed to be hanging out with his teammates, I decided to go to the gym. He was there jogging around the track with a beautiful, petite blonde. In terms of appearance, she was the complete opposite of me. The way their bodies brushed against each other without flinching and the way they looked so comfortable together, I knew he was sleeping with her." I stopped again, tears threatening to spill from my eyes.

"Hatty, you don't have to keep going."

Oh yes I do. The spigot's wide open.

"Jack confessed right away when I asked him about it. He told me he simply had more in common with Hilga from Germany than with Hatty from America. He was so matter-of-fact about it, and that really hurt. He used to say looking at me was like seeing a movie star from the early days of Hollywood. I thought it was a lovely compliment, but after I found out he cheated on me, it made me feel frumpy. So you can see why I'm kind of mystified by the fact that you want to spend time with me."

I took a deep breath, willing the lingering anger to settle down.

John reached across the table and took my hand, squeezing it gently. "The woman I loved is named Claire Léglise. Her family owns one of the most popular casinos in Monaco. I courted her. She knew I was close to proposing, but she chose to end our relationship."

Close to proposing. A cocktail of excitement, nervousness, and expectancy prompted my brain to dust off a memory of my seven-year-old self wearing a wispy white nightgown and my mom's slip as a veil. But the prospect of John proposing, even at some distant date, worried me. What would that mean for my career?

It was almost imperceptible, but I was staring at him so intently, I noticed the flicker of pain in his eyes. I squeezed his hand. A twinge of jealousy confirmed my budding affection for John.; clearly, he still cared for Claire, and clearly, that bothered me.

"She blamed my family because she thought they weren't sufficiently welcoming. She also didn't want to spend the rest of her life under constant scrutiny from the press. She felt it could ruin her family's business. So, we said goodbye, and I haven't seen her since."

"Since when?" *I'm not sure I want to know.*

"Since July."

"Three months ago? Are you ready to go through this process again so soon? And with someone you hardly know?"

A soft knock again stopped our conversation. Jean-Paul entered and supervised as two men brought the food to our table and served us. I gave the requisite ohh's and ahh's, but felt eager to return to the topic at hand.

When we were once again alone, I said, "John, are you really ready for this now?"

"My brother asked me the same question last night. Yes, I'm ready. I don't believe in letting the past bind you. Hatty, you're so completely different from Claire or any other woman I've ever dated. You don't hold back. You speak your mind. I need more people like that in my life."

"You might get tired of it. Before too long, you'll want me to keep my mouth shut."

"That's not going to happen."

I picked up my spoon and tasted the meat stew. "Oh, my goodness. So. Good."

"I'm glad you like it. I love Flemish cooking," he said, digging into his bowl of stew.

We spent the rest of the meal talking about our favorite movies and the books we love. Both of us laughed too easily thanks to the wine; it bathed reality in a soft, warm glow.

When we arrived in Toulene, we waited by ourselves in the train car while the rest of the passengers emptied into the station. It was time for us to leave, but he slipped his arm around my waist and pulled me close. He kissed me softly on the lips. Slower this time. It felt the way kisses in the movies look: intense, sensual, not one movement out of sync. There was a sense of restraint; we stood on the precipice of a new relationship, only beginning to get acquainted. Even so, this kiss hinted at the depth of our attraction.

"Sleep well. I look forward to seeing you soon," he said, tucking a lock of hair behind my ear. His tenderness and the way he gazed into my eyes eased my concern about his fairly recent break-up with Claire.

Before I started my car, I sent James a text: *No story tonight. The event was a bust, just a low-key family gathering.*

Turning the ignition, there was a tune simmering on my lips. *Ding, dong, the blog is dead.* I couldn't wait for Monday when I'd walk into James' office and tell him I was done with First Rate Royals. I was about to find out just how first rate the royals really were.

CHAPTER THIRTEEN

The noisy vibration of my new phone zapped me out of my dream—a surreal recap of the previous day's trip to Ghent. I thought James might be calling to chew me out for not filing a story last night; it was strange he never responded to my text. The words "No Caller ID" flashed across the top. I fumbled with the slim rectangle and answered just before it went to voicemail.

Before putting the phone to my ear, my eyes noted the time on the phone's screen: 6:30 a.m.

"Hello?"

"Hatty Brunelle?"

"Yes. This is she."

"This is Cilla d'Hiver. I'm head of the public affairs office at Belvoir. Do you have a minute?"

I grabbed my glasses and sat up in bed. "Is this about the paperwork I need to sign?" *John doesn't waste any time.*

"I'm calling about the story you wrote for today's edition of *The Morning Dispatch.*"

Surprise and confusion swished in my brain. "I didn't write a story."

"It's on your blog. It's also in today's print edition above the fold. Your story reveals information and details you collected from the prince yesterday."

I reached for my laptop sitting on the nightstand and flipped open the lid. "Hang on… I still don't know what you're talking about." Struggling to keep my voice steady, I inhaled deeply, reminding myself I'd done nothing wrong.

"I'm calling to put you on notice and say the palace has no comment…"

"Wait! My laptop's not on yet." My school-issued laptop was half a step above two Dixie cups and a piece of string.

"In the future, if you want to contact the Meinrad family, come through me. Good day."

The line went dead. What just happened?

My laptop finally woke up, and I opened my blog. The top headline tattled the precious secret John had entrusted to me:

Secret Charity Work Revealed! In Her Final Days, Princess Beatrix Established a Foundation for Cancer Patients

From staff reports

The Morning Dispatch has learned exclusively that shortly before her death, Toulene's Princess Beatrix set up and funded a foundation to support cancer patients in Ghent, her hometown.

Public tax records for the foundation reveal the Meinrad family continues to funnel yearly donations to the organization even though it provides no services to the people of Toulene.

"I can't believe the royal family is sending Toulenians' tax money outside our borders to fund a pet project of the late princess," said Assemblyman Henk Haas who chairs the finance committee.

Prince John traveled to Ghent Saturday to visit patients who receive medical supplies and other services from the foundation.

"He visits us as often as he can, usually two or three times a year," said a cancer patient leaving the foundation office Saturday.

A sick feeling rose up in my chest. Who wrote the story and

how did they get this information? I dialed James' cell phone, knowing he'd pick up even though it was early on Sunday morning.

He answered on the second ring. "Did you see the story?" he asked.

"What the hell are you doing?" I yelled into the phone.

"I'll ask you the same thing because your text said there was no story."

"John made me promise to keep the information about his mother's foundation off the record."

"Fine. But Paul made no such promise. He followed you because I knew you'd need back-up."

"Back-up? Don't you trust me to do my job?"

"The prince promised to take you to a private event. I expected him to gag you with an off-the-record request, so I sent Paul along as your wingman."

"Wingman? I didn't know he was going to be there. Look, I've done my best to earn the prince's trust and do my job. Do you have any idea how hard it is to strike that balance? And now you've ruined it." I huffed as though I'd jogged a mile, and I had runner's adrenaline screaming through my veins. "I quit. I'm done with the blog and I'm done with your paper."

"You can't quit. You'll fail your internship."

"We'll see. I'll talk to my advisor tomorrow. If I have to stay in school an extra semester, that's fine. But I'm not going to let you undermine my credibility and burn my sources." I mashed the red button on the screen to end the call. Then I threw my phone into my pillow and let my tears pour over the injustice of the situation.

After washing my face and blowing my nose, I picked up the phone to call Tilda. She'd help me figure out how to fix this cluster. I was in no shape to formulate a plan.

The lights were low, and only a couple of people remained in the front room of Finn's—Monday evenings were slow after ten.

Sitting at the bar, I nursed a diet soda. My phone showed thirty minutes had passed since I sent my napkin note to the back room where the prince, Plato, and some other guys were playing poker. The message I sent him? *I refuse to fold.*

I typed a text to Tilda, telling her our plan didn't work.

"I don't think you want to hit send," a deep voice behind me said.

John put his hand on my arm and I flipped my phone so it was facedown.

"May I sit?" A line just above his jawbone pulsed; he held his teeth together tightly.

I nodded and felt a lump in my throat. He had on his cap, coat, and glasses, the same disguise he wore the night we met. Seeing the frumpy get-up made me even more nervous about having this conversation. A lot had happened. I had more to lose now than I did the night we met.

"I got your note." He held up the napkin, looking at me expectantly.

"Right. I just want you to know I didn't write the story. Without my knowledge or consent, James had another intern, Paul, follow us. He saw us leave the foundation office, then he spoke to one of the patients when she left the building. Of course, he didn't tell her that he was a reporter—and that's terribly unethical. Then, he got the nasty quote from the assemblyman over the phone, and put the story together." John looked at me intently, which only made my nervousness flare. "I'm really sorry about the story. I wish there was a way to fix this."

"Thank you. I appreciate your explanation." The hurt in his eyes didn't disappear.

"And I quit my internship. I can't work for a publication that doesn't abide by basic journalistic standards of conduct. They treated you and your family very badly. I don't want to be a part of that." I reached out and took his hand. "What I do want is to spend more time with you."

And there it was. The moment when he'd either accept me or reject me. I swallowed hard and took a deep breath, steeling myself for a possible (probable) rejection.

He squeezed my hand. "I don't know if this can work. You're in a risky line of work as far as my family and I are concerned."

"I talked to my advisor this morning. She says she can pull some strings and find another internship for me. I'll find out Wednesday where I'm going to work. I plan to continue working on my investigative story. But I'm not going to cover you and your family."

He reached over and cupped my cheek with his palm. "Still, this won't be easy."

I laughed. "I don't do easy. Just ask my parents. I turned down a full ride to the University of Missouri Journalism School because I wanted to study in Toulene."

"In that case, I have a proposal. How do you feel about spending some time together this weekend?"

"Absolutely! I'm up for anything."

I curled my legs underneath me as I nestled into the oversized chair. Aging hipsters and university students floated through Soleil, our favorite coffeehouse, as Tilda and I sipped our drinks. We were a fixture there on Wednesday nights, our designated time to catch up since we both kept crazy schedules.

She looked at me intently. "The way I see it, this is a win-win for John. He gets the girl and he squashes your blog. What's not to love about this story?"

"Tilda. Are you serious? Can't you be a little excited for me? I've got a new internship and I get to spend time with John. That's a win-win for me."

She grinned. "I suppose. At least now I know he can't use you to plant stories since you're not covering his family."

"Okay. Professional considerations aside, can we unleash our inner sixteen-year-olds for a minute? The prince and I are dating!" I whispered the words, scared to death someone would overhear.

I'd signed the contract Tuesday evening when the Meinrad family attorney, Lars Franke, visited my apartment. He went over the details line by line. I was free to tell my parents and my closest friends all of whom I named in the contract: Plato, Sam, Tilda, and Sara. Lars told me the palace staff would have to run background checks on each of them before giving me clearance to share my news. Thank goodness none of them were wanted by Interpol.

"Of course, I'm excited for you. I'm also relieved you can still work on your investigative project." She set down her mug and rubbed her hands together. "Tell me what he's like. I only know him as the broody prince who drops into the National Assembly building to gripe about policies his family doesn't like."

Broody? I couldn't imagine it. She had her Assemblyman Aalders-colored glasses on when she saw the prince.

"He's funny, actually. He's kind of formal when he speaks, but I think it's adorable. There's also a lot of depth to him. Even you'd be impressed."

"Depth. Like how he wants to be a farmer?"

"Oh, c'mon. I thought the same thing when I heard about his Ph.D. in environmental sciences, but he's serious about his work. He told me about the experiments he's doing out by the coast."

"You're already defending him? His hooks are in deep."

"Okay. I like him. So sue me."

"I'm a solicitor. I could do it."

"Before you drag me into court, I need your fashion advice, counselor. What do you think I should pack for my weekend at the palace?"

John's handwritten invitation confirming our weekend together at Belvoir had arrived Tuesday, along with a dozen white calla lilies.

"Something sweet but sexy. You want to look good if an *Xpress* photographer shows up." Tilda stood, taking a final swig of her coffee. "I've got to go. I promised Plato and Sam I'd help them shop for their new flat. You can borrow my teal wrap dress for your palace extravaganza. But only if you agree to give me full details and most importantly, tell me if he talks politics or policy."

"Yeah, yeah. I'll tell you. And don't even joke about a photographer showing up. If the paparazzi find out we actually *are* dating, I'm guessing someone will live tweet the weekend from the bushes outside the palace gates."

CHAPTER FOURTEEN

I stuffed another pair of undies in my rolling duffle bag, and double checked I'd packed the nightie I just bought—cute but comfortable, playful but not overly sexy. I had no idea if John would even see it. Before zipping the bag, I nestled my gift for John among the folds of my sweater. I was eager to surprise him, but I'd have to wait for the perfect moment.

"Goodbye, my lovelies." I caressed the slender neck of a calla lily and poured fresh water into the vase.

Downstairs, I looked right and left—*no paparazzi!*—and got into the waiting car. The photographers had better things to do on a Friday night. I did owe those obnoxious reporters a small debt of gratitude. Their work enabled me to learn more about John's ex-girlfriend, Claire Léglise.

After our day in Ghent, I took a Google-guided tour through Claire and John's relationship. It's a special kind of torture to see the guy you just started dating in photos with a woman who's supermodel beautiful. There were snapshots of them at restaurants, on a beach, in the back of a black car. I decided to put on my blinders and block Claire from my mind. For my own sanity.

Entering through my usual door at the side of the palace, a woman I'd never seen before greeted me. She was shorter than me but older, probably in her mid-forties.

"Good evening, miss. I'm Astrid and I'll take care of everything you need this weekend." A German accent coated each word.

She was a servant, part of the palace staff. Do I shake her hand or give a quick head nod? I settled on an awkward little wave. "It's nice to meet you Astrid." Growing up middle class in Missouri meant servants were as foreign a concept to me as driving on the left side of the road.

"Follow me, miss."

She led me up a couple of short staircases and down a hall, stopping in front of a big brown door. Stepping inside the room, my eyes shot upward, registering the gold foil on the molded ceiling. I was a long way from the white popcorn-covered ceiling in my childhood bedroom. A wave of warmth ran through me at the sight of lively flames in the brick fireplace. A four-poster bed outfitted in pink, silky fluffiness dominated the room. While I slowly drank in the decor, noting with appreciation the bouquet of fresh stargazer lilies on the dresser, Astrid parked my duffle on top of a luggage rack. She opened the doors of a massive wardrobe.

"You may hang your clothes here. If you need me to iron something, please leave it on the bed. Otherwise, dial 201 on the house phone. I'll come right away." She closed the door as she left.

As I unpacked, there was a knock at the door.

"Who's there?"

"May I come in?" John's voice was muffled through the wood.

"Of course!"

John swooped into the room, wrapping me in his strong arms. He planted a kiss on my lips. My body responded by pressing into him to express my inappropriately intense desire. Would it be too forward to pull him down on top of me in front of the fire?

"We've been apart entirely too long. Nearly six days," he said, securing a loose lock of hair behind my left ear the same way he'd done Saturday night.

"I missed you too." My hands wrapped around his upper arms; I loved the firmness of his biceps.

"So, let me tell you what I've got planned. Tomorrow night, we're having dinner with Henri and my father. They both have very busy schedules over the next month, so I want you to meet them while they're home. But for tonight, how about a casual dinner, just you and me? You can wear what you have on and we'll eat in the breakfast room. Afterward, we'll watch a movie."

"Sounds perfect. I've been dying to hear about your week. Since I can't email or text, it's kind of hard to keep up with you." I hated the part of the contract that banned us from texting, calling, or emailing each other. Recent phone hacking scandals made it too risky. *Damn you, muckrakers!*

"I had a good week. I'll tell you all about it at dinner. I'm going to go so you can get settled." He took a deep breath. "What do you put on your hair? I love the way it smells."

"It's a new shampoo. It's called whatever's-on-sale-this-month-at-Boots." What else would you expect from a working girl who buys toiletries at the corner pharmacy?

"I'll send Astrid back in thirty minutes to walk you down to the breakfast room. Unless you think you can find it yourself?"

"Are you kidding me? I have a horrible sense of direction. I could end up wandering through the subterranean tunnels to another country."

Before we sat down to eat dinner, John took me into the kitchen and introduced me to the two cooks and the footmen who would serve our food. Mr. Vermeulen was there. I found out he's John's valet, which has nothing to do with parking cars.

During our meal, John and I talked about our week. I gave him the scoop on the hour I spent packing up my things in *The Morning Dispatch* newsroom (awkward), the conversation with my advisor at school (reassuring), and my new internship at *Les Valenciennes*, one of the alternative weeklies (game on).

"What kind of reporting will you do for *Les Valenciennes*?" He moved the asparagus around his plate.

Telling him about my investigative story felt like the journalist's equivalent of showing a little ankle; I didn't want to give away all my secrets on our first date.

"I'm going to finish my story on the possibility the lead smelter near Kortrijk is making people sick. Some professors from the Royal University are doing the research. They're testing soil samples, analyzing health data, looking for patterns, clusters. I keep tabs on their work and I'm in the process of interviewing neighbors who have chronic conditions. As long as I write an in-depth story that gets published, I get internship credit and can graduate in May."

"Do you feel this jeopardizes our courtship in any way? *Les Valenciennes* opposes the monarchy." A biting edge made his voice angry.

"Of course not. Whatever they say on their editorial page is completely separate from my story. Look, I gave up a full ride at the oldest journalism school in the United States to move here and study under Europe's best journalism professors, so this internship is extremely important to me. And this is my big story."

John scooted his chair, and took a sip of wine.

I fidgeted with my napkin. "I hope you aren't going to tell me I can't write this one story while I'm dating you. Because I'm going to write it. I thought I could do an internship as long as I'm not covering you and your family." The fact I had to defend any part of my educational experience irked me.

"Hatty, you're free to do whatever you want. But don't violate your agreement with us. It's not in your best interest. I'm just asking you to be careful." He tightened the grip on his fork and knife.

"I will be." I had no idea why he was being so uptight about my internship, but I needed to diffuse the tension. "Look, I don't want to do anything to ruin this. I'm just starting to believe you might actually like me."

"Of course I like you. A courtship isn't something to do on a whim. That's why I care a great deal about your internship and how it might impact our relationship."

As we moved on to lighter topics, it was easy to imagine we were a normal couple, that the people bringing out food and clearing dishes were servers in a restaurant, not palace staff.

After dinner, we walked upstairs to The Flat where we crashed on the big comfy couch. Someone had repositioned it so we were facing the massive flat screen on the wall, rather than the huge windows that dominated the sitting area.

"What'll it be, my dear?" he said with a forced Ozarks accent.

I giggled. "Well, how about a classic?" I said, trying my best to mimic the way people in Toulene speak English.

"Wait a minute. I was going for an American southern accent. What are you doing?"

"Umm. A Toulenian accent?"

"How, exactly, do you characterize the way my people speak?"

"It's weird. Like a British accent, but with a pinch of French nasality."

"Okay. Clearly, I need to schedule a history lesson during one of our dates. It might enlighten you on why we speak the way we do." He flipped through the movies that were available for streaming. "How about Charade?"

"Sure. That's an oldie, but goodie."

"Maybe you can learn something about French accents," he said with a wink.

I took one of the accent pillows and threw it at him, prompting John to reach over and pull me closer. As the movie started, I nestled into him. Astrid came by with sodas and small bowls of lightly salted popcorn. She pulled the heavy drapes over the windows before turning out the lights, leaving us bathed in the TV's glow.

About twenty minutes into the movie, John started massaging my neck and asked, "Are you cold?"

I was freezing, but before I answered, he moved me aside and retrieved a blanket from a chest on the other side of the room.

When he came back, he sat down and spread the lush folds of fabric over me as I cozied up beside him again. Those arms of his… so sturdy, strong. Our bodies bent and adjusted so we literally fit together.

My eyes widened when I felt his warm hands slide against the bare skin at my waist, inching a little higher. He leaned close to my ear. "Do you mind?" His voice was low and husky.

"No." I shifted slightly and my skin tingled as his touch skimmed along my lower rib cage before moving over the curves of my chest. Getting felt up by the prince on our first date? Yes, please.

"Your skin's beautiful. It's flawless." His hands explored underneath my shirt but they didn't go past the barrier of my bra.

"Flawless? No one's ever used that word to describe anything about me." I tried to make my breathing sound normal.

"That's a shame because it definitely applies."

Suddenly, his hands gripped my body, and he hoisted me onto his lap, facing him. Through his sweatpants, I felt the biggest compliment I'd ever gotten.

He took my face in his hands, kissing me, pushing my lips apart with his tongue. Both of us took ragged breaths, and I savored the taste of him—no mint this time, just John. The tentativeness of our first two kisses was gone. In the dark glow from the TV, we unleashed whatever secrets made us click, and it was magical. I reached down to pull my shirt over my head.

"Hatty. Stop." He spoke gently and squeezed my hands to hold them in place.

I froze. *What the heck?* Horror and confusion. Had I completely misread where this was going?

"We can't."

"Of course not." I slid off his lap and stretched the bottom of my shirt down. Total humiliation consumed me. I swallowed hard.

"Hatty. Look at me." He took my chin in his hand and pulled my face toward his. "This is not how it's going to happen. If our relationship progresses, then we'll find ourselves in many *positions* to do this kind of thing."

I couldn't help it. A big fat tear slid down my cheek. I hated myself for letting that tear escape. It screamed, *I'm pitiful!* I wiped it away roughly with my hand.

"I want you. I think you can tell I *really* want you. But I'm committed to my wife, whoever she may be, because that act is our most sacred duty to the people of Toulene. It's how this family survives." His words pierced my heart. He put the responsibility of his position, the seriousness of sex, and the commitment of marriage into a beautiful package and tied it with a bow. And it wasn't my gift to open.

"I understand. But you make sex sound like a public event rather than an intimate affair."

"Tell me: how would you feel if you knew I'd slept with Claire? We were very nearly engaged. Aren't you glad we didn't take that step?"

"So, are you a…"

"A virgin? Yes. I'm sure you know about the royals from other countries who fathered children out of wedlock, creating horrible scandals that rocked their countries and, worst of all, the children who had no say in the matter. They became pawns for people wanting to blackmail the royal families. I can't entrust that part of myself to any woman but my wife."

I didn't meet his eyes. My heart's brisk thuds reverberated through my chest. "Then, that makes me feel damaged."

"What do you mean?"

"Are you going to make me say it? I slept with Jack." Then I added in a small voice, "I guess that's a deal breaker for you, huh?"

I rubbed my forehead at the disclosure of such a personal detail. And the guilt returned right on cue. I did, after all, grow up in the Bible-loving corner of Missouri. My intimate encounters with Jack were also fraught with disappointment because they quickly went from hot lust-and-thrust to just sex, and never evolved into lovemaking. I took the blame for the fast fizzle, and convinced myself our lackluster sex life spawned his infidelity. Didn't European men get famously bored with their girlfriends and wives? When our relationship began, I was the virgin. I'd always felt it was evident to Jack I had no idea what I was doing. Remembering all the pain wound up in my experiences with my ex pricked my eyes and brought out a fresh tear.

"Oh, Hatty. Come here."

John wrapped me in a bear hug and I was nearly in his lap again. He stroked my cheek and kissed my lips with intensity, but not the urgency of the previous "lap kiss" that had led to this conversation.

"It's not a deal breaker. I'm just mad you gave yourself to someone who didn't appreciate you. And it makes me quite jealous, to tell you the truth."

"I hate myself for not waiting."

"You had no idea you'd end up here with me. You had a serious boyfriend, and you did what many people do when they're in a committed relationship."

He sounded non-judgmental, but I worried—a lot—about how this would impact our courtship going forward, especially when he said, "Why don't we say goodnight? I want us to feel fresh for the rest of the weekend."

He walked me to my bedroom, and neither of us spoke.

I opened the door. "This is good night?"

"I'll wait here while you change. Then I'll tuck you into bed."

I shut the door and peeled off my sweater and jeans, relieved to be out of the clothes I'd tried to rip off earlier. I pulled on the nicely fitted but modest calf-length gown. I also removed my contacts and slid on my black-rimmed nerd glasses. Might as well show him the real me, near-sightedness and all.

"Okay. I'm ready."

He walked in and scooped me up in his arms, no small feat considering I was only an inch shorter than him. He gently placed me in the bed, pulled the covers over me, and sat down.

"I'm not going to kiss you." His thumb grazed my lower lip. "Because I know I can't stop at a kiss. This is very flattering." His index finger moved to the neckline of my gown, headed toward my cleavage. He lightly skimmed my skin. "Hatty, I'm very attracted to you. That's why I can't let things get out of hand. I wouldn't be able to stop myself."

"Since I was ready to throw my clothes all over your floor, I think you know how I feel about you."

"I'm having a wonderful time getting to know you. I'm looking forward to introducing you to Henri and my father tomorrow. Rest, and I'll see you in the morning." He bent closer and gently kissed me on the lips after all.

I followed Astrid down the stairs, mentally gearing up to meet John's father and brother. John and I had spent the day exploring the palace grounds. I got to see the famous Belvoir peacocks up close as we meandered through the gardens. Our wandering also took us through the new plot of ground his grandmother had chosen for her newest collection of flowers and shrubbery. It sat empty but was primed to go when spring arrived. Then, we walked all the way to the fence at the very rear of the estate. It marked one of the city's boundaries and bordered a wooded area that looked positively magical with curling vines snaking around trees that stood in dense clumps.

When I returned to my room, I discovered Astrid had ironed the wrap dress Tilda loaned me. Then, she went above and beyond by helping me put my hair into a sophisticated up 'do. She completed her masterpiece with a sparkling barrette she produced from her pocket. For her next trick, I thought she might whip out a pair of glass slippers or turn a pumpkin into a Rolls.

Astrid escorted me to the dining room's closed doors. I took a deep breath to subdue my nerves and nodded. She pulled the door open, and there were the three Meinrad men, each one impeccably dressed in a suit. They stood at my arrival.

"You look lovely, Hatty," John said, extending his hand and walking to me. He led me to the man I recognized from television newscasts. "This is my father, Leopold Hendrik Franz Meinrad."

I placed my hand in Prince Leopold's, bowed my head, and bent my right knee in a slight curtsey. God bless Astrid for showing me the proper way to greet John's father before we left my guest room.

"It's lovely to meet you, Hatty."

Fear seized my chest with an iron grip. I had no idea how to address him. I wish I'd thought to ask Astrid. But now I'd just have to ask him.

"I'm honored to meet you, sir. What should I call you?"

He smiled. Being this close to Leopold Meinrad, I saw John's gleaming grin was an echo of his father's.

"Will you call me Leo? Almost no one does."

"Of course. Thank you for inviting me to dinner, Leo." I could see why almost no one called him that—it was too casual and familiar for the man destined to be Toulene's next king.

"And this is Henri," John said.

Henri leaned in and kissed my lips lightly.

I suppressed my surprise at his rather intimate gesture. "It's nice to meet you, Henri."

"Oh, no. You have to call me Prince Henri." Just as John had told me: Henri was amusing and charming.

We sat at the large, long table. The staff poured wine, and John's father cleared his throat. "Hatty, tell us how you decided to study journalism. And why you came here."

"Well, I'll have to tell you a little family history."

"Please do." Leo raised his glass of wine, nodded, and sipped, a kind of silent toast.

"My grandfather was a photographer during the early part of the Korean War, but he spent most of his career at *Life* magazine. His biggest assignment was a cover shoot in 1952 of Marilyn Monroe. He also did serious stories. One of his favorite assignments brought him here. He did a photo essay to show how Toulene had changed a decade after VE day. About a dozen photos wound up in the magazine. The rest he kept in a big red album in his study. I used to flip through the pages and imagine walking along a cobblestone street in Roeselare. Even the name of the capital enchanted me. He made journalism sound like glamorous, hard, heroic work."

Henri cut in: "Like a knight wielding a notebook and pencil."

"The pen is mightier than the sword!" John and I said it at the same time. Everyone laughed, and John squeezed my thigh under the table. We began eating the small enticing salads sitting in front of us.

"I remember when *Life* magazine ran that article and your grandfather's photos. My parents felt he did an exceptional job capturing the spirit of our people," Leo remarked.

"Thank you. It means a great deal to hear you say that."

During the meal, I answered their questions about my parents, life in Missouri, and my move to Toulene right after high school. "It was a tough transition because I missed my mom and dad. But I was ready for a dramatic change. I was the only person from my town to move overseas for college."

The servants came around to offer coffee with our chocolate mousse.

"And what do you plan to do after you graduate in May?" John's father asked as he poured cream into his cup.

"Part of me wants to go back to the U.S. and take my journalism skills for a test drive in a statehouse. Grad school is an option, too. There are so many exciting possibilities."

"And now that you're dating my son, is a relationship with him also an exciting possibility?" Leo kept his eyes on his coffee as he stirred it slowly.

"Yes. It is." Such a blunt question. What I actually wanted to say was this: *My life is not a Choose Your Own Adventure book that requires me to pick either John or my career. Also, this weekend is technically our first date. Just sayin'.*

As we finished dessert, John graciously changed the subject, and we talked about the horseback riding he had planned for the following day. It was a bummer that rain was in the forecast.

We said goodnight to Henri and John's father before making our way upstairs. I asked John to unzip my dress before I slipped into my room to change. His finger traced my spine as he pulled the zipper down below my waist.

I quickly changed into my nightgown and let him into my room. I climbed into bed.

"You were brilliant tonight."

"Do you think so? Your dad made me kind of nervous."

"He just wants to get to know you better. That's all. Sleep well, Hatty."

He kissed me goodnight and left.

As soon as he was gone, I sat up and clicked on the little bedside lamp. I reached for my purse and fumbled around for my phone. Music. I needed music. The first song that came up was one I used to play when I taught aerobics classes. That was two sizes and two years ago. Even though I loved to work out, the campus gym became no-man's land, a place where I might run into Jack. So, I stayed away.

Before I had a chance to overthink it, I hopped out of bed, threw on a T-shirt and sweatpants, picked up the phone, and dialed 201.

"How may I assist you?"

"This is Hatty. Is Astrid available to come to my room?"

"Yes, miss."

The line went dead. In about three minutes, there was a soft tap on my door.

"Astrid. I really need to exercise. Is there a place in the palace where I can work out?"

"There's a gym on this floor. I can take you there."

"No, that's okay. I don't want to disturb any of the family." In addition to John, Henri and Leopold had bedrooms on this floor. "Isn't there another place I can go? I really just need an open area where I can move."

Astrid's lips pulled to one side, like she was conflicted about something. "Follow me."

She took me to the far end of the hallway, and opened a door that revealed a stark white staircase, probably a service area for the staff. We descended several flights before arriving at the bottom. She withdrew from her pocket a small fob and waved it in front of a panel, causing it to beep. The door clicked and she turned the handle.

"Honestly, Astrid. You guys have keyless entry but still use rotary phones?"

I coughed as we walked through the dank air filling the hallway. She stopped in front of a door on our left. As she flipped on the overhead lights, I followed her inside. The wall opposite the door was covered in mirrors, and a ballet barre ran across them. In one corner, there was a small stand holding a turntable and a stack of records. Two speakers sat nearby on the floor.

"What is this place?"

"This is where the princess used to dance." Astrid spoke softly, with her hands folded as though in prayer.

At first, I didn't get it. Then I realized she meant Princess Beatrix, John's mother.

"Are you sure it's okay for me to be down here? I don't want to cause any problems."

"Please. Go ahead. Call me on the phone here on the wall when you're ready to go back upstairs."

"Thank you." She left me alone in the room. It wasn't overrun with dust, so someone came in here and cleaned on a fairly regular basis.

I didn't waste any time. I still had traces of adrenaline in my body from dinner. Quite frankly, I felt a surge of anger at Leopold's question about my future plans; it hit me wrong. Honest to freaking goodness, I thought Europe was supposed to be a bit more progressive in this regard. But John had warned me his father is very traditional, especially in his views of gender roles.

After sliding my phone into its armband holder, I put my ear buds in place. My finger searched the playlist until I found one of my kick-ass aerobics tunes, and started into a routine. My body protested when I forced it to do high impact moves to get my heart pumping.

The music ripped into the final verse, and something in the small window of the door caught my eye. I kept moving, convinced I was just freaking myself out. After all, I was in the subterranean studio of a dead princess.

As the song wound to its climax and then the powerful, punchy end, I saw it again. Just a quick movement. I yanked the ear buds out and defiantly strode toward the door. I swung it open and found five staff members in the hallway.

I stood there, unsure what to say.

Astrid spoke: "I'm so sorry, miss. We were just curious about what kind of exercise you do."

The sound of my heavy breathing filled the hallway—I still hadn't caught my breath. "Come in and I'll show you." I turned my back and walked inside.

Since I had no way to plug in my phone and play music through the speakers, I went over to the stack of records. I flipped past several classical music options and came upon Journey's Escape album. In the upper right hand corner, the name "Bea" was written neatly with flowing curves. With great care, I slid the record out of the cover, placed it on the turntable, and switched it on. I moved the needle around until I found the beginning of the song I wanted. I silently thanked Plato for letting me tag along with him on some of his DJ gigs where I occasionally helped with the turntable.

"Okay. Let's go. We're going to start by stretching our neck muscles." Astrid and the others looked at me with confused faces. "Don't you guys ever do aerobics?"

No one spoke. As the opening of the song continued, I stretched my neck, and gave instructions, hoping they'd join in.

Since I didn't have a routine ready for "Don't Stop Believin'," I just free-styled my way through the first two verses.

"C'mon, you guys!" The intensity of the song picked up.

In the mirror, I saw Astrid and another young woman do hamstring curls with me in time to the music. They followed along as I stretched both arms into an arc over my head with the long note at the end of the phrase.

"You guys look great!" I shouted over the music.

All five of them moved with me, getting most of the moves right. They smiled and I hit my stride. So, I started singing.

I busted out my harmony as I looked at my happy little group in the mirror. And there he was. John stood in the back of the room, his arms folded across his chest. I gasped and did my best not to miss a step. *This is who I am. Take it or leave it, baby.*

As the song faded, I ran over to the turntable and stopped the music.

Astrid and the others filed out, nodding deferentially to John as they passed him. Calling over her shoulder, Astrid said, "Thank you, miss. Will you need anything else?"

"No. I think I've got an escort to take me to my room." I smiled at John though his face looked... broody. Isn't that the word Tilda had used?

We were alone with the door closed. "John, I'm sorry about being down here. I just wanted to exercise without disturbing you."

"I'm just surprised. That's all. This section of the cellar is secure. Whenever anyone accesses it, my father and I get a text telling us who has opened the outer security door. When I saw it was Astrid, I was concerned. She almost never comes down here." I saw that teeth-clenching line on his jaw. It was dangerous and sexy.

"I'm really sorry if I've done something to offend you. I just needed to relax."

"So being with me and my family isn't relaxing?" Definitely in full-out brood mode.

"To be honest, dinner wasn't very relaxing. It was enjoyable, but not relaxing. I don't know why or how I've upset you." Wrap. Unwrap. I twisted the earphone cord around my phone.

He ran his hand through his hair, making it look a little greasy and unkempt. Even so, it was lovely.

"Hatty, do you know why this area is secure?"

I shook my head.

"My mother's things are down here."

"Astrid said this is where your mother danced."

We stood about five feet apart. Should I go to him or give him space? I teetered on the balls of my feet.

He took a deep breath, closed his eyes, and exhaled. Opening his eyes, he walked over to a corner where a little wooden stool sat. "I haven't been down here in years. I used to sit right here and draw while she danced. She did ballet mostly. Those records were the soundtrack of my childhood. Tchaikovsky, Brahms, Chopin."

"And Journey, right? You sang that song to me the night we met." I walked closer to him, but didn't insinuate myself into his personal space; a physical and emotional chasm gaped between us.

He pinched the area between his eyes, frowning. "Are you ready to go to bed?"

"Yes." I walked to him and took his hand.

At the door to my room, he said goodnight. I wasn't sure a good night was possible after what had just happened—and *hello*, no kiss? I watched him walk down the hall and turn the corner. Irritated that he was mad at me for no good reason, I slammed my bedroom door, hoping he heard it.

When I got out of the tub the next morning, a tray of fruit, muffins, and coffee sat on my bed, along with a note saying Astrid would come to my room at 9:30 and take me to meet John. Per John's instructions, I put on the same unflattering riding clothes I wore the first time I set foot in the palace. I looked in the mirror at my amplified thighs and pressed my arms to my side. It helped hide the flare, but I couldn't walk that way.

Astrid took me down the service staircase, but instead of stopping on the main level and going outside to the stables, she kept descending.

"I thought we were going riding."

"He's waiting for you in the studio." She flashed her fob in front of the panel and the door clicked.

In the studio, John sat on the floor with his back to me, his head bowed into his hands. I walked over and touched his shoulder; it moved with each breath. He grabbed my hand and kissed it. I sat on the ground next to him, unsure where things stood between us.

"I'm sorry for how I behaved last night. It just came as a shock to see you in this room. It brings back a lot of memories for me."

"I'm sure it does. It's okay. I'm sorry I came down here."

I reached out and stroked his cheek. Turning his head, he kissed my palm, which imbued the moment with a heightened sense of intimacy.

"I should have left as soon as Astrid told me this was your mother's studio."

"No. It actually felt good to see you in here dancing and making Astrid and the others so happy." He stood and reached his hand out to help me up. "Hatty, will you dance with me?"

"I'd love to."

Flipping on the turntable, he delicately placed the needle, and I again noticed how adept he was with his fingers. The opening notes of Journey's "Open Arms" engulfed us. We leaned into each other, and I rested my head on his shoulder. Even in this hushed moment, the heat between our bodies intensified as we swayed. It was like a scene from Dirty Dancing, minus the dirty. Instead of acting on the attraction that connected us like a live wire, we simply held each other.

After a few minutes, he sniffed loudly and looked at me. "If you've forgiven me for my lack of manners last night, I'd love to take you for a ride."

"In the woods behind the palace?"

"As you wish, my dear," he said, placing an unruly lock of hair behind my ear.

When we got back from our horseback ride and picnic (thank goodness the rain held off), I packed. My dread of leaving John grew heavier every time I added something to my duffel. *Suck it up, Hatty.*

A knock on the bedroom door interrupted my little pity party. John walked in, a hint of sadness evident in his eyes.

"Here. Let me take this downstairs for you."

"Don't you have people to do this kind of thing?" I teased him as he grabbed the handle of my duffle bag. "Hey, before we take my bags downstairs, I want to give you something."

"This sounds important. Should I sit?"

"Sure."

I grabbed his gift from the wardrobe where I'd kept it since my arrival. Holding it behind my back, I perched on the edge of the bed beside him.

"This is for you." I placed the quirky little camera in his hand. "It's a Rollei 35 millimeter that belonged to my grandfather. When he died, my grandmother gave it to me. My granddad took pictures of me with it when I was little. He called it his 'off-the-clock camera' because it was so much smaller than the ones he used at work."

"Hatty, I don't know if I can accept such a special gift. Do they even make this camera anymore?" He turned it over in his hand, looking at it from different angles.

"I doubt it, but it's loaded with film and ready to go. Since I don't get to be with you very often and all this is so new to me, I thought it would be cool if you took some photos while we're apart. That way, I can see what I miss."

He gently set down the camera and gave me a fierce hug. "Hatty, this is one of the best gifts anyone's ever given me. Thank you."

"You're welcome. I can't wait to see your photos."

"I can't wait to see you again." But he hadn't said anything about when or where our next date would be. With this realization, my heart sank.

He gave me one last hungry kiss. My eyes drifted shut, and I savored the taste of our lips converging. A desperation drove my mouth into motion because I didn't know when I'd see him again. Soon, I hoped. Very soon.

CHAPTER FIFTEEN

Shortly after I got home Sunday evening, Tilda and Sara arrived at my apartment to get all the details on the weekend while I did laundry. Such a glamorous life I led.

Tilda blew into her cup of steaming chai. "Do you think his father and brother like you? Henri seems like such a goofball and their dad strikes me as being entirely too serious."

Sara jumped in. "They're both sexy as hell. If you don't want them, I'll take all three."

"Tilda, you've got them pegged—Henri's a doll and their father is quite solemn. So get this: I asked his father what I should call him, and he said Leo. Think about his stern face. Can you imagine anyone calling him Leo?"

"Did you?"

"Heck, yes!"

"They probably thought that was cute and folksy." My Missouri charms I unwittingly put on display from time to time brought Tilda endless amusement.

"Okay. Who cares about dad and brother? Tell us about the kissing." For Sara, the world was a romance novel, its pages turning before her eyes.

"Well. He's very good at it. When he kisses me, it feels like home. Does that make sense?"

"Absolutely. A beautiful image. Does he use a lot of tongue?"

"Sara!"

"Well?"

"I guess. I mean, I don't know. How do you quantify tongue?"

"Doesn't matter. Just tell me this: did you do anything else?" Sara leaned closer.

"Well, I didn't see it, but I know he has one heck of a kingmaker."

"How do you know if you didn't see it?"

"Use your imagination."

"Not a good suggestion. I've got one hell of an imagination."

We giggled. All we needed was pizza and a handmade fortunetelling game made of notebook paper and this could pass for a high school sleepover. In those days, my friends and I stayed up late sharing every awkward detail about the boys we'd kissed.

"Back to the important part of the weekend," Tilda said, glaring at Sara.

"Hey, this stuff's very important! We need to know if they have chemistry." Sara winked at Tilda and shook her booty. *Lord help us.*

"Sara, settle down. Honestly. The really important thing is what his brother and father thought of you. Because if you don't have their approval, your relationship with the prince is doomed."

"John said they enjoyed meeting me. Good old Leo asked me a very pointed question about what I planned to do in May, and if dating John figured into my future."

"And what did you say?" Sara stopped dancing.

"I told him it does. But, c'mon, we just started dating. Suddenly, I'm supposed to be thinking about long-term plans? So ridiculous!"

"I totally get it," Tilda said. "But you're not seeing the big picture from their perspective. They're used to everyone bowing to their whims and following their schedule. And I'm sure they don't like the fact you're in journalism. Might do them good to have someone like you around."

"Yeah, well, we'll see. I'm going to call my mom in the morning and tell her. She's going to flip out."

Mom hated anything she perceived as getting in the way of my career, and I'd bet that's how she'd see my courtship with John. Note to self: don't use the word "courtship" because she'll hate that, too.

"Hey, Mom!"

"Hi, honey! How are things going with the new internship?"

"Good. They're letting me focus on my investigative story. It's the perfect arrangement. Much better than at the *Dispatch*."

"Don't you miss covering the royals? I thought you did a wonderful job with the blog. Sounded like such a fun assignment." *Oh, mom. You have no idea.*

"Well, that's actually what I'm calling about. It was a lot of fun spending time with the royal family. Specifically, the prince. John."

Awkward pause.

"In fact, it was so fun, we've decided to spend more time together."

"What do you mean?" I sensed her hackles awakening in alarm.

"I mean we're dating. Me and the prince. The prince and I. Us. Together."

"Dating? Is he the reason you left the *Dispatch*?" Mom cut straight through the bull. No wonder her students both loved and feared her.

"Well, I couldn't very well cover someone I'm dating. Once we began our courtship, I moved to *Les Valenciennes*."

"Courtship? What is this, the 1950's?" *Damn that word!*

"It's just the official term they use in the paperwork."

"What paperwork?"

"I had to sign paperwork consenting to the terms of our courtship."

"This sounds absolutely medieval. Why would you ever sign such a document?"

"Because I like him! A lot. It's fine. It's more than fine. I'm glad to be rid of that stupid blog. It was complete fluff. Now, I'm working on a story that really matters."

"As long as you don't step on any royal toes, right?"

"My story has nothing to do with John's family. Can't you be happy for me?"

"I'll be happy when I know you aren't throwing away your career for a lifetime of 'Stand By Your Man.'"

"Trust me. I'm not giving up my career for John. This is the 21st century. It *is* possible to have a relationship and a job, you know?"

"I *don't* know. I just don't know about this, Hatty."

I gritted my teeth, determined to show her I could, eventually, have it all—a successful career, an adoring husband, and two-point-five kids. Boom.

CHAPTER SIXTEEN

I holed up in my corner of the *Les Valenciennes* newsroom Wednesday, transcribing interviews I'd done pre-prince with some of the neighbors who lived close to the smelter. Leisel de Vries' voice surged through my ear buds:

"My husband and I had been trying to get pregnant for months. I finally went to the doctor to find out what was wrong. She did an ultrasound and found polyps in the area outside my uterus. She told me many of her patients from Kortrijk have similar reproductive problems."

Her voice sounded broken and tired.

I listened to my next question: "Could your doctor remove the polyps?"

"Yes, but she couldn't do small incisions. She had to cut me from here to here to remove all the polyps."

I cringed. Leisel had raised her shirt to show me the shiny, red line where the knife had traversed her abdomen.

"How long ago was that?"

"About a year."

"Have you been able to conceive?"

"Not yet. But we're hopeful."

I paused my recorder and stopped transcribing, letting the seriousness of her situation wash over me. Her desperation rang through every word. Even though pregnancy was the furthest thing from my mind, my heart was heavy for her. She had cried intermittently during our interview. Each time she dabbed at them with a wadded up tissue, I suppressed the urge to say, "We can just stop. You don't have to keep going." Painful as it was for her, Leisel wanted to share her story. Before I left, she hugged me, thanking me over and over again for listening.

Opening my reporter's notebook, I made a note to schedule an interview with Leisel's doctor, and then walked over to Sandra's desk. She was a hard-nosed reporter who had exposed a scheme by two assembly members to defraud a federal program out of millions of euros. I admired her tremendously.

"Sandra, how easy is it to interview doctors in this country?"

"It depends, I guess. What do you want to ask?"

"I want to talk to a particular doctor about trends she's observing in her patients."

"Is this for your smelting investigation?"

"Yeah."

"Then she probably won't talk on the record."

"Why not?"

"Since all the physicians in this country are government employees, and the crown owns the smelting facility, I doubt she'll comment." Sandra sounded as if she were explaining something to a child.

"What do you mean the crown owns the facility?" *Not good.*

"I thought you knew. Isn't that why you left your blog to come work here? So you could leverage your relationship with the royal family to do a worthwhile story instead of gardening updates?" She smirked. The reporters at *Les Valenciennes* thought my blog was a royal joke.

"I seriously have no clue what you're talking about."

"The royal family either owns the building for the smelter or they lease it and use it for smelting. We're not sure, but we've been trying to find out for years. They hide and alter public records, you know. Those scientists from your university are going to uncover the truth about the smelter damaging the environment. The Meinrads need to be held accountable for the problems that place has created for the people who live nearby." She turned back to her laptop.

My stomach grumbled, issuing a threat. I dashed straight to the bathroom where I lost my lunch.

I left the newsroom and got in my car, my hand resting over my stomach. Why hadn't John told me his family was one of the biggest players in my story? This was an unexpected level of douchebaggery from my new boyfriend.

On my way home, I stopped at Boots Pharmacy. As I stood in line to pay for the antacids, John's face on the cover of a magazine caught my eye. He had his arm wrapped around the waist of a beautiful woman with black hair. They both smiled conspiratorially, their heads nearly touching as they leaned toward one another. The headline screamed, "The Prince Goes for the Gold!" A little bubble farther down the cover said, "Prince John dumps journalism student for gymnast!" That stinking exclamation point stuck in my craw.

I grabbed the magazine, paid, and ran out to my car, sensing another wave of nausea settling over me.

Steadying my breaths, I opened the magazine in the safety of the driver's seat and started reading:

Did Toulene's Prince John really just take journalism student Hatty Brunelle for a ride? It appears so. Only two weeks after he whisked away the wide-eyed, aspiring reporter to Belvoir, Toulene's Prince Charming was spotted out on the town with Olympic Gold Medalist Adela Zuzen of Spain. The pair canoodled in a booth at the ultra-ace downtown eatery, Go. It was clear these two were planning to stay!

"I think they wanted to sit in the back so they could snog without anyone seeing them," said Bie Peeters, Go waitress.

I closed the cover, grabbed my stomach, and suppressed a dry heave. After a few more deep breaths, I started the car, went home, and crawled into bed. Three letters buzzed in my head like a giant neon sign illuminating my brain: WTF.

CHAPTER SEVENTEEN

A fter a night of dreaming about a self-righteous confrontation with John, I woke up exhausted. I showered and got ready to go to the newsroom.

On my way through the lobby of my apartment building, the doorman handed me a sealed envelope.

As I walked outside, I tore it open. John was sending a car to get me at 4:00 p.m. Fine. I was ready for a fight. *Bring it.*

I seethed, still unsure which made me angrier—his concealing the fact his family owned the smelting operation or his apparent fling with the Spanish gymnast. It was a close contest and the gymnast wouldn't get the gold this time.

When I arrived at the palace late in the afternoon, John greeted me with open arms, ready to plant a serious kiss on my lips. Just a day and a half ago, I would've felt an undeniable hunger, but now there was only bitterness brewing.

I let him envelop me in his arms, but turned my head when he tried to kiss me.

"Hatty, what's wrong?"

"We need to talk."

"Of course. We can go to my room." His brows pulled together. A sign of worry, perhaps? *He knows his girlfriend is a badass from the Ozarks and it's come-to-Jesus time.*

Behind his closed bedroom door, I got right to it. "When were you going to tell me about your family's role in making people sick in Kortrijk?"

"What do you mean?"

"You never told me your family owns the smelting operation that's apparently causing people to get lung cancer and have miscarriages, if they can get pregnant at all. You make me sick."

"Oh, God." His hand ploughed through his hair. "Hatty, until this week, I didn't know we still owned the buildings. We lease the facility to a private company that runs the smelter. I thought we sold off that property several years ago. I swear I was going to tell you about it because this creates a conflict of interest for you now that we're dating."

"Conflict of interest? Don't pretend like you care about my profession. And why is it I'm the only journalist in town who can't seem to keep tabs on where you go and the women you see?" I tossed the magazine at his feet, giving myself a slow clap in my head and a heaping helping of *You go, girl!*

"You're upset by this?"

"I need to know right now if you're dating any other women."

"Are you serious?"

I waited with my arms folded across my chest.

"No. You're the only one I'm dating."

"Then how do you explain this story?"

"I met Adela a couple of years ago. She was in town Monday, and asked to see me because she wants to date Henri. And do you know why she was in Toulene?"

"I have no idea. But wait a minute. She can just call you up and ask to see you, and I can't?"

"It's different because I'm not dating her."

"Apparently someone thinks you are. Since you don't make *her* follow the rules *I* have to follow, you get 'caught' with her, and now everyone thinks you guys are dating? This is so messed up."

"I'm not seeing her. She came to Toulene to host a gymnastics camp for immigrant youth. But of course, that's not sexy enough for a magazine cover so someone saw us out and took a photo."

"They just made up the story to go along with the picture?"

"I suggest you start acting like a journalist and get the facts right before you burst into my home and accuse me of being a horrible person." He turned away from me.

The room was silent, though the air was heavy with our harsh words. I walked out of his bedroom, slamming the door behind me. Astrid was dusting in the sitting area.

"I'm ready to go home." She silently led me down the staircases to the entrance I'd used just a few minutes earlier. I got in the black car parked in the curved driveway and waited. A couple of minutes later, a driver came and took me to my apartment.

A painful aching nipped at my heart, overriding the anger. This breach of trust heralded the end of my courtship with John. This was a different kind of royal flush—our relationship was sliding down the toilet.

CHAPTER EIGHTEEN

Despite my confrontation with John, I slept deeply. It helped that I'd gotten very little rest the previous night.

Friday morning, I went to my media ethics class where I got into an argument with a Latvian student over whether news bloggers ought to follow the same ethical standards as other journalists. *They totally should.* Then, I came home, put on sweats, and curled up with my textbook. I read and sipped lukewarm coffee, trying to ignore the hollowness I felt inside. A news ticker of headlines about our breakup ran through my head, a ceaseless ribbon reinforcing my misery.

I was about to get up and go to the bathroom when someone knocked on my door. I looked through the peephole and saw John standing there with two members of the Royal Guard. Adrenaline shot through my body. What the heck was he doing *here*? He was dressed like any other twenty-something who might live in my building; he wore a ball cap, slouchy jeans, and a long-sleeve T-shirt under a khaki field jacket. In one hand, he had a black bag that looked like a soft-sided briefcase.

I unlocked the door and opened it. "Just happened to be in the neighborhood?"

"May I come in?"

I stepped out of the way, and he walked inside. The plainclothes guards stayed in the hallway.

"They're kind of conspicuous. I guess it's a good thing my neighbors hardly know who I am. Do you want to sit?"

As he walked into the tiny apartment, my nerd glasses slid down my nose. I shoved them into their proper place and pulled back my hair, knowing there was no way I looked presentable, but also not caring—the man had seen me looking like a wet dog and that hadn't repelled him. I walked over to the couch and plopped down.

"Hatty, I'm sorry to come here unannounced. I wanted to see you at home. At your home. The last thing I want to do is change who you are because there's so much about you I love." *Trotting out the l-word? This must be serious.*

"Okay."

He sat beside me. "I also want to say I'm sorry I didn't call you the minute I found out my family is still in the smelting business. It was wrong of me to wait. I was afraid you wouldn't want to have anything to do with me and I couldn't bear that. Can you forgive me?"

"Yes. But how do I know you were really going to tell me?"

"Whether it's the factory or that photo of me with Adela, you have to trust me." He took my hand in his.

"I want to trust you. But it's hard because I trusted Jack too, and look where that got me."

He turned my chin toward him and looked into my eyes. "Please don't compare me to your ex-boyfriend or punish me for his mistakes. I don't compare you to Claire. I think we both want the chance to have something different than what we experienced in the past. Isn't that why we're dating?" The blaze of sincerity in his eyes sent a surge of affection zipping through my heart. But the journalist in me didn't lie down and roll over so easily.

"Of course." I turned my whole body to face him. I needed to see him straight on as he answered my next question; it was too important. "But tell me this: how can you pursue a doctorate in environmental science and give lip service to protecting farmland yet turn a blind eye to what's going on in Kortrijk? There's something in the soil and ground water that's making people sick. This one woman I interviewed… You should hear her voice. She can't get pregnant, but she doesn't know why. I want to help these people because they deserve answers."

"And we want to help them. A generation ago, they begged the monarchy to bring jobs to their town, and that's what we did when we leased the facility to a private company so they could open the smelter. The fields in that area were dead and residents couldn't farm. So, we gave them the opportunity to earn decent wages and improve their lives. Hatty, there may be something in the soil out there, but it existed prior to the smelter coming online."

"What were they doing at the facility before your family cleared the way for the smelting operation?"

"A private investor built the facility in 1897 and opened an asbestos plant. Our government spent millions of euros cleaning up the contamination after we bought the property. Then we let Ren Corp. start up a lead smelter. Of course, we want to know if it's creating more pollution. But so far, the dots don't connect."

"Why are you just now finding out your family still owns the buildings?"

"Granny, my father, and Aunt Elinore talked extensively about selling it a couple of years ago and turning the entire place over to Ren Corp. It sounded like a done deal. I was finishing my master's degree at the time, so I didn't follow every detail."

"What are you getting at here? That I can't do my story?"

"Not if you plan to continue to have a relationship with me. And if you end our courtship, you can't report on any of the details I've disclosed because of the agreement you signed."

"Okay. Damn it. Why does this have to be so hard for us?"

"I warned you this would be tricky."

"Look, if I back off of this story, you have to promise me you're going to check into the situation out there. I don't want to leave those people hanging. They need our help."

John stood. "I understand, and we'll stay on it. You know, there are so many people who need help, and I think you're just getting warmed up." He reached into the black bag by his feet and pulled out a laptop. "This is for you. I believe in you and your talent as a writer. I know you're going to do great things."

I took the laptop and set it on the coffee table. My fingers glided across the smooth silver top. I'd told him only once that my laptop was a loaner from the university, so I'd have to return it when I graduated.

"I can't believe you did this. Thank you so much."

As I wrapped my arms around his neck, I fought back tears. *A laptop from the guy you're dating? Seventeen-hundred euros. Knowing he listens when you talk? Priceless.* In that moment, I adored him, and apparently, he felt the same way about me. My mental news ticker with its headlines detailing the end of our relationship stopped dead in its tracks.

"I'd like us to spend more time together… if that sounds good to you," he said.

"I'd like that very much."

"Great. If it works with your schedule, I'd like you to accompany me to Berlin tomorrow. From there, we'll drive to Potsdam. My cousin Pru is having her birthday party at Sanssouci. Have you heard of it?"

"No, but it sounds like fun. I'd love to go with you. Thank you for inviting me."

"Thank you for agreeing to come with me on such short notice. I'll send a driver over at nine, and I'll meet you at the airport. How does that sound?"

"Perfect! What should I wear?"

"Hmm…" He looked deep in thought as he pulled me closer, and his hands slid down my back. Even after reaching my waist, his hands kept going. When they grazed my ass, he gave it a playful squeeze before moving up again to my lower back. "I'd say a short black dress is in order."

I melted into him, gently patting his cheek. "You're lucky, mister. I just happen to have a little black dress."

"We're staying only one night, but it will be one hell of an evening. Gatherings at Sanssouci are notorious."

"Notorious for what?"

"I'll say this: I have a second cousin who supposedly was conceived there."

"So, it's a bunch of cousins getting their freak on? Sounds like a *royally* good time."

"Very funny. I'm going to go so you can pack."

He leaned in to kiss me, and my lips parted. Our tongues were well acquainted, and did their own seductive dance. His hands slid around my waist and then down. This ass grab was longer, more intense. The sensation of his fingers caressing a part of my body that rarely enjoyed another person's touch electrified me. A tingling ricocheted around my stomach before settling between my legs. When he let go, he took a step back.

"I can't wait to see you all dressed up for Pru's party. I guarantee I won't be the only one wanting to grab your ass."

"Maybe. But yours are the only hands I want touching my body." I reached for his arms just above the wrists and placed his hands on my rear again. His breathing became uneven as he gave me one last, deep kiss.

After he left, my stomach thrashed at the thought of an evening spent meeting and greeting royals and anyone else famous and rich enough to get invited. At least I'd have John by my side; his presence would help slay my nervousness.

CHAPTER NINETEEN

On our flight to Berlin, John and I sipped wine in the comfort of wide leather seats. A small table set up between us held the photos he'd taken with my grandfather's camera. There was a snapshot of Henri eating breakfast at the palace, multiple pictures around Roeselare taken through a car window, and shots of people walking the halls of the National Assembly building.

"See how boring the life of a prince is?" He finished his wine and handed it to the only flight attendant on our private plane.

"Hardly." After passing off my empty glass, I held the photos in my hand relishing the novelty of it—most pictures I encountered existed as pixels on a screen not as tangible artifacts of daily life. "I'm impressed you figured out how to develop the film."

"There are a few perks that come with being a member of the royal family."

"A secret dark room in the basement of the palace, for instance?"

"I can't say. I'm sworn to protect state secrets." He winked at me.

"Here's a secret you can protect: I'm nervous about the party."

"Don't worry. We'll stay together."

A soft ding told us it was safe to leave our seats. John unfastened his seat belt, stood, and offered me his hand. "I want to show you something."

He pulled me to the rear of the aircraft and opened one of those folding doors you typically see on an airplane lavatory. He stepped into the dark space and drew me to him, closing the door behind us. Shadows and the scent of John engulfed me. He threaded his fingers through my hair and kissed me. His lips moved to my neck; he flicked my skin with his tongue.

My arms wrapped around him, and I reached underneath his shirt, hungry to explore. Hard, undulating muscles welcomed my touch. Another hardness asserted itself, this one below the waist, unavoidable in the tight space forcing extremely close contact. Still, we didn't have room for much except caressing and kissing, ensuring we couldn't get too carried away.

"There's plenty of oxygen in here, right?" I gasped.

"No idea. Just try to stay calm." *As if.* His hands eased toward my chest, and though they stayed outside my sweater, he skimmed over my breasts. I inhaled sharply, nervous and aware of what I considered to be a major shortcoming.

"Sorry they're so small." I squeaked out the words between breaths that came too quickly, exposing just how turned on I was.

"Shh. You're perfect." I barely felt his touch through the sweater and generously padded bra.

"You don't know that. You've never seen them. And anyway, this is like false advertising," I said, taking his hands and squeezing his fingers around the bra cups. "Hang on." I reached around to my back to undo the hooks, wiggling to the side while leaning forward to achieve enough clearance to accomplish the task in our confined quarters.

"Mind if I help?" His arms encircled me, and his hands moved under my shirt. With one twist, he finished the job. He may be a virgin, but this wasn't his first time unhooking a bra. The cups loosened and slid up, offering easy access to my breasts.

His eager fingers and my primed flesh met beneath the threads of my cotton sweater. I moaned softly as he caressed me.

"See? I told you that bra was false advertising," I muttered.

"Shh. Let me enjoy this." His authoritative tone increased my pleasure. He kissed my neck while intensifying his handy work. Under the spell of his squeezing, rubbing, and gentle tugging, I hardly registered the muted ding. Then, the plane hit a pocket of air. We jostled into each other, and my knees went wobbly.

"We'd better go sit down, right?" I didn't like to fly, and I certainly didn't want to be bumping around a tiny closet while we ploughed through rough air.

Bang, bang! A knock on the door, and then, "Your highness. The pilot wants everyone seated."

"We'll be right there."

Another bump, harder this time, threw him against me, smooshing me into the wall. "Are you hurt?"

"No. But let's get out of here," I said, reaching for the door handle.

He got there first and opened it. I braced myself in the door frame and stepped into the galley.

"Wait. Turn around." He hastily lifted the back of my shirt and fastened my bra. Trying to look presentable was probably pointless because the flight attendant and guards up front certainly knew what we were up to in the closet.

When the air smoothed out again, the flight attendant came by with small, warm towels. After she walked away, I leaned across the table between me and John. "She totally knows what we were doing back there. Do you think she'll tell anyone?"

"Of course not. She's been on my family's payroll for the last decade."

After our plane landed, we went to an expansive, tastefully decorated apartment that John's family kept in Berlin. A maid named Jana greeted us at the door with cold drinks and homemade pastries. *Seriously, ya'll. This isn't helping my thighs.*

We freshened up and changed into our party clothes before hopping in a convertible and tearing our way toward Potsdam. Thanks to the unseasonably warm weather, we put the top down, but there was enough wind that I had to wrap up in my coat.

It was the first time I'd been in a car with John driving. When he wasn't shifting gears, he had his hand on my thigh, pushing up the hem of my dress and inching closer to the sweet spot that longed for his touch. But alas, he didn't quite get there during the drive. What a tease.

Luminaries lined the driveway outside Sansssouci, their flames protesting winter's early darkness as it enveloped the landscape. In contrast, the lights inside the palace blazed like high noon on a summer day.

"Here we go. Are you ready for this?" John asked as he threw the car into park and waited for the valets to open the doors.

"I think so." I grabbed the bottle of wine we'd selected as a birthday gift for his cousin. "Are you sure no one's going to photograph us or talk to the press?"

"No one here needs the money. And they're just as sensitive as I am about reporters snooping in their private lives. We'll be fine."

We walked up to the massive doors and a man in a tuxedo pulled them open for us. Hyper rhythms of a lively jazz number pumped out of hidden speakers and electrified the air. It was hard to know where to look. The entryway to the palace was an elaborate foyer—airy, immaculate—a showcase for a series of portraits that lined the walls. But the people standing around in clusters were so elegant, they almost made the décor look shabby. Scattered throughout the entryway and in the ballroom just beyond, most of the women wore fashionable cocktail-length dresses in neutral colors like slate, chocolate, and muted gold. As I mentally thanked John for encouraging me to wear black, a bright-eyed woman in a short, fitted coral dress accosted us.

"John! And you must be his beloved Hatty!" Someone I'd never met threw her arms around me in a big hug. But she'd called me John's beloved, so I liked her instantly.

"Hatty, this is my cousin, Pru."

"It's so nice to meet you! Happy birthday!" I presented her with the bottle of wine.

"Lovely accent! Come in! We're just warming up!"

Without looking at the bottle, Pru handed it to a waiter who walked past us.

She linked arms with us, putting me and John on either side of her, and escorted us into a big open room with molding that looked like fancy scrollwork. The golden accents on the walls paled next to the glam groups of people scattered throughout the room talking and drinking. If I'd walked onto a movie set, the people would not have been more perfectly outfitted, coifed, and put together.

"John. Do you mind if I steal Hatty? Since Lucas hasn't arrived, she's going to be my date. Everyone's dying to meet her." Pru pushed John away and steered me in the opposite direction.

Though she'd been born in Toulene, Pru had spent most of her life in Australia, and it showed every time she spoke. So did her enthusiasm. She effervesced, and I couldn't imagine she ever got tired. With her quick, urgent steps, she took me to a small circle of women who looked close to my age, maybe a little older.

"Attention!" Pru said, affecting a heavy French accent while softly clapping her hands. "This is Hatty." The way she said my name made it sound like a scandal.

Faint smiles beamed back at me. With their flawless complexions, impossible curves, and over-styled hair, these women were cartoon princesses come to life. Pru ran through their names so quickly, none of them registered in my brain.

"Hatty! The American! How did you ever meet our darling John?" The redhead asked in a high-pitched, saccharine voice. I half expected her to reveal a seashell bra, pull a crab out of her purse, and start singing about crap she found in a shipwreck.

"Oh, I know how they met!" said one of the blondes, holding up her gloved hand as though she wanted a teacher to call on her. "She was modeling lingerie for a charity event, and John was in the audience!"

Dear Lord. "Well, that's not exactly right." Please don't envision me in lingerie. Let's just not go there.

"I heard you were wearing ripped fishnets when he met you in some dark and sinister pub," said another blonde.

"Well, you need to double check your facts." I tried to make my voice light, like I was amused—ha, ha—and not pissed by their inaccurate information. "I did dance in a charity event a couple of years ago to raise money for a school in Ethiopia, but John wasn't there. It's true we met in a bar, though it wasn't exactly dark or sinister."

The awkwardness of the conversation pushed a trickle of sweat down the middle of my back. Where the hell was John?

Before anyone else jumped in and asked for clarification on what I wore the night we met, I asked, "What are you drinking?" I gestured to the group's one brunette.

"*J'sais pas!* Pru, what are they serving? Something with bubbles."

Pru grabbed a flute as a waiter passed by and handed it to me.

"*Merci.*" I drank it the way I used to down cold glasses of lemonade on hot Missouri afternoons.

"Hatty! You drink like an American!" Soft laughter rippled around the circle.

"I'll take that as a compliment. Where's John?" A surge of panic gurgled up in my throat as I scanned the room.

"Oh, who knows? He hates these soirées. Come. You're in high demand." Pru linked arms with me again.

For a full hour, she took me from group to group and introduced me as the "hard drinking American" despite the fact I'd had only the initial few gulps of wine. Still, her guests, some of whom were clearly a bit tipsy, fussed over me. Several peppered me with questions. When I answered them, they looked bored, so I quickly came up with brief responses to move us through the formalities. The whole time, I tried and failed to get a visual on John.

I grabbed Pru's arm when we were between groups. "Where's the powder room?"

"The what?"

"*Toilette?*"

She led me out of the ballroom through a side door. We stepped into an open area. She pointed to the right.

"Over there. I'll wait for you inside." She headed into the ballroom.

I pushed open the heavy door and stepped into the ante room where there was a large, rectangular ottoman-type-thing positioned in front of a brightly lit mirror. I walked into the next area where there were walled off stalls with floor-to-ceiling doors. Europeans like their bathrooms small and private.

When I was done, I washed my hands and perched uncomfortably on the edge of the ottoman in front of the mirror to check my make-up. Out of the corner of my eye, I saw another woman sit at the other end.

"Are you Hatty?"

I turned to look at her. Of all the impeccably dressed people I'd seen, this woman took the cake and the plate it was sitting on. She must've stepped into Sanssouci right off the pages of *Vogue*. Brilliant white teeth gleamed from between red, glistening lips. Flawless skin was set against dark, smooth hair. A square neckline plunged low and tight, plumping up the tops of her breasts into supple mounds.

"Yes. I'm Hatty Brunelle." There was uncertainty in my voice. I knew I hadn't met this woman—I'd remember her perfection for the rest of my life. Still, she looked very familiar.

"John was right. You're cute, even if you are unrefined."

"I don't think we've met," I said, offering a smile, despite her unkind words.

"No. We haven't, but John told me all about you. I'm Claire." She leaned over the ottoman and extended her hand.

"Léglise?"

"*Oui*. It's so nice to meet you."

It was the hair. In all the online photos I'd seen, she had blonde locks instead of brown. *Maybe she lost her peroxide and toothbrush.*

"*Enchanté*," I said weakly, squeezing her hand. A hyper awareness of my shortcomings made me want to smooth my dress, fluff my hair, and check for lipstick on my teeth. "I'm sorry. Did you say you and John were talking?"

"I bumped into him right after you two arrived. I found a quiet little spot for us to have a *tête-à-tête* and plied him with liquor. Now, he's ready to have a good time. You know how much he hates these parties, even if he does adore all the attention he gets."

"How lovely to meet you. And thank you for ensuring John had a few drinks. I like how that makes him more handsy." I raised my arms and lightly bounced on the ottoman, as though testing its give. "If he keeps drinking, maybe we'll come in here for a quickie later. You know how much he loves the no-pants dance. Excuse me." I stood, grabbed my small purse, and left the ante room.

My heart raced and my breathing came in heavy huffs. I didn't give a damn who was next on Pru's must-meet list. I'd just met the most important person in the entire place.

Not caring what other people might think, I slung open the big doors to the hall. I walked over to a chair in the corner, kicked off my shoes, and stood on it. Aha. John was over by the cartoon princesses. They'd migrated to the other side of the room, but they were still all together, the sisterhood of the traveling implants. As John talked, he prompted small outbursts of polite laughter from the group.

"So, people from the Ozarks really don't wear shoes."

I looked down and gasped. A man with shiny dark hair held out his hand. He was at least fifteen years older than me. Golly, he was hot. He had the refinement men acquire with age and experience; he looked utterly at ease and relaxed.

I placed my hand in his and stepped down. His other arm wrapped around my waist firmly, with complete command of the situation, as though he routinely wrangled barefoot gals off chairs in fancy ballrooms. Planting my feet on the floor, I had to look up to see his chiseled features.

"Thank you. And to whom do I owe the pleasure?" I asked, feigning a formal tone.

"I'm Count Gerhard Hohenstaufen, John's cousin. And you're Hatty Brunelle." *Count Whose-it?*

He kissed the back of my hand softly, making me forget momentarily about Claire and my urgent need to find John.

"Has anyone shown you the gardens?"

"Not yet."

"May I?" He took my hand again and started to lead me away.

"Wait! I need to put my shoes on." I felt like a total hick.

"Please." He gestured for me to sit down.

My tight dress allowed me only to sit on the very edge. Gerhard knelt in front of me, retrieved one of my pumps, and then cradled my bare foot in his hand. I watched as the German count slid on the shoe in a smooth, adept motion. Maybe he did do this kind of thing often. *Rawr.* He lifted my other foot, cupping it in his large, warm hand. Just as his fingers lightly caressed the bottom of my toes, someone close by cleared their throat.

I nearly fell out of the chair when I saw John standing over us.

"Gerhard. You've found my lady in distress. Thank you for helping her. I can take over from here." John bent down and took my foot from Gerhard. That sexy line just above his jaw bone pulsed, signaling a flash of anger.

The count stood and pulled down on the ends of his jacket. "Your lady was indeed in distress. I was going to show her the gardens since you left her all alone."

"Thank you, Count, for your help," I said, sensing trouble brewing between these two cousins. I wanted to avert any arguments.

"*Adieu*, my dear." The count backed away, maintaining eye contact with me a second too long to be polite. It was an invitation, and I flinched.

John smiled up at me. "I'm sorry I left you with Pru long enough for the wolves to circle. Pru gets bored easily, and Gerhard can't resist a beautiful woman."

I closed my eyes for a moment. "I have to tell you something. I met Claire. She said she'd spoken to you and you guys had several drinks. Is that right?"

John stood and walked away. How dare he! I caught up with him and grabbed his arm.

He looked straight ahead as he spoke. "I know we already have trust issues, but I confess: I knew she'd be here. She and Pru are friends. I didn't tell you because I thought you might not come, or you'd worry unnecessarily."

Walking through the crowd, we tried to look like we weren't having a serious conversation. Given the setting, there was no way we could have it out.

I tried a different approach. "It's fine. So, tell me more about your cousin, the count."

"Gerhard? He's one of Germany's most notorious philanderers."

"He's certainly very skilled at helping women get what they need."

"I'm just glad I intercepted you when I did. Were you really going to the gardens with him?"

"Is 'going to the gardens' some kind of euphemism?"

John laughed. "Here it is. If you'd gone with him, he'd be caressing a lot more than your toes right now."

"And how would that make you feel?"

"I'd simply have to defend your honor," he said as we stepped through a doorway into the cool air. So much for unseasonably warm.

We walked around the end of the palace. I saw a wide terraced garden with a lighted fountain at the bottom of a long staircase.

I slipped off my heels. Again.

"What are you doing?" John asked.

"Catch me." I took off running down the stairs.

The hard, cold pavement smacked my feet, which only made me move faster. John's footsteps pounded behind me. What was I thinking? He plays rugby. He'd overtake me in a matter of seconds.

I darted off the stairs and onto one of the terrace ledges. It was wide, so I wasn't afraid of tumbling over the edge. As I approached the dead end, I scrambled in search of an escape route. A hand grabbed me and tugged at my dress. Something gave way and my dress slipped down to my waist.

I stopped and covered my bare chest. "Oh God!" I said. Cold air teased my breasts.

John's hands were on my sides, and he spun me around facing him. He pressed his lips to mine and his hands pulled at my arms, which were still wrapped across my chest. I halfheartedly tried to resist and he yanked harder. He kissed my neck, forcing me to lean backward as I struggled to stay covered. Exposing myself outside in the middle of winter wasn't my idea of a rocking good time.

My back arched and his arm reached around to support me. He must have known it was an unsustainable position because he lowered me down into the grass and gravel. I saw his face in shadow, partially lit by a small light on the terrace wall by my head. Soft giggles and heavy breathing drifted up to us from a couple of terraces below. You people have a mansion with a thousand bedrooms and you go for a romp in the freezing garden?

John squeezed my shoulders and slid his hands onto my bare back, pressing me into him. We kissed and I tasted alcohol.

"John. Stop. Not like this."

He drew back instantly. My words echoed the sentiment he'd spoken to me on the couch at Belvoir. He didn't say anything as he helped me onto my knees, and turned away as I adjusted my dress, moving it back into its proper position.

"Let's go find your shoes."

He took my hand and led me back up the stairs. After grabbing my pumps, we walked inside. The staff was gathering the guests for dinner. Tables filled another ballroom on the far end of the palace. I tried to smooth my hair; I suspected we both looked a bit disheveled from our terrace almost-tryst.

"Did you show her the gardens, John?" Pru asked with a twinkle in her eyes.

"Very funny." John sounded moody.

Of all the important friends and family at Pru's party, she included me and John at her table. We laughed and chatted our way through dinner. John drank only water.

After dessert, he kissed me on the cheek and whispered in my ear: "I'm going with some of the guys to the game room for darts and drinks. I'll come find you later. Are you okay on your own?"

"Sure. Go have fun." The prospect of navigating the next couple of hours alone filled me with dread.

"Just promise me you'll stick with Pru and stay away from Gerhard," he said, already standing.

"I'll take care of her, John." Pru grabbed my hand and patted it.

After dinner, we went back to the ballroom. The overhead lights were off. Strobes flashed and swirled. The madness of a rave replaced the elegance of the ballroom. Some kind of glowing rope snaked along the walls. I didn't see Claire Léglise the rest of the night.

I discarded my shoes for the third time that evening and danced with Pru and her crew of princesses. Lubed with liquor, they were more human, less cartoonish. They even took off their shoes.

In the middle of dancing, a pair of hands touched my waist. Afraid it might be Gerhard, I tensed my body until I realized it was John. We said goodnight to Pru and left the ballroom. Instead of heading to the entryway, John led me down a hallway lined with doors. He opened one for me, and I walked into a cozy, plain bedroom. "Are we spending the night?"

"Yes. I've had too much to drink. I can't drive to Berlin." Even when smashed, he remembered the weight of the family's reputation rested on his shoulders as an heir to the throne.

He slipped out of his shoes and took off his jacket. It was only 11:30 p.m. and I heard the muffled party music still going full swing back in the main ballroom. Our little bedroom had an adjoining bathroom, and John went in without closing the door. *Well, this is a whole new level of openness.*

Trying not to hear what he was doing in the bathroom, I distracted myself by opening a bureau drawer. Empty. I don't know what I expected to find. Maybe a shirt I could sleep in.

John came out and plopped onto the bed. "I'm sorry I didn't tell you about Claire being here. She loves her family more than she loves me, you know."

"Sleep," I said, exasperated by his sloshy lack of self-editing. I unfolded a blanket at the bottom of the bed and placed it over him as he closed his eyes.

I blinked into consciousness, looking at the room and trying to remember where I was. Not at *the* palace, but a palace. Then the memories of the previous night flooded my mind. I turned my head to find I was alone in bed.

I threw back the covers and stood up. There was a knock.

"Come in."

John cracked the door, stepped inside, and closed it behind him.

"I brought you some clothes. I'm really sorry we ended up crashing here." He walked over to me with a black duffle bag. "Good morning." He kissed me softly on the lips. "You look beautiful, by the way."

"I bet it looks like I slept on a weed-eater." My hands assessed my tousled hair. Über messy. I opened the bag and found a sweatshirt and shorts. "I'm dying to get out of this dress." I reached around back for the zipper.

"Here let me." John stood behind me and slowly pulled the zipper down, causing the front of my dress to collapse to my waist as it had done the previous night on the terrace. I turned around to face John, amazed at myself for being both bold and vulnerable.

"You wanted to see this part of me last night. It's better in the light of day with both of us sober, don't you think? Since I now know what Claire looks like in person, you need to see me for who I am. I don't look like her. It's not even a contest."

John's eyes were wide and his mouth hung open slightly. He blinked hard once before pulling me close to his chest and kissing me. My bare skin produced goose bumps in response to the gentle friction from the soft, thin fabric of his dress shirt. I began unbuttoning it.

"Hatty, you're beautiful. You're perfect," he whispered between kisses. His hand cupped the bottom of my right breast. His thumb grazed my nipple, and I sucked in a quick, rough gulp of air. He ran his tongue down my neck, and moved toward my chest. Then, he stopped. Just like that. He turned and reached into the duffle bag.

"Let's get you dressed so we can say goodbye to Pru." He held up the sweatshirt, covering my chest.

"Does that mean you don't want to have your way with me?"

He took my hand and placed it on the front of his pants. "It means I do, but I'm going to stop myself." He pulled my hand away. "Do you mind getting dressed in the bathroom so I can cool down? I can't walk out there like this."

He sat down on the bed and took out his phone. I headed for the bathroom, stopping once to glance back at him; he was watching me.

"If you don't get dressed, it's going to take a lot more than boring emails to take my mind off your amazing body."

His words, the look of longing in his eyes, and the way he'd touched me moments earlier went a long way toward squashing the fresh insecurities that meeting Claire had spawned.

CHAPTER TWENTY

Pushing up my sleeves, I thrust my just-washed hands into the flour, sugar, egg, and butter mixture. I was eager for John to taste chocolate chip cookies made from my mom's recipe.

"So this is how people in the Ozarks do it? *Sans* utensils?" John looked over my shoulder into the bowl, an eyebrow raised to emphasize his skepticism.

"Sure! Why not?"

John kneaded the muscles of my upper back mimicking my hands and fingers working the ingredients into a stiff dough.

"It seems I'm not the only one in this relationship who's good with their hands," he said as he ran his palms up and down my arms, squeezing intermittently to work those muscles too.

"I hate to have you stop what you're doing, but do you want to add the chocolate chips?"

He picked up the bag, put one between his lips, and kissed me. The chip melted under the friction of lips, teeth, and tongues. *Délicieux!*

"That chocolate kiss is certainly an improvement over the one we shared the night we met," I purred.

"Much better." He leaned into me, pushing my lower back against the wooden work table. He never seemed to care about the palace staff walking in on us, but it terrified me. What would John's father think if he found out? John's hands dove below my waist, gripping my ass.

Loud footsteps froze us. "Take it to a bedroom, Your Hiney-ness."

Henri snorted as he walked over to the bowl sitting on the table behind me. He dug his index finger into the mixture. John shoved him away.

"Don't stick your fingers in my lady's dough." John glared at Henri, then burst out laughing.

Henri picked up a handful of flour and threw it in my hair.

I gasped in surprise. "Will they lock me in a tower if I kill you?" I laughed in spite of my irritation.

"All of you out so I can finish." Hilda the Deutsch baker interrupted the horseplay. 'Hilda' means buzzkill in German.

"See? If you boys behaved, I'd get to finish something for once in this kitchen." I huffed dramatically as we left Hilda to shape the dough into balls and put them in the oven.

"Now what?" I turned on the two handsome brothers in the hallway outside the kitchen.

"Up for another movie?" John asked.

"Always." I squinted my eyes at Henri, daring him to comment.

"Confirmed. You two are the most boring couple in palace history. Baking, movies. You're like an old married couple."

I gasped and huffed, preparing to protest his accusation that we were boring. Before I had the chance, Henri turned and headed down the hallway. "I'm going for a walk." He gave a single wave, grabbed his coat from a hook, and walked out a heavy door leading outside.

John took my hand and guided me in the opposite direction toward the staircase. "It seemed like that bothered you. Did it?" He asked the question without looking at me.

"What? Henri accusing us of being boring?"

"No. Of acting married."

As though waiting for this cue, sweat sprang out from the pores around my temples and armpits simultaneously. How is it possible to have such coordinated sweat?

"Nothing Henri says bothers me. Anyway, it sounded like a compliment to me."

"That's how I took it. I just wanted to make sure you felt the same way." John squeezed my hand, a now-familiar gesture he used to punctuate a conversation. "So, what are we going to watch? We've got 'The Painted Veil' from your list and 'A Scanner Darkly' from mine."

"Either one's fine with me. But do you mind if I wash the flour out of my hair first?"

"Sure. But only if you let me help." His suggestion dripped with possibilities.

I nodded and John led me to the bathroom I used when I spent the night at the palace. He closed the door and turned the lock with a sharp click.

He grabbed my arms, just below the shoulders, and nipped at my neck. "I don't want to get your shirt wet. Mind taking it off?"

I looked into his simmering eyes and nodded my consent. In a single swoosh, he pulled the long-sleeve T-shirt over my head, forcing my arms into the air. Before I lowered them, his hands squeezed my ribcage below my bra and he brought his kisses south, closer to my cleavage. I wore a new black bra, the successor to the one I'd worn when I got soaked outside the preschool. He stopped and retrieved a towel, spreading it on the wide, raised area surrounding the lip of the jetted tub.

"Lie down." I did as he instructed. He guided my head over the tub, cradling it in his palm. With his other hand, he opened the faucet.

"Do you like it hot or cold?"

"Hot, please."

He pulled the attached nozzle and rained the warm water over my hair. Next, he squeezed the pearly pink shampoo onto my hair and got to work.

"You're so beautiful."

His declaration stood on its own; it didn't come in the heat of intense kissing or groping. He was really examining my face, so his words held more weight.

"Beautiful? Maybe. But only from this angle."

"From every angle." He set the nozzle down. "Look at me. I love you. That's all that matters. Stop being so hard on yourself."

It was the first time he'd said those three simple words. The inflection of his voice, the concern in his eyes consumed me. Not only did he love me, but he worried I wasn't getting it. My ears rang with the ancient love song every devoted couple knows by heart; its wordless melody told me yes, I knew he loved me, and I loved him, too.

Without regard for my sopping hair, I sat up, took his face in my hands, and kissed him. I pulled back and looked him in the eyes. "I love you, too."

He smiled and lightly brushed some suds off my cheek. "Let's get you washed up."

I leaned back and closed my eyes, letting his fingers massage my scalp and lace their way through my hair. Devotion infused his movements; never had anyone doted over me like this. After the rinse, he squeezed my hair, pulling the excess water into the tub.

"Sit up." He grabbed a towel from a nearby shelf.

After patting my hair dry, I nuzzled into his chest. "Thank you."

"Well? How did I do?"

I stood and walked to the mirror. "Not bad. I may have to let you try a few more times… practice makes perfect and all that."

"Just say the word." His tenderness overwhelmed me.

INCONCEIVABLE!

Three weeks before Winter's Feast, the annual post-Christmas gala at Belvoir, there was an unusual flurry of activity in the driveway at the side of Belvoir. It caught my eye when the driver pulled up in front of my usual door. John met me, and led me inside.

My feet expertly navigated the halls and stairs; this was the 17th time I'd been to Belvoir since we started dating. (But who was counting?) I was such a frequent visitor I thought about leaving a toothbrush and other essentials in the bathroom connected to my bedroom. Afraid John's father would find out and freak, I rejected the idea and kept packing and unpacking my rolling duffle for each visit. Whatever.

I planned to make savory stuffed dates during this visit, having given John my ingredients list when I was at Belvoir a couple of days earlier. The palace staff got any ingredient I requested. Most impressive was their ability to supply me with sweet, luscious strawberries, even though they were out of season, for my grandmother's strawberry bread. Since they went to so much trouble for the main ingredient, I improvised the buttermilk with milk and lemon juice. The loaf still turned out right: dense and cake-like.

Instead of leading me to the kitchen, John took me to The Flat.

"Straight to your bedroom, huh? You haven't changed your mind about your virginity, have you?" I said with innocent fluttering eyes as he shut the door.

"Don't you wish!"

The weather was cold and the paparazzi was hot. Their speculation about John's love life ran rampant like the season's flu, spreading rumors across glossy printed pages and social media. Since they were so desperate to find out about the prince's "latest fling" and why almost no one saw him in public these days, we stayed at the palace most of the time. My name surfaced a couple of times as a possible contender for John's affections. But we gave them so little to go on, it came off as pure speculation.

I slipped off my shoes and John grabbed my arms, pulling me tight against his body. Falling onto his bed, he promptly rolled on top of me. Through my jeans, I felt him coming to attention, a sensual greeting. *Hi, honey, I'm home!*

"What's this all about?"

"Hatty… Spend the rest of your life with me." He was a bit out of breath.

Did I hear that right?

I gently pushed on his chest. "Seriously. What's going on?"

He sat up, but I remained on my back. Ever so lightly, his fingers traced the peaks and valleys of my face. "Hatty, will you marry me?"

I sat up quickly, too quickly, because little silver stars exploded in my field of vision. "I'd better lie back down."

I eased back into a reclining position on the comforter. He lay down beside me, our faces an inch apart.

"I love you, and I want you to be my wife." *John wants me. Forever.* My very core lit up at the prospect of spending the rest of my life with him, and I had to stop myself from screaming, "Yes!" Because it wasn't quite that simple.

He held up a platinum ring, reached over, and took my right hand, the traditional place for wedding rings in Toulene. "Hatty, would you do me the honor of being my lifelong partner?"

He slid onto my finger the most beautiful ring I'd ever seen. It had a large center stone sitting among a circle of small diamonds. *Holy bling-bling, Batman.*

His proposal didn't come as a complete surprise—at the conclusion of our last date, the royal family's private attorney accompanied me home to go over some new paperwork. Lars Franke explained how my life would change if John and I got married. In order to have a title, Duchess was the most likely, I'd have to give up my U.S. citizenship. The title was necessary to fulfill legal requirements for marrying a member of Toulene's royal family, a law implemented after that messy Fergus-Emmaline business. Lars also told me if we got engaged before March, I'd have to forgo my final semester and delay graduation. He said in Toulene, royal engagements traditionally last no more than six months, so I'd be too busy planning the wedding and preparing to move to focus on my studies. There was also the little matter of my internship. I'd need time to work with my advisor and develop a plan that fulfilled the university's requirements and didn't involve coverage of the royal family or the National Assembly.

I frowned at the thought of having to halt my education.

"Oh God. What's wrong?" John's eyes were open wide and his lips wilted in concern.

"I'm going to be completely honest with you. I want to marry you. I want it more than anything. But your lawyer said if we get engaged, I can't graduate in May. Is that true? Why can't I do both?" I said it with my eyes closed, willing the tears to stay away.

He held my hand and rubbed it gently. "I understand. I'm asking so much of you. I knew the thought of delaying graduation would upset you. But I received some exciting news today from London. A family friend sits on the editorial board of The Guardian. He wants to be your mentor and help you become a writer for the paper's editorial page. I'm guessing the university will count that as your internship, even if you work remotely."

His face shone with satisfaction because he'd solved my problem. Except he hadn't. It smacked of favoritism. No one in their right mind at The Guardian would agree to work with a young journalist without a degree unless she were poised to wed a prince.

"Don't you think I can find an internship on my own? Before we met, I was well on my way to completing a degree without royal intervention."

"Yes, I realize you can find your own opportunities. But I thought you'd love the idea of working for such a prestigious paper. And they want you to write about poverty, education, and children's issues. I thought you'd be thrilled."

"I'm surprised. That's all."

"I'm sure you realize there's no way you can be married to me and work as a reporter of any kind. Reporters are the enemy of this family."

Boom. There it was. I suspected he felt this way, but he'd been careful not to say it explicitly. Now that we were in this thing deep, the truth emerged.

"So am *I* the enemy then? I was a reporter."

"Of course not. I'm talking about the men and women who nearly kill themselves and others trying to get a photo of me with a family friend or cousin so they can spew lies about who I love." His voice was loud. "And when we're married and have a palace full of beautiful children, I'll be damned if I'm going to let some fool with a camera hurt or exploit them in any way."

I'd never seen him this angry or heard him raise his voice so loudly. I sat up and took his hand, rubbed his back.

"Yes. John, I love you. When I think about what would make me happy for the rest of my life, all the pictures in my head include you." It was true. Going back to my pre-John life wasn't an option.

He kissed my palm, and squeezed my hand. "This spring will be busy. After the wedding, whenever that is, we'll move to Langbroek Palace to give ourselves space and distance from my family. Once we're settled, I promise to do everything in my power to make it possible for you to finish your degree. And in the meantime, you can begin working with Hans Friedman."

"Hans Friedman?" He was one of Europe's most revered journalists, though I hadn't seen his byline recently. I didn't realize he sat on The Guardian's editorial board. "Fine. If it were anyone else, I'd say no." I smiled in spite of myself, exhilarated to have the opportunity to work with one of the biggest stars in my field.

"Just embrace the fact your position is always going to open doors for you. You're a royal now, baby." His playful smile weakened my lingering resolve to argue.

"Fine. Now, I have an important question: why me? Why do you, the Prince of Toulene, want to marry a gal from the Ozarks?" My heart thumped faster; I was eager to hear his answer.

He turned to face me, and caressed my cheek. "All my life, I've been surrounded by pretty things—exquisite paintings, gorgeous heiresses, opulent palaces. While I appreciated the aesthetics, none of them appealed to me. When I met you, I understood why. They're all fake. But you… You're exactly who you are. And you know, I can't do that. I always have to play the part, be perfect, and be 'Prince John.' You aren't trying to be something different. You're just you. Hatty, you're my kind of beautiful." He leaned in and gently brushed his lips against mine.

I drew in a deep breath. "For the record, I love the real you. That 'Prince John' guy is great too because he knows how to be gracious to all the asshats he meets—and that's a real gift. You've shown me it's possible to be good and kind, even under extreme pressure. But I love you most when you're not being Prince Charming. I like it when you curse, hit your brother, and laugh until you snort. It reminds me even though you're a prince, you're still just a guy. It's really fun to see that side of you."

Our lips met again, and his hands wove themselves into my hair. He gently tugged, exposing my neck. His tongue licked an invisible line along my jaw and neck as he mapped his way toward my chest. His familiar pattern of kissing me stoked a fire between my legs.

But then he stopped. "I have an idea for how to share our big news. Let's announce our engagement at Winter's Feast."

"Oh, good call. I like that."

"And I want your parents to be here. They can fly from Springfield to Chicago and then try out the direct flight to Roeselare."

"I think I'm going to explode with happiness! It's been more than six months since I saw my parents. I can't wait for you to meet them! Do you want to hang on to the ring until Winter's Feast?"

"No, you keep it. Just don't wear it until then."

"How would you feel about letting me invite some of my friends? If we're going to announce our engagement, I'd like Tilda, Plato, Sam, and Sara to be there."

"Absolutely! I'll make sure they're on the list. Invitations go out tomorrow."

"So, what am I supposed to wear?"

"Don't tell me the future Mrs. Meinrad is afraid she'll look 'dudely' at Winter's Feast. Is that the right word?"

I lightly punched his arm. "Yeah, that's it." I never should've told him about my high school fashion horrors.

"Well, you could wear the nightgown from your first weekend at the palace." His fingers skimmed the neckline of my shirt.

"A bit scandalous, don't you think?"

"You're right. We try to avoid scandal at all costs, so no nightgown on the blue carpet."

"What's a blue carpet?"

"It's our version of Hollywood's red carpet. The guests for Winter's Feast walk a blue carpet from the street to the palace door. We let photographers set up on the west lawn and cover the arrivals. The idea is to give them some access so they don't climb over the fence to get pictures. But I think you should stay here the night before so they don't see you make a grand entrance."

"Yeah, I like that idea. We don't want to tip our hand." That, and I hated the idea of being on the lens-end of a journalist. "What will your family say about our engagement?"

"Dad, Henri, and Aunt Elinore knew I was going to propose to you today and they're completely supportive. I also briefed Granny. She trusts my judgment, and I know she'll adore you. By the way, did you know she gets to choose our wedding date?"

INCONCEIVABLE!

My new in-laws are total control freaks! When I told Tilda that Lars had come to my apartment to go over the details of a possible engagement, she mentioned the queen would have the authority to set the wedding date as well as the location. It was a little nugget Tilda had gleaned from a law school class on the monarchy. Of all the concessions I had to make, these seemed relatively minor.

"That's fine. What else do they get to decide? Whether or not my wedding dress has straps?"

"That's entirely your choice, though I know a tailor in Paris who'd love to help you with both your wedding dress and your dress for Winter's Feast."

A French designer wants to dress me? Maybe there's hope for me on the fashion front after all.

"And is the plan still for me to meet your grandmother for the first time at Winter's Feast?" Nervous energy bounced around my stomach at the thought of meeting Toulene's queen.

"She'll arrive a few days before, and I expect that's when you'll meet her. We have to follow her schedule and her lead."

The queen kept a lower profile than 007. Only a few people knew she holed up at an estate in Phuket, Thailand October through February. Her physicians recommended the warmer climate because apparently, she was prone to respiratory problems that got worse when winter arrived in Toulene. This explained why John was so unwilling to discuss his grandmother's schedule and change of plans when I interviewed him the first time. She'd never intended to visit that preschool herself. Promoting her appearance was part of the ruse to make people believe she was still in Toulene. Learning this bit of information assured me I was fully behind the curtain seeing the inner workings of the monarchy. Or so I thought.

"Stand up," John said. "I want you to see something."

He stood behind me, wrapping his arms around my waist. We looked at ourselves in the big mirror hanging on his bedroom wall.

John's hands slid around my midsection. "Our children will be kings and queens. On top of that, they'll be devastatingly gorgeous. I mean, look at us."

Intense desire surged through my body. Carrying John's child was the most intimate expression of love I could imagine. *Swoon.*

CHAPTER TWENTY-ONE

As my friends and I ambled along Rue Delambre, I kept tabs on the building numbers so we wouldn't miss the designer's atelier. It was Thursday night, and I resented the fact we had to leave Paris tomorrow evening because well, it was Paris and I loved it. During our walk, Sara, Tilda, Plato, and Sam debated what they were going to wear to Winter's Feast.

While I was in the City of Light choosing my dress for the upcoming party, John and Henri were in Paphos, Cypress visiting a tailor whose family had made special occasion clothes for generations of Meinrads. As much as I worshipped Paris, I wanted to go with them to Paphos because the projected high temperature during their trip was 75 degrees. John said no. He was paranoid and didn't want us photographed together until after we announced our engagement. The press was still snooping, getting more suspicious that John's public appearances had taken a nose dive. But so far, his plan was working: I hadn't seen one camera flash since the paparazzi gave up on me shortly after I got whisked away with John in the limo. *In your face, reporters!* I appreciated the small victories since I knew news of our engagement would unleash a media maelstrom, a vortex swirling around me and John. I dreaded it, but accepted it as part of the package. Growing up in the Ozarks, I'd learned that spring brings out nature's beauty, but the warmth that awakens the flowers also breeds tornadoes; you have to accept the bad with the good.

"How are things going in Cypress with the boys?" Sara always wanted to know every detail when it came to John.

Even though we were still supposed to follow the ban on electronic communication, John called me every night from Paphos to give me the highlights of his day.

"They're having fun. They got measured yesterday for their black, boring tuxes."

"Boring or not, his tux won't draw attention away from his beautiful girlfriend," Sam offered.

"I love you, Sam," I said, throwing my arm over his shoulder.

"Are you trying to steal my boyfriend?" Plato cut in, shoving my arm off Sam.

"Them's fighting words." I knocked Plato's hat off his head.

"We need crowd control for the Americans over here." Tilda called out with her hands cupped around her mouth.

"Hatty. Do you think John's cousins will be at Winter's Feast? What's the name of the one from Germany? Prince von Sexy-stein?"

"I'm sure Count Hohenstaufen will be there." Sara had begged me to divulge all the details of my weekend at Sanssouci, and seemed particularly interested in hearing about Gerhard.

"I'll be his HO-henstaufen anytime." Sara stopped on the sidewalk to put her hands over her head and wiggle her hips.

"Honestly, Sara!" I laughed at her unbridled enthusiasm. "You have to stop watching American rap videos because one day, I'm afraid you'll up and run away to L.A."

I grabbed her hand and pulled her along as we both cackled.

"This is *la place*!" Plato said, opening the red door for us.

We filed inside. A black and white checkered floor gave the entryway a vintage feel, and an enormous spiral staircase provided drama.

"Hatty? *Enchanté!*" The voice came from a man who looked to be in his seventies. He handily descended the stairs.

"Monsieur Bonhomme?" John had shown me photos of the world renowned designer with his mother. The man approaching me had sparkly, kind eyes, suggesting his surname's meaning rang true. I figured if he could help me find a beautiful gown, he'd be a damn good man.

Monsieur Bonhomme embraced me and softly planted a kiss on each cheek. He knew I was bringing an entourage, so I introduced my friends.

"My dears. Please. Call me Mathias. Now, I would be delighted to make a dress for you, Hatty, but I want to show you a few finished gowns, in case you like one of them." He pronounced the words with a thick French accent. John told me to speak to Mathias Bonhomme in English, not French, because he wanted to practice with an American.

We followed Mathias up the staircase to the first landing, where he opened a door off to the right. Inside, floor to ceiling windows allowed the fading sunshine to saturate the peeling wallpaper. Though the room looked a bit dilapidated, the racks of dresses shone like brand new stars in Mathias' universe. He led us to a rack with three gowns.

"These should fit, or I can take them in, if they are too big. Shall we begin with these?"

My friends watched in hushed awe as I examined each gown. The first was an orange-red strapless dress with rhinestone accents on the bodice. A matching stole hung next to it. It had a full skirt that flowed out from the bottom of the bodice, hiding all manner of below-the-waist flaws; I loved it immediately. There was also a silk pewter dress that seemed a bit too old for me, and a light lavender gown with spaghetti straps. As I'd expected, the orange-red dress looked the best on me. My little gang agreed. I was ready to call it a day when Mathias spoke up.

"If I may, mademoiselle. I have one more gown to show you. Come with me, but let me ask your friends to stay here," he said as he headed toward a door at the back of the room.

"I'll be right back, guys." They were already milling around, taking advantage of the opportunity to examine the dresses hanging on other racks.

"Take your time. Maybe I'll find something here I can wear," Sara said as I followed Mathias.

He took me to a large dressing room outfitted with a small stage, a massive tri-fold mirror, and more racks of dresses.

"Mademoiselle, will you try this one for me?" In his wrinkled hands, he held a black gown devoid of bling, though the fabric was shiny. It was a strapless mermaid dress, a style that hugged the body until just above the knees where fluffy folds of gauzy black fabric cascaded in expansive layers.

"It's beautiful, but not for me. Do you know how huge this will make me look?" I patted my thighs.

"*S'il vous plait.*" He offered it to me with his head slightly bowed. Not knowing how to respond to such a gesture, I took the dress, stepped on the little stage, and placed the hanger on the top edge of the mirror.

"*Oui. Pour vous seulement.*" Only for you, Bonhomme.

He turned around as I took off my shirt and pants and stepped into the dress. I had to wiggle as I gently tugged it up around me. I held it up and asked him to zip it.

When he was done, he stood beside me and we gazed into the mirror.

Yes, my hips and thighs looked big, but that's how they were supposed to look. The flare at the bottom brought them into perfect balance, giving me an exaggerated feminine shape.

"This is the one, mademoiselle," he said, not taking his eyes off my reflection.

"*Ouais*," I agreed.

"Don't show the others. Surprise them and *Monsieur le Prince* the night of the party."

I nodded. "*Merci. Merci beaucoup.*"

I took the dress off and put my clothes back on, knowing the black gown was the perfect choice for what essentially was my debut as John's fiancé. I could hardly wait to see his reaction to my selection.

"We will send this dress to the palace early next week." Mathias Bonhomme took my hand in his, put it to his lips, and placed a gentle kiss on it. "Hatty, it has been a long time since such a beautiful woman from Toulene's court paid me a visit. *Merci*, and I hope you will come see me again. You've made me very happy."

"Me too, Mathias."

When I walked back into the larger room, my friends stood huddled around Sara who cradled a phone in her hand. They looked up at me with wide eyes.

No one spoke. Sara handed me the phone.

Prince John Spotted in Cypress With Ex-Girlfriend

By Clarence Watson

December 12, 2013

After weeks of almost no public appearances, Toulene's Prince John was spotted at a quiet bar near Tzelefos Bridge in Paphos, Cypress with ex-flame Princess Juliana of Holland's royal family.

The two dated more than a year ago, though neither the Meinrad nor Orange family ever confirmed the pair were in an exclusive relationship.

A tourist snapped this photo of the two cozied up in a booth at the back.

Belvoir Palace staff did not respond to requests for comment.

The photo was dark and grainy, but I'd recognize that gorgeous man-hair anywhere. His head was bent toward a ravishing blonde as though they were deep in conversation. I handed the phone back to Sara.

"I'm sure it's all a big mistake. Would you excuse me for a minute?"

I walked out of the room, down the spiral staircase, and into the entryway. I twisted a heavy brass knob on a door to my right, and stumbled into a massive closet. I pulled the chain hanging from the ceiling, bringing a bulb to life, and closed the door.

Breathe, Hatty. My fingers shook as I dialed John's cell phone number for the first time, not giving a shit I wasn't supposed to call him.

CHAPTER TWENTY-TWO

W e're *engaged*. Doesn't that mean anything to you?"
My words blasted into the phone, sending my
anger across the miles right into his ear.

"Of course it does. How can you even ask such a question?
Look, she's an old friend and she invited herself out for drinks. It
was her last night in town. I couldn't say no."

Face palm. "Of course you can. You say, 'No. I'm engaged. This
wouldn't look right.' I think you *like* being seen in public with lots
of different women. What I can't figure out is why you never want
to be seen out with me."

"Hatty, we'll be seen in public soon enough, and then there's no
going back. I want to guard our privacy as long as possible. In fact,
I want you to move into Belvoir."

"If you think—" My righteous indignation froze. "What did you
just say?"

"It's easier to protect you from the press when we're together.
And, I want to spend more time with my soon-to-be wife." *God,
who could argue with that?*

"But isn't that risky? What if they find out I'm moving in?"

"They won't if we're careful. I'll make all the arrangements."

"So, we're not renting vans, collecting empty boxes from the grocery store, and getting our friends together for moving day?" *Because that's how we'd do it in Missouri.*

He chuckled. "Not unless you want to do it that way."

"Fine. You've twisted my arm. I'll let you and your 'people' handle it."

Silence. Then, "Hatty, I miss you."

"I miss you too."

We said goodbye. My fury over the news story didn't evaporate, but it dissipated as I imagined living just a couple hundred feet away from my fiancé.

It was Christmas Eve, and what I thought of as "Orange-gate" with the Dutch princess was behind us. Though my journalistic skepticism stayed aroused, John's lack of suspicious behavior starved it. *Rest in peace, skepticism.*

As I got ready to go downstairs and join John's family for dinner and a gift exchange, my stomach thrashed with anticipation. The queen had arrived from Thailand earlier in the day. She was in Roeselare to celebrate Christmas and then Winter's Feast on December 29 before heading back to Phuket on January 2. As an early Christmas gift, John gave me a black velveteen dress with a delicate lace slip that deliberately hung below the hem line. I thought the exposed lace was an elegant touch, but I worried about the reaction it would elicit from the queen and John's fuddy duddy father.

I walked into the dining hall to find John, Henri, and Leopold gathered around a side board, inspecting liquor bottles. John set his down when he saw me.

"Hatty! You look stunning." John kissed my cheek and squeezed my hand to reassure me as he led me to the queen. She sat at the head of the massive table with Aunt Elinore standing beside her. Beneath the queen's flawless make-up, her skin was tan. She wore a navy blue suit with a stylishly wide collar and a string of pearls.

"Granny, this is my Hatty," John said, transferring my hand to his grandmother's. I gave her a deep curtsy, bowing my head and lowering my eyes.

"Your Majesty." No one had to tell me how to address the reigning monarch.

"Hatty Brunelle of Southwest Missouri. Daughter of a school teacher and nurse. Do I have that right?" She released my hand.

"Yes, your majesty." I kept my back straight. The queen's presence made me want to maintain the best posture.

"Are you a reporter? You know we don't really like the press in this family." She gave me a playful wink that made me smile.

"So I've heard. I was a journalism student at the Royal University, but I'm taking a break from school to get to know your grandson better." I stopped myself without mentioning my previous internship at *Les Valenciennes*, remembering the alternative weekly opposes the monarchy.

"Trading a future Pulitzer for a prince? I think you've chosen wisely, though admittedly, I'm a bit biased."

"Are you tired from your trip?" I wanted to move away from the painful subject of my on-hold education.

"Oh yes. It's always exhausting. Maybe someday I can convince Leo to bring the boys to Phuket for the holidays." She lifted a wine glass to her lips.

"But we'd have to cancel Winter's Feast!" Aunt Elinore said dryly. Since she shouldered most of the event planning responsibilities, she had a love-hate relationship with the annual celebration.

At that moment, the butler, Herr Schroeder, came into the dining hall and sounded a gong. A pretty brunette slipped into the room behind him, taking a seat next to John's father. This was

Louisa, a much younger "friend" of Leopold's, according to John. Yes, he actually used air quotes when he described her to me.

Toulenian tradition called for an elaborate Christmas Eve dinner with family. The staff served course after course of holiday fare. Fresh winter vegetables filled our salad plates, and the table held baskets of bread best enjoyed with slabs of rich Irish butter. The main course consisted of roast turkey along with a Cornish game hen for each person at the table. I hardly had the capacity to entertain the two rounds of dessert—cheese and fruit.

After our overindulgence, we moved to the parlor with the blue textured wallpaper and white-and-gold molded embellishments. The gift exchange had the potential to be terrifying. I mean, what do you buy a queen, a duchess, and three princes? It sounded like the beginning of a bad joke. And there were rules. The meaning of the gift was more important than its size or monetary value, and you had to give everyone in the family the same gift.

"Hatty. You may go first." The queen smiled at me and a sharp terror ran down my arms. What if they hated my gift? Too late to second guess it now.

I passed out the weighty green boxes. They looked festive with a sprig of fresh holly on top. "You each get a dozen chocolate chip cookies made from my mother's recipe. Instead of regular chips, I used chocolate chunks from Pierre Marcolini's shop in Brussels. I hope you love every bite." The cookies had a subliminal message: they showed how blending a recipe from Missouri with fine chocolate from Europe could lead to something beautiful. *See what I did right there?*

"I'm already in a food coma, and you're giving me more to eat?" Henri groaned with dramatic flare before devouring an entire cookie in one bite.

There was an exquisite outburst of ohh's and ahh's as they each tried the cookies.

Even Leopold seemed pleased. "Did John tell you Pierre Marcolini is our favorite?"

"I confess. He deserves credit for recommending that particular shop." I patted John on the cheek.

John went next, giving each of us a little black book with a leather cover, just like the one he used during our trip to Ghent. He encouraged us to find a creative use for our notebook. Aunt Elinore said she'd jot down her final to-do list for Winter's Feast. In a burst of inspiration, I announced I'd use mine as a sketchbook.

"Are you an artiste, Hatty?" The queen stared at me.

"Not really. I'm not very good, but I love to doodle."

Henri handed out bottles of wine made from the first harvest of grapes in Burgundy, France the year he was born. "It was a good year!"

John's father gave us each a platinum watch. As he placed them in our hands, he noted he'd like the family to be known for being on time in the New Year.

"Louisa picked them out." We all pretended like we hadn't heard him. *Royally awkward.*

We each received a personalized photo album from Aunt Elinore. Underneath my name were the words "Winter's Feast 2013."

"Don't store all your photos on your phone," she admonished us.

The queen went last. She raised her hand to Herr Schroeder who stood by the parlor door. He disappeared, and just a few seconds later, returned with a string of servants. They delivered a box to each of us.

"Go on. Open them." The queen waved her hands before sipping her tea.

Inside, I found a small wooden box. Carved on top were a series of arched characters I didn't recognize.

"It means 'family' in Thai." It was one of the seven languages the queen had mastered.

I opened my box and inside was a single pearl and a tiny slip of paper. "Welcome to our family" was written on it in tiny cursive. I looked up in surprise at the queen. I mouthed the words "thank you" and she smiled broadly.

After our gift exchange, John and I politely excused ourselves and headed upstairs. Instead of walking me down the corridor to my room, he opened the door to his bedroom.

"I can't stand the idea of having you wake up alone in your bed on Christmas morning. How about you sleep here tonight?"

"Of course. And I assume when you say 'spend the night,' you mean literally just sleep together." *Let's just be clear.*

"Yes, my dear."

"What will your family say if they find out we've spent the night together? They'll think I tried to seduce you."

"No they won't, and they're not going to find out. Since tomorrow's Christmas, the staff will have the morning off. So, Henri will prepare breakfast for Father, Granny, and Aunt Elinore, and they'll eat at eight. Just sneak back to your room to get ready while they're having breakfast."

How could I say no?

"All right. I'm going to change clothes. I'll be back."

When I returned, I tapped on the door. John opened it, wearing a fitted tee shirt and soft cotton drawstring pants. Not even Pierre Marcolini's chocolate looked this delicious.

I went in and he quickly closed the door behind me. We looked at each other and laughed nervously.

"We're acting like horny teenagers," I said with a giggle.

"Well, since we're a bit older, we have to show more restraint." John, always the sensible one.

"I suppose you're right."

He walked me over to the bed with its blankets and sheets peeled back. After he helped me up onto the high mattress, I handed him a little box.

"Merry Christmas," I said as he opened it and picked up the piece of canvas. "I know this is cheesy, but I wanted you to have something from America that also honored your mother's memory."

John held the micro painting close to his eyes. "Where did you find this?"

"My mother bought it from a Toulenian artist living in Missouri. After your mother died, this artist did a series of paintings to honor her. My mom bought one, but never had it framed. I asked her to send it to me so I could give it to you for Christmas."

"Thank you. I've never seen this painting. It's extraordinary."

His mother died December 26, 1998 when John was nine and I was seven. He lightly rubbed the painted fabric of his mother's face with his thumb. I suppose enough time had passed to smooth over the rough edges of his grief.

He set the square of canvas on the dresser, turned off the light, and got into bed.

As my legs glided between the sheets, it felt cool and summery, even though winter reigned outside. I hoped it would always feel this good being in bed with John. We pulled the layers of covers over us and snuggled into each other as dull light seeped into the room around the edges of the heavy drapes.

"Hatty, you fill a hole in my heart that opened up when Mum died. I love you for that." He nuzzled my neck.

"Have I told you how much your mother meant to me?"

He stopped and propped his head up on his hand. "No. Please tell me."

"Okay. Well, it was the beginning of first grade. I was six years old. My teacher asked us to make a collage using photos of someone we admired, and I chose Princess Beatrix. I'd seen pictures of her helping children in Africa in some of my mom's magazines. I cut them out for my project and glued them to a big pink poster board. She was so beautiful, stylish, and smart. But above all, I imagined she was compassionate."

"I think you'll follow perfectly in her footsteps as my wife and mother to our children." He kissed me on the forehead. "I wish you could've met her. She would've loved you."

John lay down and I placed my head on his chest. We soon fell asleep.

CHAPTER TWENTY-THREE

The day after Christmas, my parents arrived at Toulene International Airport on the very runway John helped christen a few months earlier. I met them at the arrivals gate with open arms and tears.

"Hatty! You look wonderful!" Mom was as effusive as ever in complimenting me.

Dad gave me a big hug, briefly lifting my feet off the ground. "Don't they feed you over here?"

"A little too much. You'll see. Belvoir has an amazing kitchen staff."

We walked out the front doors to a black limo idling at the curb in front of a Do Not Park sign.

"Is this really necessary, honey?" My mom handed over her suitcase handle to the driver.

"No. But John insisted on sending this monstrosity instead of one of the cars. He wants you to travel first class all the way to the palace."

"Well, he sure didn't put us in the cheap seats on the plane," my dad said. "But you still feel the turbulence in first class, so your mother was a Nervous Nelly the whole way."

During the drive to Belvoir, I pointed out some of the city's sights.

When the black limo swung into the side gate at the palace, my mom gasped. "This place doesn't look real."

"Isn't it wild?" My giddiness burst through every word.

Astrid met us at the door, and led us upstairs to a bedroom two doors down from mine.

"Thanks, Astrid." I turned to my parents. "John thought you guys might want some time to relax. I'll be back in a couple of hours and we can walk downstairs together for dinner. It's completely casual so don't get dressed up. I can't believe you're actually here!"

I hugged them again and left. My parents were at Belvoir Palace in Toulene to meet my future husband who also happens to be the future king of this country. Their grandchildren would inherit the throne one day. *That's crazy, ya'll!*

When we arrived in the breakfast nook, John extended his hand to my parents. "Mr. and Mrs. Brunelle, it's very nice to meet you!"

My mom went in for a hug. "You're much cuter in person!"

I laughed. "I told him the same thing."

My dad shook John's hand. "Nice to meet you. I hope we're not a royal pain in the ass!" Yep, there it was, that Brunelle compulsion to use corny jokes and puns to lighten the mood. It must literally be in our genes. My dad's belly laugh probably startled the staff.

During the meal, John told my parents about the things we'd done at the palace the last few weeks. He also peppered them with questions about their lives, our family, and the Ozarks.

After the staff placed dishes of fresh fruit on the table for dessert, John cleared his throat. "Mr. and Mrs. Brunelle, I've fallen in love with your daughter." He took my hand in his and kissed the back of it. "With your blessing, I'd like to marry Hatty. I promise I'll love and protect her our whole lives."

I froze a smile on my face and spoke quietly through clenched teeth, hoping my parents wouldn't hear. "I thought we were going to wait to tell my parents at Winter's Feast."

John answered through his teeth as well. "But I need to ask your parents' permission."

Mom and Dad showed no signs of shock at the news—they probably figured things were serious if John was willing to fly them across the ocean—but John had caught them off guard. The silence grew long and awkward.

Then Dad spoke up. "Someday, John, you'll have a daughter. And you'll understand how difficult it is to think about her belonging to someone else, especially when that someone lives on the other side of the planet."

"I don't belong to anyone!" I said a little too loudly. "Don't talk about me like I'm not in the room."

"Yes, George, she's not chattel. Crawl out of the Dark Ages. You, too, Hatty. I mean, what happens to your career if you get married?" Cue mom's theme music because she was here to save the day. She might even need a cape.

"Mom, John's helping me meet some important people in my field, and there are some exciting possibilities on the horizon. My journalism career is still very important to me."

"What do you mean?" John jumped in, also raising his voice. "You agreed you were done with reporting." Time for John's teeth clenching.

I glared right back at him. "Reporting, yes. Journalism, no."

"Wait just a minute. You're done with reporting? I don't think so," my mom said in disbelief, making her I-have-no-words huffing sound.

"Look. John and I love each other. I'm the happiest I've ever been in my life. He's an honorable man with honorable intentions. I'll finish my degree, eventually. We'll see what happens after that. Please just be happy for us." Get your shit together, Brunelles!

"Hatty, of course we love you and if this is what you want, we support you completely. John, welcome to our family." Thank God for my dad and his ability to diffuse the tensest situations, a skill he'd honed during his years in the ER.

Mom kept her arms crossed, needing time to cool off.

"John, I think my parents have had a very long day." Hint, hint.

"Yes, of course. I'm sorry to spring all of this on you at a time when you're likely exhausted."

"Sleep sounds good." It was all my mom managed to say. She looked pissed, haggard.

And to think, they'd only met John. Couldn't wait to see how they'd mesh with his family.

CHAPTER TWENTY-FOUR

T he statement was ready to go. The palace public affairs office drafted three sentences announcing our engagement, and John and I gave our blessing. I dreaded the coming media frenzy. The palace staff planned to email reporters at midnight, several hours after we shared our big news with family and friends during Winter's Feast.

All of that was hours away. I sat at the breakfast table with John, my parents, and my inner circle. Mom and Dad sipped coffee, still battling jet lag while Plato, Sam, Tilda, and Sara chattered about the palace and the evening's festivities. Seeing so many people I loved sitting around one table warmed my heart. I wanted to bottle up the moment and hold on to it forever.

"John, will you introduce me to your cousin from Germany?" Sara asked between bites of muffin.

"Of course. But I should warn you. Gerhard doesn't like to dance."

"We'll see about that." Her eyes smoldered, ready to slay a German count with a single glance.

After breakfast, John arranged for a driver to take my parents to one of the biggest shopping centers in Europe. It was fifteen minutes from the palace, depending on traffic. My dad forgot to pack dress shoes for the suit he planned to wear to Winter's Feast.

While my parents handled their fashion emergency, John and I took my friends on a tour of the palace grounds. This was John's first opportunity to spend any significant amount of time with them. Except Plato. They saw each other at regular poker games.

It was just after 1:00 p.m. when John said, "We'll have lunch delivered to our rooms so we can begin getting ready for this evening. Shall we head back inside?"

Sara pulled my arm and held me back as the others walked ahead of us.

"Do you think I have a shot at one of his cousins?" Sara was a party girl, game to do anything and anyone.

"Sure. Why not?"

"I hope so because I need to bag a nob. A girl could get used to this kind of royal treatment."

My hair sat in a messy bun on my head, and I wore glasses instead of contacts. Tilda and Sara helped me into the black mermaid dress Mathias had sent to Belvoir. Their eyes were large and unblinking when I pulled it up.

"Zip me?"

Tilda nodded and moved behind me to secure the dress. "Hatty. This is absolutely gorgeous. John's going to propose to you on the spot." *Oh, Tilda, if you only knew!*

"This is, by far, the nicest dress I've ever worn. I have to admit, I kind of like it. Am I betraying my nerdy-girl roots?"

"No," Tilda said, looking me up and down. I adjusted the position of my glasses; I hadn't yet put in my contacts. "You're a nerdy fashionista—a nerdista!"

"I love it! But I'm definitely not wearing my specs downstairs."

Tilda slipped into a classic gown in navy with a fitted bodice and flowing taffeta skirt. Sara's short, tight dress showed her legs that wouldn't quit.

"Am I slut-errific or what?"

"If I say yes, is that a compliment?" I handed Sara her lipstick.

"Oh yeah."

When we descended the stairs at 5:30 p.m., about fifty people stood in groups around the grand foyer. John came over to us right away with Sam and Plato on his heels.

"Hatty. You're simply radiant." John kissed my cheek, then whispered in my ear, "I want to peel that dress off and have my way with you."

My eyes widened and I laughed lightly, suppressing my body's urge to writhe with desire.

We left my friends by the stairs and John took me around for a meet-and-greet. I recognized some of the faces from Sanssouci, but most were new, a who's who of European royalty and old money. The high ceiling in the foyer did nothing to dissipate the cloud of cologne and perfume that hung over the gathering. My eyes watered from the aromatic barrage as John led me to a group of twenty-somethings.

"Hatty, this is Percy and Jos. We played together at Cambridge."

A shot of nerves threatened my composure as I shook hands with international rugby star Jos de Haven. He was kind of a big deal. Though his nose sat crooked, it didn't diminish his dashing good looks.

"Nice to meet you both. I know Jos still plays, but how about you, Percy?"

"I traded the field for the court. I'm a solicitor now."

"I'd like to get both of these guys back in the game," Jos said, grabbing John's shoulder roughly. "I'm thinking about putting together a celebrity match for charity. People would pay a lot to see the prince and one of the country's top solicitors get the snot knocked out of them. Don't you agree, Hatty?"

No. Blinking. Way. The thought of John participating in such a brutal game against professional players made me cringe.

As John, Jos, and Percy reminisced, I caught a brief glimpse of my parents. They were in deep conversation with a couple I recognized from Sanssouci. John had assured me Aunt Elinore would introduce them to other couples, and ensure they didn't end up standing alone.

Herr Schroeder sounded the gong, interrupting conversations to signal it was time for dinner. There were tables set up all around the Regents Room. To my surprise, several wall panels were gone so that the room was nearly double its usual size.

As we took our assigned seats, the queen stood and rang a small bell to quiet the massive room. "Please join me in raising a glass to get our celebration underway. In the scarcity of winter, may we celebrate our bounty. Winter's Feast reminds us even though the land looks barren, the potential for life sleeps just below the surface. Fill your stomachs with food and your hearts with hope!"

The crowd responded with a loud and unified, "Prost!" as they observed the customary opening toast.

I lifted my plate and removed a glossy brochure. It outlined the many courses we'd enjoy throughout the evening. There were vignettes and photos featuring the farmers who produced what we were about to eat.

The meal consisted of bite-sized samples of food from farms across Europe. At first, I was taken aback by the tiny portions, but the sheer quantity and variety of food helped the dinner live up to its moniker. From dainty micro-salads to fruit samples to petite meats, the courses kept coming.

John leaned over between courses. "Don't you love this? Farmers competed fiercely to earn a spot on your plate tonight."

"Talk about the cream of the crop!" *Snort, snort.*

"Well done, Hatty! You're a scream." Pru lightly smacked my arm. She appreciated my wonky sense of humor. Her boyfriend Lucas, a sandy-haired Aussie with rugged features, didn't react to my lame attempt at being punny. His eyelids were heavy from lingering jetlag.

As the courses changed from meat to sweet, Leopold Meinrad stood and rang the small bell.

"We have an announcement to make this evening, and I'm happy so many of our dearest friends and family are under one roof to hear our news. John?"

My heart nearly sprang out of my chest as John prepared to announce our engagement. I reached into the small sachet I was using for a purse and slipped the sparkling diamond onto my right ring finger.

"Friends, thank you for being here. In life, there are only a few things I've absolutely had to get right: math on the exit exam, the winning play in my last rugby match, and the choice of a partner who will help me build the future of my family and this country."

Someone nearby sucked in a quick breath.

John continued. "Even though I didn't get the first two quite right, I know I've succeeded with the third. It's with extraordinary happiness I introduce to you my future wife, Hatty Brunelle of the United States of America."

Before I scooted my chair back and stood, the room erupted in applause. And I heard other chairs scooting. As I rose to my feet, so did everyone else.

In an instant, the people we loved most in the world surrounded us: his brother and aunt, my parents (at last, looking elated), Tilda, Plato, Sam, and Sarah. In all the hugs, clapping, and wiping of tears, I didn't see the queen. What was her reaction? I turned and looked in her direction. There she stood at her table, smiling in approval. John and I left the hubbub to go to her. She took both of my hands in hers.

"My dear. I have only one piece of advice: make your own happiness. You'll do just fine." She cradled my cheek in her hand before opening her arms to officially welcome me into the family.

After our announcement, the staff brought out flutes of golden, bubbly goodness. The happy hum of excited conversations, laughter, and glasses clinking floated through the hall. The conclusion of the meal brought no fewer than six dessert courses. After the waiters served the last dish, people began making their way out of the Regents Room.

I turned to John. "Where's everyone going?"

"To the grand ballroom. The after-party is just as amazing as the meal."

We lingered in the Regents Room, accepting congratulations as some of the guests formed an impromptu receiving line. Astrid slipped behind us and gave us cups of coffee, made slightly sweet by the whipped cream dollop floating on top. What I really needed was an IV with caffeine drip. Stat.

We headed to the hallway, the promise of karaoke luring us toward the ballroom.

"Hey. I need to stop in the restroom. You go ahead. I'll meet you in there." I let John's hand slip from mine.

"I'll wait for you."

"No. Go. People want to talk to you, Mr. Prince-man."

"And you. You're like a breath of spring at our Winter's Feast." *Melt.*

He left and I slipped into the bathroom. As soon as I sat down in the first stall, the door to the hallway banged open.

"Adela! I'm sorry, okay? I'm such an ass."

I sat motionless on the toilet as complete silence followed Henri's outburst. I saw his black shiny shoes outside the stall.

"Umm, it's Hatty."

Henri exhaled loudly and banged the stall door. I jumped up at the sudden noise and used the opportunity to get my clothes back in place. I pushed the door open and we were almost nose to nose. I gently put my fingertips on his chest and pushed him away.

"Sit," I commanded.

"Fine." He spoke heavily, flopping into a chair by the full-length mirror near the sinks.

I washed my hands and walked over to my soon-to-be brother-in-law. "What's up, Buttercup?"

"It's not funny. This is serious."

"Okay, but I don't even know what 'this' is."

He looked miserable. The reddish glow of his cheeks revealed he had a first class ticket to Hangover-ville.

"Adela's mad. She thinks I'm too flirty."

"Well, are you?"

"No. Not intentionally."

I sat on the arm of the chair and reached around his slumped shoulders to give him a squeeze.

"Look. Her worst fear is probably that she'll get snookered into thinking she's the one you love, only to find out through the tabloids you've dumped her for another woman. Not that you'd ever do that. *Right?*"

"Give me more credit than that."

"I do. But she may feel a tad insecure. And seeing gorgeous women hanging all over you pushed her over the edge. You need to go find her and make it better."

"I think I love her." He rubbed his eyes.

"Then let's go look for her."

As he stood, he took a piece of chewed gum out of his mouth. He grabbed my right hand and placed the wad in my palm. "You're my sister now."

"So, this is what it's like to have a little brother?"

"Pretty much."

We both laughed and I put the gum in my mouth.

Sister. It was the first time anyone had used that word in reference to me, the chronic only child.

Henri leaned against my side and slung his arm around my waist as I guided him into the hallway.

When we found Adela, she was leaning against the handrail of the grand staircase. Her long, fitted red dress was sleeveless, exposing strong, shapely arms folded across her body. I knew immediately she wouldn't take any crap from him.

I whispered to Henri, "Don't screw this up. Make it right."

He nodded and went to her.

CHAPTER TWENTY-FIVE

Opening the doors to the ballroom, a whole new feast sprawled before me. There were jugglers, a guy on a unicycle, and a clown. A scantily clad woman on a trapeze swung above the dancing, thrashing crowd. A waiter stopped in front of us with tiny glasses.

"Absinthe?" the waiter asked.

John politely declined, but I grabbed a glass and threw it back in a single swig. The taste of licorice with a bitter edge coated my mouth. Only moments later, the strong alcohol made my head swim.

"Every hour, a shower of confetti rains on the crowd," John said, pointing to the ceiling. "It's like celebrating New Year's Eve over and over. There's a countdown one minute before."

"Should I expect an acid-dropping midget in a bowler hat to ask me to dance? This looks like a scene from a Baz Luhrmann film."

"Baz!" John raised his hand and waved. A dashing man with silver hair swirled over to us with a blonde woman in his arms.

"Baz, this is my fiancé Hatty. She knows your work quite well."

My eyes were wide as Baz kissed me on each cheek.

"Congratulations, you two! It's so nice to meet you, Hatty. This is my wife, Catherine Martin."

"You're a costume designer, and you guys worked together on The Great Gatsby, right? We loved that movie!" *I'm a total fangirl.*

"Thanks, Hatty. Your gown is exquisite, by the way." Those words coming from Catherine Martin nearly knocked me over.

"Hatty, it's nice to meet you," Baz said. "I'll let you two make your way through the crowd. If you're feeling adventurous, stop at the water tank at the far end. You put in your legs and tiny piranhas eat away the dead skin. It's popular in Thailand at the spas. Your grandmother told me about it. Very invigorating!" And with that, the Lurhmanns moved on.

I couldn't see the tank (and there was no way I was going to feed my flesh to piranhas), but at the far end, I spotted the karaoke stage.

"You don't really think you can outdo me at karaoke, do you? Maybe we should sing a duet," I offered.

"You're on your own, my dear. I always sing solo."

"Well, aren't you a cocky so-and-so? Don't you know I've spent the last three and a half years singing my heart out in karaoke bars throughout your fair kingdom?"

"Before we go mic-to-mic, let's get a drink. What do you want?"

"Just water. I don't want to impair my performance with more booze or caffeine."

As John walked away, I set my sights on the five cartoon princesses standing together looking ridiculously over-the-top in nine inch heels and slinky dresses. They also wore scowls.

"Hey! It's nice to see you guys again. Isn't this amazing?" *Cause, ya know, I'm like the belle of the ball, tonight.*

One of the blondes looked at me with an expression that screamed, *You've got to be kidding me.* Instead, she said, "Congratulations on your engagement."

"Thank you! I'm so happy we got to share the news with everyone tonight."

But none of the princesses smiled back at me.

The redhead spoke up. "We're sure you'll eventually become the kind of girl who fits with John and his family."

The backhanded compliment took my breath away and released a flood of self-doubt.

Before I could respond, another woman spoke up. "Yes, if you need any advice on how to blend in, we'd be happy to help you. It's clear you're out of your league. I'm sure this all seems so… foreign to you." The inflection of her voice made the word "foreign" an insult, a slap across the face.

"What do you mean?" I spat back at her.

"You're too unrefined, and all that has to change. No more karaoke in pubs, dancing barefoot, or speaking your mind so freely. Good luck with all that." The red-head laughed lightly as if she'd just made a joke.

Plato caught my eye and waved me over. *Thank goodness.*

"Excuse me." I turned my back on the women and left, wanting to punch someone.

I nearly ran to Plato. He grabbed my arms and furrowed his brow. "Hatty, what's wrong?"

"It's nothing."

I couldn't repeat what they'd said without having a complete breakdown or knocking someone out. I think part of me felt like they were right—I didn't fit in and I wasn't refined. I belonged outside the walls with the rest of the nosy journalists who just wanted to get their story and go home.

"Hatty. You look pissed. Did those witches say something to you?" Plato put his hands on my shoulders and stared at me. I nodded, still wrestling the knot in my throat as the anger simmered inside me.

"C'mon. I have an idea." Plato led me the length of the ballroom to the stage. The DJ was bopping along to the dub-step blaring through the single headphone he held against his ear.

"Hi! We're ready for karaoke. Do you have "Raise Your Glass" by Pink?" Plato grabbed my hand and squeezed it. On this karaoke stage, he'd definitely have my back.

The DJ nodded and began swiping and tapping on the tablet he had plugged into the sound system. "When this number ends, okay, mate?" Like the Luhrmanns and Lucas, the DJ sounded like an Australian import.

We went on stage and stood behind the two microphones. I scanned the room for John, but didn't see him anywhere. People noticed us standing there, and turned to see what we were about to do.

When the song ended, the DJ spoke into his mic. "Ladies and gentlemen, the next princess of Toulene." *Hey, that's Duchess, buddy.*

The crowd stood still and every eye was on us. I took a deep breath and smiled, finally seeing John holding two glasses back by the entrance. Even this far away, his broad grin gleamed in the blue-white light.

Watch your crazy American fiancé show you how it's done.

The song began and Plato grabbed his mic. This number was our favorite. It's the one we always sang when we did karaoke together.

People smiled appreciatively as Plato rocked through the first verse. Sam came to the front of the stage with Tilda and Sara. They grooved and danced in their free-spirited way.

We ripped into the chorus, and the cartoon princesses stood in a hideous huddle sneering at us. My only thought when it was my turn to sing a verse? *In your face, bitches.* I grabbed the mic from the stand and yanked it to my lips. I spat the words, sending them like darts toward their frozen frowns. They were the only people in the entire place who weren't jumping, dancing, or lifting their drinks as the song gained momentum.

More people joined the dancing when we cranked out the second chorus. Wine sloshed out of glasses as they bounced up and down singing with us. As we neared the end, the entire place exploded in a riot as people sang with us and kept dancing. Baz dipped his wife; they were wrapped up in their own little world. Mom and Dad stood just off the dance floor smiling at me, probably happy and relieved that I was comfortable enough in this setting to let loose.

When the song ended, people screamed, clinked glasses, and rushed the stage. Plato raised a shot glass, handed me one, and we clinked them together. I took a healthy sip, but didn't suck down all of the liquid; I was still a bit unsteady from the absinthe. I handed the glass back to Plato and floated to the edge of the stage. Gerhard was there in an instant, swooping me off the platform before I could object.

He cradled me in his arms. "Hatty, never let them change you." Gerhard lowered my feet to the floor.

John immediately took my hand.

"Sorry," I yelled over the roar of the crowd. "We were probably a little over the top."

"You were spectacular. I'm going to whisk you away before you have to do an encore." John led me toward a side door.

In the hallway, we were alone. John's strong hands formed a vise on my hips, roughly pulling my body into his while pushing me toward the wall.

"I love how you look and feel in this dress." He slid his hands over the slick fabric to my backside, squeezing me while he kissed my neck. "Claire had nothing for me to grab back there."

I grabbed his chin in my hand and turned his face down to mine. "Let me kiss her name out of your mouth." Our lips slammed together hungrily.

John brought one hand around to the front of my strapless dress. I wriggled my body closer to his, making it easier for him to reach inside.

A stern voice stopped us: "John."

John immediately pulled away at the sound of his father's sharp tone. My fingers curled, digging into my palms. Embarrassment and panic filled me, mixing into dread.

"You can't let your wife do that." Leopold narrowed his eyes at us.

"What are you talking about?" John turned, putting himself between me and his father.

The queen was there, too. "Leo, leave them. Let's go inside." She stepped closer to us, gesturing toward the doors leading back into the ballroom.

"Hatty, you can't go on stage in front of our family and friends singing such wildly inappropriate songs if you're going to marry John. You were practically screaming the lyrics, words like 'panty snatcher.' My God."

The tension in Leopold's voice warned me of his simmering irritation. It was the same way John sounded when he was trying (and failing) to control his anger. But I didn't give a crap. My inner Ozarks redneck woke up.

"Let me get this straight. You object to 'panty snatcher?' Maybe you find it offensive because it hits too close to home. By the way, where's Louisa?"

I gasped at my bad manners. Clearly, the liquor had loosened my tongue.

John squeezed my hand hard. I didn't blink.

The queen lightly touched my arm. "What Leo is trying to say is the public announcement of your engagement puts you in the spotlight. People will be looking at you, judging you, perhaps even expecting you to fail because you're not from Toulene. Don't give them a reason to hate you. You're now a part of our family, and how they feel about you impacts how they feel about us. Be the best possible version of yourself. Now, go enjoy the evening, my dears."

And with that, the queen took Leo's arm and pulled him toward the door to the ballroom.

I awoke the next morning in John's arms. He'd crashed in my bedroom at 3:00 a.m. when we decided to leave the party, even though it was still going strong. John told me it didn't wind down until 5:00 a.m. and officially ended at seven.

We were scheduled to have a late brunch with John's family and my parents. I gently shifted John's arms, wiggled out of his embrace, and crawled out of bed. In the shower, I let the hot water wake me up. I came out of the bathroom wearing only undies and a plush terrycloth robe.

"Good morning, dearest," John said from the bed. He rubbed his eyes and yawned.

"Good morning, sunshine! I hope I didn't wake you."

"No. You're fine. I was already awake when you got out of bed."

"Why don't you stay in bed and I'll join you?" I went over to him and crawled under the covers.

Nervous smiles, then our lips met to exchange tender kisses. John pulled back and placed his finger over my lips. He slid his hand between the folds of my robe and stopped over the spot where my longing concentrated itself into a beautiful ache. He pressed, rubbed, and stroked, applying the right pressure. Bonus: he knew how and when to vary his touch as he manipulated me through the thin fabric of my lacy undies. The harp wasn't the only instrument from which his fingers extracted thrilling sounds. Under his intense gaze, I moaned in delight and my quick breaths transformed into lustful panting. Reaching under the covers, my hand seized him through his cotton pants. In a matter of moments, his eyes rolled back and his pleasure culminated in my hand. My body gave in, too, and I savored the intensity of the moment. This wasn't sex but it was already so much better than anything I'd ever experienced with Jack.

Reveling in our newfound intimacy, my body thrilled in the wake of his touch, ready to respond again, if the opportunity, ahem, arose.

"I give that two thumbs up. Way up," I teased.

"And that was just the trailer. Imagine how earth-shattering the full length feature will be."

I ran my hand through his hair. It was the first time I'd let myself do it. It felt soft and each section sprang back into its perfectly messy place.

"I'm a little nervous about our families getting together for brunch. My mom should *not* sit near your dad, agreed?" *Feminist and the Beast.*

"Agreed. I asked Astrid to take one final look at the placards to make sure they're not together just before we come downstairs."

"That's why I love you. You think of everything."

The start of our big family brunch was smooth. Mom was at the opposite end and side from John's father. The queen sat at the head of the table. As things wrapped up, and the staff came around to refill our cups with tea and coffee, the queen spoke.

"Hatty. John. Your parents and I have spoken, and we've settled it. You will marry one week from today at St. Joseph's Cathedral, and we will serve dinner afterward here in the Regent's Room. Your parents and I are changing our travel plans so we can be here for the happy occasion."

What the what?

I just stared at her. Speechless. Thank goodness John spoke up.

"Granny, I think that's a lovely plan. Thank you for making the arrangements so both of our families can participate."

John sounded a little too practiced. I wondered if he was in on it. I was caught completely off guard.

I looked at my parents. Mom smiled and Dad gave me a thumbs up. Really? They weren't going to speak up and say this is happening entirely too fast?

John squeezed my hand.

"Thank you, Your Majesty," I managed to say.

I had a million questions, none of which I wanted to articulate in front of our families.

After brunch, I didn't get time alone with John, damn it. Instead, I went to say goodbye to my friends and tell them they'd have a royal wedding to attend next Sunday. Shock and excitement registered on their faces. I told Sara and Tilda I wanted them to be my bridesmaids, along with John's cousin Pru. The people in Brussels could hear their excited screams. Plato, Sam, and Sara left, but Tilda offered to stay a few more hours to help me plan the details. Even though she kept the royals at arm's length professionally, Tilda was elated at the prospect of helping map out my wedding.

Astrid led me and Tilda to a cozy study I'd never seen before.

Aunt Elinore was waiting for us. "Ladies. We have much to do. Shall we get started?"

She turned on a large flat screen mounted on the wall, and it displayed what was on her laptop. She'd already done a great deal of work on the schedule for our wedding day. It was presumptuous, but I had to let it go. I'd never get this thing pulled together without her help.

Under Aunt Elinore's guidance, we worked through the details. The queen had already signed the necessary paperwork to confer on me a title: Duchess of Reines. She chose that city because it's where I'd lived the last three and a half years. Aunt Elinore said I'd meet with the family's attorney Friday morning to sign the final legal documents, which would include a renunciation of my U.S. citizenship, the final step in my journey to becoming royalty. *Is this really happening?*

"Now, we always use the same florist, caterer, bakery, local tailor, and musicians for events at the palace. These people all have background checks and clearances, so it's ideal to let them handle the wedding. Agreed?"

"I guess." I clenched my fists and tapped my foot.

"What's wrong, Hatty?" Tilda, best friend extraordinaire, didn't miss anything.

"I'm cramming months of planning into hours. This isn't how I imagined doing it."

"Then let's make the most of the hours we have." She pulled out her smartphone, maxed out the volume, and played a Mary J. Blige song we both loved.

"Give me that," Aunt Elinore snapped.

Tilda sheepishly handed over her phone. Aunt Elinore pulled out a cord and connected it to the flat screen. The music blasted through the speakers.

"If you're going to enjoy Ms. Blige, ladies, you've got to 'pump up the volume.' Can I interest you in a drink?" She produced a shiny silver flask from a desk drawer.

Warmed by the liquor, we selected champagne and scarlet as my colors. I agreed to carry a bouquet of tulips down the aisle, a nod to the Dutch heritage of some of the country's population. Given the time of year, though, the tulips would come from northern Africa. At least they'd get processed through the flower market in Aalsmeer, Holland. I'd wear a veil of Belgian lace that would include the pattern from the swath John bought me during our trip to Ghent. Besides having the lace pattern that symbolized fertility draped over me, this was also my way of acknowledging those in Toulene who traced their roots to Belgium.

One playlist, two hours, and three flasks later, we were done.

"When you arrive in Paris tomorrow for your fitting, Monsieur Bonhomme will send his assistant to pick you up at the train station. So, I think you're set." Aunt Elinore closed the lid of her laptop. "I suggest we all get some rest."

John came by my bedroom to tell me goodnight. He wrapped his arms around me and I turned my head away from him.

"What's wrong, love?"

"What's wrong? Are you serious? Ask me how I feel about your grandmother setting our effing wedding date one week from today."

"I don't think I have to ask."

"Don't we have a say? There are so many details to work out, though it seems Aunt Elinore's happy to take care of most of them on my behalf."

John pulled me closer. "Aren't you ready to marry me?"

"Yes, of course. I can't wait to be your wife. It's the wedding part that I'd hoped to spend a couple of months planning. Don't you get that?"

"I do. But here's the real reason for the short engagement. Granny wants to extend her stay in Thailand until June, and she doesn't want to make a second trip back to Toulene between now and then. It's absolutely exhausting for her to travel so far, and when she's very tired, she's more vulnerable to getting sick. Aside from Granny's wishes, I don't know how much longer I can wait for this."

John slid his hands below my waist, squeezing my ass and pulling me closer to him. Our lips met in a hungry flurry.

When there was a pause in the action, I pulled back a little, still trying to wrap my head around how we'd get this wedding pulled together in one week. "And I guess all the family and friends you want at the wedding are still here for Winter's Feast, so they'll just stick around for another week?"

"That's right."

John led me to the little bench at the end of my bed and we sat. "There is one more thing I need to tell you. Granny requests we follow Toulene tradition that requires the bride and groom to stay apart the week before their wedding. The idea is to build anticipation. Even though I'll miss you, I think it's terribly romantic."

"What? You've got to be kidding me. This whole thing is crazy, you know."

"Yes, but I appreciate you being so understanding. We have to be careful about letting Granny get too exhausted. She looks strong, but she's had some significant health problems in the past couple of years: pneumonia, bronchitis."

"I get it. But isn't this like throwing a match into a barrel of gasoline? The paparazzi will spiral into a tizzy speculating about the reason for the short engagement. God knows what they'll say."

"They'll suggest you're pregnant. Or that Granny's on her death bed. Or my father is forcing me to marry you against my will."

The list of possible headlines made me sick; my heart pumped too hard and my stomach bucked. I rubbed my forehead and looked down at my lap. What was I getting into here? I felt utterly unprepared.

"Look at me." John raised my chin and our eyes met. "Regardless of when we get married, the press is going to have mean-spirited things to say. We ignore them, and the rumors die. At least this way, coverage of our actual wedding next weekend will drown out the speculation about our brief engagement."

I took a deep breath. "I'm going to miss you this week."

"Yes, but the next time we see each other will be at the altar. I can't wait." He leaned in and kissed my neck before migrating to my lips. I loved the way our mouths moved together, adjusting, exploring, expressing a longing that words alone failed to convey.

"I wish we could freeze this moment and bottle it up," I said, pulling back from his lips.

"Instead of hanging on to it, let's promise to spend our lives creating more moments like this one."

"I love you, John."

"I love you, too, Hatty."

More kisses and then he left.

Sitting in bed alone, I pulled up the *Xpress* website. News of our wedding was the top story.

T-Minus One Week to Royal Wedding: Queen Shocks Prince John and Duchess Hatty With Wedding Date

by Clarence Watson

December 29, 2013

INCONCEIVABLE!

Just hours after announcing their engagement, Prince John and his American bride-to-be received word from Her Majesty that their wedding date is Sunday, a source close to the royal couple tells Xpress Euro exclusively.

"Hatty is trying to cram months of planning into just a few days. She's a little nervous!" said the insider.

Speculation abounds about why the queen wants a short engagement. Royal observer Nic Capucine says the wedding may be a precursor to even bigger news. "It's time to go on bump watch!"

Could the newly-minted duchess be pregnant? So far, there's no word either way from Belvoir Palace.

Meanwhile, the duchess reportedly had a wild night Saturday at the Winter's Feast after-party. She took the karaoke stage with her American friend Plato Jones to sing a couple of raunchy songs.

"I'm guessing she'll get etiquette lessons from the palace staff after that!" the insider said of the duchess.

Hatty Brunelle has spent the night at the palace on multiple occasions. The former journalism student only met the prince for the first time in October, and they reportedly began dating shortly after that initial meeting.

CHAPTER TWENTY-SIX

I still can't believe they think I'm pregnant. Do I *look* like I'm pregnant?"

"Of course not!"

Tilda pulled another airy bite from the baguette and I sipped my wine. It always tasted better in Paris. Even though I didn't want anyone to recognize us, it wouldn't be the worst thing in the world for a photo of me with booze to go viral. It might help refute the pregnancy rumor… or make it worse.

"At least there aren't pregnancy memes swimming around the Internet," Tilda offered.

"But have you seen the ones about my hair?"

"No."

I swiped and tapped my phone's screen. Shortly after news of our engagement went public, pranksters unearthed one of the photos of me exiting my apartment building the morning after John let me ride with him from the preschool. In the snapshot, I looked flustered, and worst of all, a gust of wind had blown my hair into a hot mess partially covering my face. It was the paparazzi photo I hated the most. Handing my phone to Tilda, I exhaled loudly.

She scrolled through the images. "Mane squeeze? Brush with destiny? Hair's looking at you?" Tilda snorted.

"And don't forget my personal favorites: The Prince is wild about Hairy and Hair today, queen tomorrow."

"Did you see this one?" Tilda turned the phone to reveal a new-to-me caption: Wedding Invitation: Comb one, comb all.

I rolled my eyes. "I give most of them three out of five stars. If you want props for your meme, you've got to animate that shit."

We laughed at my assessment and clinked our glasses before we each took a gulp.

Despite the wild rumors and snark, Tilda and I enjoyed the sites and tastes of Paris for a couple of days without anyone recognizing us. Even on New Year's Eve, no one noticed as we joined the countdown at Restaurant Ciel in the 9th arrondissement. We ate crêpes and toasted the New Year in the lounge surrounded by revelers, twenty-somethings too drunk to recognize me. Also, I wore a beret to ensure I screamed *tourist!*

A handful of photographers knew we were in the city for my wedding dress fitting, and evading them proved tricky. Monsieur Bonhomme fielded questions from one reporter, but he convinced the guy we weren't staying anywhere near his design studio. We also had Astrid in our back pocket; she advised us on how to keep a low profile with hats, cash, and taxis (no black car service this trip).

"Let's go. I need to finish packing. And that bartender's making me nervous," I said, draining the last drop of merlot from my glass.

I left a wad of bills on the table, suppressing my urge to look at the clean cut man in his neat white shirt polishing glasses methodically. I didn't want to arouse his suspicions.

We headed back to the little apartment in Monsieur Bonhomme's building where we were staying one more night before heading back to Roeselare.

A massive bouquet of red roses greeted me Thursday morning when I arrived at my Belvoir bedroom. There was also a note from John resting on top of a pink, leather-bound book.

You once said getting your spouse a book was romantic. So, I took your suggestion and had one commissioned for you. Phillipa of Hainault gave her husband a book of laws, but I'm giving you the opposite.

I opened the cover, and there was the title, *A Book of Grace: Beloved Prayers and Poems of Toulene*. The table of contents revealed a collection focused on love and marriage. I pressed the book against my chest. John loved me and wanted to make me happy. I knew these things, but the book provided tangible proof. *Be. Still. My. Heart.*

Thursday brought more wedding-related festivities. First up: lying on a table and spreading my legs.

Egads! A white pain shot up from my crotch.

"Damnation, that hurts!" I raised my head, glaring at the woman inflicting trauma as she removed my pubes with gobs of hot wax. No bride-to-be should have to endure this agony mere days before her wedding.

Sara cackled. "Get used to it. I'm guessing John likes all of his play things to be immaculate."

"I'm not one of his possessions!" Indignation flamed through my body, tensing my muscles.

"Relax, miss." The woman gently patted my leg with her gloved hand.

Sara and Tilda lay on their own tables, also getting Brazilians in a show of sisterly solidarity. Tilda and I were newbies. Sara, however, had a standing appointment to keep herself hairless.

"Hatty's right, Sara. This is killer. I'm going on the record right now and saying I'm not marrying anyone who wants me to look this way. This is bullshit."

We hee-hawed at Tilda because she almost never swore. I owed her—not only for enduring this painful process with me but for booking our appointment at a salon-slash-plastic-surgery center in

Roeselare known for its discretion. It was where assembly members, staffers, and mistresses of assemblymen came for various treatments and procedures.

I filled my lungs with air as amber threads of hot wax dripped from the wooden stick onto my flesh. It hurt, but it also gave me little twinges of pleasure—the heat, open legs, and a pair of eyes intent on that part of me. It was weird and kind of wonderful.

"Maintenance tip, ladies," Sara said, raising up on her elbows and looking over at us. "If you're going to keep up a Brazilian, don't shave between salon visits. It's better if it grows out just a little. But Hatty, since you're going to be gone a whole bloody month for your honeymoon, take a razor so you can get rid of any hairs that start to grow back during the trip. No man wants to see a five o'clock shadow on his wife's lady parts."

Her choice of words sent us into hysterics, prompting dirty looks from the women trying to finish the tedious work on our nether regions.

After a few more moments, the woman hovering over me stopped. She asked if I wanted her to wax all the way to the back.

"Say yes!" Sara yelled, pumping her fists in the air. "I call it a rear cheer! You don't want to be smooth everywhere except around your back door."

"Sara! Okay, fine. Go ahead."

I flipped onto my stomach as the gloved woman instructed me to do. I braced for what was sure to be a painful experience. As she dripped and ripped, it wasn't that bad, especially compared to the earlier torture.

"See? That's actually the easy part. But no one wants to tell you that." Sara was already on her stomach, too, getting her rear cheered.

After our waxing session, it was time for my bachelorette party. Pru met up with Tilda, Sara, and me for drinks in the back room at Finn's. We sat at a round table, throwing back drinks and talking. This was as wild as it was going to get—there were no strippers on the agenda. Across from me, there was an entrance to the kitchen, and behind me, a door leading into the main pub. The owner promised us the door to the pub was locked. Still, Bernard the Guard stayed in the room with us as we talked and let the liquor flow.

"Are you nervous?" Sara asked me between sips of her cosmo. She didn't look up from her near-constant texting.

"Nah, I'm not nervous. I was kind of mad about the queen springing this on us so quickly, but I've decided it's fine. The wedding is just the opening line for the story of our lives together. So, it should be memorable, but what counts most are the words that fill all the pages that follow."

"You're practicing your toast, aren't you?" Tilda guffawed.

"Do you like it?"

"Yes! I love it!" Pru interjected.

"It's really lovely." Tilda's voice had an uncharacteristically sentimental ring to it.

Pru thrust her glass in the air. "I propose a toast to John. He's ridiculously perfect and completely loyal. He's a loyal royal. Pfft!" The laughter burst through her loose lips and tears seeped from her eyes. Her giggling heightened into a playful squeal.

"How do you embroil a loyal royal in the U.K.? By remembering he'll *pound* anything." Tilda lightly tapped her fist on the table as she howled at her own joke.

"So, do you know where John's taking you for your honeymoon?" Since we arrived at Finn's, Sara had peppered me with questions, and it was starting to irritate me.

"I have no idea. Now that there's so much buzz in the press about us, I can't imagine we'll stay in Europe."

Tilda took a swig from her wine glass and said, "On your honeymoon, you know he's bringing his scepter, right?"

"Oh yeah. He'd better." I knew where this was going.

Pru joined in, suppressing a chortle. "John has the most

important scepter in our family. We're relying on you to polish it, rub it, and stroke it."

"Am I the only one who's responsible for maintaining his scepter?"

"Heavens, no! John's been polishing that thing for years." Pru chuckled. "But he's ready to give the job to someone else. Think you can *handle* it?"

"I have just the place to put it." We cracked up, and I topped off everyone's wine glass.

Without warning, the door leading from our room to the pub flew open and flashes sent shockwaves of bright light toward us. We let out small shrieks and covered our faces. Bernard was at the door in an instant, pushing the men back and shutting them out on the pub-side of the door. He spoke briefly into his sleeve to call in back-up.

"God! That was crazy!" Sara said. "I'll be right back. I've got to go to the restroom."

"She's been throwing back more drinks than usual." Her phone buzzed on the table, tempting me to pick it up. "What's that all about?"

"Who in the world has she been texting all night?" Tilda leaned over for a peek at Sara's phone. She gasped. "It's a text from Clarence Watson!"

"What?" He was the biggest a-hole of all the reporters who stalked the royal family. In addition to slinging mud for *Xpress*, he had his own television show on E! Europe.

"What does it say?" My whole body jittered.

Pru was the first to grab the phone. "If there's a spy among us, ladies, we need to smoke her out."

Pru slid her finger on the screen, which apparently required no password, glanced at it, and handed it to me.

There was a long string of texts between Sara and Clarence. She'd told him we were going to be here tonight. I scrolled back through the older messages. Apparently, they started texting a week before Winter's Feast. Shock and anger surged through my body like poison, making me lightheaded. Just then, the door to the kitchen swung open and Sara walked into the room.

"Hey! What are you doing with my phone?"

"Finding out exactly what kind of backstabbing bitch you are." I hurled the words at her, holding tight to her phone. "Bernard, would you kindly escort her out?"

He approached us, his imposing presence daring Sara to move. He put his hand over his mouth, turned his head, and spoke into his sleeve.

Sara grabbed my arm. "Hatty, listen to me…"

"I don't have to listen to one word from you. You've been eaten alive with jealousy since I first started dating John. It's killing you that a royal chose me. As if you ever stood a chance with any member of his family."

"As if *you* did. You're just his rebound relationship from Claire Léglise. Why do you think the queen wants such a quick wedding? So John won't change his mind. None of them like Claire or her family. So, a fat American no one likes is better than the daughter of an alcoholic casino owner who's up to his greasy armpits in debt. Try to keep up, dearie. You really should read some of the magazines that cover you."

I briefly considered slapping her, but the kitchen door swung open and two palace guards rushed toward us.

"Miss. Please come with us," the taller man said. I handed the other guard Sara's phone.

As she walked out between them, Sara turned to me. Mascara-streaked tears ran in rivulets down her cheeks. "Hatty, I'm sorry."

Even though she apologized, her hateful words found their mark and pierced my heart. Did the Meinrad family really believe John wouldn't want to marry me if we waited several months? I had a lump in my throat the size of an apple.

"Let's get you home," Tilda said, putting her arm around my waist.

"C'mon, you." Pru wrapped her arm around me from the other side.

Bernard spoke into his sleeve again and held the door open for us. We walked through the kitchen to the back exit.

Bernard stopped us. "There are a lot of reporters with cameras out here. We've moved them back. Duchess, how do you want to proceed?"

"Open the door, Bernard. We'll just walk to the car."

He did, and we did. The cameras flashed. The reporters yelled. Anchored by Tilda and Pru, I walked to the car and got inside as though it were just another day in the life of a duchess. And I suppose it was.

PART II

CHAPTER TWENTY-SEVEN

Prince John Weds American in Lavish Private Ceremony
By Clarence Watson
January 5, 2014

Sorry, ladies! It's official! Prince John is taken. The bells of St. Joseph's Cathedral in Roeselare rang out the news of the nuptials Sunday as a select group of guests witnessed Prince John Meinrad and Duchess Hatty Brunelle, originally from the United States, exchange vows.

"They couldn't take their eyes off each other," a palace insider told Xpress exclusively.

Sources close to the happy couple say the queen kept the pair apart after she set their wedding date. She announced the date just hours after the palace released news of the engagement.

The Timing

Speculation abounds about the spectacularly short engagement.

"There are any number of reasons for a quick ceremony," said royal observer Nic Capucine. "The most obvious one is Hatty's pregnant. We know securing the line of succession will be their first order of business, so if she's already expecting, the palace will just call it a 'honeymoon baby.'"

Publicists for the pair sharply denied the timing had anything to do with the duchess being pregnant.

What They Wore

Duchess Hatty reportedly walked down the aisle in a dress custom-made by Mathias Bonhomme. He's the chief designer for Valise, the same fashion house in Paris that made many of the outfits worn by John's late mother, Princess Beatrix. The strapless dress had a sweetheart neckline with a fitted bodice. The elegant full skirt swirled out from her waist. The bodice was adorned by a few flowers and vines that echoed the lace pattern on the veil.

Bridesmaids were Lady Prudence Hanover of Sydney, Australia (cousin to Prince John), and Tilda Mburu of Roeselare (Duchess Hatty's closest friend and chief of staff to Assemblyman Hans Aalders). Lady Pru and Tilda wore dresses made of champagne-colored raw silk. These gowns came from a tailor in Roeselare who reportedly turned them around in record time.

Prince John's brother Henri, their cousin Count Gerhard Hoehenstaufen of Leipzig, Germany, and the Australian boyfriend of Lady Pru were also in the wedding party. Prince John accompanied them to Cypress where they were fitted for black tuxes. A tailor on the island has a long-standing relationship with the Meinrad family. Their black tuxedos offered a stunning contrast to the bridesmaids' dresses.

Luxurious Honeymoon

Mum's the word on the honeymoon location! The palace won't say where they're spending their first days as a married couple, so we asked some of our Xpress staff to weigh in on the possibilities.

"I think he'll whisk her away to the Caribbean. What's more romantic than the sun setting over clear blue water?" asked Suzette Schultz, Xpress advice columnist.

"He'll surprise her with a safari in Kenya where they can behave like a couple of wild animals. Grr!" predicts Jean Piquet, Xpress Europe fashion editor.

"These two lovebirds will cozy up in a posh ski resort in St. Moritz, Switzerland where they can lie in bed together and NOT watch it snow," speculated Genevieve Hastert, Xpress beauty editor.

We'll just have to wait and see if this is a honeymoon or a babymoon!

CHAPTER TWENTY-EIGHT

I crept into the bathroom, trying not to awaken John. When I pulled down my underwear, there was a wet, bright red spot.

"Damn it." I hated having any kind of "personal stain" on my clothing since I didn't do my own laundry. It was like making an announcement to the entire staff: *clean up in aisle five!* Of course, I could just trash the panties, but it seemed too wasteful. I blamed my Ozarks upbringing for my inclination to be frugal.

I took off my silk pajama bottoms and underwear, and went to the sink. The cold stream of water helped me rub out the blood. As I continued to work on it, John walked in.

"Did I catch you with your panties off?" I could be holding a dead rat, and as long as I was partially naked, he wouldn't notice the animal carcass.

I turned off the tap and dropped my underwear into the sink. He walked over. cupped my right breast through my pajama top, and kissed my neck.

"You might want to stop right there. It's *that time* again." I nodded toward my panties soaking in cold water.

"Are you sure? I thought you'd be nine months late this time," he said between kisses.

"Good grief! We've only been married for five months. What's your hurry? I'm selfish. I want more time to have you all to myself. The Baby King can wait." I loved the silly nickname we used for our future oldest child.

I firmly pressed my hand against the front of his pajama pants. "Even if we can't do the deed, we can still have fun." I stopped and walked back into the bedroom. As he followed me, he peeled off his clothes.

"Hatty, this is David Steiner and his wife, Shelly," John said while shading his eyes from the afternoon sun.

"So lovely to meet you both."

The U.S. Ambassador to Toulene shook our hands to welcome us to the July 4th VIP reception on the back patio of the embassy. Their three small children, Chase, age five, Karissa, age three, and Jax, age two, were decked out in red, white, and blue outfits. Jax toddled around us with a red popsicle dripping onto the front of his tiny flag-themed polo. The other two kids pulled on the hem of their mother's skirt. Shelly maintained her composure while repeatedly removing the kids' hands and smoothing her clothes.

"Hatty, I loved the piece you wrote for The Guardian last month about the need to implement stronger early childhood education programs across the continent. Your research was sound and the arguments were compelling."

"Thank you, Mr. Ambassador."

"Please call me David. Do you enjoy being a contributor to the paper?"

"It's a dream job. The editors paired me up with a wonderful mentor, a senior writer, who's coaching me as I transition into writing for the editorial page. It's quite a change, and it's a little difficult working from home instead of being in the newsroom. But I love it."

"Good. Keep those insightful editorials coming. The continent needs that kind of perspective." The ambassador turned to John. "While I have you here, I wanted to ask about the protests at the smelter. Are the local law enforcement officers in Kortrijk handling the situation or will they need back-up from some of the surrounding communities?"

"We feel confident the police in Kortrijk can keep things under control. The protesters aren't local. Our investigators believe a radical environmental group recruited them in other countries and brought them inside our borders."

It must have sounded like boring grown-up talk because the Steiner children got a bit noisier and Shelly furrowed her brows in distress. I saw a stack of children's books on a bench in the corner.

"Which one of you likes to read?" I bent down closer to the kids' eye level.

"Me!" Three little hands shot into the air.

"What do you say we read some of these books?" I offered, pulling the three children away with me to the bench.

I picked up *Don't Let the Pigeon Drive the Bus* and started reading. The children knew the drill and they yelled, "No!" every time the pigeon asked to get behind the wheel. John and the ambassador looked our way, still talking, while Shelly threw back a highball.

As I continued reading to the kids, I watched John shake hands with the ambassador and make his way around the room. From where I sat, I observed what people outside our bubble saw: a confident man who always had something interesting to say, but wasn't so insecure he had to dominate the conversation or be the center of attention. I loved watching him smile in that charming, self-effacing way that made him seem accessible. He knew how to come across as a regular guy. These were the characteristics that caught my attention before I ever met him in person. It's why everyone fell in love with him.

Shelly came and escorted the children into the building behind us. When I was alone, John walked over to me.

"Children love you. Do you know why?"

"Because they think 'Hatty' is a funny name?"

"It's because you're not pretending to be someone else. Kids can sniff out pretense a mile away. You had them in the palm of your hand."

"I could say the same thing about you and the people you met just now."

"Then I suppose we're a damn good team."

He squeezed my hand and led me to the bar.

After I got off the phone having wished my parents a Happy Fourth, John and I sprawled across the couch at Langbroek Palace. We'd moved in two weeks earlier, happy to have a few kilometers between us and Belvoir. We watched the recording of last year's *A Capital Fourth* concert featuring the National Symphony Orchestra playing in Washington, D.C. I loved the patriotic music because it reminded me of the July 4th celebrations of my childhood—sweaty hair, hands covered in sticky watermelon goodness, and live bands playing on the town square.

John's phone buzzed in the pocket of his shorts. He snorted as he woke up. He always dozed off when we stayed up past 10:30.

"Turn that off, please," he said, his eyes on the glowing screen in his hand.

"What's wrong?" I paused the concert.

He turned the phone around. It was a text from Henri: *At Adela's. It's positive.*

"What does that mean?"

"He told me earlier this week she was late." *Late. As in late-late. Yikes.*

John dialed and then held the phone to his ear. "Take her to Belvoir. I'll meet you there," John said when Henri picked up.

After another moment, he disconnected, and rubbed his forehead. "We need to have the staff ready your old room."

"Let me handle that part of it." I started to stand, but John grabbed me and pulled me onto the couch.

He smoothed my hair with his hand. "You were worth the wait."

He kissed me with an intensity that bordered on harshness. I opened my eyes while our lips were locked and moving. His face was scrunched up, almost in agony. He pulled back, clenched his teeth, and took a deep breath. "I can't believe Henri let this happen."

I put my hands on his face. "It's going to be fine. We need to focus on keeping this quiet. Let's go."

Gloom hung over John's frowning face as we ate breakfast at Langbroek. He stood and took one more gulp of coffee.

"Try to have a good day." I kissed John gently. Deciding a comforting kiss wasn't enough to improve his outlook, I followed an impulse and rubbed his crotch through his khaki pants. "That's the teaser for tonight's double feature."

He smiled for the first time since he rolled out of bed. "Naughty girl." He kissed my forehead, squeezed my breasts, and left. *Leave him wanting more. That's how I roll.*

I left the breakfast nook and headed to our bedroom. Lord, I didn't think I'd ever get him out of the palace. With him gone to the assembly for the day, I had time to investigate the small book I discovered last night at Belvoir when I was helping Adela get settled in my old bedroom. When I went into the bathroom to see whether the hair dryer was still stored under the sink, I flicked on my phone's light and flashed it inside. After finding the hair dryer stowed neatly in its place, an old metal box sitting in the back right corner glinted in the light and caught my eye. I reached inside and pulled it out. There was a tiny lock on the latch that popped open when I tugged at it. Sitting inside the box on an old silk handkerchief was a notebook. It was black like the one John used on occasion, except this one was bigger. I flipped open the cover and recognized the neat handwriting with flowing curves. It was the same cursive that was on the Journey album cover I'd found in Princess Beatrix's dance studio. Realizing I held a treasure, I resisted my desire to start reading while I sat there on the bathroom floor in Belvoir. I didn't want Adela to walk in and find me thumbing through the journal. Instead, I stuffed it in my purse and put the box back inside the cabinet.

Alone and sitting on the couch at Langbroek, I cracked open the journal.

January 21, 1988

Happy birthday to me! This notebook is a present from my dear husband. He says it's a useful gift for his newly-minted 19-year-old wife because I'll need a place to keep track of my schedule and obligations. During the three months since our wedding, I've made only one mistake, agreeing to speak at a luncheon for career women when I'd already committed to helping fold brochures at the AIDS in Africa office. So, here's to no more mistakes, Little Notebook! You're my new best friend!

As I read through the entries, the details revealed more than her schedule. I got a glimpse of the inner workings of Princess Beatrix's marriage to Leopold. It felt wrong reading such intimate details about John's parents. After devouring the entries through April, which included some rather racy revelations, guilt trumped my curiosity. My days of investigative journalism were behind me and I didn't want to be a snoop. I closed the journal and tucked it away in a shoebox at the back of my wardrobe.

CHAPTER TWENTY-NINE

W ith as much subtlety as possible, I adjusted my body in the hard wooden pew at the front of the church. Something along the back zipper of my dress poked mercilessly into my flesh.

"Weddings make you uncomfortable, Mrs. Meinrad?" John whispered and my hand went to my eyebrows for my patented "I'm stressed" gesture.

"Of course not. Something's poking me back there."

"Hey, that's my job." He pushed my hem up an inch and squeezed my thigh.

The pipe organ lurched into a melodic chord progression, and the entire church stood. John tried to adjust my dress to avert the poking. As he jiggled and pulled the area around the zipper, the hem of my dress slid up.

"Careful," I whispered. All we needed was a tabloid report about me flashing the congregation at my brother-in-law's wedding.

By the time Adela passed our pew with her chin slightly lifted, the sharp poking was gone.

John moved from our spot in the front row to the altar where

209

he stood by his brother.

During the ceremony, the vicar led Henri and Adela through the vows and other rituals. St. Andrew's Cathedral was smaller than St. Joseph's where John and I exchanged vows, but it was a stunning venue with an interior that boasted an airy palette of white, mint green, and pink.

Henri and Adela looked at ease as the vicar prayed over the communion elements. He had no knowledge of the circumstances that led the couple to his altar. And while the tabloids had snarked on and on about how a pregnancy scare spurred me and John to get married post haste, they made no such allegations about Henri and Adela.

A young boy stood and began singing Ave Maria.

Ave Maria
Gratia plena
Maria, gratia plena
Ave, ave dominus
Dominus tecum
Benedicta tu in mulieribus
Et benedictus fructus ventris
tuae, Jesus.

I translated the words in my head, remembering them from my high school choir days: Hail Mary, full of grace, the Lord is with you. Blessed are you among women, and blessed is the fruit of your womb, Jesus.

The fruit of Adela's womb remained a secret thanks in part to the sweeping gown she wore. It swallowed her small, muscular frame, but it did the job of concealing even the tiniest trace of a belly swell.

The thought of the baby inside her sparked an unexpected pang of jealousy. My period had arrived Friday, right on schedule. Aside from being a few days late in July, I'd had regular 28-day cycles. Now that it was August, we'd had eight straight months of unprotected sex. What the heck was going on?

Seeing Adela so radiant and imagining the joy that would literally come from her body, a beautiful blending of her DNA with Henri's, I felt strongly for the first time that I was ready, perhaps even eager, to get pregnant.

Riding in the car toward Belvoir for the reception, I whispered to John, "I want to have your baby." I smiled, realizing those were the lyrics from the silly song I sang at Kamikaze Karaoke the night we met.

He smiled back and squeezed my hand. "I know."

John came to bed at 1:00 a.m. We were exhausted from the wedding, reception, and after-party. I slid out from under the covers when I heard him snoring. I removed my laptop from its case and crept into the den. I searched words like "infertility," "trouble getting pregnant," and "trying to conceive."

I cringed as I read about how endometriosis and polycystic ovarian syndrome hinder a woman's ability to get pregnant. Then I poured over websites featuring treatments with scary names like ovarian drilling. The acronyms also made my head spin. On the infertility discussion boards, the women used them in their posts: DH doesn't want another IUI. He thinks we won't get a BFP until we do IVF.

I found the meaning of each set of letters and translated: Dear Husband doesn't want another In Utero Insemination. He thinks we won't get a Big Fat Positive until we do In Vitro Fertilization.

I read about one woman who was on her eighth in vitro fertilization cycle. Eighth! Another woman was preparing for some kind of exploratory surgery to find out why she couldn't get pregnant. I also saw the story of a couple struggling with the husband's problem: he didn't have any sperm in his ejaculate.

What I read overwhelmed me and fanned my fears. A headache threatened, so I shut the laptop and went back to bed.

CHAPTER THIRTY

The taper candles flickered, sending shadows dancing across John's handsome features. We gave Brigitta, our chef, the night off and I cooked dinner. At my request, John dismissed the rest of the staff for the evening. The requisite number of royal guards stood outside Langbroek Palace. For us, this was being left alone. I needed to discuss an issue with him that caused me tremendous anxiety, and didn't want to risk anyone, not even staff, overhearing us.

One of the perks that came with "couple time" was John's harp playing. The instrument sat unused in a corner most of the time. But after Brigitta left, I cooked and he strummed, creating a beautiful soundtrack for my preparation of the pasta.

Now that we were finishing our meal, nervousness gnawed at my stomach.

"So, I was reading some stuff online, and I think I need to buy a thermometer." I tried to sound casual.

"A thermometer? Are you feeling ill?" He wrinkled his brow in concern.

"No. I feel fine. Actually, I don't feel fine. What I mean is I'm not sick, but I'm worried."

"What do you have to worry about, love?"

"I'm concerned I haven't gotten pregnant yet." There. I'd said it, despite the growing tightness in my chest. Why did this discussion make me feel so weird?

"Are you trying to tell me you want to have more sex?" His eyes lit up and he raised his eyebrows.

"I'm always up for more sex. But don't you think it's odd I've been off the pill for nine months and we haven't had any luck getting pregnant? I thought I might get a thermometer and track my basal body temperature."

After multiple adventures into the depths of online infertility discussion sites, I knew it was time to begin monitoring my ovulation in this way.

"I don't even know what that means, but it sounds extreme. I don't think there's anything wrong, but if it would make you feel better, go see Dr. Cloutier."

Rather than comforting me, the suggestion I see the royal family's physician filled me with panic. Worry-filled thoughts niggled my mind.

"Okay. I'll ask Astrid to make an appointment. Do you want to come?"

John pulled out his phone and didn't look up. "If you want. But I can't imagine he'll have much to say to me. I'm going to Belvoir tomorrow at nine for a briefing on the protests at the smelter. I'll be gone until after lunch."

"Okay." Disappointment filled my chest. I wanted him to show support by going with me to see Dr. Cloutier. I disliked the Meinrad family's physician. He was kind, but emotionally removed.

I was glad to hear John was headed to Belvoir in the morning. *That gives me plenty of time to creep on the discussion boards and obsess over how to get pregnant.*

The harsh paper crinkled noisily under my bottom as I scooted toward the end of the exam table. A thin white sheet covered me below the waist and draped over the sides of the table to the floor.

"That's good. You can stop there, Duchess," Dr. Cloutier said with his thick French accent. He refused to call me Hatty despite my request that he use my first name. Being in such a compromising position, legs propped and parted, made me realize how little titles mattered. When Dr. Cloutier looked at so many women *down there*, could he really tell us apart? I doubted it.

He conducted the exam with efficiency and emotional sterility. A cold poke here, a bit of pressure there.

"You may sit up, my dear."

I adjusted and held the sheet tighter over my lower half as I sat on the edge of the table. My legs dangled like a child sitting in a grown-up's chair.

"I think you're merely overanxious about getting pregnant. There appear to be no problems, and we don't even consider an infertility diagnosis for a woman your age until you fail to conceive after one year of unprotected sex. Stop worrying because that will make you less desirable to your husband, and desirable you must be." He smiled and winked before turning to my file. His wrinkled hand scribbled something on my chart.

Those were the words he said. This is what I heard: *It's your fault. Your worrying is causing you not to get pregnant. So, stop it. Focus on how to entice your husband and not on getting pregnant. It will happen.*

Basically, the plan was to have more sex. We could totally do that.

Every time I swallowed, it was like sending a knife down my swollen, aching throat. The pain reminded me of the time I had strep as a kid.

I threw on some sweats and climbed into bed. Lying on top of the covers, my eyes drifted shut; fatigue overtook my body.

But the sound of John's voice finishing up a phone call just outside our room sent me into a panic, and I jumped out of bed. Spurred by adrenaline, I sprang for the door and locked it to give myself a chance to change into something sexier. The egg white-like substance on the toilet paper this morning told me it was my most fertile day this cycle. I'd learned online this was the body's primary evidence of pending ovulation.

We'd started our day with slow, luscious sex when my throat felt merely scratchy. But I wanted to squeeze in one more romp to maximize our chances of getting pregnant, sore throat be damned.

The knob jiggled. "Hatty? Are you in there?"

"Just a minute." Ugh... it even hurt to talk. Naked and chilled, I shoved the sweats under the bed. Forget the lingerie; I answered the door in the buff.

"Sorry. Did you need something?"

"I do now."

John pushed into the room, pressing his lips to mine. I turned my head. "Be careful. I might be getting sick. Kiss me anywhere but my lips."

He held me in his arms and twisted his lips to one side. "Are you up for this?"

I laughed and patted his cheek. "For sure. I'll spread my legs, but not my germs."

He grabbed my ass and licked my neck before walking me backward to the bed. He lifted me onto the mattress. I watched him undress, kicking out of his pants and popping a button off his shirt as he tore at it too roughly. I ran my fingers over various sweet spots, knowing he got aroused more quickly when I gave him a show.

My desire to move things along intensified as gunk streamed down the back of my raw throat. I wondered whether we had any cough medicine in the bathroom.

John didn't bother taking off his socks before he climbed on top of me, pushing my back into the mattress. A desperate need to cough concentrated itself in my throat. I swallowed in hopes of making it go away. As he entered me, a violent cough exploded from my mouth and the force pushed him out.

"Go again," I choked, putting a fist over my mouth in case I coughed again.

"I don't think you're up for it."

"But you are." I grabbed him down there, not wanting him to lose his concentration. "We've got to do this. Please?"

He laid his hand across my forehead. "You're burning up."

I relaxed, letting my feet touch his legs and he jumped. "Your toes are ice cold. We're done."

He went over to the dresser and grabbed a pair of thick socks.

"My sweats are under the bed." I stood as he retrieved my clothes. He helped me get dressed and tucked me into bed.

After he put on his robe, he came to my bedside. "I'll be back. Do you need anything?"

"Your semen. But if you aren't willing to give me that, then some ginger ale would be nice."

"Okay. I'm going to ask Astrid to call Dr. Cloutier's office and arrange for him to see you tomorrow morning."

He kissed my forehead before leaving the room.

CHAPTER THIRTY-ONE

The scientists from the Royal University prepared to release their findings about the environmental impact of the smelter. Toulene's Ministry of Agriculture received a courtesy copy of the results one day before the scientists went public. Things didn't look good. John and his family couldn't believe scholars who worked for a university they supported could produce such a scathing report. The findings blamed the monarchy for failing to intervene and initiate an environmental clean-up program.

"Their conclusions are complete speculation because they're not supported by the science." John paced the parlor at Belvoir, running his hand through his hair.

Aunt Elinore, Granny, and Leopold were also there. Cilla, the family's public affairs guru, sat on the arm of the sofa, listening intently. She intimidated me. It went back to that Sunday morning call early in my relationship with John when she confronted me about the story Paul had filed exposing Princess Beatrix's foundation.

"John. We were going to sell the plant anyway because it's a money pit. At least this study gives us cover to make that move now," Aunt Elinore said.

"I don't care about the public relations aspect. I care about the science. This report rests on thin evidence produced by shoddy research. And we could've avoided being caught in the middle of this if we'd sold the property several years ago, as we'd planned to do," John countered.

I coughed, still recovering from my cold, then cleared my throat. "Then why don't you hold a press conference and refute the findings?"

All four of them looked at me like I'd just suggested John run naked through the streets.

"Hatty, if John holds a press conference about this issue and doesn't take questions, the reporters will erupt in a frenzy. God only knows what they'd write. We can't allow that to happen," Aunt Elinore explained.

"Okay. Then, don't call it a press conference. He can just read a prepared statement and walk off stage. The longer you go without issuing some kind of response, the longer the story stays alive. Talk about the researchers' shoddy work, you get coverage for a day or two, and then the press goes back to reporting on what Claire Léglise is wearing for her wedding." Claire was set to wed a British royal at a ceremony outside London in two weeks. The woman who broke up with John because she didn't want media attention regularly talked to reporters about the preparations for her big day. *I heart hypocrisy.*

"I think Hatty has a point," Cilla said, standing. "If we draft a statement, have John read it, and leave, we might prevent this story from growing into something bigger."

John sighed, shaking his head, his irritation apparent. "Hatty, this isn't going to work. You've never dealt with anything like this."

"But I know what journalists will think if you don't respond. Your failure to comment will become the story. Giving a statement means you'll have coverage for twenty-four, maybe thirty-six hours. Then, they'll move on to the next big thing. It's a way to shut it down."

John paced, his hands behind his back. "Look, you don't know how this works. Reporters don't just let us walk on stage, read a piece of paper, and walk away. They always try to get in their questions. This is way beyond anything you experienced as an intern."

That stung. "But I do know how editors think, and how newsrooms operate…"

John exhaled noisily, exasperated. "Hatty, please let us handle this. You don't have a degree and your experience is still quite limited."

Oh no he didn't. Oh yes he did.

"Excuse me? *Excuse* me? Who's fucking fault is it that I don't have a degree? Don't take away the value I bring to this discussion. I worked for several months in two newsrooms. I write guest columns for The Guardian. I'm telling you, reading a statement is the right thing to do."

P.S. Did I just drop the f-bomb in front of the Queen of Toulene?

The queen stood. "Cilla, if *you* think it's the best move for John to read a statement, I can go along with that. Please brief the reporters and let them know John won't accept questions. If any of them try to shout questions at him afterward, have their credentials revoked."

I looked at John, triumphant. *Mic drop.*

That evening, John burst into our bedroom at Langbroek and slammed the door. I didn't look up. I sat in bed typing a message to Kendra27, one of the women who frequented the same infertility discussion board as me. Where else but online could the infertile share tips, encouragement, and the occasional pregnancy test photo?

"How dare you speak that way to me in front of my family," John huffed.

I threw down my phone and jumped out of bed, ready to have it out. "You dismissed me like I'm some kind of hick who doesn't know anything. That was hurtful and embarrassing. Get your head out of your ass, prince."

He stomped over to me, and I took a step back, unsure what he was about to do. He grabbed me by the arms and pulled me to him. He kissed me with a fierceness I didn't anticipate. It left my knees wobbly.

"I'm sorry. I shouldn't have said that. Your turn," he said, letting go and stepping away.

"My turn for what?"

"To say you're sorry for behaving like a child."

"I'm not sorry I called you out on being a jerk. But I'm sorry I did it in such a blunt way. Next time, I'll use more tact. There. Are you happy?" I turned to climb back into bed.

His hands wrapped firmly around my ribs, right under my breasts. "You're not allowed to go to bed angry."

He turned me toward him and kissed me, leaning into me until I sat down on the bed. He unbuckled his pants and removed his shirt. An intensity that was both sensual and angry-looking colored his face.

I laughed. "Are you requiring make-up sex?"

"Yes. And you're going to enjoy it."

Hot damn. He was right.

After the last of the thrusting and a final, strong heave, John started to climb off me.

"Hey, stay inside!" He froze in place, though I felt him already going limp.

Keeping him inside me a couple of minutes after he climaxed was one of several "tricks" I'd discovered online for improving the odds of sperm arriving at their destination inside my uterus.

"Okay. You can get up." I patted his arm. He kissed my cheek and headed for the bathroom. I kicked my legs into the air and supported my pelvis with my hands, using gravity to assist the little swimmers.

John came back into the bedroom and gave me a funny look. "I bet that's uncomfortable. How long do you have to stay like that?" Embarrassment brought a flash of heat to my cheeks as my husband looked at me in what was probably the least flattering position known to humans.

I lowered my legs, peeled back the covers, and slid underneath.

"That's it. Just a couple of minutes."

John clicked off his bedside lamp, leaving us in darkness. As I cozied my body into his, satisfaction brought a smile to my lips. I was doing all I could to maximize our chances of getting pregnant. Surely, it would happen this cycle.

CHAPTER THIRTY-TWO

C an you believe Prince Henri and Prince John married those two commoners? Honestly. They must be after their money. Don't you think?" Adela batted her eyes at the handsome Frenchman who brought our entrées. His face was blank; he didn't recognize us.

"I do not know." He responded in stilted English as he set our plates on the table.

"I think that Adela girl will look hideous when her belly gets really big." Adela puffed up her cheeks and reached her arms in front of her abdomen, fingers entwined. "Can you believe she got pregnant so soon?"

Adela, you're killing me! And her emerging bump was, in fact, killing me on the inside. My jealousy was an untamable beast that nickered at every reminder of Adela's pregnancy.

"Excusez-moi, s'il vous plait." Our garçon made a hasty retreat.

I laughed too loudly at the poor guy's awkwardness. I needed to adjust my volume from Ozarks holler to Paris café. "I can't believe you just said that! Do you think he knows who we are?"

"Not a chance. I'm Camilla Madiera and you're Jill Larson. Are those the fake names we decided to use?"

"You picked them. Your name sounds like a movie star and mine sounds like a farmer's wife."

"You *are* a farmer's wife. Kind of."

"He's an environmental scientist, thank you very much. Let's finish in the next twenty minutes so we can head up the hill before traffic picks up."

Sacre Cœur was our destination. Adela was Catholic, and wanted to visit this church before giving birth. It was the pretext for what I viewed primarily as a wives-only shopping excursion to Paris. I craved a new pair of boots as much as I craved another bite of brie.

As we rode through the streets, Adela looked at something on her phone. "What does John say about the protesters?"

Protests resumed at the smelter with new vigor after John made his statement to the press condemning the scientists' findings.

"He says they're orderly, so that's good. He's hoping the town will implement a curfew so the queen doesn't have to step in with a heavy hand."

Strategy sessions about how to handle the protests consumed a great deal of John's time, so I loved getting to spend the day with Adela. It was the first time we'd been together for any significant length of time.

"You know, you're a riot. Why haven't we done this sooner?" I offered her a piece of gum.

"We're too busy coddling our princes. But we should plan more escapes like this." She popped the spearmint nugget into her mouth.

I looked at my bag from *Au Printemps* sitting in the floorboard. It held black silky lingerie, exactly what I needed to fulfill Dr. Cloutier's advice to focus on making my husband happy as the main means to getting pregnant. This little something-something promised hours of baby-making fun. Even though all my post-sex pelvis-lifting efforts hadn't yet brought positive results, we had to stay the course. I did my best to bring an optimistic spirit to our baby-making efforts, but a hollow sensation in the pit of my stomach grew more intense with each passing month. Having to watch Adela swell into new, beautiful proportions only increased the pressure for me and John to conceive.

At *Sacre Cœur*, our plain clothes guards walked ahead of us. The crowd was light, so we easily found a bench, the ideal place to sit and take in the sights of the basilica.

Adela bowed her head in prayer, and guilt sat heavy on my shoulders. I was interested in the church simply as a tourist. My heart clung to my anxiety over our inability to get pregnant, crowding out everything else, including God. I remembered all the verbiage I'd learned growing up in church about "casting my cares on the Lord," but the words now had a tinny ring.

Instead of praying or reading the Bible, I read and meditated on the stories of other women who were trying to conceive. I especially loved reading about those who struggled for months or years, but through one method or another, finally saw those two glorious lines on their pee sticks. They were the saints, the women who had worked miracles. So, I was religious about my fertility rituals: taking my temperature every morning before getting out of bed, ensuring we had sex daily, and doing pregnancy tests as early as five days before my period was due. Instead of a rosary, I gripped that piece of lace John bought me in Ghent. Many of the delicate strands were now broken, unable to withstand so much handling.

"Care if we move on?" Adela stood.

"That's fine. Did you want to light a candle?"

We walked over to a small table. She dropped money into a wooden box and took a white tea light. She placed it in a tall candleholder, and with one hand on her belly, she lit it. Every time her hand floated to her lower abdomen, my jealousy stirred. *Shh. I'm happy for them. I really am… kind of.*

"Why do you guys light candles?"

"It's a symbol of hope."

"Then I want to light one, too." After making my donation, I placed my candle beside Adela's. "To hope."

We walked around the perimeter to a small alcove toward the back where several benches sat in front of a statue of the Virgin Mary. Adela picked a seat and I heard her doing Hail Mary's under her breath in Latin. I sat close by, listening to her quiet, rhythmic recitation and staring at the statue in front of us. I almost laughed out loud at the realization I was the anti-Mary. She got pregnant without a man so much as looking at her while John and I were trying all kinds of positions during and after sex to improve our chances of conception and it still wasn't happening. And here beside me was a woman who had gotten pregnant "by accident."

Hey, Mary. For the record, I'm not praying to you because I'm not Catholic and I don't believe in praying to anyone but God. And I can't even do that right now. But, if you hear me, can you tell God I really, really want a baby? I'm asking you to do this for me because I think you get it. You know how important it is to be a mother. And I want to be a mom. I want it so bad it hurts.

I stopped my train of thought, unsure how to end my non-prayer conversation with the statue. Adela reached over and squeezed my hand. She stood and walked away. I got up, looking at the open hands of the stone woman and simply said, "Thanks."

CHAPTER THIRTY-THREE

B ernard, I'll be right back," I said, motioning toward the women's restroom at the back of the café. My stoic guard merely nodded in acknowledgement. I was on a mission and I wanted to accomplish it before Tilda arrived for our Christmas gift exchange.

Once inside with the door locked, I dug around in my purse and found one of the long, slender white packages. I tore it open and held the stick in my hand.

"C'mon, baby," I said softly as I put the tip between my legs.

When it was saturated, I placed it gently on a flat, dry area at the side of the sink. I set the timer on my phone for five minutes.

I finished up and washed my hands, resisting the urge to peek at the results window on the stick. Looking in the mirror, I fluffed my hair. Just as I applied a fresh bit of lipstick, the timer went off. My eyes darted to the stick. Were there *two* pink lines, indicating I was pregnant? I picked it up and brought it closer to my face, unsure if the faint second line was my imagination or a trick of the low bathroom lighting.

I stopped the timer, turned on my phone's bright light, and

directed the beam at the results window. Sure enough, there was a very light pink line next to the control line. Because I was addicted to reading online discussion boards, I knew the darkness of the line didn't matter, so long as there was a second line that had coloring; gray lines were no good. Many of the women even posted cell phone photos of their results, asking for opinions on whether their test was positive. These women were obsessed.

I placed the lid over the tip, slid the entire pee stick back into its packaging, and put it in my purse. I suppressed the surge of joy that threatened to explode from the core of my being. With Christmas five days away and our one year anniversary next month, this was the best gift I could give John. My parents were also due to arrive in two days for Christmas, so I'd get to share the news with them in person. I put my hand on the door knob and stopped. Digging around in my purse again, I pulled out the test. Just one more peek at those glorious double lines. *Woot!* I tucked it back in its white wrapper and dropped it into my purse. After a single fist pump, I unlocked the door and walked out calmly.

Tilda was sitting at our table, talking in a low voice into her phone. She wrapped up the conversation, got up, and hugged me.

"Merry Christmas, darling." She handed me a beautifully wrapped package.

"Oh, Tilda. Did you wrap this?"

"What do you think? Sit. Open it!"

I carefully pulled off the ribbons and bow and removed the lid. Nestled among white tissue paper was a fluffy green blanket. On top of it was a small card: "For the Baby King (or Queen)." I picked up the card and saw the letter "M" for Meinrad embroidered near the blanket's sateen edge.

Tears filled my eyes.

"When it happens, you'll be an amazing mum," Tilda said. She reached across the table and squeezed my hand. During our bi-weekly phone conversations, I'd alluded to my anxiety about the fact I wasn't yet pregnant.

I pulled the blanket from the box and skimmed my fingers through the soft material. "Thank you. It's beautiful and perfect."

I folded the fabric and put it back in the box. The small gift I placed in front of Tilda was also wrapped in exquisite paper. Astrid had done well.

"I *know* you didn't wrap this." She inspected the small box that fit in the palm of her hand and gingerly pulled off the ribbon. "Oh, Hatty!" She removed the earrings from the box.

"There's a man in De Haan who makes jewelry from the seashells he finds on the beach at sunset. I thought they'd look lovely on you."

She put on the delicate, shapely earrings. Against the dark spirals of her hair, they positively radiated.

"How do they look?" I reached into my purse to grab a mirror. As I pulled my hand out, the pregnancy test package fell onto the table. I quickly shoved it back inside and handed her the mirror. Concealed in the unmarked white wrapper, she probably had no idea what it was.

"Is that a pregnancy test?"

Dear Lord. "Maybe."

"Are you late? Are you pregnant?"

"No. My period was supposed to start today. Here. Look at your earrings." I handed her the mirror, hoping to move the conversation away from my cycle.

"Hatty, these are brilliant! Thank you so much."

Just then, the barista arrived and took our order. Imagining that faint pink line in my purse, I asked for decaf coffee.

"How are things with the smelter protests?" Tilda and her boss at the assembly kept close tabs on what happened in Kortrijk.

"Off the record, okay? You can't tell Assemblyman Aalders about any of this." My how things had changed. I was the one requesting off-the-record conversations.

"Yes, of course."

"We think the cold is keeping the protesters away for now. But when the weather's better, John says there's reason to believe they're going to come out in larger numbers. He's working with Cilla and the rest of the public affairs team on how to respond when the protests resume. Okay… Enough smelter talk. Tell me about your date last Friday."

Tilda went through datable men like I went through pregnancy tests.

"This guy is chief of staff for another assemblyman. Gustav is his name. I mean, can you see me dating someone named Gustav? So, he had one strike against him right away. Then, after dinner, he *removed* his *front tooth*. He cleaned it with his shirt, and slid it back into place." She shook her head in disbelief.

I guffawed. "It's pretty ballsy to whip out your false tooth on a first date. I mean, that's the kind of threshold you don't typically cross until the third date."

"Well, I'm done with blind dates. That's my New Year's resolution. No. Blind. Dates."

When it was time for me to return to Langbroek Palace, we said our goodbyes. As she left, I looked at Bernard and motioned to the restroom. He nodded and sat back down.

Locking the door, I pulled out the positive pregnancy test and stared at it. Again. I tilted it and checked the line from various angles. Yep, it was positive! I placed it on the edge of the sink and took out a fresh pee stick. I went through the motions and waited. There was no second line this time. Even with the help of my phone's light, I didn't see so much as a shadow next to the control line. Of course, I'd had plenty of coffee and water to drink, which meant my pee might be too diluted to produce a second pink line. And I hadn't held it for a minimum of four hours. That recommended timeframe came from the women I'd "met" through the online infertility discussion sites. Despite my attempts to rationalize it, the negative test stared back at me, announcing another failure.

My hands shaking, I dialed Dr. Cloutier's office. I listened to the automated menu and pushed the button to connect to a nurse.

Once I got a live person on the phone, I said, "Yes, I'm one of Dr. Cloutier's patients. I had a positive pregnancy test about an hour and a half ago and did another test just now and it's negative. Do I need to come in and see the doctor? What should I do?"

"Is your period late?"

"It's due to start today."

"Your urine may have been too diluted to produce another positive result so soon after the first one. Wait and test again when you wake up tomorrow morning. The concentration of the pregnancy hormone is typically highest after you've held your urine all night."

See? You just need to hold it in and do it again!

"What happens if I get a negative test in the morning?"

"Nothing, unless you want to come in for a blood test to find out for sure if you're pregnant. Now, if you *are* pregnant this early and have a miscarriage, there's nothing we can do to stop it. In that case, you'd only need to come in if you had excessive pelvic pain or blood clots larger than two and a half centimeters. Is there anything else?"

"I guess not. Thank you." I hung up, feeling nauseated. If the beginnings of a baby were inside me, it could be dying and there was nothing I could do to save it. On the other hand, I might just need to wait and retest in the morning. It was the not knowing that intensified the gnawing angst.

I needed to move along or Bernard would come tapping on the door to make sure no one had assassinated me while I was on the toilet. I pulled out the two pregnancy tests and held them side by side. There clearly were two lines on the first and only one on the second. I put both of them in their packages, secured them in the depths of my purse, and walked out the door.

The next morning, I dashed into the bathroom to do a new test; John was still asleep. While I waited for the result, I lined up the two tests from the day before alongside the new one. Five minutes passed without a second line. Sometimes the tests take up to ten minutes to show a positive result. So, I waited.

No dice.

My fist slammed against my lips to block the loud scream I wanted to release. I bit into my knuckles, squeezing my eyes closed, and my shoulders shook. Tears seeped from between my eyelids. I fanned myself and checked the results one more time. One test with two pink lines and two tests with one line each.

I dug out a plastic bag and wrapped it around the two negative tests before tucking them into a box in my closet. I'd toss them later when John was gone. But the positive test I kept. I brought it close to my eyes, marveling again at the double pink stripes. They were real. I found an empty make-up bag and placed it inside, unable to get rid of it just yet.

A sensation of cool air on my lady regions reminded me I'd failed to pull up my pants after doing the test. I went to the toilet, wiped, and there it was. The telltale sign of failure, even more definitive than a negative pregnancy test: bright red blood. If it had been brown, I might have tried to convince myself it was bleeding from the embryo implanting in the lining of my uterus. But nope. This was the red carpet my body rolled out to announce the monthly arrival of dear old Aunt Flow.

Despite my profound sadness at the turn of events, I had to get on with the day or at least go through the motions. I took a deep breath, pulled up my pants, and wiped my eyes. I didn't want to tell John about this. There was no need to upset him.

CHAPTER THIRTY-FOUR

The door shut, and we were alone in front of the Ghent altarpiece. John arranged to have the church closed to the public for an hour while we visited. It was a huge request, asking the church to turn away tourists on a Saturday, but being a prince had its privileges.

"Do you remember our first kiss?" John placed his hands on my waist as we faced each other, ignoring the masterpiece beside us.

"Of course. What I remember is how you tasted. Minty, delicious. But I was in shock because I totally wasn't expecting to lock lips with you. I thought I was here as a reporter, remember?"

"I do. I'm glad you didn't slap me or run screaming from the church. Happy anniversary, love."

One year of marriage. Wowsers.

After a make-out session in front of the altarpiece, we walked down the street arm in arm. Every shop window displaying baby clothes caught my eye. A physical ache rose up in my chest as I thought about going in and picking out organic cotton onesies for our baby-to-be. It didn't matter I wasn't yet pregnant. I would be soon, by golly, and I wanted to nest.

After passing the fourth baby clothing boutique, I told John to wait. A small bell jingled a welcome as I went inside. The ancient hardwood floors had an attractive luster, making the tiny clothes on miniature hangers seem even more delicate and luxurious. A light green sweater caught my eye. I took it from the rack, walked to the counter, and paid for it. Cash, of course. Didn't want to leave behind any evidence.

When I emerged from the shop, John smiled. "Find something you like?"

"Yes. It's darling."

I pulled the sweater from the bag, realizing how reckless this was. If someone recognized us and saw me with baby clothes, it would be international news within minutes. But the streets weren't crowded and no one was paying attention to us. We were unremarkable in our winter coats and hats.

"Baby King will love it," John said, kissing me lightly on the cheek.

Sitting in front of my wardrobe at Langbroek, I held the sweater, marveling at its impossibly small size. The fabric felt soft against my cheek. I placed a light kiss on the garment before I wrapped it in white tissue paper with reverence and placed it in a plastic storage bin. The container also held the baby blanket Tilda gave me for Christmas, a pair of white crib shoes (Astrid placed the online order in her name), and my childhood copy of Goodnight Moon. Mom didn't ask any questions when I asked her to mail it to me. But I was pretty sure she knew I was in baby mode.

As I slid the storage bin into the floor of my wardrobe, I remembered the other treasure I'd put in there last summer and my curiosity grumbled. I decided to make time to read a little more in Princess Beatrix's journal. I decided to wait to tell John about it because I was afraid I'd no longer have the opportunity to read it. That seemed horribly selfish, but I never knew his mother. Reading her journal allowed me to get to know her through her own words rather than John's memories. I was eager to read more.

CHAPTER THIRTY-FIVE

D r. Dreesen will be ready to see you in about fifteen minutes. Would you please just wait here?" The nurse left us alone in the waiting room. Our guards stood in the hallway.

John screwed up his lips on one side; he looked torqued. He never had to wait for anything or anyone.

I adjusted in my chair, creating a loud series of squeaks. I looked at my phone and the date jumped out at me. Adela's due date, March 22, was rapidly approaching.

"Adela's getting close, you know?"

John didn't look up from his phone. This is why I almost never talked about the infertile elephant in the room. It was a miracle he was accompanying me to the doctor this time.

"Why can't I be happy for them?" I asked because I really wanted to know.

"Because you aren't happy for us. We seem to be stuck, and they're about to cross the finish line."

Get off your blinking phone and look at me!

"It hacks me off," I said. "They didn't wait to have sex until after they were married, and now they're being rewarded with a baby. I'm an awful, terrible person for feeling that way."

The door opened. "Hatty? John?"

Our first names. Nice touch. We stood and followed the nurse down a bright hallway with taupe walls.

Our attorney Lars Franke visited this doctor's office last week and took care of the necessary paperwork, adding an extra layer of privacy protection on top of the country's already-strict patient confidentiality laws. Having the medical staff sign additional confidentiality documents was a routine matter anytime a member of the royal family needed to see a specialist. That, and we always had our appointments after hours. Because we were seeing an OB/GYN who specialized in infertility, we *really* wanted to keep this on the down-low. In fact, John had asked Lars not to mention our appointment to anyone in the family.

The nurse led us into a spacious, neat exam room. "Dr. Dreesen will be right in to see you."

John sat stiff and upright in the chair. When we were alone, I took his hand. "Thank you for coming with me."

"Of course. I'm interested in hearing what she has to say about you."

"It's kind of a team effort, you know. I can't get pregnant on my own."

I tried to be patient with him, but it wasn't easy. I think it was the sight of Adela's emerging bump that nudged John's emotional barometer; since December, he randomly asked questions about our efforts to get pregnant. Him: Do you think we're having enough sex? Me: I think sex every day definitely hits the mark. Him: Tell me again why you take your temperature every morning. Me: To track my basal body temperature so I know if I've ovulated.

I checked the time on my phone. Ten minutes after six. An alert flashed silently on the screen, telling me I had a new message from

Kendra27. I read the first few words: "Good luck at the doctor…" I quickly darkened the screen and flipped my phone so it was facedown. I worried what John would think about me sharing a few details about my situation with a woman I'd "met" through an online infertility discussion site.

There was a short knock and the door opened. A petite woman with dark hair and a sizeable baby bump walked in. She extended her hand to each of us. "I'm Dr. Dreesen. It's nice to meet you both. Tell me what's been going on."

I explained to her I'd gone off birth control pills in December 2013, less than a month before we were married. "I think Dr. Cloutier's office sent you my records. I saw him late last summer, and he didn't think anything was wrong. He told us to keep trying. What's not in my chart is that in early December, the day my period was due, I did a pregnancy test. I saw two lines, but the second line was really faint. About an hour and a half later, I did another test. It was negative. The next morning, my period started."

John squeezed my hand. Oh right. I'd never mentioned the tests to him.

"Was your period heavier than normal?" she asked.

"Yes."

"How long are your cycles typically?"

"Usually twenty-eight days. I was about five days late last July."

"Do you have any pain with your period?"

"I went on the pill in high school to help with cramping. Since I went off the pill, I've had some pain, but I just take medicine for it."

"How about during sex? Any pain then?"

John shifted in his chair. I knew this was way outside his comfort zone.

"No. Well, sometimes a little, but not enough that we have to stop." Another tidbit I'd never shared with John.

"And not bad enough that she's ever told me about it," John said, looking past me to the doctor.

"Hatty, I'll give you a minute to undress. I'd like to do an exam and we'll also draw blood. I'll be back in a few minutes."

When she was gone, I got undressed and for the first time, my nakedness didn't stir a reaction from my husband. He sat there looking uncomfortable, nervously checking his phone.

My frustration with his emotional distance boiled. "Are you expecting a call?"

"No."

When Dr. Dreesen returned, she completed the exam, and then drew blood from the crook of my arm. "We didn't want to ask someone to stay late just to get your blood."

She and I watched the red liquid snake its way through the tiny tubing attached to the needle in my arm. She slid the needle out after filling two vials and covered the tiny bleeding spot with a bandage.

"Hatty, you can get dressed. John, since we're doing a fertility work-up, we'll need to check your sperm count. We'll look at the morphology and motility—the shape of the sperm and how well they move." She opened a drawer and took out a plastic cup with a sealed lid and blank label.

"Take this in the bathroom…"

"I'm sorry. I need to go." John left the room.

You've got to be kidding me? I just went all spread-eagle for this lady and you can't pop some off into a cup?

Dr. Dreesen and I didn't speak for a couple of seconds. I sat under a sheet on the exam table, my legs cold and my face burning in anger and embarrassment. "I'm sorry. I think this is all very strange for him. It's weird for me too."

"This process is overwhelming. Take this container with you. Perhaps you can convince him to do it at home. Just don't use any lubricants or saliva. After you have the ejaculate in the cup, put the lid on and place it in your bra. You'll need to keep it warm against your body and bring it to the office right away. Do you think you can do all that?"

"Oh yeah. I'll get it done. Thank you for your help."

"My nurse will call and schedule a follow-up so we can review the results."

That night, I lounged on the couch in our den with my laptop open. I was reading up on the best food to eat when you're trying to get pregnant. I paused momentarily to give my two cents on whether Kendra27's pregnancy test looked positive. After the requisite five minute wait, she'd snapped the plastic case apart and pulled out the test strip. (This had become one of my go-to moves, too, when I thought there might be a hint of a second line.) With the strip exposed to fluorescent lights in her basement, she'd taken a photo. Then, she ran the snapshot through several different filters, and posted the results on the discussion boards. You had to hand it to the sepia filter. It made faint lines on pregnancy tests look bold and solid, the kind of positive result I dreamed about getting.

I really liked Kendra27, even though I knew her only through the online community. She said she lived in Virginia near D.C. I told her I was an ex-pat living in Europe. That's about all I could reveal. So few people knew what was going on with our attempts to get pregnant. Tilda was a part of the inner circle, and so was Astrid. She scheduled the appointments, and most importantly, kept me secretly supplied with embarrassing quantities of pregnancy tests. Our royal guards knew about our appointments with Dr. Dreesen, but John and I trusted them. They knew everything about John's family and said nothing.

"What are you doing?" John crept up behind me and I nearly jumped through the ceiling.

"Nothing! Just reading." I started to close the laptop lid.

"Wait. What's that?" He leaned over the back of the couch, pushing the lid open.

He skimmed the messages from Kendra27. "Please tell me she doesn't know who you are." A low angry tone crept into his voice.

"Of course not! I just need to talk to someone who understands how I feel because, apparently, you don't get it." Without warning, hot tears streamed down my cheeks.

He walked around the couch and remained standing. "Maybe I don't get it because you're keeping secrets from me. Why didn't you tell me you had a positive pregnancy test in December?" His nostrils flared.

"Look, you do *not* know how it feels. It's my body every month that screams, 'YOU FAILED' in big, red, angry gushes."

"But you had a positive test in December. Why didn't you tell me?"

"Tell you what? That I had a positive test for an hour and a half? I called Dr. Cloutier's office when the second test was negative. The nurse said there was nothing they could do if it was a miscarriage." I nearly choked on the last word.

John sat beside me, wrapping me in his arms. He pulled me to his chest. "Shh. Look. It will happen. I know it will."

I tried to believe him.

About ten minutes later after our mini fight, John went to the kitchen. While he was out of our bedroom, I snuck in and retrieved his mother's journal. I took it to the den and slipped it under one of the couch cushions. When he returned, he kissed me goodnight before heading into our bedroom and closing the door. I waited about fifteen minutes before sliding the journal from its hiding spot underneath me.

Flipping through the pages, a splash of red caught my eye. I stopped and went back to it. She'd written the entry in red ink. The slant of the handwriting made it look angry.

September 21, 1988

Why isn't my body cooperating? My period came today with a vengeance. It was three days late this time, and I thought for sure there was a baby growing inside me. Leo says if I don't get pregnant soon, I'll have to take medication to move things along. I'll do everything in my power to make this happen. He looks at me as though the waiting is breaking his heart. I can't stand the thought of disappointing him.

I flipped ahead, my heart pounding in my chest. It seemed John and I weren't the first royal couple to experience fertility problems.

December 30, 1988

Happy (Almost) New Year! We're in Phuket with Leo's mum for the holiday. Such a beautiful country. I could live the rest of my days at this beach. I'm glad to get to relax before I begin taking the new fertility drug. Dr. Cloutier says it will boost my ovulation and dramatically increase our chances of conception. I'm so excited I could be pregnant and holding my first child in the New Year!

John was born October, 1, 1989. I did the math and scanned the entries for late January until I found it.

January 25, 1989

It happened!!! We went to the doctor early this morning, and they confirmed I'm pregnant! I've felt cautiously hopeful the last few days because I've been ill in the morning and my period was due last Saturday. Leo was with me when the doctor delivered the news. I've never seen him look so relieved. The doctor said my due date is October 1, and I should come back in a few weeks for a check-up.

Punctual from the start, John had arrived on his due date. That was the last entry in the book. I wondered if she had bought a new journal to track her pregnancy, and if so, where she'd squirreled it away.

Maybe we'd also find a pill or procedure that would help us get pregnant. I felt hopeful as I thought about our next doctor's visit. Dr. Dreesen would know why we weren't getting pregnant, and she'd have a plan to fix it.

I was lying in a funny position. My neck rested at an odd angle and my hands were splayed across my lower abdomen. The energy of life pulsed inside it.

I slowly moved my hands over my skin. As though they were endowed with the power of ultrasound, my hands revealed the grainy picture of the baby growing inside me, projecting it onto the wall. I saw the little body in its reclining position. The flow of energy from my body to his showed up as a pulse on the ultrasound image. I felt so alive and so did my baby. What would happen if I reached inside my belly and touched it?

At that thought, my eyes shot open. My hands were still moving across my abdomen. I'd fallen asleep on the couch. In a panic, I jumped up and searched for Princess Beatrix's journal. I grabbed it and hid it under the couch before turning off the lamp and going to the bedroom.

Tiptoeing to my nightstand, I opened the drawer and pulled out the plastic cup Dr. Dreesen gave me, the one intended for John. I set it on top of the table next to my glasses.

Burrowed under the covers next to my husband, I rode a fresh wave of hope brought on by how real and vivid my dream had been.

Instead of hopping out of bed, I stayed still, going through my plan one last time. John usually woke up shortly after I did, so I waited. In a few minutes, he rolled over toward me, moaned softly, and yawned. I migrated my right hand toward his side of the bed. It made contact with the front of his sweat pants, a thin barrier between me and the hardness underneath. We were facing each other, and at my touch, his eyes drifted open.

"Good morning, wife." A sweet smile spread over his thick lips.

"There's something I need you to do. And if you'll let me help, it will be so much fun," I said, encouraging him with my hand.

He inhaled deeply. "I'll do whatever you say." His eyes closed in a moment of pleasure.

My right hand stayed busy while the left reached over to the nightstand for the cup. *Hatty 1, Infertility 0.*

John opened his eyes, catching a glimpse of the cup. "Okay?" I wanted him to acknowledge that he was on board with this.

He sighed, then smiled. "Let's do it." He brought me close. Our lips converged moments before he moaned. Then, he whispered, "Anything for you."

CHAPTER THIRTY-SIX

We have your results." Dr. Dreesen sat down behind her desk, looking at the computer screen, which she kept turned away from me and John.

"Your sperm count is well within normal ranges. The motility is good and the morphology is also normal. So, no problems there."

Relief washed over John's face. At the same time, I must have turned green because I knew the blame rested on me.

"Hatty, all of your labs were normal. There are no areas of concern at this point."

"But how is that possible if I'm not getting pregnant?"

"We call it unexplained infertility. We just don't know what's preventing you from conceiving."

"Can I ask a blunt question? Am I too fat to get pregnant?"

"You're not fat. You're in the upper range of what's normal for your height and build. Compared to most women in Toulene, you have a larger frame, but your weight is fine and it's not impacting your fertility."

"What happens now?" I worked to keep panic out of my voice.

"Well, we have several options. I can do what's called a

hysterosalpingogram or HSG test. We flush a special dye through your fallopian tubes and use X-ray equipment to watch how well it flows. It's a way to see whether your tubes are blocked.. Sometimes, this diagnostic procedure can remove tiny obstructions that may be interfering with the egg getting to the uterus and increase fertility."

"That sounds like a reasonable next step." This is where my online obsessing paid off. I knew exactly what she was talking about with the procedure she described.

"There's another option I want to discuss. The last time you were here, you said you went on the pill in high school to ease menstrual cramping. You also mentioned that you sometimes have pain during intercourse. All of this may point to endometriosis. That's where the tissue that normally lines the uterus grows in the abdominal cavity. For some women, the presence of this tissue interferes with ovulation or impacts the quality of the eggs. A laparoscopy allows me to make very small incisions in your abdomen and see if there are any structural issues."

"What are the other options? I don't want Hatty to go through that kind of surgery." John rubbed my back.

"We can also try several cycles of assisted reproductive techniques. Hatty would take an ovary stimulating drug. She'd use an ovulation predictor kit at home to pinpoint when she's about to ovulate. Then, you'd supply us with your sperm so we can prep it and transfer it into Hatty's uterus." It was all business as usual for Dr. Dreesen.

"I appreciate knowing our options. Could we also just keep trying on our own and see what happens?" John looked a bit pale.

"Of course. Why don't you discuss how you'd like to proceed? When you're ready, give my office a call."

We thanked Dr. Dreesen and left. When we arrived at Langbroek Palace, John went into the study and shut the door.

I walked onto the balcony outside our second story bedroom. I shuddered in the cold of January's early evening air as I gazed over the back lawn. The air was brisk, and twilight had slipped its orange-red mantel over the daytime sky. I pulled the chunky sweater tighter around my body, closed my eyes, and listened. There was the dull roar of traffic outside the fence that separated our grounds from the public street. I heard the low mewing of the cat. He was a gift from John for our one year anniversary. As I picked up Booters and turned to go inside, I paused at the sound of a child's laughter. It was like half hearing a secret hastily whispered in a crowded hallway. So soft and brief, I wasn't sure I'd heard it at all.

CHAPTER THIRTY-SEVEN

John sent the cue ball cracking into a big cluster at the far end of the table, scattering the balls in all directions. His father stood back with his cue stick in one hand and a glass of beer in the other. Leopold had invited us to Belvoir for dinner, and suggested a game of billiards afterward. It was a pleasant ending to a day that brought a flicker of hope: I'd had an HSG that morning and both of my tubes were clear. I was thrilled and relieved. Maybe the very act of sending liquid shooting through my tubes would improve our chances of conceiving. I'd read multiple stories online about women who got pregnant the cycle after their HSG.

Energized by my new optimism, I sipped hot tea in a comfy chair by the window; I ditched alcohol altogether in case it was having a negative impact on my fertility.

"How did it go with Dr. Dreesen?"

John looked at his father, unsure what to say. Someone couldn't keep a secret. So, Leopold knew what we were doing? *Awesomesauce.*

"It went fine. She ran some tests, and there are no obvious problems. She offered some advice and options for how we might move forward." John sounded non-committal, casual.

"You know, if things don't work out, you two will have to get a divorce." Leopold took a final swig of his beer and I nearly did a spit take. I caught myself before any tea left my mouth.

"What the hell are you talking about?" I blurted.

John stared down his father. "She has no idea what you mean and I can't believe you'd say such a thing in front of her. Hatty, there's an antiquated section of our legal code that makes it possible for male members of the royal family to initiate a divorce or have their marriage annulled if the wife can't conceive. But you don't have to worry about that."

"I'm not worried. I know you love me. Leo, you can take that law and shove it right up your ass."

John's father took a step toward me but directed his words at John. "I bring it up only because I did everything in my power to make sure your mother got pregnant with you so Granny and I never had to have this conversation."

"I don't understand," John said, his hands gripping the cue stick. *He's going to break it.*

"I took your mother to see Dr. Cloutier, and he gave her a new fertility drug. The next month, she was pregnant with you. I suggest you and Hatty do whatever is necessary to fulfill your obligations to the people of Toulene."

"We'll do whatever Hatty wants in terms of medicine and procedures. But I am not divorcing her, even if she never gets pregnant. And I forbid you to speak to her again about any of this."

John slammed the cue stick onto the table, grabbed my hand, and pulled me out the door.

Astrid set a paper bag on the dresser in our bedroom. "Here's your medicine, Madam."

"Thanks, Astrid."

After she left the room, I walked over and picked up the bag. I liked the name of the ovary stimulating drug: Overa. It sounded hopeful, and reminded me of the word "overcome." Astrid's name was listed as the patient, yet another layer of protection for us.

John burst into our bedroom, his eyes huge and his mouth open.

"What's wrong?"

"There was an explosion at the smelter," he said with almost no inflection in his voice.

"The one near Kortrijk?" A sinking feeling opened in my stomach because I knew damn well there was no other smelter.

"Yes. We have to go to Belvoir. Now."

On the fifteen minute drive, John gave me the details. No one had been killed or injured when a homemade bomb exploded inside one of the hallways. It went off in an area that was empty on the weekends, thank goodness. The authorities suspected an employee had something to do with it.

At Belvoir, the public affairs staff was in overdrive. Though they offered advice, their job was to follow our decisions on how, when, and what to communicate to the public through the media. Cilla asked me and John to step inside her office.

"Hatty, there's already chatter on social media about the investigation you did as an intern into the environmental impact of the plant. You need to tell me everything." Cilla had a pen and notepad in hand. We'd gone over this once before.

I told her about the interviews I conducted and the spreadsheets I created. All the work was saved on my school laptop, which I'd returned to the university's computer help desk. I watched them wipe the hard drive. All my handwritten notes were in a big box in storage at Langbroek.

"It looks like the source of the social media posts is *Les Valenciennes*. I'm sure they feel some level of betrayal since you left them to join the institution they adamantly oppose," Cilla said in a matter-of-fact tone.

I hardly knew what to say. "I didn't do anything wrong."

"Of course you didn't. But that doesn't matter to them. They deal in speculation and innuendo." She turned her laptop around so I could see it. "Look at this post from one of your former colleagues. 'The Duchess set out to help the people of Kortrijk by investigating how the smelter is harming local residents, but the crown bought her silence.'"

I was standing at the bottom of a ravine looking up as the wolves descended.

CHAPTER THIRTY-EIGHT

J ust relax, Hatty." *If only.*

John stood beside me as I reclined on the exam table. The cold instrument filled me when it reached its destination between my legs. Dr. Dreesen smiled and after a moment, removed it.

"That's it. You did a beautiful job."

If by 'beautiful job' you mean spreading my legs, then yes, it was gorgeous.

"Now we wait?"

"Yes. And you can sit up. We'll see you back in two weeks for a blood test to see if the IUI worked."

She left, and John kissed my lips. "Let's go celebrate our first and only in utero insemination with popcorn and a movie."

"Sure. You pick the movie. I don't want anything mushy or sappy. Okay?"

"Agreed. No sap. No mush. Inglorious Basterds it is."

Smudged cheeks surrounded me and tiny fingers tugged at my dress. We were eight days post-IUI, visiting a preschool to make a push for early childhood education funding increases. The assembly was debating federal appropriations, so we needed media coverage of our position. After John made prepared remarks to the three reporters we allowed inside the childcare center, it was play time.

"What's your name?" A little boy with spiky blond hair put his hand on my arm.

"Hatty. What's yours?"

"Hat-EE! Do you like hats?"

"Yes! Do you have one I can wear?"

He turned and walked away. I looked over at John. The teacher had lined up all the little girls who wanted to see him. One of them had a tiara perched askew atop a mop of stringy brown hair. She held a baseball bat over her shoulder. *She doesn't trust this prince guy.*

"Here, Hat-EE!"

The blond boy held a triangular pirate's hat, which had an eye patch attached to it. I put it on, and slid the patch into place. "Arr, mateys!"

The group of kids around me laughed, and some replied with their own "Arr!"

"Hat-EE! Where are your kids?"

"What's your name?"

"Adrian Raske."

"Well, Adrian Raske, I'm not a mom yet. But when I have kiddos, I hope they're half as cute as you!"

I placed a gentle kiss on his forehead. Adrian smiled as a chorus of delighted squeals erupted from the other children. The one photographer we allowed inside the center clicked his camera repeatedly.

This was our first post-bomb public appearance, and we wanted to keep the focus on the preschool funding issue. The three reporters followed the rules we set out and didn't ask us any questions.

As we left through a side door, we encountered a line of angry-looking reporters. They shouted questions at us because there were no rules out here.

"Duchess, will you release your investigative work on the environmental impact of the smelter?"

"Your Highness, will you take seriously the allegations of environmental harm in Kortrijk caused by the smelter?"

We had extra guards with us, and we made it through the gauntlet to the safety of the waiting car with only their words accosting us.

Prince John and Duchess Hatty Refuse to Answer Questions about the Bomb… AND, Is the Royal Couple Trying for a Baby?

By Xpress staff

March 9, 2015

At an appearance this morning at Regent's Primary School in the capital city, the first public sighting of the pair since the explosion at the Kortrijk smelter, the Prince and Duchess took no questions from reporters about the incident. They also refused to comment on the investigation the Duchess was doing on the environmental impact of the smelter prior to her marriage to the prince.

But the Duchess did chat up the children inside. She reportedly told a child "I'm not a mom yet." Her comment feeds speculation we may soon hear the sound of little feet running through the halls of Langbroek Palace.

"By saying, 'I'm not a mom yet,' she's making it clear she and Prince John have started trying to get pregnant," said Anna Fetke, a historian whose work chronicles the last five decades of Toulene's royal family. "It's no surprise they'd want to have a baby now. They've been married for more than a year!"

Meanwhile, baby watch is heating up for Prince Henri and Duchess Adela as they prepare to welcome their first child this month. The duchess was spotted shopping for baby clothes in the upscale Vrel neighborhood. Speculation over the baby's gender continues as the due date approaches!

CHAPTER THIRTY-NINE

J ohn tapped on the door and we heard Adela's sweet Spanish accent: "Si! Come in!"

She lay in bed looking completely worn out but lovely as she cradled the new little life in her arms. Henri stood and hugged John. Their embrace lasted longer than I expected, and when they pulled apart, Henri was wiping away tears. We stood beside the bed and Adela pulled back the blankets exposing the scrunched up face of our nephew.

"Oh, Adela. He's perfect." I swallowed hard to keep back my own tears.

A flash of jealousy and longing ripped through my body. Henri and Adela didn't know our first in utero insemination had failed. They didn't even know we'd had an IUI. Raw grief lay in wait, poised to creep around the corner and hijack any thought it wanted to overtake.

"Mum would be so ecstatic," John said, almost in a whisper. I squeezed his hand.

"Does he have a name?" I consciously steadied my voice.

Henri looked at his brother and said, "Juan. Named for the man I admire most."

John's face took on a new light. "I don't know what to say… This is an unexpected honor."

Adela shifted toward me and extended the baby in her arms. "Hatty, would you like to hold him?"

I nodded as I sat on the bed and let her place the infant in my arms. For the first time since we arrived, he opened his eyes. I pulled him close to my face and smelled the clean newness of this tiny being. Closing my eyes, I imagined I was holding *my* baby. The minute the thought entered my head, I pushed it away. If I let my mind wander in that direction, John would have to carry me home in a weeping heap.

"You're a natural, Hatty! I can't wait for Juan to have some cousins," Henri said, oblivious to all we were doing to make that happen. I looked up at him and smiled, intense heat radiating through my body. The hot flashes were an annoying side effect of the ovulation stimulation medication.

We stayed only a few minutes more, excusing ourselves so Adela and the baby could rest.

"What do you say we go to De Haan after the IUI next week?" John asked, taking my hand in his as we descended the stairs.

"Sure. I'll never turn down a trip to the beach."

"I just think it might be good for you to be in a more peaceful setting, away from the madness that's going to envelop Belvoir now that the baby is here."

As we made our way to the car, I felt relief at the thought of escaping the media frenzy surrounding the new prince. Outside Belvoir's fence, men and women with still and video cameras were lined up, waiting for something to happen. When they saw the gates open and our car emerge, they flipped into overdrive, clicking their cameras and yelling. I blocked it out by imagining our little cottage in De Haan holding us within its cozy walls, our own protective womb.

When our car cleared the reporters, I released a gush of air and twin tears ran down my face. John put his arm around me and pulled me close, kissing my forehead.

CHAPTER FORTY

My cell phone buzzed while John and I ate breakfast. It was Cilla. She asked me to put her on speaker phone after I confirmed we were alone.

"Hatty, does the name Leisel de Vries sound familiar to you?"

I thought for a moment. I'd met so many people since John and I had been together. I had a hard time keeping track of names, though I was pretty good at recognizing faces.

"I don't know. Should it?"

"The Royal Guard arrested her last night. They think she's involved in the bombing. When they questioned her, she told them you had interviewed her when you worked at *The Morning Dispatch*. Is that true?"

Of course. Leisel de Vries was one of the women in Kortrijk. I'd interviewed her during my internship. Her story flooded my mind.

"Yes, that's right. She told me she and her husband had trouble getting pregnant, and they believed their infertility was somehow related to pollution from the smelter. But why do they think she was involved with the bombing?"

"She and her husband recently had their third unsuccessful in vitro fertilization cycle. They appealed the national healthcare system's three cycle limit. Two days before the bombing, Leisel received news the appeals board voted to deny their claim," Cilla said dismissively.

I nearly gagged on her words. Had my failure to follow through on my investigative story led to this? If I'd kept digging and my story had run, maybe Leisel and the others would've received some additional financial and medical help from Toulene's government. The dots might not connect directly, but I felt hugely responsible for Leisel's desperation. It felt similar to the desperation I felt every time I saw a single pink line on a pregnancy test.

"Hatty, are you alright? You look ill," John said, coming around the table to me.

"I'm okay."

"Cilla, do you need anything else from us?"

"No. Just wanted to find out if Leisel's claims about Hatty interviewing her were true. Hatty, tell me one more time no one else has copies of the work you did on this story." Cilla sounded uncharacteristically nervous.

"No one has my work."

We got off the phone and I had to lie down. I'd failed a sister soldier in the fight against infertility.

The black car sat in traffic. We were headed to Dr. Dreesen's office for a second round of IUI.

"When we get to the office, and you have to go do your thing, take my phone with you." I handed it to John.

"Why?"

"Watch the last movie I made."

He pushed the home button and started scrolling.

"Hey! Not now."

Bernard sat up front with the driver. I didn't want either one of them to know what I'd done. I reached for the phone, but John was faster. He leaned away from me and hit play.

"I can't believe my wife is such a bad girl," he whispered.

"Save it for later," I hissed. "I just thought you might like some... *inspiration*." I knew he hated having to go into a room and "perform" on cue.

"This will do nicely. Thank you." He leaned over, kissed me, and grabbed my breast through my shirt. My eyes darted to the front. Bernard and the driver were looking straight ahead.

I sat on the table in the exam room, waiting for Dr. van Noort to do the in utero insemination. Since our IUI last month, Dr. Dreesen had delivered her baby and was now on maternity leave. So, we put our fate in the hands of young Dr. van Noort, a Dutch man with floppy blond hair. For me, this part of the process was fast and clinical. Otherwise, it was just too weird to think about another man putting my husband's sperm inside of me.

I didn't ask John to join me for the painless procedure this time.

Dr. van Noort worked quickly and in a matter of moments, the IUI was done. John came in afterward while I lay horizontal on the table.

"Look at you, Wonder Woman. You can get pregnant without your husband in the room," John said, stroking my cheek.

He placed his hand on top of the sheet above my abdomen. "C'mon, Baby King. You've set the stage for a grand entrance. It's time."

"Yes! This is your mother speaking to you. Get your booty in gear, Baby King. You're late!" I laughed at my own silliness to keep from crying my eyes out.

"Knock, knock." I peered through a crack in the door.

"Hey! Come in."

I walked into Tilda's office in the assembly building, closing the door behind me.

"I'm really sorry to barge in on you like this." That's as far as I got before my desperation erupted in hot tears. My lungs demanded air in hiccupped gulps.

Rushing around her desk, Tilda encircled me with her arms.

"I'm sorry. Do you know how much I hate to cry?"

"Shh. Just breathe," Tilda instructed, squeezing me close to her.

I nodded and she released me. Taking a couple of slow, deep breaths, I pushed my despair into the basement of my heart as I did almost every day. An online post from a high school friend announcing she was pregnant with her second baby—morning sickness again? What a drag!—had released my sorrow from its usual hiding place.

"Aren't you guys leaving for De Haan today?" She handed me a tissue.

"Tomorrow."

She let go and gave me a tissue. Wiping my eyes, I confessed: "I have horrible thoughts, you know. This whole infertility thing—it's not about John. It's not even about the baby. It's about me being a failure."

"You're not a failure. You can't beat yourself up over this. It's not your fault."

"And I have to keep up a positive front. Even to John. What if this IUI doesn't work?" A small shriek and then more tears and hiccupping. The possibility of failure weakened any remaining shred of optimism, leaving hopelessness in its place.

Tilda set her hands on my shoulders, shaking me gently. "Then you'll think of something else. This isn't the end of the line. You've got plenty of time and lots of options. Have you guys talked about adoption?"

"No. I'm open to it, but I have no idea what fresh weirdness that conversation might spawn. If I brought up adoption, John would think I'm admitting defeat. And I'm not."

"Of course not. Look, go to the beach and relax. When can you test to see if the IUI worked?"

"The day after tomorrow. Will he hate me if I can't give him children? I have one job, Tilda. One job!" I bit my knuckles to prevent more shrieks and tears.

Tilda hugged me again. "Don't stress, okay? That's definitely not good. No one gets pregnant with this kind of pressure hanging over them. It's going to be fine."

Yeah, right. Fine was a faraway country, inaccessible to me.

CHAPTER FORTY-ONE

W e walked along the sandy shore in De Haan, bundled up in field jackets and knitted caps. We didn't resent the cold because it kept the tourists at bay until June and allowed us to walk unnoticed, even on the public beaches.

"Tomorrow's the day, right?" John kicked a shell with the toe of his sneaker.

"Yep. I've got two pregnancy tests in case we don't believe the first one."

"Only two? I'm not sure I believe you. I know about the massive stash in your armoire at home. How are you feeling?"

"Good. A little nauseated, I guess."

"Is that a sign you're pregnant?"

"I don't know. I sometimes feel this way when I have my period." A few days before my period was due, my body tortured me. Every month, it produced what I inevitably misconstrued as early pregnancy symptoms. Sore boobs? Check. Weird cravings? You bet. Lower back pain? Without fail. Even though I knew—KNEW—this happened every month, I still got excited when my breasts became tender and the cavalcade of other pregnancy signs made an appearance. It was a cruel deception I endured cycle after cycle.

I bent over and examined a band of shells embedded in the sand. Most of them were broken with their shiny pink interior facing up.

"I can't wait to bring our kids here," I said, lifting a delicate scallop shell, and putting it in the pocket of my jacket.

"Me too."

"Growing up, we'd go to Destin, Florida every year. We stayed with my aunt, uncle, and four cousins. They had this rambling old house with banged up hardwood floors. We'd stuff the cars and haul to the beach every day. When we were older, my cousin Katie and I were probably sophomores in high school, we promised we'd bring our own kids back to that beach to play together."

"You will. I promise. You know what I like to think about? I like to imagine how gorgeous our children will be. Thank goodness you're bringing straight teeth into this family."

"Oh, c'mon. Your slightly crooked smile was one of the first things I adored about you because it let me know you weren't actually perfect. It helped me not feel intimidated by this amazing hair." I reached up and touched his gorgeous locks.

He took my hand and kissed it. I envied his confidence, and tried not to be annoyed by his inability to wallow with me in self-pity.

The metallic clicks of the timer were the soundtrack of our wait. I'd left the pregnancy test on the bathroom counter to prevent myself from sitting and staring at it for three minutes. I'd become attached to this one brand of pee sticks that took only three minutes to show the result.

My superstitions around getting pregnant were endless. We were using a kitchen timer instead of my cell phone because I'd come to associate its sound with seeing a single line, and somehow I'd convinced myself changing the timing device might change the test result.

Ding! The minute we heard the bell, we joined hands and walked from the kitchen into the bathroom. Panic dried my mouth and dampened my palms. I was a nervous wreck. I stepped onto the cold tile floor ahead of John.

A single line proclaimed another failure. All emotions evaporated, leaving behind only a husk, dry and empty.

"Maybe something's wrong with this test. Could you do another one later?"

"I can. But when you do the test first thing in the morning, it's your best shot because the pregnancy hormone is more concentrated and the urine is less diluted. That's what I read online, anyway."

"But what if you try again tomorrow?" It was the endless parade of "what ifs" that exhausted me. But he was right. I'd test again in the morning.

"Yes, I'll do another test in the morning." Who was I kidding? I'd do another one this afternoon.

I left the test on the counter and walked back into the kitchen. I scooped up my phone and sent Kendra27 a quick message because she'd been "crossing her fingers and toes" and "sending good vibes for a positive!"

I saw a new email from Plato. Sitting on a stool by the kitchen island, I opened it:

SAVE THE DATE! Saturday, August 15. We're doing it! We're getting married. I'm dragging Sam to Iowa to meet my family and we're tying the knot. I know it's an impossible thing to ask, but we want you guys to come. Puh-LEAZE! Also, remind John he's on the hook to play with Jos in the charity rugby match. My cousin and the kids in Ethiopia thank both of you! By the way, I will get you to Ethiopia sometime in the next twelve months. It will straight up change your life. Love you, girl!

I hit reply:

I'll see if we can come to the wedding. But only if you promise right now you guys won't get pregnant before us. The game is on John's calendar. I won't let him wiggle out of it. Ethiopia's on my radar, so we'll see. OXOX

I looked up when I heard John walk into the kitchen.

"We've got to do more." He held the test in his hand, his eyes wide—he looked shell shocked.

"Look, I'll test again tomorrow. You do realize you've brought the urine-soaked test into the kitchen, right?"

"What are we going to do if you still aren't pregnant?"

Helplessness filled his face, and relief overtook me because I sensed he'd hit rock bottom at last. Finally, we were in the same place at the same time on this journey, both of us falling into the pit. *Welcome to a whole new level of misery, honey.*

I grabbed a napkin, took the test from his hand, and threw it in the trash can. "I really resent you coming so late to the game. You can't sit on the bench for three quarters and then swoop in with five minutes on the clock and ask how to win. It's like I've been doing this by myself."

He approached me, pointing an accusatory finger. His nostrils flared; he was seething. "That's a lie. You can do a lot of things on your own, Hatty, but you can't get pregnant by yourself. I've done everything I can to make it happen, except agree to the laparoscopy. I still don't want you to go through that kind of surgery."

I stood toe-to-toe with my husband, not blinking. "'You've 'done everything' you can? Oh, c'mon. This whole thing makes you so uncomfortable. You've just been phoning it in."

His fist slammed against the granite island. "You can't 'phone in' sperm!" he yelled.

"And by the way, there is no magic bullet. I don't know how to fix this!" I screamed the final words into his face and threw my arms into the air in exasperation. I didn't give a damn if Bernard and the other two Royal Guards heard us from their posts outside.

He took two steps back and blew out air, trying to calm down.

"But you spend hours online trying to figure out how to get pregnant. What's next?"

Even though I wanted to believe we'd get pregnant this time, I'd already been thinking about what we'd do if this month's IUI failed. Developing Plan B was a critical part of keeping hope within reach. If this fails, then there's this. Hope and despair were neighbors, coexisting with a quiet tension in my heart.

"Since we don't really know what's keeping us from getting pregnant, in vitro fertilization may be the best shot we have. From what I've read online, it has relatively high success rates."

John rubbed his eyes, a gesture I knew so well because it conveyed his exasperation with this entire process.

"I'm so sorry," I sobbed.

John wrapped me in his arms, and I pressed my head against his shoulder. "I feel like if I hadn't slept with Jack, I'd be pregnant. This is a punishment, you know? It's all my fault."

"That's ridiculous. You know that's not true. There's a way to fix this and we'll do whatever it takes."

CHAPTER FORTY-TWO

I s Duchess Hatty Really a "Barren-ess?"
By Clarence Watson
April 13, 2015

Duchess Hatty has been receiving fertility treatments, according to two sources who spoke to Xpress. They cited firsthand knowledge of the couple's appointments with Dr. Hilda Dreesen, a highly regarded fertility specialist in Roeselare.

Though there are no details on what procedures the couple has undertaken, it's clear they're eager, and perhaps desperate, to get pregnant. At an appearance earlier this year, the Duchess told a young boy she wasn't a mother "yet."

"It would be highly unusual for a couple that's as young as the prince and duchess to have problems conceiving. They certainly face a great deal of stress and as we all know, that can contribute to fertility problems," said Dr. Heinz Baden, a gynecologist who does not treat the royal couple.

Representatives for the couple refused to comment for this story.

"The expectations are very high. They've been married for nearly a year and a half, and Prince Henri and Duchess Adela have already produced an heir. Maybe Prince John and Duchess Hatty could use some pointers from *their younger rivals!" said Anna Fetke, a historian who writes about the royal family.*

I stood in the tidy concrete hallway outside the locker rooms with my arms wrapped around John's neck.

"Just be careful, okay?"

"I will be extra careful."

I'd felt uneasy about the rugby match ever since John told Plato he'd play. I hated the game. It was so rough and they didn't wear helmets.

"Am I interrupting, love?" I looked up at the sound of my ex-boyfriend's voice. Jack swaggered toward us.

"Hello, Jack," John said. I saw the telltale line on John's jaw, so I knew he was clenching his teeth.

Jack looked right at me. "Hatty, what's this I hear about you trying to get it up the duff?" A big smile spread across his face.

I cringed at his crude reference to mine and John's attempts to get pregnant. I stared at him as I kept my arms around John.

"Maybe you just need a ride with a real man. You remember what that's like, right?" Jack stood a couple of feet away.

John moved me aside, and rushed toward Jack. Grabbing the front of his jersey, John shoved him against the wall. They were about the same height and build, but John's anger gave him the upper hand.

"Don't you ever speak to my wife again," John said quietly through his teeth.

Jack pushed back and John stepped away, coming over to me. "Save it for the field, Meinrad. You're going to need it out there." Jack walked away.

"What's his deal?"

I turned at the sound of Jos de Haven's voice. He came into the hallway from the locker room.

"Nothing," John said. "Are you ready for this? It's been a long time since we played together. I hope I can keep up with you and the rest of the guys who do this for a living." John bent over to straighten his socks.

"So, how are things, Hatty?" Jos gave me a bear hug. "I keep meaning to get in touch with Astrid so Gabs and I can arrange a time to come see you."

"We'd love it. How about sometime this summer?" Jos and Gabs were an adorable couple.

"I think that would work out nicely for us. There's something we want to discuss with the two of you." Jos looked around to verify we were alone. "It took us a long time before Gabs got pregnant with Alina. It was our first in vitro cycle that made it happen."

"I had no idea," John said.

"No one knows we got pregnant that way. Not even our family. But when I heard you and Hatty were getting help, I just wanted to say… well, it's a lonely road, brother." Jos' eyes welled up. Was this hulking man on the verge of tears before what was sure to be a brutal match?

John nodded, his face blank. My husband hated everyone knowing that we were having trouble getting pregnant. Cilla and I talked him out of calling *Xpress* and demanding they retract the story with the "Barren-ness" headline. I didn't show him the latest meme using my messy hair photo. Someone added the caption "Bad heir day" after *Xpress'* story about our infertility broke. I feared he'd try to call Google and ask them to stop including it in search results.

Jos slapped John on the back and sniffed loudly. He wiped his nose with the back of his hand. "Alright. Let's go kill somebody." Jos headed back into the locker room.

I gave John a quick kiss on the lips. "If you do kill someone, make sure it's Jack."

Team Led by de Haven Crushes Opponents in Charity Rugby Match

INCONCEIVABLE!

By Alain Schwartz
April 25, 2015

Jos de Haven and his Blue team, which included Toulene's Prince John, dealt a serious blow to the opposing side earlier today during a match at Pentuk.

De Haven's rivals were the Red team, led by Daniel O'Shea. One of O'Shea's teammates, Jacques Giteau, took a particularly hard tackle from de Haven and Prince John. Paramedics had to take Giteau off the field on a stretcher. Organizers of the match said Giteau was resting and was expected to make a full recovery. Proceeds from the match benefit a school and orphanage in Ethiopia. Final totals weren't available yet, but organizers expected to raise €50,000.

CHAPTER FORTY-THREE

The queen and I sat alone reading in the parlor after dinner. John and Leopold were playing darts in the game room on the other side of the palace. The queen had summoned us to Belvoir to celebrate John completing his Ph.D. With Henri, Adela, and Baby Juan on vacation in southern France, it was a quiet meal.

The queen closed her book. "Hatty. What's all this business about you and John trying to have a baby?"

"We've been hoping to get pregnant for a while now. We may see a doctor when we're in the U.S. in August for our friends' wedding."

"I trust you'll have Lars take care of all the security and paperwork. The privacy laws are different in your country."

"Yes, Your Majesty. And Toulene is my country now." I set down my book.

"I hope for your sake this American doctor is very good."

"For my sake?"

"Yes. If you're unable to get pregnant, John will divorce you." She didn't blink as she stared at me.

"I don't believe you."

"Under our laws, the only obligation you have as his wife is to produce an heir. Failure to do so nullifies the marriage."

"Which is it? He'll divorce me or you'll request our marriage be annulled?" *Get you story straight, Queenie.*

"If he refuses to divorce you, I'll order the marriage annulled. Either way, he'll be free to find a new wife who can fulfill her obligations to our country."

The injustice of her words choked me. I cleared my throat. "But it's not my fault! The doctor said we don't know why we can't get pregnant!"

"Everyone knows you slept with that rugby player before you met John. I was willing to look the other way because you came to us with no other baggage. But now that you're unable to accomplish one of the most basic biological functions, I'm withdrawing my support."

"So, let me get this right. You don't want a wife for John. You want a body to carry his baby." I nearly spat the words at her.

"I want him to have both. John needs a partner who can help him give our country the one thing only he and Henri can provide: heirs."

She stood, and so did I.

"I'll be damned if you're going to destroy my marriage. I told Leo to shove it, as you probably know, and now I'm respectfully passing along the same memo to you, too... Your Majesty."

I walked out of the room and went into the service stairwell. I huffed, out of breath and horrified by the queen's threat to annul my marriage.

I texted John: *I've decided. We will definitely do IVF in St. Louis.*

Within seconds, he texted back: *If you're sure, then I'm on board. I'll call Lars in the morning.*

PART III

CHAPTER FORTY-FOUR

F resh sunshine penetrated the shutters we'd closed the night before, breathing life into the villa's bedroom. Even though our bodies were still adjusting to Maui's time zone, the sun called us to come and play. I wanted to tell the sun to shut up and go away so I could sleep.

I rolled over and inhaled sharply. "Oh, God. You scared me."

John was lying there awake and staring at me. I yawned, careful to blow my morning breath out the side of my mouth, away from John.

Instead of speaking, John reached over, cradled the back of my head in his hand, and began kissing me. His movements took on a sense of urgency.

He continued to hold my head while his other hand navigated the sheet and comforter to find the bottom of the long shirt I wore. With one quick movement, he pulled it up. My hunger for him flared when I saw he'd removed his boxers while I'd slept.

Unlike many of our intimate encounters during the last year, the timing of this one didn't match-up with my ovulation. We just wanted it. He took me with unusual force, and I responded purely from instinct. I didn't think about whether the position of our bodies would make it easy for the sperm to reach an egg.

After a few brief moments of intensity, I expected this bliss to end as abruptly as it had started. But instead of hitting a high point, John stopped moving, grasped my hips, and turned me over.

This definitely isn't sex for procreation. I got on all fours. It was a position we hadn't used in a very long time, but it felt so good, illicit even. That thought pushed me over the edge mere moments before John went over it, too. As his movement slowed, his breath sounded more ragged than normal and his hands continued to grasp my sides. I turned and looked up at his tear-streaked face.

I turned and melted into him. "What's wrong?"

I stroked his hair as he hastily wiped at the tears. This was the first time I'd seen him cry.

"I think about it all the time, how to fix it. What's it going to take to get you pregnant? But just this once, I wanted to have you. I wanted sex to be about me and you, not about the baby." His face was damp from sweat and tears.

"Good work. I definitely wasn't thinking about sex for procreation just now." I winked and smiled, a lame attempt to lighten his mood.

He grabbed the glass of water on the nightstand and took a long drink. "This baby, who doesn't even exist, controls us. He's always around. It's like he's waiting just off stage. And nothing I do can bring him into the light. I don't know how much longer I can stand it. Sometimes, I hate him. I'd go to the fucking ends of the earth for him, but I hate him for what he's done to us."

"What do you mean, 'done to us?'"

"The thought of what you're going to do to your body for the IVF cycle is killing me. I hate watching you go through this for me and my family, for the whole country."

"News Flash: I'm not going through all these hoops to get pregnant for your family or the country. Even if we were just Joe and Mary Smith, I'd be this intent on making it happen. I don't care about conceiving the future king of Toulene. I want to be the mother of your children." I stroked his hair and face.

He kissed me, placing his hands on my cheeks before leaving the bedroom.

I stayed on my back in bed. "Fine, God. I'll try to pray because I feel like I'm being punished or taught a lesson, and I can't take it anymore. Neither can John." I clenched my fists. "Please, please make me a mother. And if you can't or won't, stop this pain for both of us by just erasing the desire for children from our hearts and minds. Take it away. Take it away!"

I wiped at the tears that oozed down my temples.

Prince John and Hatty Search for Answers to Fertility Problem
By Clarence Watson
August 3, 2015

Prince John and Duchess Hatty are taking an extended tour of the United States, but only after reportedly visiting a doctor of Chinese medicine in Toulene for acupuncture treatments.

"It's clear the desperation is setting in if they're looking at alternative therapies to help them get pregnant," said, Nic Capucine, a longtime observer of the royal family.

During their visit to the states, the couple will spend a week in Maui, and then attend the wedding of two friends in Iowa. Next, they'll travel to Missouri where Prince John will spend several weeks in St. Louis meeting with local and state officials to learn about the environmental problems that led to the closure of the lead smelter in Herculaneum, Missouri.

A press release from the palace about the couple's visit to America said the prince hopes he can gain insights from Missouri officials as Toulene's government considers what to do with the smelter near Kortrijk. There are still occasional protests meant to highlight claims that pollution from the facility is causing health problems for local residents.

Representatives for Prince John and Duchess Hatty had no comment on reports of the couple's ongoing infertility struggles.

CHAPTER FORTY-FIVE

After the acupuncturist came to the townhouse we were renting in St Louis, John and I headed to Zia's. It was a lovely little place on The Hill, a neighborhood renowned for its Italian restaurants. The owner let us have a private room anytime we wanted to dine there.

When we finished eating, I checked my phone. "It's time. Do you mind if I do it here at the table?"

"Of course not," John said, and he pulled out his phone.

He was reading a book by Dr. Matt Marche, the man overseeing our IVF cycle. It explained the process in detail. There was a list of the drugs we'd use to suppress my body's natural cycle so we could accelerate the growth of follicles on my ovaries. The book outlined the surgery I'd have to remove the eggs from the follicles so Dr. Marche could work his petri dish magic. He'd inject John's sperm directly into each egg. If the eggs and sperm fell in love and stuck together, the doctor would then transfer the resulting embryos from the petri dish to my uterus. All the while, I'd continue injecting myself with the medications that kept my body on track to nurture these little lives. *Freaking amazing.*

I removed the "pen" from its case and made sure I had the appropriate dose remaining. I twisted the top and set it on the table. We'd had a private class with a nurse to learn how to do all the injections for the cycle. I pinched the flesh on my abdomen, inserted the needle at the end of the pen, and released the skin. Then, I pushed the top down until it clicked.

As I removed the thin needle, I looked up and saw John watching me. "I love you more than you'll ever know." He reached over and squeezed my hand.

"If that's true, then grow a beard."

Since we'd been in the states, he'd gone a day here and there without shaving, just long enough to achieve a nice five o'clock shadow. I hadn't thought it was possible for him to be any sexier until I saw his scruffy face.

"You know what? With all the stuff you're doing to your body, growing a beard is the least I can do to be a supportive husband." He handed me the small round bandage to cover the place where I'd inserted the needle.

"Are you serious? Don't tease me. Ozarks girls totally dig beards."

"I'm serious. No more shaving until the end of our two-week wait after the embryo transfer."

"I'm holding you to it, mister!" I leaned in and kissed his lips. "That'll feel different when your beard comes in. So sexy. And speaking of beards, I still can't believe Sam had a beard for their wedding!"

"Plato grew up in Iowa. Maybe he likes beards too. Have you heard from them since they left for Ethiopia?"

"Plato sent me a photo of Sam on top of a building. He said they were installing a new roof on an orphanage."

"Celebrating their love by showing love to others. It makes perfect sense." John picked up the needle pen from the table and handed it to me.

"You know, they want me to come with them to Ethiopia sometime.

"I certainly wouldn't want you going there once you're pregnant. Maybe after Baby King's a bit older."

Before we left the sanctuary of our little room at Zia's, I opened my large purse and placed the needle in the bright red sharps disposal bin I had to carry with me.

"I'm glad I caught you before your hot date," I said into the phone. I was elated that Tilda had finally found someone who made her swoon.

"Please. We're literally going for coffee. Boring." The delight in her voice betrayed her words.

"Well, I always knew you'd find a man who wasn't intimidated by your beauty and success."

"Okay. Enough talk about me and Kellan. How are things going there?"

"So far, we're on track. They had to increase the dosage for my ovary stimulating drugs because my follicles weren't growing as fast or as big as they wanted. I go back for an ultrasound tomorrow to check for progress."

I left out the part about how, during the first two ultrasounds, the technician had failed to find any measurable follicles. Without big follicles, Dr. Marche would cancel the cycle.

"Did your parents come to St. Louis?"

"No. We're planning to visit them after the embryo transfer. I just want to focus on taking care of myself and being with John."

"So, have you told him about your conversation with the queen?"

"Not yet. I just don't know how to bring it up."

"How about we hang up right now, and you walk over to him and say, 'Hey! Your grandmother says she's going to order an annulment of our marriage if we can't get pregnant. What are you going to do about it?'"

"Like it's that easy."

"It is. Didn't you learn how to ask tough questions in one of your journalism classes?"

"Okay, I'll do it. But only because I can't stand having the weight of this on me."

"And the stress could impact the success of the cycle. I'm going to let you go. We'll talk again after you've got those little babies nesting in your uterus. Love you! Miss you!"

After I hung up, I walked downstairs. John was running on the treadmill we had set up in the spare bedroom.

"Can I talk to you?"

"Of course." He kept running without slowing down.

"Okay. Well, before we left Toulene…"

"Sorry. Could you hand me that towel?"

I grabbed it from the bed and slung it across the side of the machine.

"Now what were you going to tell me?" He scrutinized the meters on the treadmill's control panel as he wiped the sweat from his neck.

"Never mind. We'll talk about it later. But let me ask you something else. Would you ever consider adoption?"

He kept jogging with his eyes on the digital display. "I've never considered it because it's not possible. We have strict laws in Toulene about the line of succession, including a restriction that says only a natural-born son is considered an heir."

"But how can you just dismiss the idea? I grew up with a girl who was adopted from China. Her parents also adopted a girl from Korea. They were such a sweet family."

"I'm sure they were. And adoption is beautiful but it's not for us." He stopped the treadmill, wiped his face, kissed me on the forehead, and walked out of the room.

John had just raised the stakes for our IVF cycle. I had held adoption in the back of my mind as the ultimate Plan B if we couldn't get pregnant. Now, that wasn't even an option. I went to our bedroom upstairs, opened my laptop, and began typing a long post to the women on the infertility discussion boards. I needed to vent.

"We removed all three. Dr. Marche's office has the eggs and your sperm," Dr. Barnes said to John.

I kept my eyes closed as I lay on the hospital bed, the perfect set-up for eavesdropping.

"So, his office will call and tell us what happens next?" John's voice revealed his stress.

"That's right. You know, we were lucky to get three eggs because her ovaries had a surprisingly weak response to the stimulating drugs. If you end up doing another cycle, at least we'll know to start her on a stronger dose right from the beginning. She should wake up soon, and the nurse will be in to check on her shortly."

I heard footsteps as Dr. Barnes left the room. He had done the egg retrieval; Dr. Marche would oversee the petri dish work and then transfer the embryos to my uterus in five days.

I kept my eyes closed. Three eggs retrieved. *Suck it, infertility!* I silently thanked God. The ultrasounds leading up to the retrieval revealed three follicles was the best my body could do, even with a high dosage of the follicle stimulating drugs. It was a depressingly low number for a woman my age. Most women in their twenties who do IVF produce eight or more eggs with one IVF cycle. At least, that's what I'd gleaned from the infertility discussion boards. More eggs meant a better chance of having embryos left over to freeze and use later. I did feel grateful for the three little eggs my body had grown to maturity. It certainly could've been worse.

"Hey. How do you feel?" John asked, walking over to my hospital bed.

"Sleepy. Happy. He got three, right?"

"Three little miracles. Dr. Barnes says they're on their way to

Dr. Marche so he can inject the sperm and wait for them to grow into embryos. Hatty, I think we've found the answer. I believe it's going to happen." He tucked my hair behind my ears.

"Me too." I closed my eyes. "Give me my phone, please." I dialed my mom's cell phone. She answered immediately.

"What's the news?" Anxiety rang in my mom's voice.

"Three. They got three eggs." *Happy dance!*

"Oh, hon. That's wonderful. We're so excited for you. Do you need anything?" My mom wanted to be right in the middle of our IVF drama, so I appreciated her willingness to keep a respectable distance. I just wanted to keep this low key and low stress.

"No. We're fine."

"Are you and John still planning to come down here after the embryo transfer?"

"Yes, as long as there aren't any hitches. We don't know how many of those eggs will become embryos. There might not be anything to transfer." The very thought of failing at this point made me want to hurl. Surely, *surely* it would work.

"Hatty, I want to tell you something."

I waited and heard her fidgeting.

"Your dad and I tried to give you a brother or sister."

"What do you mean?"

"We tried for years to get pregnant after you were born. But it never happened. My doctor could never figure out the problem. It took us two years to get pregnant with you."

"But I thought you guys only wanted one child." I remembered the conversations we'd had from time to time when I was young. The issue of a sibling came up whenever one of my friends welcomed a new baby sister or brother.

"It was just easier to explain it that way instead of sharing our heartbreak with you."

"So, what does that mean?" Admittedly, I was a little pissed they'd lied to me.

"It means I understand how you feel. And I'm proud of you and John for pursuing your dream to be parents, even with all the mean things they say about you in the tabloids. It's a testament to how much you love your child."

My free hand reached down to my abdomen; it would soon hold my baby.

"Thanks, mom. I love you."

"I love you too. Call me after the embryo transfer and let me know how it goes. We'll see you in a few days."

The metal stirrups were cold enough to penetrate through my socks, making me shiver.

Before I could truly ponder the awkwardness of my body's position, Dr. Marche spoke. "Hatty, I need you to scoot your bottom down to the end of the table."

I did as he asked, putting myself in just the right position for the embryo transfer.

"John, talk to her. Help her relax." Dr. Marche reached around to the tray behind him.

"We're walking down the beach, feeling the water as it runs over our toes." John spoke soothingly.

Dr. Marche didn't believe in using anesthesia for the embryo transfer, preferring the patient to stay awake but completely relaxed. As John kept talking through the guided meditation, Dr. Marche turned back to me with a metal instrument in his hand. It looked like there was a string of spaghetti on the end. I knew it held the three embryos, three little spheres of potential life. They'd outgrown their petri dish and needed a home. I could give them one.

In a matter of a few more moments, Dr. Marche was done. "It was flawless, Hatty. Let me help you up."

With him and John on each side of me, I removed my feet from the stirrups and stood. They helped me to the recovery room next door where I was allowed to lie down for a few minutes.

"Stay here as long as you wish, but there's no medical need to rest. You're free to go whenever you feel ready."

"And what about sex?" John asked.

"I'd recommend waiting five days. You're good to resume normal sexual activity after that."

Before Dr. Marche left the room, I said, "Thank you. Thank you, so much."

"You're most welcome."

When he was gone, John whispered. "Normal sexual activity, huh? I wonder what he considers abnormal sexual activity?" I laughed and appreciated John's ability to interject some levity into the moment. The hard part was behind us.

I closed my eyes and imagined the embryos floating inside my uterus and willed them to find a soft, welcoming spot to land. There was only a one percent chance all three would survive, but I sometimes imagined life with triplets. It would be like a starving person devouring a large pizza in one sitting: overwhelming and divine.

CHAPTER FORTY-SIX

The Fairfield Dairy here in Nixa made an ice cream flavor in honor of your visit: Chocolate Royale! And we're going to serve it for dessert." The pastor of my parents' church boomed into the microphone.

The fifty people gathered in the fellowship hall cheered and laughed at his announcement.

After the embryo transfer, John had three days of smelter-related meetings in St. Louis. Then, we'd boarded a chartered plane and flew to Springfield with Astrid and our guards in tow. My parents met us in the General Aviation lobby and drove us to their house in Nixa. To wrap up our visit, we were about to enjoy Sunday lunch with some church folks.

"Hatty, John. Before we eat, I'd like to say a blessing over you."

I nodded. This was par for the course in my corner of Missouri.

"Heavenly Father, thank you for bringing Hatty and John here to us. And we thank you for Hatty's precious parents who raised such a God-fearing daughter. We thank you for the leadership you've entrusted to John and Hatty, and ask that you give them both wisdom as they guide their country in a way that honors and glorifies you. Now, bless this food to the nourishment of our bodies and bless the hands that prepared it. Amen."

I doubted John had ever been the object of this kind of prayer. He grinned and looked appreciative, even though this form of religion was completely foreign to him. We sat at a table with my parents, three members of the United Methodist Women's group, and Nixa's mayor.

"Hatty, you're positively glowing. Married life agrees with you, sweetie."

"Thank you, Mrs. Hammond. I'm very happy."

"Don't worry about getting pregnant. I know it'll happen in the Lord's time."

Is it the Lord's time for me to crawl under the table to escape this conversation, Mrs. Hammond? "Yes. Thank you. We're just trying to be patient."

I reached under the table and squeezed John's leg.

"What are we having for lunch? I hear you ladies are wonderful cooks." He knew how to redirect conversations like a pro.

"Well, it's a chicken casserole Mildred makes only on very special occasions." Mrs. Hammond gave a little nod to Mildred Hagler who sat beside my mom.

"It sounds delicious," John said with a smile. I was fairly certain he'd never tasted a casserole in his life.

"Well, John, were your meetings in St. Louis productive?" I didn't know Mayor Jim Swafford, but my parents disliked him. How obnoxious of him to ask about such a sensitive issue.

"Yes, they were. Thank you for asking."

We listened as the mayor droned on about the importance of protecting watersheds, an issue near and dear to his heart, he said, as long as it didn't impinge on the city's budget priorities. I quieted my desire to put on my reporter's hat and call out the contradictions in what he said.

After lunch, I lost track of how many dead-fish handshakes I endured; it didn't bother me in the slightest because each person at the church loved my family. John had multiple lipstick prints on his cheeks.

When we were outside the church with my parents, I handed John a tissue. "Here. The ladies of Nixa United Methodist Church marked you."

"They're lovely."

"They're my people. This is where I'm from. Now you know why I'm so direct. People here don't pussyfoot around sensitive issues."

"Did you just say 'pussyfoot?'" He gave me a wicked smile.

"Oh, no. Look at the time. We need to head out," I said, not wanting my parents to hear John mistakenly imply the word "pussyfoot" had something to do with sex. *Très embarrassing.*

"I can't believe you have to go back to Toulene already! Four days isn't enough time." Mom embraced me.

"I know. But you guys can come this fall or for Christmas. You can help me decorate the nursery." My hand dropped to my lower abdomen. "Just a week and a half until we find out if it worked."

"Oh honey, it will. I'm sure of it." Mom gave me another squeeze.

Then it was Dad's turn. He gave me and John big hugs. "Let us know if you need anything."

"I will, Dad. I love you."

"John, take good care of my girl."

"I always do, sir."

CHAPTER FORTY-SEVEN

John reorganized the book shelves. Then, he dusted the TV screen. This was the first time I'd ever seen him do any cleaning.

"I can start up an aerobics routine, if you want, so you'll have something to do," I teased.

"What are you talking about? I don't need anything to do." He rubbed the dust off a vase with the bottom of his T-shirt. "What time are they supposed to call?" John's hair looked exceptionally unkempt and gorgeous.

"I don't know. Sometime this afternoon. You're the future king. Can't you go down there and demand they give us the results right now?"

I'd gone to Dr. Dreesen's office that morning for a blood draw so they could run a pregnancy test.

"How are you so relaxed?" He ran his hand through his hair, his eyes wider than normal.

"It's out of our hands. There's nothing we can do at this point to change the outcome. Why worry?"

The truth was I'd peed on a stick every day since I'd gotten an injection of the pregnancy hormone to prepare my eggs for retrieval. The first pregnancy test produced bold, brightly colored double lines. But I couldn't celebrate because it was due to the shot. Then, each morning, the second line got lighter. Until one day, it didn't. It was about the same intensity as it had been the day before. I knew this because I kept all the tests and lined them up for comparison. Then, the second line started to get darker in the days that followed. John was in on my little experiment. While the continued positive tests were wildly encouraging, we remained cautious; only a blood test would confirm it was a pregnancy and not just residual hormones from the shot.

Just then, my phone rang out its melodic tone. It was Dr. Dreesen's office.

"This is Hatty," I said, activating the speaker.

"It's Dr. Dreesen. Your beta number is one hundred! Hatty, you're pregnant!"

I gasped and my vision blurred with tears. Hearing those words meant more than the double lines on the pregnancy test. John wiped at his eyes.

"Thank God! I'm so relieved. What happens next?" I was eager to do whatever was necessary to keep the pregnancy chugging right along.

"You need to come back Monday morning, and we'll do another blood test. We'll want to see the beta number continue to rise to confirm the pregnancy's progressing as it should."

We cleared one hurdle, but a track full of obstacles was ahead of us and we'd have to clear each one over the next nine months. I tamped down the worry and allowed myself to celebrate the news I'd waited so long to hear.

When we ended the call, John scooped me up in his arms and kissed me deeply. He carried me into our bedroom and shut the door.

"Mom? I'm pregnant."

"Oh, thank the Lord! How wonderful!" Her voice broke on the

last word and she sniffed.

"I've got to go back to the doctor's office Monday and make sure my beta numbers go up. What if they don't? I'm so worried. How did you stay calm when you were pregnant with me?"

"I wasn't relaxed. I worried every minute of every day until I held you in my arms. And after you were born, the worry grew. That's what parents do—obsess over their children. Welcome to parenthood. You're going to be a wonderful mother."

The jingle-tingle of the queen's bell quieted the family's noisy chatter in the dining room. She raised a glass.

"Tonight, we celebrate the wonderful news John and Hatty received this week. She has the future of our family growing in her womb. We're thankful and relieved."

My face flushed as heat rose to my cheeks. *Relieved? Ugh.*

"On the heels of this blessed announcement, I have a bit of news to share myself," the queen continued. I looked at John and he gave a little shrug and shook his head.

"I will be abdicating and passing the crown to Leo at the beginning of next month. And when I leave for Thailand this time, I'll be moving there permanently."

Only Leo and Aunt Elinore didn't have a shocked look on their face.

"Granny, are you sure you're ready for this? It's a huge decision," John said. This move put him literally one heartbeat away from being king.

"My dear, I'm completely ready and the time is right. With Juan and your baby on the way, the future of the family is secure. I've been thinking about this for a long time."

No one else spoke up. It was a retirement announcement, and no one seemed to know how to react.

Herr Schroeder entered, followed by staff carrying trays of food.

The meal began and the casual banter slowly returned.

I leaned over to John and pretended to wipe my mouth with a napkin. "What about Louisa?" Leo's mistress had become a fixture at Belvoir. I was surprised she wasn't joining us for dinner.

John shook his head, and I dropped it. But I was curious how this turn of events would impact her.

I looked at my profile in the big bathroom mirror. I was only wearing panties so I could see the full length of my upper body. Even though I knew there was no way I'd have a bump this early, I couldn't resist looking. I closed my eyes and imagined what it would feel like when my abdomen was full and round with new life.

So far, everything with the baby was right on track with my beta numbers increasing at the right pace. John reached around me from behind and put a hand on my lower abdomen.

"I've never seen you like this. There's a glow about you." He swept my hair aside and kissed the back of my neck.

"Okay. I'm sorry to break the mood. But now can I ask you about Louisa?" *Inquiring minds need to know what the heck's happening!*

He frowned. "He'll either have to marry her or end it. Their relationship can't continue the way it is."

"And you want him to end it. What do you think he sees in her?"

"I think he sees a bit of my mother."

"What? I can't believe you'd think that. They look nothing alike and more importantly, Louisa can't compete with the grace and kindness your mother seemed to have."

"I don't mean they're truly alike, but I think Louisa's youth helps him relive the way he felt when he and my mother were young. I don't know if that's true or if it even makes sense, but that's the only way I can stand to think of it. Otherwise, it's just about the sex."

"You're making me blush, Your Highness."

"I'm about to make you do a lot more than that."

He spun me around to face him. Pressing my almost-naked body into his, he kissed me before stepping back to remove his clothes.

CHAPTER FORTY-EIGHT

I placed my feet in stirrups and waited for the ultrasound tech to return to the room. I was naked from the waist down except for a thin sheet spread across my lap. It reminded me of my only infertility-related appointment with Dr. Cloutier.

There was a brief knock before the handle turned and a woman who looked about my age entered the room.

"This is a trans-vaginal ultrasound, just like the ones you had to monitor the follicles during the IVF cycle." She picked up the wand with her gloved hand.

"Too bad that thing doesn't vibrate." I forced a nervous chuckle.

"Who says it doesn't?" She raised an eyebrow and laughed.

I lifted my head and craned my neck to see the monitor as she inserted the wand and moved it around.

"I see the sac. I'm looking for a heartbeat." She stared intently at the screen.

I took a deep breath and waited. I counted the squares on the ceiling.

"Any luck?" I asked, trying to sound cheerful.

"No. I can't find it."

"What does that mean?" Panic rose in my throat.

Her friendly demeanor evaporated. "It may be too early for a heartbeat. Your doctor's office will call you with the results."

As soon as she left the room, I got out my phone and called Dr. Dreesen's office. I asked the nurse to have someone call me as soon as they had the images from the ultrasound because I was worried.

I got dressed, gathered my things, and met John in the private room where he was waiting. I didn't say anything.

"Well?"

"No heartbeat. The tech said it might be too early though."

Just then, my phone rang. I put Dr. Dreesen on speakerphone.

"The sac measured four weeks and four days. That's too small for a heartbeat. At this point, you shouldn't worry. But at your next ultrasound in three weeks, we definitely have to see a heartbeat. For now, relax and just give me a call if you need anything."

We rode in the back of the car in heavy silence, both of us uneasy. When we arrived at Langbroek, dusk was erasing the day, darkening the sky into night. We went into the bedroom and shut the door. I didn't think the sac measurement was right for how far along I was supposed to be. The inconsistency niggled my brain.

"Are you going to get the progesterone?" I called after John as he went into the bathroom.

"Yes."

"Would you mind getting the ice pack? I don't think I can handle it unless you numb me up first."

John had to administer intramuscular shots of progesterone in oil each night. He gave the shot below my waist between my lower back and rear. Even though we alternated sides, that entire area was incredibly tender. I couldn't even wear jeans anymore because the waistband rubbed against those painful spots.

I pulled my sweatpants and underwear just below my rump and felt the chill of the ice pack as he gently set it on my lower back. He ran his fingers over my flesh as we waited.

"Okay. I think it's numb." I grabbed a gulp of air and held it in anticipation.

John pinched a section of my skin, and inserted the needle. As he released his pinch, I exhaled, feeling the sharpness travel through my muscle millimeter by millimeter. He slowly pressed down on the syringe and I gritted my teeth against tears as the medicine entered my body. Even as he pulled it out, the needle continued to assault my muscle, sending out pulses of pain.

"Baby King had better appreciate all this." I wiped my eyes.

"You're doing an amazing job. I love you."

I looked up at him as he sat on the bed beside me. "If this doesn't work, are you going to leave me?"

"No. I won't leave you. No matter what happens. Why would you even ask such a question?"

"So, will your family exile us if I can't get pregnant? The queen told me she'd have our marriage annulled."

"She won't. She'll get over it."

As we kissed, he finished undressing me.

After we were spent, I rolled over and laid my head on his chest. "You know, Plato wants me to go to Ethiopia. I know you don't like it, but don't you think a pregnant lady could make that journey?"

"Only if her knight in shining armor accompanies her."

"Too bad I married a prince." He smiled and rolled his eyes. "C'mon. I'm only teasing."

We left Langbroek to spend some quiet time in De Haan. John thought I'd feel more relaxed at our beachside cottage during the first trimester. Brigitta came with us so I wouldn't have to cook, unless I wanted to whip up something. Unlike most pregnant women, I didn't dread the weird cravings or morning sickness. I'd longed for this experience, and I wasn't going to complain about any of the unpleasant aspects of pregnancy—I finally had what I wanted.

As we walked on the beach in the early evening, my tennis shoes sinking into the soft sand, I picked up shells and put them in a little plastic bucket.

"Did you know today's Halloween?" I added a conk shell to my collection.

"No. Growing up, I envied American kids and their Halloween fun. I wanted to dress up and ask my neighbors for candy."

"It was always one of my favorite holidays when I was little. My mom decorated the house with cardboard cut-outs of skeletons and scarecrows. And I loved letting my imagination go wild with costume planning. One year, I was the ghost of Marilyn Monroe. I remember thinking I had to be her ghost because just going as Marilyn wasn't original enough. I had this sheer dress, big earrings, and a platinum blonde wig we borrowed from a woman in our neighborhood. She'd worn it after her hair fell out during chemo. Isn't that crazy?" I took John's hand.

"Please tell me your mum has photographic proof of you wearing someone's chemo wig."

"I'm sure there are pictures. But you wouldn't have known it was a chemo wig if I hadn't told you!"

As we walked, I had the sensation of peeing on myself. "That's strange." I hadn't relaxed my bladder.

"Hatty! You're bleeding!" John yelled.

I looked down at my sweatpants and dropped the bucket. Instead of urine, a dark red stain spread from my crotch, creeping down the inside of both pant legs.

"What's happening? I need to get to a hospital!"

We looked around us. The beach appeared deserted. I looked way down the shore to our cottage. A single Royal Guard stood on the stairs leading up to our house, but he was too far away to hear us. We saw a man near the dunes, sitting on a blanket.

"Hey!" John said, waving his arms frantically.

The man got up and jogged toward us as I hobbled, not in pain but in hopes of preventing any additional bleeding. John had his phone out and was punching the touchscreen frantically.

"Oh, madam. Are you okay?" The man looked at my pants. Then realization dawned on his face as he looked from me to John and back to me. "Duchess, let me help you."

At the same time, I heard John yelling into the phone. "Send someone down the beach. Something's wrong with Hatty!"

As the man and John helped me hobble toward the cottage, I tried to think rationally for a moment. Was there any possible explanation for what was happening?

I looked down at my pants, evaluating the quantity of blood. It no longer felt like it was pouring out of my body, but the warm, sticky liquid had spread farther down both legs. There was no way this was normal.

Blink, Hatty. When my eyes fluttered, tears spilled onto my cheeks.

Bernard ran toward us, pointing to a parking lot to our right, just off the beach. I heard the wail of the siren before I saw the pulsing red lights of the ambulance. It made me think of the blood pulsing and leaking out of my uterus. As I looked at the men unloading the white stretcher, I realized there was only one plausible explanation for what was happening: miscarriage.

The curtain provided a thin barrier between me and the hubbub of the emergency room. An invisible hand squeezed my uterus producing agonizing cramps. I curled up my legs in hopes of making it stop.

Despite the pain and the gravity of the situation, I babbled nonsensically. "Did you know in Germany, they call ambulances 'Krankenwagens?' It sounds like 'cranky wagon.' I can't believe I had to come here in a cranky wagon. I'm sure everything's going to be fine. Just peachy, because there's no way you can come this far and have your pregnancy go to pot."

"Hatty, the doctor's here." John rubbed his eyes.

A tall man with dark hair walked to my bedside.

"Your beta numbers are low. You're having a miscarriage. Did you even know you were pregnant?"

I let out a single, choked laugh. I wanted to spit in his face.

"Yes. We knew," John said quietly.

"I need to go to the bathroom."

John helped me up and I realized there was a gigantic, thick pad between my legs. It felt like I was straddling a hay bale. When did that get there?

I waddled into the tiny bathroom. When I was done, there was a streak of blood on my hand. I glanced in the toilet bowl. The water was bright red and filled with black clots. Part of a Bible verse came to mind: "The wages of sin is death."

My baby was in pieces, floating in the hospital toilet.

"This is death," I said aloud.

Then, I wailed, my throat producing a sound I'd never heard before.

John was by my side in an instant, holding me up, preventing me from crumpling. He carried me back to the bed. And just like that, exhaustion overtook me. I stilled my body and let John rub the blood off my hand with a rough white washcloth. The metallic smell rankled my stomach.

The doctor wrote something on his clipboard.

"We'll go ahead and send you home. You'll need to visit your doctor in a week to see if your body has cleared all the tissue or if you'll need a D and C. If you're in pain, I can write you a prescription for something that will help." The doctor's professional demeanor irritated me.

"Yes, I'm in pain," I whispered.

"Would you like the nurse to send this to the hospital pharmacy? It's open late."

"Yes, please," John said.

I reached for the doctor as he started to go. "Do I need to keep doing the progesterone shots?"

"This was an IVF cycle?"

"Yes."

"Then continue the shots until your obstetrician tells you to stop."

The doctor left and I closed my eyes.

A loud crash interrupted my thoughts. I opened my eyes and saw the little metal trash can overturned. John had apparently kicked it over. He was digging the heels of his hands into his eyes and rubbing.

"Don't. You can't fall apart now," I said, shaken, even in my state, by John's outburst.

He inhaled noisily and pulled his hands away from his face.

"Let's get you out of here," he said.

We'd come to the emergency room without my purse, and I'd arrived in the blood-soaked sweats. A nurse brought me a set of blue scrubs, and John helped me slide them on.

Shakiness took hold of me as an orderly held my arm and supported my back. I lowered myself into a wheelchair. He spread a white sheet over my lap before rolling me through a side door where our black car was waiting. John ran back inside and got my medicine from the pharmacy. We rode to our cottage in silence.

Booters, my little gray cat, followed me into the bathroom. I closed the door and scooped him up. He let me cradle him like a baby. I held him and wept, crying from the depths of my emptying womb. He didn't wiggle or try to escape. I spoke softly: "Why?" I repeated it over and over again, a dirge for my baby.

I don't know how much time passed before I set Booters on the counter and went to the toilet. The bowl again filled with bright red blood and blackish clots, but they weren't big enough to warrant another trip to the ER. The nurse said I shouldn't come back unless they were larger than a quarter. The cramping had eased under the influence of the pain medication.

I grabbed a clean pair of sweats and one of John's old T-shirts.

When I went back into our bedroom, John was there. "If you feel up to it, we'll go back to Roeselare tomorrow. I spoke to Astrid and she's made an appointment for you to see Dr. Dreesen." He paused, looking uncertain. "It's time for the progesterone shot."

"No. There's no way I'm doing any more of those shots. If there was a baby in me, it's gone now. I'm not torturing myself anymore."

I rolled over and buried my body under the heaping covers. John set down his phone, and crawled onto the bed. He stayed on top of the blankets and put his arm around me.

"I'm sorry, Hatty. I'm so sorry," he whispered.

"Me, too." I let the black curtain of a heavy sleep close over me while John held me tightly.

We shared news of the miscarriage by phone with my parents and John's father the next day. I wanted to get it done because telling it meant reliving it. Both calls included the requisite untruth: "I feel fine. I'll be okay. I don't need anything."

While my parents shared my agony in their tearful, quiet way, John's father responded with predictable disappointment devoid of sympathy. Leopold insisted this was a good test run, and assumed we'd do another cycle right away. He also said this would not change the queen's plans to abdicate.

When we got home to Langbroek, I sat on our bed, staring out the floor-to-ceiling window, seeing nothing. Thinking nothing. Feeling nothing. My heart thumped inside a cocoon of numbness. I'd unpacked my emotions and reached the bottom of the suitcase. Instead of finding a secret stash of peace or comfort, I found nothing. It was empty. *Barren.* The only emotion that sometimes crept up on me was a sense of wonder at my inability to cry more. The tears had dried up after those phone calls to our parents. An accusatory voice in my head snipped, *What kind of mother will you be if you can't wail and scream over the loss of your baby?*

"Hey. Do you need anything?" John sat beside me on the bed, taking my hand.

"Do you?" Kicking that trash can at the ER was the only emotional release I'd witnessed from him.

He pinched the place above his nose and closed his eyes. "No." He raised his head and looked out the window. "I don't know what's next."

I pushed out a gush of air. "Do we just go on with normal life?"

"I don't know what normal is anymore." He squeezed my hand, walked to the bathroom, and closed the door. I'd heard a soft hiccupping sound coming from the bathroom earlier, though he'd emerged later with dry eyes. I supposed he wanted to stay strong in front of me. Even though it seemed my tears had dried up, I hungered for a few more moments of shared grief. But I couldn't bring myself to ask him to sit and wallow in pain with me. Shouldn't that sort of emotional synchronicity happen naturally? Yet another disappointment to add to the pile.

Royal life's driven by ceremony and scheduled events. But there was no prescribed way to recognize our loss, mourn it, and achieve closure. No funeral, no proclamation, no announcement. Instead, we faced another kind of ceremony: the queen's abdication.

CHAPTER FORTY-NINE

I took my seat at the long table beside John for what was sure to be the most awkward family meal in Toulene's history. The lunch was a precursor to the abdication and coronation ceremony, which was set for 3:00 p.m. at St. Joseph's Cathedral.

Seated across from us waiting for lunch to be served, Henri and Adela hid their pity behind weak smiles. Cousin Gerhard sat on the other side of Henri, a bit miserable since there were no women at the table with whom he could flirt. The rector of the church sat on the other side of me, chatting with Aunt Elinore about the expected turnout and how the intermittent rain showers might keep people away. Then there was Leopold and the queen. They looked placid, and for some reason, that worried me.

The servers came around with our first course and refilled our glasses. My stomach turned as I heard the tinkle of the queen's little bell.

"Dearest ones. This is a day to celebrate. And I want to thank the rector for always opening the church for these special occasions. It's a place that's appropriate for both beginnings and endings," she said, looking directly at me on the last word. "Lift your glass as I end my reign and we welcome my capable son onto the throne."

"Prost!" The sound of wine glasses clinking together rang out.

On impulse, I pushed back my chair, stood, and held up my glass. "I'd like to propose a toast. To the woman who is my queen. She upholds the rule of law in all cases, no matter the cost to her family or the ones they love. So, cheers to you, Queenie!"

There was a pause before I heard subdued murmurs of "Prost."

I sat back down and after a moment of awkward silence, people resumed their conversations. John firmly pressed his foot on top of mine, at the same time looking at me and smiling.

Yeah, well, at least I didn't drop the f-bomb.

From my seat on the platform behind the pulpit, I gazed out at the solemn faces looking toward us from the pews. Long banners hung from the balconies inside St. Joseph's, displaying the Meinrad family's coat of arms. The rector began the ceremony with an opening prayer.

John was the first family member to speak; he introduced his grandmother. Just as he did every time he spoke in public, he used a tone that was reassuring and strong. He made people believe the future would be fine, regardless of what it held. With my body still working to rid itself of residual tissue, I no longer took comfort in his confidence that things would work out. They hadn't.

I took a deep breath to stave off my tears and joined the polite applause as the queen took her turn at the pulpit. John sat down beside me on the raised platform and took my hand. I nodded to reassure him he'd done a great job.

"It is with deepest gratitude I come before you today to pass the crown in this peaceful ceremony to my only son, Leopold Hendrik Franz Meinrad. I know he plans to continue to focus on advocating for full funding of my early childhood initiative, Read to Succeed. I once again call on the assembly to make this vital program a budget priority. Expect our next monarch to roll out a strong agenda that takes into careful consideration the needs of our people. And now, I want to leave you with a few words from the Common English Bible. It comes from Romans, chapter 8: 'If we see what we hope for, that isn't hope. Who hopes for what they already see?' I can't see the future, but I know it will be glorious. So it is with hope and expectancy that I leave you. The prosperity we desire for our country is waiting in the distance. My son will lead you there."

With the grandeur of thundering applause and Toulene's national anthem as her backdrop, the queen walked to a table and signed the abdication papers, making it official.

As the anthem ended, it was Henri's turn to speak. He approached the pulpit looking pale and sweaty as he shuffled his notes. I quickly glanced at Adela; she stared with a worried expression at her husband's back.

Henri took a deep breath. "Fellow citizens. Not everyone has the opportunity to bear witness to the peaceful transfer of power, and our own history demonstrates this process often is not an easy one. At times, it's been fraught with violence and betrayal. So, it is with tremendous pride I stand here today to be a part of this joyous ceremony. It is our privilege to honor the longest reigning monarch in our country's history. Queen Sophia Gisila Victoire Meinrad has led Toulene with dignity and grace for more than thirty years. And I expect my father will continue the role she established of an active monarch who champions policies that are in the best interest of the people. It's my honor to present my father, Prince Leopold Hendrik Franz Meinrad. I look forward to seeing the plans you have for our country. You make me proud." Leopold came up to Henri, and they embraced.

As Leopold began his remarks, Henri stumbled a bit before reaching his seat, and Adela and I went to him. We helped him off the side of the stage. I held open a door leading into a hallway.

Before closing it behind us, I looked back at John. He wore a helpless expression on his face. As the heir apparent to his father, he was required to be present during Leopold's coronation; he couldn't leave the stage.

In the hallway, Henri leaned into me. "I'm going to be sick."

Adela slung her arm around him, and I looked around for a trash can. There was one sitting a few feet away. I grabbed it and rushed over to Henri as his lunch left his mouth.

"Just breathe," I said. Adela stepped away, looking like she was going to be sick. Yep, the person who just had the miscarriage was the only one not barfing.

"Adela, go get a cold rag so we can cool him off," I said, guiding Henri farther down the hall toward a chair.

As he sat, Henri looked at me. "How did I do? You'll tell me the truth, won't you, sister?"

His sweet, youthful face shone through the sweat. Bits of goop were plastered around his mouth.

"You were marvelous. You Meinrad boys are quite talented."

Adela came back with a damp communion cloth. "Thank you, Hatty. I can handle him now. You go enjoy the rest of the ceremony," Adela whispered.

I slipped away, but instead of going into the cathedral, I found an exit and escaped into the cold afternoon. Autumn's air was alive, scented by fires in the fields and whispering stories of the coming snows. I closed my eyes involuntarily and opened them when my cell phone vibrated. I hadn't realized until that moment I'd been clenching it in my hand.

I looked at the new email, a plea from Plato: he and his cousin really needed some help in Ethiopia at one of the orphanages. Would I be willing to come?

I wondered how late autumn smelled in the horn of Africa.

CHAPTER FIFTY

I added two pairs of socks to my suitcase, unsure whether I'd wear anything other than sandals during my time in Ethiopia. "Do you think I need socks while I'm there?"

John didn't look up from his phone. "Maybe. I don't know."

There was a knock. John set his phone aside and opened the door to our bedroom.

"The car is ready," Astrid said.

"Would you please send Mr. Vermeulen upstairs in half an hour to get the suitcase?" Astrid nodded and John closed the door.

"Half an hour? I'm almost ready to go." I felt trapped in my own bedroom.

"I'm going to miss you." John sat on the bed and pulled me onto his lap. "Are you sure you want to do this?"

"Absolutely. Plato's been asking me to go with him to Ethiopia since we got married." I avoided my husband's eyes.

"It just feels like you're trying to shut me out." He placed my hair behind my ear, a gesture that still made my heart flutter with anticipation. "Don't push me away." The tenderness in his voice made me want to weep, but I didn't want to cry anymore.

"I'm not pushing you away. I just need some space to sort out my feelings. It's the pressure that's making it hard for me to think straight."

"We can try again. I think it's encouraging you got pregnant. Don't you?"

"I don't know. I just need a mental 'reset' so I can figure out what's next. And while we're talking about what's next, do you know how hopeless it makes me feel that you won't even consider adoption?"

"You know it has nothing to do with my feelings on adoption itself or the children..."

"Yes. You've made it clear Toulene's laws dictate your position on adoption, a position that's silly and old-fashioned. If you really wanted to adopt a child, you could."

"I'm not going to argue this point with you because it's not up for debate. I don't want to fight before your trip."

"Come with me," I said, suddenly hopeful. "Maybe we both need a break from all this. I'd rather not go by myself."

"My schedule is full for the next week. But I'll miss you."

He kissed me, and then I stood to go.

"I love you. I'll see you next Saturday. Try not to worry. I'll text you when I arrive."

En route to the airport, I asked the driver to stop at Toulene's only prison for women. It was outside the capital set among pastures where sleepy cows grazed.

Bernard, my faithful guard, followed me inside, fully aware of the arrangements Astrid had made at my request. The uniformed woman at the front desk had a visitor's badge ready. She walked around her desk, unlocked a heavy door, and held it open for us. Bernard and I headed inside, and from there, she led us to what looked like a conference room.

When she left us, I turned to Bernard. "Would you wait outside, please?"

"I'm sorry. I can't leave you alone with someone who's been convicted of a violent crime."

"Fine."

Just then, the door opened and the woman from the front desk escorted into the room a person I barely recognized. Leisel de Vries looked smaller than I remembered, frail almost, but hyper alert as she sat across the table from me. Her once-beautiful brown hair hung in limp, dry sections.

"Leisel, thank you for agreeing to see me."

"Do you want to interview me again for a story you'll never write?" She punctuated the question with a small, sharp laugh.

"That's why I'm here. I regret not telling your story. It pains me, to tell you the truth. But more importantly, I want to say how sorry I am you never became a mother."

Leisel looked at me and narrowed her eyes. "So it's true? You can't get pregnant."

"I know what it's like to have a failed IVF cycle, yes."

I reached across the table for her hand. She sprang back in her chair, pulling her hands into her lap. Bernard shifted closer, and I shook my head slightly to let him know he didn't need to intervene.

"I was…" I took a breath, then swallowed. "I got pregnant, but it didn't stick."

"But you'll do another cycle. And another, and another until it does. You don't know how it feels to be told by people who have children you only get three chances at IVF. Then, if you can't afford to pay for more cycles yourself, you're done. Just like that, hope is gone." She spread her fingers and smoothed her shirt, emphasizing her flat abdomen.

"That's what I wanted to talk to you about. I'm going to lobby the assembly for extended fertility treatments for women like us."

"We're not alike. I'm done," she said, pushing back from the table.

Before the uniformed woman escorted Leisel out the door, I stood. "Leisel, I'm truly sorry."

She shrugged her shoulders and left the room.

Walking out the front door, I turned to Bernard. "Remember. Not one word about this to John or his family."

By the time our plane landed in Addis, having bounced its way through banks of clouds on the descent, I felt like I was drowning in "me soup." I'd given my brain permission to throw a pity party during my trip. *If I die in a plane crash, my biological footprint will be gone. No trace of me will live on in the world. Biology itself has declared John and I are incompatible. Even senseless animals can accomplish what we can't. The universe is trying to tell us something. God is punishing me for sleeping with Jack when we weren't married.*

At the airport, I waited by myself in a room for forty-five minutes while Bernard got our visas. As John's wife, having a member of the Royal Guard with me at all times was just part of the deal, even if I wanted to escape to another continent. At moments like this, I appreciated having Bernard on hand; he was out there navigating immigration on my behalf.

After we left the secure area of the airport, we were in a mass of people. Through the crowd, I caught sight of Plato jumping and waving. We hugged and he kept me close to his chest.

"You look gorgeous. Even tired and without make-up, you're still a nerdista. I'm so glad you came. This is our driver, Mamush. C'mon, let's get your bags."

"It's nice to meet you, Mamush. Isn't Sam here, too?"

"Nope. He's back home. Someone has to work and fund these luxurious trips." Plato guffawed because we were definitely south of luxury and east of comfortable in the crowded baggage claim. I thought I heard chickens clucking.

Mamush, who looked about eighteen years old, loaded our suitcases on top of his van and secured them with ropes and cords. We bumped our way along the streets of Addis Ababa. I gazed out the window, wondering about daily life in a city where poverty and death lived under the same roof.

When we arrived, Mamush pulled through an iron gate and drove behind the main house where Plato's cousin, Desta, lived with her family. She was married to an Ethiopian man named Tariku.

There was my home for the next few days, a small cottage with concrete walls. Mamush carried my luggage inside. Chickens strutted around the yard like they owned it, and a couple of goats chewed on something over by the fence. Desta and Tariku emerged from the cottage.

"Hatty, we're so happy to have you here! Are you tired?" Desta embraced me.

"No. I feel good. Thank you for letting me come."

"We eat breakfast in the main house at eight. You're welcome to join us. Then, we'll head over to the orphanage and start painting."

I heard a slight twang when she spoke. Though Plato grew up in Iowa, Desta had spent most of her life in a suburb of Nashville.

"That sounds perfect." I placed my backpack beside the small kitchen table.

Desta showed me around the cozy cottage, explained how to get hot water for my shower, and then she and Tariku left me alone. I inhaled slowly, experiencing the rich new aromas that drifted in through the screens that separated me from the mosquitoes and animals milling around the yard.

I plopped down on the white blanket spread across the low bed. This was a definite departure from palace life. I took out my phone, happy to see two bars. Addis was only one hour ahead of Toulene, so I knew John was still awake. I sent him a text to let him know I was getting settled.

He wrote back, "Have fun and be safe. Love and miss you. Whatever you're searching for, find it. I need you back here."

CHAPTER FIFTY-ONE

Mamush's van was full of volunteers from a church in Virginia. We'd stopped at a guest house to pick them up. I introduced myself as Hatty Meinrad, and saw small flickers of recognition on some of the faces. Though John and I certainly received some coverage in the U.S., it wasn't close to the level of attention we got from the media in Europe.

I sat by a window in the back next to Bernard and listened to some of the volunteers talk about their impressions of Addis Ababa. As we drove along in stop-and-go traffic, I willed myself not to get carsick as I'd done when I was a child riding on back roads in the Ozarks.

I pushed open the window as far as it would go to let in a bit of fresh air. We stopped at a traffic light, and a hand touched my arm. I looked out the window and saw a woman standing in the road reaching up to me through the narrow opening. Her right breast was exposed and a sluggish baby was latched onto it. Just then, the van moved.

"Here. Give them one of these." The woman sitting in front of me handed over a granola bar.

"Okay. Thanks."

Shoving sugar-filled processed food stuffs at these poverty-stricken beggars seemed insulting and terribly insufficient. As I looked at the dusty, parched faces along the roadside, I tried to reframe my own infertility struggle. See? These people have real problems. Survival problems.

The van turned into an alley that sloped downhill. We slowly rolled over rocks in a road that looked like a creek bed. It probably was in the rainy season.

Ten minutes later, we turned down an even narrower path that ran between green corrugated fences. The van stopped and Mamush hopped out. He opened a gate off to the right. As he pulled the van into a wide driveway, I saw clotheslines covered in damp baby outfits and children's clothes, a brightly painted metal swing set, and a plain one-story cinderblock building. Another van sat empty, having brought in another set of volunteers ahead of us.

Plato and Desta sorted us into groups and sent us into the orphanage's main building. I was supposed to help the nannies move the infants because their room was about to get a fresh coat of paint.

Just as the others had done before entering the building, I slid off my shoes by the front door. The textured tile was pleasantly cool under my feet. When I got to room A, I stood in the doorway, unsure what to do. All the nannies sat on the floor; most of them held two babies. A few infants sat propped on little pillows, their heads angled to drink from a bottle resting next to them on blankets.

"Hi. Desta said you need help." How ridiculous. It was obvious they needed more help than I could give them.

A nanny with a slender, elegant face smiled at me. I went to her and she nodded toward a baby on a pillow. I scooped up the infant and the bottle propped on the blanket beside her. As soon as I tilted the bottle into the optimal position, the baby came to life and drank with enthusiasm. I smiled at the big brown eyes that locked on my face.

"She's a girl, right? Why is she making that grunting sound?" I asked without knowing whether any of the nannies spoke English.

"She has a throat problem," a nanny sitting across from me said with a light accent. "Hold her up. It is better."

I raised up the baby girl and the sound softened considerably. She also seemed to be drinking with less effort.

"What's her name?"

"Tigist," the nanny said, pronouncing a hard G sound in the middle. "We call her Tidgie." Baby Tidgie was the cutest June bug I'd ever seen.

"My name's Hatty. What's your name?"

"Alemtsehay."

I watched as the babies drifted from drowsy to deep sleep. The nannies deposited each infant into a painted wooden box that had a thin pad in the bottom. Tigist was the only one still awake and drinking.

Alemtsehay sat down next to me. She began to sing softly: "Tidgie-ay, konjo. Tidgie-ay, nay-konjo."

Tigist's top and bottom lashes slowly met over her eyes. The gradual motion reminded me of the tiny Venus Flytraps my grandparents had years ago, and how they slowly closed to capture the food they needed to survive.

I followed Alemtsehay to the remaining wooden box and placed Tigist inside with great care. The tiny baby started snoring like an old man.

"Does she always do that?"

"Oh yes. Throat problem." The nanny pointed to her own neck for emphasis.

With all the babies asleep and secure, the nannies and I moved the boxes down the hall to a room with bright white walls. The air was heavy with the smell of fresh paint. I wondered about the impact of the fumes on such tiny lungs. Once the boxes were all inside, two nannies went around opening windows and I turned on the ceiling fan.

"Are you from the states?" Alemtsehay motioned for me to sit with her on the floor where she folded blankets.

"I grew up there. But I live in Toulene, in Europe. My husband is there. Are you from Addis?"

"No. I'm from a village in Sidamo. Aleta Wondo. You've heard of it?"

"I don't think so."

She laughed. "I suppose not."

"Where did you work in Aleta Wondo?"

"At the orphanage. I came here to see the city. But I may go back to my village. The orphanage director left, and they need help."

I lost count of how many blankets we folded while the babies slept in their boxes around us. Baby Tigist's grunt-like snores floated through the room as we worked.

As I got to the last blanket, Mamush stuck his head in the room. "Lunch, Hatty?"

I excused myself and got in the van.

"We're going for pizza," one of the volunteers told me.

"Pizza? In Ethiopia?"

"Yes. Mamush says Ethiopians love Italian food, even though they drove out the Italians in 1941 after a six-year occupation."

Bumping along in the van toward an air conditioned café, I wondered where the nannies ate their lunch.

My hands shook as I read the email on my phone a second time. I tried not to convey my alarm to the people at my table. They laughed and talked too loudly as they finished their pizza.

It was from James Compson, my former editor at *The Morning Dispatch*. I had no idea how he'd gotten my personal email address.

He explained he'd left his position at the paper to work for

Xpress. As a "courtesy" to his former colleague, he wanted to give me an advanced copy of the story he was about to drop. I knew he was fishing for a comment from me.

Palace Insider Says Duchess Hatty Had Miscarriage; She and Prince John are Separated

By James Compson for Xpress

November 17, 2015

The Belvoir source, who asked to remain anonymous, says Duchess Hatty had a miscarriage in late October following a cycle of in vitro fertilization. As Xpress previously reported, the couple has been trying to get pregnant for months without success.

Now, it appears the strain of the infertility treatments, the details of which have been kept secret, has torn the pair apart. Xpress has confirmed Duchess Hatty left Roeselare Monday and flew to Addis Ababa, Ethiopia. She's reportedly there to do humanitarian work with a longtime friend. Public records show she has no return ticket.

Meanwhile, Prince John is still in Roeselare, and his public schedule doesn't show plans to travel to Ethiopia. The palace source says the trip is a trial separation.

Royal observers say the situation doesn't bode well for a couple already under extreme pressure to produce an heir.

"The last thing they need is to spend time apart. How is Hatty going to make up for her miscarriage by getting pregnant again if she isn't even on the same continent as her husband?" said Nic Capucine, royal observer.

Belvoir's public affairs office did not return calls for comment.

James concluded his email with a zinger: *Hatty, you should've listened to me when I was your editor. You could've been one hell of a reporter.*

"Hatty? You look sick. Are you okay?" The question came from the woman sitting across the table and two people down from me. She furrowed her brows. I recognized her as the person who'd given me a granola bar to hand out to the beggars. "Do you need something else to eat?" She reached in her purse. *Prepackaged food can't solve everyone's problems, lady.*

"No. I just need to make a phone call."

"Time to go, everyone." Mamush announced from the head of the long table where we sat.

I fumbled in my haste to pull up my phone's keypad. Once I had it, I dialed John's cell. *Call Fail* flashed across the bottom. Great. No bars. I typed a quick text and hit send. A couple of moments later, a red exclamation point appeared by the text message, punctuating my status: incommunicado.

That night, I wanted to see if James' story had hit, but I still had no bars on my phone and the Internet connection at my cottage was out. I opened my laptop to type a long message I'd email to John when someone revived our lifeline to the world.

I wrote a confession: I've fallen in love. Someone has filled the emptiness of my heart. I wrote about how Baby Tigist caught my attention and wouldn't let it go. Even as my fingers clicked on the laptop, I worried about how she'd get fed overnight when there were fewer nannies. What if she woke up screaming and no one went to her?

I shared in my message to John the story Alemtsehay told me after lunch about how Tigist came to the orphanage. A woman from her village had walked into the city carrying the sickly child, begging for someone to help her. She said Tigist's birth mother had died, and no one knew who the birth father was.

In conclusion, I wrote: *John, I know this sounds crazy, but I may stay here a bit longer than a week. Will you please come to me? I miss you so much. And I love you.*

Exhaustion overtook my worry for Tigist as I listened to the noises of the city penetrating the thin walls. In a way, the jagged city cacophony reminded me of the soundtrack of Roeselare, except here, the mix included roosters crowing and goats grunting.

CHAPTER FIFTY-TWO

When I arrived at the orphanage the next morning, I couldn't wait to check on tiny Tigist. I bounded out of the van and went inside. Smiling nannies greeted me when I stepped into the freshly painted infant room. Once again, my bare feet registered the cool temperature of the tiles.

I scanned the room. "Where's Tigist?" An alarm sounded in my head.

"She's in the clinic. We had to move her because her cough got worse," one of the nannies said as she changed a baby's diaper. The day before, Tigist had coughed some after I fed her, but it sounded like a minor cold.

"May I go see her?"

"Yes. Go through the middle hallway, through the kitchen, and out the back door. It is a small building. You will see it."

Almost before she finished giving me directions, I was on the move. The front room of the clinic was dark. Nannies sat on small cots holding babies who were bundled tightly like flies bound by a spider's thread. A nanny wearing a kerchief had a sizeable toddler on her lap. The child's eyes moved in strange ways and weren't in sync. I scanned the room but didn't see the baby who mattered the most to me.

"Tigist?" I directed my question at a nanny in the corner.

She motioned toward the door to my right. I walked through it and found Tigist lying in a tiny bed, head shaved and an IV inserted in her scalp. Medical tape held the needle in place. She had the same glazed look I'd seen on Baby Juan when he had been ill a couple of months earlier. Alemtsehay was in the room, folding clothes and putting them in a pile.

"May I?" I asked, indicating I wanted to hold Tigist.

She nodded and came to help me. Tigist was hooked up to a bag of liquid suspended from a hook above her head. Alemtsehay pulled up a wooden chair next to Tigist's bed. I sat and she put the baby in my arms. Tigist looked at me a moment before coughing harshly. I put the back of my hand across her forehead. She felt warm but not hot.

"What's wrong?"

"Pneumonia."

At lunchtime, I tried my phone and got a signal. John answered quickly.

"Hatty. You have to come home. Did you see the story in *Xpress* claiming we're separated? My father planted it." Aha. So, James' article had hit.

"What? Why would your dad talk to the press and lie about us being separated? That's unconscionable."

"It is. But he told me he did it. He says the story lays the groundwork for the order he's about to issue to annul our marriage."

"You can't let him do that. And I can't leave Ethiopia. There's a sick baby here who needs me. She'll die if I abandon her." Panic raised the pitch of my voice as, for the first time, I articulated my fear that Tigist might not make it.

"Come back so we can formulate a plan to deal with Leopold. He says if you refuse to do another round of IVF, he's going to sign the annulment papers."

"Threaten him."

"What? He's the king. I could go to jail for threatening him."

"I don't mean physically. Threaten to leak the story of his relationship with Louisa. You think they still see each other, right?"

"I know they do. I'll have to think about it."

Sigh. I have to do everything. "You can't think about it. You have to do it. I'll see if I can catch a flight out of here this afternoon. I can probably be in Roeselare by tonight. We're going to set your father straight. Then we're both coming back here tomorrow. This baby needs us."

CHAPTER FIFTY-THREE

J ohn and I slammed into each other, embracing and kissing deeply in the midst of the crazy bustle at Toulene's International Airport. Bernard held back several people trying to snap photos. *Let 'em rip, baby. Show the world we're together and we're in love.* It's about time something true about me and John made the rounds on social media.

"Are you ready to do this?" John scooted into the seat next to me in the back of the black car.

"Like we have a choice. My goal is not to drop the f-bomb in front of Leopold again."

"If ever a situation called for a fuck or two, this is it."

"Listen to your mouth! I'm gone for a few days and you start swearing? Makes me wonder what would happen if I'd stayed in Addis for the whole week."

Herr Schroeder told us where we'd find Leopold. When we burst into the game room, Louisa sat on the billiard table, her skirt hiked up. Leopold stood between her legs.

319

They looked shocked and pissed at our intrusion, but Leopold didn't let irritation seep into his voice. "Let me guess. You want to announce a divorce rather than endure the embarrassment of having me annul your marriage. I think that's commendable."

I held up my smartphone and snapped photos.

"Stop it!" Louisa yelled. She scrambled, bringing her legs together, and hopped off the table. Leopold didn't move.

John stared at his father and I put my phone in my back jeans pocket.

Leopold spoke again in a casual way that betrayed the weight of his words. "I know you didn't want your relationship with Hatty to end like this. But your commitment to this family, to our country, is much bigger than the vows you made to Hatty."

John remained still and silent.

"I'd say the reaction to the article has been neutral at best. There's no outcry over the break-up of your marriage. The people of our country realize what you don't: she's just an American who caught your eye after Claire cut you off. It's time to move on. Be a man, John."

"He's more of a man than you," I interjected. "And if you don't leave us alone, I'm going to hit 'send' on every photo I took and shoot them to my friend James Compson at *Xpress*. You're not the only one with connections to that cesspool."

Leopold ignored me and spoke directly to John. "I know if you loved Hatty as much as I loved your mother, you'd do everything you could to avoid an annulment. I was the one who sent Bea to Dr. Cloutier. He gave her an experimental drug to stimulate her ovaries. It worked two times—for you and Henri. She kept taking the pills, hoping she'd get pregnant a third time, but the medication caused cysts." Leopold walked to the sideboard and poured himself a drink.

"You mean the pills brought on the cancer?" John's face was pale.

"Dr. Cloutier told her the pills were causing the cancer to grow, that taking them was like throwing gas on a fire. But she was committed to fulfilling our dream for this country." Leopold swallowed the drink in one gulp and threw the glass against the wall. Louisa jumped back as shards flew toward her.

"I will *never* sacrifice Hatty like that." John was making fists and curling his fingers tighter.

"Your mother knew exactly what she was doing. She risked her own health, her own *life* to bring you into this world. I won't let you walk away from your duty."

"Promise you won't annul our marriage or we send out the photos." John paced. His movement reminded me of footage I once saw of a caged lion.

"As with your mother, I'm doing what I must to protect the country."

John walked over to his father and punched him square in the jaw. Louisa squealed. We walked out of the room.

We made our way across Belvoir to the wing that now belonged to Henri, Adela, and Juan.

A staff member I didn't recognize led us to their sitting room where they were watching a movie.

"How did you guys get in here?" Henri said with a half-smile.

"What's going on? Hatty, I thought you were in Ethiopia," Adela said.

"I was."

John sat in a chair across from his brother and Adela. "Our father planted that story about me and Hatty being separated."

"Planted the story? I thought you guys really were going through a trial separation," Adela's eyes grew wide.

"Hatty and I are leaving in the morning for Ethiopia. Does that sound like a trial separation? Look, our father is determined to break up my marriage and I won't stand for it."

"But if you leave, are you coming back?" Henri's voice was thick with concern.

"Yes. I'll come back, but I don't know when. I'm going to Ethiopia to be with Hatty, and we'll decide as a couple when it's time to leave. She and I have a lot to discuss. But, I'm not coming back to be king."

At this, Henri's mouth fell open. So did mine.

"Granny just abdicated. You can't give up your place in the line of succession now." Henri's cheeks bloomed with red blotches as he realized what John was saying.

John walked over to his brother and put a hand on his shoulder. "You're ready for this. When I see you with Juan, the patience you have and the love you show him, I know you're going to be the kind of king Toulene needs. And you come with a baby in hand. So maybe everyone can just relax."

"Actually, if you're leaving the country, there's something I want to tell you face to face before you go, and we know the timing is terrible." With a furrowed brow, Henri clasped his brother on the shoulder. Adela took my hand, her face full of concern. Oh no. Did one of them have a serious illness?

Henri continued. "Adela's pregnant. We're going to have another baby. I wasn't sure how or when to tell the two of you because I can only imagine how this makes you feel."

To tell the truth, it was a punch in the gut. Even though my life seemed to be moving in a new, exciting direction, my miscarriage still cast a pall over this moment. But, I'd be damned if I'd let the shadow of what might have been ruin Henri and Adela's announcement. By rote, I squashed my grief, longing, and heartache, making them compact enough to bury in the recesses of my heart.

John embraced his brother and I enveloped Adela in my arms. "I'm so happy for you. What's your due date?"

"June 6th. A late spring baby!"

I inhaled quickly. "That's when our baby would've been due."

322

Another punch. The grief threatened to erupt, but I suppressed it. At least we'd be out of the country, and I wouldn't have to watch her body bloom into fertile fullness. It was a wretched thought because I loved Henri and Adela and would miss them terribly. But my line of thinking wasn't about them; it was about self-preservation.

"I'm glad our family will get to welcome a new baby next June after all," John said. His words brought palpable relief to the conversation. He conferred our blessing, giving permission for the family to celebrate Henri and Adela's news. I silently thanked John for having the ability to speak those words.

We embraced them again and said goodbye. A driver took us to Langbroek. In the car, I sat next to John, dabbing at my eyes when they threatened to overflow with tears.

In our bedroom, John's suitcase sat open on the bed, partially filled with the clothes he wanted to take to Ethiopia. I shut the door.

"Okay. Why, why, *why* did you tell Henri you're giving up your claim on the throne? You can't do that."

"I can and I will. I once asked you to give up things that mattered a great deal to you: your degree, your citizenship, your career as a reporter. And now, it's my turn. I'm willing to make the same sacrifice for the woman I love."

"But you were literally born to be king. I can't let you do this."

"I've made up my mind. My father isn't going to leave us alone until you give birth. We can't live under that kind of pressure. It won't go away unless I step aside. I'm going to call Lars and ask him to get everyone lined up to come over in the morning so I can sign away my life. He can break the news to my father. But first, tell me about this baby in Ethiopia and why you're so smitten with her. What's her name?"

"Tigist. Isn't that such a cute name? She's seven months old and she's very sick. The nannies say she has a throat problem. She can't get milk from the bottle when they prop it beside her. That's what they have to do at night because they don't have enough staff at the orphanage to hold the bottles while they feed the babies. They think she's choking on the formula as she drinks it, and that's why she has pneumonia. When we get there tomorrow, I want to ask if I can bring her to the cottage to stay with us. Do I sound like a crazy person?"

"You sound like a mother. I can't wait to meet your little Tigist."

While John finished packing, I went to my wardrobe and took out the box containing the baby items I'd squirreled away. I transferred each treasure to my small duffle. When I came to the green sweater I'd bought in Ghent, I lifted it to my cheek. Nestled there, the sweater's softness and petite perfection embodied all my pregnancy hopes. I refolded it and placed it inside my bag. Then, there was the blanket Tilda gave me for Christmas. It, too, attested to my desires to be a mother. At last, I had a baby who needed these things.

The next morning, John, his father, Henri, family physician Dr. Cloutier, and Lars Franke sat around a table set up in the Regent's Room. Lars shuffled papers.

John broke the uncomfortable silence. "Henri, remember how we used to bring paper and crayons in here so we could create our own versions of the paintings?"

"Yeah. The best part was how all the women we drew ended up with moustaches and beards and the men had oversized bosoms, earrings, and hair bands."

"Please tell me you never tried to draw on the actual paintings." I asked from my chair by the wall.

"Never. Do you remember how mum laughed when we gave her our pictures?" John chortled.

Leopold slammed his fist into the table. "Don't mention your mother as you're about to piss all over the one dream she had for your life." Leopold's sour face looked incapable of joy.

Lars cleared his throat. "Dr. Cloutier, you need to sign first." Lars slid a paper across the table. "This document verifies you believe John's making this decision with a sound mind."

Dr. Cloutier signed and rose from the table. "John, I wish you and Hatty all the best. I suppose now that the pressure's gone, she'll be able to get pregnant." He laughed awkwardly.

He still didn't get it. Infertility is not a state of mind.

Leopold shook hands with Dr. Cloutier, and thanked him for his time. As the elderly man left the room, I wondered how a physician could be so clueless as to suggest stress alone had stood in our way of conceiving.

"John, it's your turn to sign. I need your signature here, here, and here. Each page outlines the terms of the abdication. As you know, this decision is irrevocable and takes effect the moment you sign. Do you have any questions?" Lars slid off his reading glasses and stared at John.

"No. I understand." John was already moving his pen across the signature line of the first page.

Leopold sighed as John finished. Henri watched, his face uncharacteristically solemn.

Flipping to another page, Lars pushed the paper to Leopold. "Your Majesty, you sign here, primarily as a witness."

John handed the pen to his father who hastily added his signature.

"And Prince Henri, your signature acknowledges your new place in the line of succession."

Henri completed the process by quickly signing his name.

"That's all. I'll just make sure we get the requisite number of copies made, and I'll file them in the proper places. I know you may not announce this news right away. But the law requires me to place the papers in the public archive today. I'll be as discreet as possible. But an enterprising journalist could find these."

Lars' words stirred my dormant career aspirations. A part of me still longed to be a reporter. Being a columnist was rewarding, but I missed the thrill of digging and investigating.

"Thank you, Lars," Leopold said. Then he turned to John. "You know, I never thought I'd see this day. Your mother wouldn't believe this." Leopold drummed his fingers on the table.

"Mum would be glad I'm happy," John said with certainty. "I wish you and Henri all the best. Father, I want to apologize for punching you. I know you have the country's best interest at heart, even if at times, that's put me and you at odds. I forgive you and hope you'll forgive me."

John turned to Henri and they embraced.

"I look forward to hearing about whatever you end up doing in Ethiopia," Henri said, smiling. "I know the Internet connection is unreliable in such a remote place, but do stay in touch."

"Of course. And if we're still in Ethiopia when the baby arrives, I expect to see photos of my new niece or nephew from *you* before they're plastered all over Xpress.com," John said.

They hugged one last time. Leopold remained seated, and John laid a hand on his father's shoulder, giving it a gentle squeeze.

"Goodbye, Dad."

John and I walked out of the room. Lars followed us.

In the hallway, John shook hands again with Lars.

"Thank you, my friend. I'm sorry to part on a somber note, but we need to be on our way to Ethiopia. Hatty's helping take care of a baby girl who's quite sick."

"Is she an orphan?"

"She is," I responded. "One of the nannies told me they have paperwork for her adoption, but they haven't matched her to a family because she's so sick. When she recovers from pneumonia, I think they plan to find someone to adopt her."

"Maybe they already have. Would the two of you ever consider being her parents?

"I think it's a possibility. It's an option that's on the table now that I'm no longer bound by Toulene's laws of succession," John said.

I looked at John in surprise. "Wait. So, you're interested in adoption?"

"I'm free now, Hatty."

"If you do decide to adopt her, let me know. I can take care of all the paperwork here, and I have a colleague in Eritrea who can travel to Ethiopia and help with the necessary filings there."

John put his arm around me. "I suspect we'll be in touch."

At John's words, happiness overtook me, causing my hands to shake. Were we going to be parents? And not parents to just any child, but the child who'd already carved out a cozy place in my heart? The possibility conjured up such joy, tears swelled in my eyes. I wiped away the pockets of water with my sleeve before anyone saw.

CHAPTER FIFTY-FOUR

Mamush stood at the arrivals gate, beaming and waving to us as we walked into the busy terminal. Traveling with John meant breezing through customs and immigration thanks to the diplomatic clearances on his passport, a perk afforded exclusively to world leaders and royalty. They could travel anywhere without the usual visa hoops the rest of us faced. John's passport had no expiration date, a perk that remained in place because he retained his title.

"Do you know how Tigist is doing?" I hugged Mamush.

"Still in the clinic, but she is stable. Alemtsehay wanted me to tell you she's been feeding Tigist herself while you've been away."

"That's a relief. I'm sorry, Mamush. This is my husband, John. And of course, you remember Bernard." Good old Bernard still had to travel with us, even though John abdicated.

Mamush extended his hand, and John hugged him. "Nice to meet you, Mamush. Show me where we get our bags."

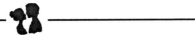

Mamush drove us straight to the orphanage. When we arrived,

Tigist was asleep, snoring loudly. The IV was gone, and her skin felt cool. Still, they'd kept her in the clinic for observation.

"She is doing much better," Alemtsehay said, wiping her hands on her apron.

John bent over the low bed. Then, he got down on his knees and lifted Tigist's right hand. He stroked the back of it.

"She casts a spell, doesn't she?" I put my hand on John's shoulder.

"Can we take her with us?"

"I don't know. Alemtsehay, what do you think?"

"Ask Desta. She will decide."

John rested his lips on Tigist's forehead before we left. Desta must have heard we were here. She met us on the front porch of the clinic building.

"John. It's so nice to meet you. What do you think of our little Tigist?"

"I think she needs to come with us. Is that possible?"

"We can probably arrange that. But how long will she stay with you?"

"As long as we're in Ethiopia," John said.

"And how long will that be?" Desta glanced at me.

"We'll stay as long as someone needs us," John replied. "I know you're short-staffed here. I want to make sure Tigist gets the care she needs. Hatty's willing to do it and so am I."

"Come to my office. We need to sign some papers before I can let you take her." *More paperwork? God help us.*

I cuddled against John on the tiny sofa in the cottage, the rough fabric grating against my legs. Though we had none of the luxuries of Langbroek Palace, I felt completely at peace, truly at home. Actually, there was one remaining luxury: Bernard and whichever guard would come every few months to relieve him.

We might have to fold our own clothes, but we wouldn't have to worry about pickpockets.

"Does she always snore like that?" John nodded toward the bedroom where Tigist's breath noisily pushed in and out of her throat.

"Yes. We probably won't sleep tonight," I said, pulling my hair back into a ponytail. The sun was already gone, and evening ushered a nice breeze through the cottage.

I heard John inhale deeply. "Is the condition in her throat a lifelong problem?"

"I don't think so. The doctor at the orphanage said she'll outgrow it. In the meantime, she needs someone to feed her or she'll keep aspirating the formula. That's what causes her pneumonia." I sounded like Hatty Meinrad, M.D.

"And that's where you come in, making sure she has the bottle in the optimal position each time she drinks." John squeezed my arms as he usually did when he was offering to give me a massage. I repositioned myself to let him work his magic.

"How did you ever learn to do this? You were a king-in-waiting, so weren't you on the receiving end of most massages?"

"True. But when you've had so many massages, you figure out how to do it." He dug his strong fingers into the tight muscles of my shoulders.

"How long are we staying?" With my back to him, I felt more comfortable broaching the topic.

"I wanted to ask you the same thing," he said as he kneaded my back.

"I don't know. I suppose it hinges on the health of the little snore machine in the other room. I know she's not mine, but I can't take her back to the orphanage. My need to protect her isn't something I can just set aside."

"I understand. She's so precious. And did you see the way she pulled the spoon to her mouth when I fed her dinner? Then she grabbed my finger with such strength. It surprised me given her size and health problems."

I heard a sparkle in his voice. It had been MIA for months. In the span of a few hours since we arrived, Tigist had captured him with her long Venus flytrap eyelashes and sweet smile.

"So, what do we do?" I wasn't sure I wanted to hear his answer.

"I'm here with you now. Isn't that enough?" he said, stroking my hair in the tender way that had become so known to me during our marriage.

As he removed my clothes, I released my expectations. I let go of my ideas about the way things were supposed to be. We made love by doing what pleased ourselves and each other rather than optimizing sex for procreation. Our passion and inventiveness (let's give this position a whirl) reminded me of the early days of our marriage, the time before infertility joined us between the sheets.

After we finished, I rested in John's arms.

"You know, we're completely untethered. At the risk of tarnishing my tough girl image, I have to admit I'm a little scared. You're out of a job, man. I guess I can keep writing for The Guardian. But what are we supposed to do now?"

"You make it sound like we're penniless. We'll always have access to my family's resources."

"I know. It's just that we don't have a plan. For the first time. Ever."

He stroked his chin, deep in thought. "I can grow a beard. You keep submitting your columns and finish your degree. We'll figure it out"

"I like it. Sounds like a plan, Stan."

CHAPTER FIFTY-FIVE

Tilda, we'll be there, I promise! I wouldn't miss walking you down the aisle for anything!" I said into the phone.

I nearly LOL'd every time I thought about me and Tilda strolling toward the front of the church together so I could give her away. Her boyfriend became her fiancé Monday when he handed her a stack of printed bills his boss was co-sponsoring with Assemblyman Aalders. A platinum diamond ring sat on top of the papers.

"I can't wait to see you and meet Tigist!" Tilda was practically squealing. We now had full custody of this darling baby, even though she wasn't legally our daughter… yet. John was the one who suggested we take her to a children's hospital in London during our trip to Toulene for Tilda's wedding. A team of doctors planned to evaluate her so we could take whatever steps were necessary to prevent the recurrence of pneumonia.

"Do you remember how I told you that not getting pregnant made me feel like a complete failure?"

"It was that day you came to my office."

"That's right. I still feel that way sometimes. But then I remember pregnancy wasn't my goal. What I wanted was to be a mom. And I've got that now."

"Yes, you do. I love you, Hatty. Now, get yourself to Toulene so I can squeeze you and Tigist."

"I will. Hey, I've got to go. The connection's breaking up. Love you! Talk to you soon!" I said as the static increased. The line went dead.

I walked into the living room where John was reading a book to a wide-eyed Tigist who sat in his lap. Standing in the doorway, I watched as he took her finger and rubbed it on the soft fur of the bear in the book.

Tears stung my eyes as I saw the ways in which John and I were becoming parents. It didn't happen in a single moment, like we once thought it would, in a hospital with a baby meeting us, and the world, for the first time. Instead, the transformation was incremental, measured in teaspoons of mashed peas, ounces of formula, and milligrams of teething biscuits.

Tigist's eyes were heavy. Her head drooped to the side as her loud snoring cranked up. I reached for her, and John shook his head. He stood, careful to keep his balance, walked past me, and laid her in the crib in our bedroom.

When he returned, we sat on the couch.

"Tilda said your dad is issuing a decree stating the royal family will cover the costs of all infertility treatments for couples who exceed the coverage limit under the federal healthcare program. Is that right?"

"Yes." John flipped on the television, filling the room with Ethiopian Orthodox hymns.

"How did you manage that?" I picked up the remote and clicked off the TV. "Tell me."

He smiled. "I told my father if he didn't step up on this issue, we'd release the photos of him and Louisa to *Xpress* tomorrow. I also said if he expands infertility coverage, we'd delete all the snapshots."

"Are you kidding me? I'm not getting rid of those pictures."

"Of course not. But he doesn't have to know that."

"Why did you do it?"

"I didn't want you to have any more reasons to visit Leisel de Vries in prison."

"Damn it. Why can't anyone keep a secret?"

"Because we're royals. At least, we were. *C'est la vie*, baby." He pulled out a deck of cards and began to deal. "Want to play?"

Streaks of burning orange ripped through the inky darkness of the sky, heralding the coming sunrise. I sat outside the cottage, sipping my coffee from a chipped white mug, watching chickens peck around the ground by Desta and Tariku's back door. I'd gotten up while John and Tigist were still asleep, desperate for a few moments of consistent Wi-Fi.

I scanned the coverage of Henri and Adela's second pregnancy. Almost all the articles framed the pregnancy news to convey the sense of relief it brought to John's family in light of my continued failure to conceive. Intellectually, I knew what I was reading was speculation, innuendo, and outright lies. Still, my heart ached at some of the words in the *Xpress* article.

Baby Dos! Prince Henri and Duchess Adela Bring an Heir to Spare to Roeselare

By James Compson

November 27, 2015

A palace insider says the Meinrad family is heaving a collective sigh of relief at the news, especially after Prince John and Duchess Hatty reportedly experienced a miscarriage. They underwent in vitro fertilization this fall during a visit to the United States. Sources say the stress from that failure continues to plague the pair, who are seeking counseling for their marital strife.

Duchess Adela, originally from Spain, said in a written statement she and Henri are exploding with joy over their big news. "It's truly a blessing to bring another child into this wonderful family."

Meanwhile, no one's seen Prince John or Duchess Hatty in recent days, fueling speculation their marriage is in trouble over Hatty's inability to produce an heir.

"I wouldn't be surprised if we see an official statement about their pending divorce by the end of the year," said Nic Capucine, longtime royal observer.

Still no news of John's abdication. When would Cilla decide to drop that bomb? She and Leo were probably still trying to figure out how to spin it.

"Hatty!" John's frantic voice pierced the morning air. I set my mug on the concrete porch and rushed inside.

"Her breathing doesn't seem right. And she was coughing in a weird way," John said, cradling her body. Tigist looked glassy-eyed, her breaths coming in gasps.

"Is her throat constricted?"

"I don't know. She was like this when I checked on her."

"Bring her to Desta's," I said, holding open the front door.

We sprinted across the small yard between our houses, John cradling Tigist in his arms, and I banged on the door. Tariku appeared, dressed and holding a newspaper.

"What is wrong with the baby?" he said, instantly assessing the situation.

"We don't know. I heard her cough in a funny way, so I got out of bed to check on her. She looks sick and her breathing isn't right." Adrenaline accelerated John's speech.

"Come. We must get her to the clinic." Tariku grabbed a set of keys from his pocket.

We were in a private room at the orphanage clinic. John had not let go of Tigist since he'd first scooped her out of the crib. A clear plastic mask was over her nose and mouth so she could receive a breathing treatment. The doctor, a new staff member, said she had croup, a potentially serious childhood illness. He also told us

Tigist's "throat problem" is actually a floppy larynx that makes her airway somewhat crowded. It was the reason she snored loudly and aspirated formula, propelling droplets into her lungs where they developed into pneumonia.

Tigist drifted to sleep as the soft hiss of the nebulizer sent the mist of medicine to her nose and mouth. When I looked at John, I saw a tear streaming down his cheek.

"Hey," I said, placing by hand on his arm.

"When I picked her up from the crib and felt her body limp in my hands, I thought we might lose her. I didn't want her to die without a mother and father. That's the loneliest thing I can imagine." He rubbed his cheek against his shoulder to wipe away the tear.

"She's not going to die. And it seems to me she has a mother and father." I stroked her cheek. Her dark brown skin was smooth and soft.

As I sat back in my chair, my mind permanently captured the image of Tigist nestled in John's arms. My heart grew to encompass them both; this moment cemented them as a package deal: father and daughter.

Chapter Fifty-Six

J ohn and I strolled with our arms linked as we let the smells, sights, and sounds of the Addis Mercato envelop us. Known as one of the largest outdoor markets on the continent, it was an epicenter of commerce and culture. We passed rudimentary cages holding chickens, rows of cookware piled on the ground, and shacks selling piles of dried leaves known as khat, a mild narcotic that was wildly popular.

"Don't you want to try it?" I held up a handful of the leaves.

"No, thank you. You wouldn't want to kiss me if I had a mouth full of that stuff."

"You're right." I smiled at the vendor as I put the leaves back in his pile and laid a few bills on top since I'd handled his product without buying it.

Desta, Tariku, and Plato were our guides. They named the unlabeled bins of spices we passed. We were on the hunt for a brightly colored wicker basket that would hold injera, the slightly sour, thin, and bubbly bread that was a staple of the Ethiopian diet.

We came to a small shack that was serving coffee, and took seats around a plastic table. Plato ordered drinks for us.

"I can't tell you how happy we've been to have you both here. I know you haven't decided what your long-term plans are going to be, and I understand your desire to care for Tigist has complicated things, but I wanted to ask you something," Desta said, rubbing sanitizer on her hands.

I looked at Plato. He was grinning but also trying to stifle it.

"You may have heard from our staff that our sister orphanage in rural Ethiopia, in the village of Aleta Wondo, has lost its directors. I wondered if the two of you might be willing to spend some time there... Just until we can find permanent staff to take over," Desta added the last bit hastily, as though she didn't want her proposal to sound like an imposition.

John squeezed my hand. "Do you need an answer now?"

Desta laughed. "That would be ideal, but I know you may need to discuss it before making a commitment."

"Hatty, John. If I may offer you some wisdom as you consider this opportunity." Tariku shifted in his seat and leaned across the table toward us. "There is an Ethiopian proverb that says 'the long nights end with the breaking of days.' It means we can't escape the darkness without breaking our routines, our habits, our way of thinking about things. This would certainly be a clean break."

The coffee arrived and Desta told us more about the orphanage in Aleta Wondo and the difficulties it faced being in such a remote location. As she spoke, a watercolor image of our future unfolded in my mind. It was frightening and beautiful, utterly overwhelming.

John and I left the heavy door open and closed the screen so we could sit on the porch and still hear the loud snores emanating from the bedroom. We'd come to appreciate her nighttime noises because it gave us assurance she wasn't struggling to breathe.

"So, what do you think about Desta's proposal?" I tried to sound neutral, though my mind was set on a plan.

"I think it's an interesting offer. I'm not sure it's right for us. What happens if we're in this remote village and Tigist gets croup again?"

"There are two doctors who take shifts at the orphanage in Aleta Wondo. If their clinic set-up is similar to the clinic here, I think she'd receive excellent care."

"Would you have any concerns about our safety?"

"Isn't that why we have Bernard?"

"Okay. You're great with children, but what would I do there?"

"First of all, you're also fabulous with children. They follow after you like a herd of sheep. Second, aren't you essentially a farm doctor now that you have your Ph.D.? Couldn't you help local farmers with whatever problems they're having?"

"I suppose."

"And maybe I can do more writing. The world needs to know about the kinds of situations that lead birth families to place children in orphanages. I mean, Tigist is with us because her birth mom is dead. But Desta told me about two-thirds of the children in the orphanages are there because their parents can't feed them. That's an outrage. No parent should ever have to give up custody of their children to prevent them from going hungry."

John reached over and grabbed my hand. He kissed the back of it. "These children need a voice, and you could share their stories with the world. You could do that kind of writing from here. Or from Roeselare, for that matter, if we ever decide to go back. I'm just thinking out loud here. I don't know. I need to sleep on it."

CHAPTER FIFTY-SEVEN

The heat in the kitchen made me feel slightly dizzy. As I worked with the cooks to prepare our own version of Winter's Feast, I savored the smells and textures of the vegetables and fruits in my hands.

John and I hired local restaurant workers to create the many courses for the celebration. All of the produce and meat for the feast came from farms in and near Addis Ababa. With the help of a man from the Ethiopian Institute of Agricultural Research, John had selected all of the food we were about to eat.

He came into the kitchen, grabbed me by the waist, and pulled me out the back door. We stood on a rectangular concrete porch alone except for a mangy dog peering at us through the fence that marked the orphanage grounds.

"Close your eyes. Hold out your hand." I did as John asked. He placed something small in my palm. "Open your eyes."

Encased in its signature silver foil, the single chocolate candy also had the tiny tab of paper rising from the wrapper.

"A kiss?"

"A chocolate kiss, different than the ones we've shared

before, but it's just as delicious. That's how I think of our lives here: different than what we imagined for ourselves, but fulfilling and lovely."

His lips met mine, and a surge of deep love radiated from my heart. Even with my eyes closed, a tear escaped and slid down my cheek.

The door swung open behind us and Desta reached for my arm. "Everyone's seated! They're ready."

John and I walked into the room that normally served as a gymnasium for the older kids at the orphanage. A large group of volunteers had arrived from Illinois over the weekend. They helped us set up the tables and were watching the children so that most of the orphanage staff could enjoy the feast. The volunteers who weren't helping with the kids agreed to serve the food. Tears stung my eyes at the sight of these men and women tying aprons on each other so they could give our staff a well-deserved evening of appreciation. I was an emotional mess.

John stood beside me at the head table, and I wiped my eyes. In lieu of the delicate bell the queen always used to quiet the crowd at Belvoir when she was ready to make a toast, I rang a cow bell. Everyone fell silent and turned toward me.

"Good evening, friends. During the celebration of Winter's Feast in Toulene, we usually talk about remembering our blessings. It's a way to remind ourselves to be thankful for all we have, even in the bitter depths of winter's darkness. I want our first Winter's Feast in Ethiopia to focus on the same thing: the many blessings we have in spite of the challenges we've faced this year. I've learned in the last few months there is no Plan B. There's just life." My voice started to falter as the truth of the words rang through the room.

John put his arm around me. "What Hatty's saying is we never imagined we'd be here, adopting an Ethiopian baby who stole our hearts, and preparing to help run the orphanage in Aleta Wondo."

Applause exploded in the room at this announcement. Chairs scooted and everyone stood. Desta, Tariku, Plato, and Alemtsehay gathered around us for a group hug. I wept at the symmetry of the moment, remembering how on a previous Winter's Feast miles from here, the people we loved surrounded me and John as we celebrated the news of our engagement.

After the clapping subsided and everyone took their seats again, I held up my cup to propose a toast.

"Please raise your glass with me. To endings that are really beginnings, much happier and more beautiful than we could ever write for ourselves. Cheers!"

John kissed me on the cheek as we clinked our glasses and began the feast.

JOHN'S EPILOGUE

Aleta Wondo, Ethiopia
May 20, 2016

I pulled the rag from my back pocket and wiped away the snot creeping from Bereket's right nostril. She was my shadow, the one child out of the whole orphanage who never left my side. The tiny child clung to my waist as I stepped through the doorway into the bright morning sun, already baking us with its ninety degree heat. It reminded me of the ongoing challenge I faced in helping the farmers in and around the village. They struggled in this unusual heat wave to keep their crops irrigated, but rainy season was just getting started. Soon, we'd be battling the overabundance of rain. We had a couple of ideas we were testing. Today would be a good day to gather some field data.

"Who was that?" I nodded toward the white man walking down the path.

"Oh, just some man with a camera. He had an accent like yours. He asked to meet you, and I asked if he'd like to meet the children in the TB ward. He politely declined," Alemtsehay said as she draped a limp, faded onesie across the clothes line.

"Ah, I see." Not even living in a remote area of Ethiopia could keep the paparazzi away. "Here, let me and Bereket help you with the laundry."

Reaching into the basket with her only hand, Bereket fished around for something pink. "I hang it."

I lifted her onto my shoulders and helped her place the tank top on the shaky clothes line.

"He take my photo?" Bereket pointed in the direction the man had gone.

"Not this time, love. Too bad he left without meeting our glamorous Bereket. Let's go take your photo out by the roses. We'll see what Hatty's up to."

With Bereket perched on my shoulders, I headed around the corner of the orphanage's main building.

We found Hatty sitting on an old quilt spread across the ground under a tree. Tigist sat beside her playing with an array of new toys that had arrived in the mail from her Uncle Henri and Aunt Adela. Tigist looked up intermittently as Hatty read "Don't Let the Pigeon Drive the Bus." The sweet sound of accented English floated through the air as the children shouted, "No!" "You can't drive!"

She finished reading and closed the book. "Hey! Do you want to take over? I've got a deadline this afternoon. I promised my editor I'd send my column by 8:00 p.m. their time," she said, looking calm and radiant even as she stared down a killer deadline for one of the world's biggest publications.

Hatty's holistic approach to orphan care, which focused on programs to keep children with birth families, earned her widespread respect. Her testimony last month to a congressional subcommittee in Washington, D.C. focused on ways to eliminate the need for orphanages like the one we now ran in Aleta Wondo.

"Sure!" I said. "But first, I promised Bereket I'd take her picture by the roses." I pulled the phone from my pocket.

"You stand with me, Hatty?" Bereket held out her hand.

"I will pose with Bereket Rose!" Hatty said in a sing-songy voice as she approached us.

"My name is not Rose!" Bereket protested with a smile.

As they stood laughing and discussing the merits of changing Bereket's middle name to Rose, I snapped photos. On my phone's screen, I saw a child and a mother, a mother whose arms enveloped every child in the orphanage, whose heart was full of love for children she did not birth but who belonged to her all the same.

ACKNOWLEDGEMENTS

Special thanks to Hayley Stone for being an amazing critique partner and friend. Many other writers and editors assisted me at various stages with encouragement or feedback. I want to thank Naomi Hughes, Bob Stephens, Michelle Hauck, Lora Douglas, Esher Hogan, Margarita Montimore, Laura Heffernan, Anne Lipton, and Jessa Russo.

I want to express my deep appreciation to Curiosity Quills for publishing my book. I'll never forget the moment I saw the comment from Alisa Gus on my Pitchmas entry: she wanted to see the first few pages of INCONCEIVABLE. The next thing I knew, I had a request for the full manuscript from acquisitions editor Vicki Keire. I can't thank you enough, Vicki, for seeing the potential of my manuscript and advocating for its publication. I love the vision that Vicki and Alisa have for the romance genre and the fact that it's big enough to include books like INCONCEIVABLE. I'm exceedingly grateful for my super talented CQ editor, Christina Ferko, who helped me take the manuscript to a whole new level. Christina, you were the perfect editor for this book. Thank you for bringing such a personal touch to your reading and editing of INCONCEIVABLE. I'm forever grateful. I want to also thank Matthew Phillips who designed my book's gorgeous cover. Alisa Gus said it best: it's stunning! Many tips of the hat to Eugene Teplitsky, Andrew Buckley, Nikki Tetreault, Clare Dugmore, and the rest of the CQ team who work passionately to put outstanding books in the hands of readers. I appreciate your patience and kindness as we journeyed together to "birth" my book. You've made my dream of being a published author a reality! I love being a part of the CQ family, and appreciate my fellow CQ authors who generously share their expertise. You guys are tops!

I must surely thank you, dear reader, for investing your time and dollars in this story. In purchasing this book, you're a part of changing other people's stories: I'm donating half the royalties from INCONCEIVABLE to Baby Quest and Half the Sky Foundation. Pamela Hirsch brings such passion to her work with Baby Quest, an organization that helps infertile couples afford medical procedures in their pursuit of parenthood. I applaud you, Pamela, for your dedication and hard work. And thanks for being so enthusiastic about my book from the first moment I reached out to you. The other organization that's receiving support is Half the Sky Foundation. Its sole purpose is to improve the lives of orphans in China.

Finally, I thank God for giving me a story and the courage to tell it.

ABOUT THE AUTHOR

The best compliment **Tegan Wren** ever received came from her sixth grade teacher: *"You always have a book in your hand!"*

Guided by her love of the creative process, Tegan grew up acting in theatre productions and writing poetry, short stories, and plays.

She turned her eye to writing about real life when she worked as a journalist, producing reports for various radio and television  stations in medium and large markets in the Midwest and also filing some stories for a major national news network. She spent several years writing online content, which ranged from creating descriptions of toilets for a retail website to composing a blog post about visiting Maui.

She's had the opportunity to travel overseas, and uses those adventures to inform her writing. She also draws inspiration from her own struggles and life experiences. Tegan and her husband, Patrick, experienced infertility for five years before becoming parents through adoption.

Thank You for Reading

Please visit http://curiosityquills.com/reader-survey
to share your reading experience with the author of
this book!

The Rearranged Life, by Annika Sharma

Nithya comes to terms with the idea of an arranged marriage, a tradition her conservative Indian family has held up for thousands of years. Enter James St. Clair, the smart, challenging and heartbreakingly handsome American. As Nithya and James fall in love, she questions the future she and her parents have always planned.

Now, Nithya has a choice to make. The decision she comes to takes her on a journey that transforms how she sees her future, her relationships with loved ones, and how she learns to put herself back together when even her best-laid plans fall apart.

Game of Love, by Ara Grigorian

A struggling tennis star whose celebrity status is out of control, realizes that trusting those around her is a luxury she can't afford, especially when everyone wants something from her, until she meets her kindred spirit, that's when love takes on a whole new meaning on and off of the courts.

Peace Cottage, by Lisa Kent

Peace Cottage is an inspirational story about new beginnings in trying circumstances. It's a quiet story about powerful feelings. With the sea as its background, this book asks for a comfortable chair and a hot cup of tea. Lose yourself as you follow Lucy Cook in her journey to home and love.

Who is Mr. Plutin?, by Rebecca Strong

Yesterday Vika Serkova was in New York, eating takeout alone in her closet-sized apartment. Today she wakes up with a wedding ring on her finger, next to a man who claims to be her husband. In a designer flat in St Petersburg, Russia. The Cinderella story shatters when her husband drops the bomb about why she's forgotten everything, about the work she does with her father, and about her current assignment for the Russian President. To save herself and the family she is beginning to remember Vika needs to fool them into defecting. A perfect plan but only if she can manage it with her Russian memory MIA and her opponents set on destroying each other even before Vika's manicure dries.

CPSIA information can be obtained at www.ICGtesting.com
Printed in the USA
LVOW08s1115081215

465928LV00003B/306/P